# Burn Marks

**Also by Sara Paretsky**

Blood Shot
Bitter Medicine
Killing Orders
Deadlock
Indemnity Only

# Burn Marks

# Sara Paretsky

Delacorte
Press

Published by
Delacorte Press
Bantam Doubleday Dell Publishing Group, Inc.
666 Fifth Avenue
New York, New York 10103

Library of Congress Cataloging in Publication Data

Paretsky, Sara.
Burn marks.

I.  Title.
PS3566.A647B87     1989     813'.54     89-23418
ISBN 0-385-29892-7

Manufactured in the United States of America
Published simultaneously in Canada

Design by Andrew Roberts

March 1990

10  9  8  7  6  5  4  3  2  1

BVG

*For Patti Shepherd, Jayanne Angell,*
*and Bill Mullins,*
*who believed in my writing before I did*

# Thanks

Angelo Polvere of the Mayfair Construction Company in Chicago provided me an overview of how a general contractor builds a major project and how a contractor's office works. Jay Meyer took me to the top of a sixty-story high rise going up in Chicago and walked me back down, explaining the different stages of construction. I experienced the terrors of an unenclosed concrete deck firsthand. Ed Keane made these connections for me. My ignorance of big projects greatly exceeds my knowledge—any errors of fact should be credited to my poor understanding rather than to these excellent teachers.

Ray Gibson shared different research tools for covering the kinds of things V.I. looks into in this book. Dr. Robert Kirschner, Chief Deputy Medical Examiner for Cook County, gave me a grand tour of the county morgue. It was not pleasant but it was enlightening.

As is always the case in V.I.'s adventures, no reference is made to any real public figures currently serving time or in office. Boots Meagher, Ralph MacDonald, Roz Fuentes, Alma Mejicana, and Wunsch and Grasso are products of my perfervid imagination. Nor is the construction at Rapelec Towers based on any building now standing or under construction in Chicago.

Courtenay, Cardhu, and other friends supported me through the various trials that beset me in writing this book.

# Contents

# Burn Marks

# 1

# Wake-up Call

**M**y mother and I were trapped in her bedroom, the tiny upstairs room of our old house on Houston. Down below the dogs barked and snapped as they hunted us. Gabriella had fled the fascists of her native Italy but they tracked her all the way to South Chicago. The dogs' barking grew to an ear-splitting roar, drowning my mother's screams.

I sat up. It was three in the morning and someone was leaning on the doorbell. I was sweaty and trembling from the dream's insistent realism.

The urgent ringing recalled all the times in my childhood the phone or doorbell had roused my father to some police emergency. My mother and I would wait up for his return. She refused to admit her fear, although it stared at me through her fierce dark eyes, but would make sweet children's coffee for me in the kitchen—a tablespoon of coffee mixed with milk and chocolate—and tell me wild Italian folktales that made my heart race.

I pulled on a sweatshirt and shorts and fumbled with the locks to my door. The ringing echoed through the stairwell behind me as I stumbled down the three flights to the front entryway.

My aunt Elena stood on the other side of the glass door, her finger pressed determinedly to the bell. A faded quilt made an ungainly cloak around her shoulders. She had propped a vinyl duffel bag against the wall; a violet nightgown trailed from its top. I don't believe in prescience or ESP, but I couldn't help feeling that my dream—a familiar childhood nightmare—had been caused by some murky vibrations emanating from Elena to my bedroom.

My father's younger sister, Elena had always been the family Problem. "She drinks a little, you know," my grandmother Warshawski would tell people in a worried whisper after Elena had passed out at Thanksgiving dinner. More than once an embarrassed patrolman roused my dad at two in the morning to tell him Elena had been busted for soliciting on Clark Street. On those nights there were no fairy tales in the kitchen. My mother would send me back to my own bed with a tiny shake of the head, saying, "It's her nature, *cara,* we mustn't judge her."

When my grandmother died seven years ago, my father's surviving brother, Peter, gave his share of the Norwood Park bungalow to Elena on condition that she never ask him for anything else. She blithely signed the papers, but lost the bungalow four years later— without talking to me or Peter she had put it up as collateral in a wild development venture. When the fly-by-night company evaporated, she was the only partner the courts could find—they confiscated the house and sold it to meet the limited partnership's bills.

Three thousand remained after paying the debts. With that and her social security, Elena had been living in an SRO at Cermak and Indiana, playing a little twenty-one and still turning the occasional trick on the day the pension checks arrived. Despite years of drinking that had carved narrow furrows in her chin and forehead, she had remarkably good legs.

She caught sight of me through the glass and took her finger from the bell. When I opened the door she put her arms around me and gave me an enthusiastic kiss.

"Victoria, sweetie, you look terrific!"

The sour yeasty smell of stale beer poured over me. "Elena— what the hell are you doing here?"

The generous mouth pouted. "Baby, I need a place to stay. I'm desperate. The cops were going to take me to a shelter but of course I remembered you and they brought me here instead. A *very* nice young man with an absolutely gorgeous smile. I told him all about your daddy but he was just a boy, of course he'd never met him."

I ground my teeth together. "What happened to your hotel? They kick you out for screwing the old-age pensioners?"

"Vicki, baby—Victoria," she amended hastily. "Don't talk dirty —it doesn't sound right coming from a sweet girl like you."

"Elena, cut the crap." As she started a second reproach I corrected myself hastily. "I mean stop talking nonsense and tell me why you're out on the streets at three in the morning."

She pouted some more. "I'm trying to tell you, baby, but you keep interrupting. There was a fire. Our lovely little home was burned to the ground. Burned to an absolute crisp."

Tears welled in her faded blue eyes and coursed through deep furrows to her neck. "I hadn't gone to sleep yet and I just had time to stuff my things into a suitcase and get down the fire escape. Some people couldn't even do that much. Poor Marty Holman had to leave his false teeth behind." The tears stopped as abruptly as they began, to be replaced by a high-pitched giggle. "You should have seen him, Vicki, my God, you should have seen what the old geezer looked like with his cheeks all sunk in and his eyes popping out and him shouting in this mumbly kind of way, 'My teeth, I've lost my teeth.' "

"It must have been hilarious," I said dryly. "You cannot live with me, Elena. It would drive me to homicide within forty-eight hours. Maybe less."

Her lower lip started to tremble again and she said in a terrible parody of baby talk, "Don't be mean to me, Vicki, don't be mean to poor old Elena, who got burned out of her house in the middle of the night. You're my own goddamn flesh and blood, my favorite brother's little girl. You can't toss poor old Elena out on the street like some worn-out mattress."

A door slammed sharply behind us. The banker who had just moved into the first-floor-north apartment erupted into the stairwell, his hands on his hips, his jaw sticking out pugnaciously. He was wearing navy-striped cotton pajamas; despite the bleary sleep in his face, his hair was perfectly combed.

"What the hell is going on out here? You may not have to work for a living—God knows what you do all day long up there—but I do. If you have to conduct your business in the middle of the night, show *some* consideration for your neighbors and don't do it out in the hall. If you don't shut up and get the hell out of here, I'm calling the cops."

I stared at him coldly. "I run a crack house upstairs. This is my supplier. You could be arrested for complicity if you're found hanging around out here when the police arrive."

Elena giggled, but said, "Don't be rude to him, Victoria—you never know when you may want a boy with fabulous eyes like that to do something for you." She added to the banker, "Don't worry, sweetie, I'm just coming in. We'll let you get your beauty sleep."

Behind the closed door to one-south a dog began to bark. I ground my teeth some more and hustled Elena inside, snatching her duffel bag from her when she began wobbling under its weight.

The banker watched us through narrowed eyes. When Elena lurched against him he made a face of pure horror and retreated hastily to his apartment, fumbling with the lock. I tried moving Elena upstairs, but she wanted to stop and talk about the banker, demanding to know why I hadn't asked him to carry her bag.

"It would have been a perfect way for you two to get acquainted, make things up a little."

I was close to screaming with frustration when the door to one-south opened. Mr. Contreras came out, a staggering sight in a crimson dressing gown. The golden retriever I share with him was straining against her collar, but when she saw me her low-throated growls changed to whimpers of excitement.

"Oh, it's you, doll," the old man said with relief. "The princess here woke me up and then I heard all the noise and thought, Oh my God, the worst is happening, someone's breaking in in the middle of the night. You oughta be more considerate, doll—it's hard for people who have to work to get up in the middle of the night like this."

"Yes, it is," I agreed brightly. "And contrary to public opinion, I am one of those working people. And believe me, I had no more desire to get out of bed at three A.M. than you did."

Elena put on her warmest smile and stuck out her hand to Mr. Contreras like Princess Diana greeting a soldier. "Elena Warshawski," she said. "Charmed to meet you. This little girl is my niece, and she's the prettiest, sweetest niece anybody could hope for."

Mr. Contreras shook her hand, blinking at her like an owl with a flashlight in its face. "Pleased to meet you," he said automatically if unenthusiastically. "Look, doll, you oughta get this lady—your aunt, you say?—you oughta get her up to bed. She ain't doing too great."

The sour yeasty smell had swept over him too. "Yep, that's just what I'll do. Come on, Elena. Let's get upstairs. Beddy-bye time."

Mr. Contreras headed back into his apartment. The dog was annoyed—if we were all having a party she wanted to join in.

"That wasn't very polite of him," Elena sniffed as Mr. Contreras's door closed behind us. "Didn't even tell me his own name when I went out of my way to introduce myself."

She grumbled all the way up the stairs. I didn't say anything, just kept a hand in the small of her back to propel her in the right direction, urging her on when she tried to stop for a breather at the second-floor landing.

Back in my apartment she wanted to ooh and aah over all my possessions. I ignored her and moved the coffee table so I could pull the bed out of the couch. I made it up and showed her where the bathroom was.

"Now listen, Elena. You are not staying here more than one night. Don't even think I'm going to waffle on this because I won't."

"Sure, baby, sure. What happened to your ma's piano? You sell it or something to buy this sweet little grand?"

"No," I said shortly. My mother's piano had been destroyed in the fire that gutted my own apartment three years earlier. "And don't think you can make me forget what I'm saying by raving over the piano. I'm going back to bed. You can sleep or not as you please, but in the morning you're going someplace else."

"Oh, don't look so ugly, Vicki. Victoria, I mean. It'll ruin your complexion if you frown like that. And where else am I supposed to turn in the middle of the night if not to my own flesh and blood?"

"Knock it off," I said wearily. "I'm too tired for it."

I shut the hall door without saying good night. I didn't bother to warn her not to rummage around for my liquor—if she wanted it badly enough, she'd find it, then apologize to me a hundred times the next day for breaking her promise not to drink it.

I lay in bed unable to sleep, feeling the pressure of Elena's presence from the next room. I could hear her scrabbling around for a while, then the hum of the TV turned conscientiously to low volume. I cursed my uncle Peter for moving to Kansas City and wished

I'd had the foresight to hightail it to Quebec or Seattle or some other place equally remote from Chicago. Around five, as the birds began their predawn twittering, I finally dropped into an uneasy sleep.

# 2

# The Lower Depths

The doorbell jerked me awake again at eight. I pulled my sweatshirt and shorts back on and stumbled into the living room. Nobody answered my query through the intercom. When I looked out the living-room window at the street, I could see the banker heading toward Diversey, his shoulders bobbing smugly. I flicked my thumb at his back.

Elena had slept through the episode, including my loud calls through the intercom. For a moment I felt possessed by the banker's angry impulse—I wanted to wake her and make her as uncomfortable as I was.

I stared down at her in disgust. She was lying on her back, mouth open, ragged snores jerking out as she inhaled, puffy short breaths as she exhaled. Her face was flushed. The broken veins on her nose stood out clearly. In the morning light I could see that the violet nightgown was long overdue for the laundry. The sight was appalling. But it was also unbearably pathetic. No one should be exposed to an outsider's view while she's sleeping, let alone someone as vulnerable as my aunt.

With a shudder I moved hastily to the back of the apartment. Unfortunately her pathos couldn't quell my anger at having her with me. Thanks to her, my head felt as though someone had dumped a load of gravel in it. Even worse, I was making a presentation to a potential client tomorrow. I wanted to finish my charts and get them turned into transparencies. Instead, it looked as though I'd be spend-

ing the day hunting for housing. Depending on how long that took, I
could end up paying as much as quadruple overtime for the transparencies.

I sat on the dining-room floor and did some breathing exercises,
trying to ease my knotted stomach. Finally I managed to relax
enough to do my prerun stretches.

Not wanting to see Elena's flushed face again, I went down the
back way, picking up Peppy outside Mr. Contreras's kitchen door.
The old man stuck his head out and called to me as I closed the gate;
I pretended not to hear him. I wasn't able to be similarly deaf when
I got back—he was waiting for me, sitting on the back stairs with the
*Sun-Times,* checking out his day's picks for Hawthorne. I tried leav-
ing the dog and escaping up the stairs but he grabbed my hand.

"Hang on a second there, cookie. Who was that lady you was
letting in last night?" Mr. Contreras is a retired machinist, a wid-
ower with a married daughter whom he doesn't particularly like.
During the three years we've been living in the same building he's
attached himself to my life like an adoptive uncle—or maybe a bar-
nacle.

I jerked my hand free. "My aunt. My father's younger sister. She
has a penchant for old men with good retirement benefits, so make
sure you have all your clothes on if she stops by to chat this afternoon."

That kind of comment always makes him huffy. I'm sure he
heard—and said—plenty worse on the floor in his machinist days—
but he can't take even oblique references to sex from me. He turns
red and gets as close to being angry as someone with his relentlessly
cheerful disposition can manage.

"There's no need to talk dirty to me," he snapped. "I'm just
concerned. And I gotta say, cookie, you shouldn't let people come
see you at all hours like that. Least, if you do, you shouldn't keep
them down in the hall talking loud enough to wake every soul in the
building."

I felt like wrenching one of the loose slats from the stairwell
railing and beating him with it. "I didn't invite her," I shrieked. "I
didn't know she was coming. I didn't want her here. I didn't want to
wake up at three in the morning."

"There's no need to shout," he said severely. "And even if you wasn't expecting her, you could'a gone up to your apartment to talk."

I opened and shut my mouth several times but couldn't construct a coherent response. Anyway, I'd kept Elena in the hall in the hopes she'd feel hurt enough to just pick up the duffel bag and go. But even as I'd done it I'd known in my heart of hearts that I couldn't turn her away at that hour. So the old man was right. Agreeing with him didn't make me any happier.

"Okay, okay," I snapped. "It won't happen again. Now get off my back—I've got a lot to do today." I stomped up the stairs to my kitchen.

Muted snores still seeped through the closed door from the living room. I made a pot of coffee and took a cup into the bathroom with me while I showered. Bent on leaving the apartment as fast as possible, I pulled on jeans and a white shirt and stopped in the kitchen to scratch together a breakfast.

Elena was sitting at the breakfast table. She'd put a soiled quilted dressing gown over the violet nightie. Her hands shook slightly; she used both of them to lift a cup of coffee to her mouth.

She produced an eager smile. "Wonderful coffee you make, baby. Just as good as your ma's."

"Thank you, Elena." I opened the refrigerator door and took stock of the meager contents. "I'm sorry I can't stay to chat, but I want to try to find you someplace to sleep tonight."

"Aw, Vicki—Victoria, I mean. Don't rush around like that. It ain't good for the heart. Let me stay here, just for a few days, anyway. Get over the shock of living through that inferno last night. I promise I won't bother you any. And I could get the place cleaned up a little while you're at work."

I shook my head implacably. "No way, Elena. I will not have you living here. Not one night longer."

Her face puckered. "Why do you hate me, baby? I'm your own daddy's sister. Family has to stick by family."

"I don't hate you. I don't want to live with anyone, but you and I lead especially incompatible lives. You know as well as I that Tony would say the same if he were still around."

There'd been a painful episode when Elena announced her independence from my grandmother and moved into her own apartment. Finding solitude not to her liking, she'd shown up at our house in South Chicago one weekend. She'd stayed three days. It wasn't my fierce mother who'd asked her to leave—Gabriella's love of the underdog somehow could encompass even Elena. But my easygoing father came home from the graveyard shift on Monday to find Elena passed out at the kitchen table. He put her into the detox unit at County and refused to talk to her for six months after she got out.

Elena apparently also remembered this episode. The pouty puckering disappeared from her face. She looked stricken, and somehow more real.

I squeezed her shoulder gently and offered to make her some eggs. She shook her head without speaking, watching me silently while I spread anchovy paste on toast. I ate it quickly and left before pity could overcome my judgment.

It was well past nine now. The morning rush was ending and I had an easy run across Belmont to the expressway. When I neared the Loop, though, the traffic congealed as we moved through a construction maze. The four miles on the Ryan between the Eisenhower and Thirty-first, supposedly the busiest eight lanes of traffic anywhere in the known universe, had finally crumbled under the stress of the semi's. The southbound lanes were closed while the feds performed reconstructive surgery.

My little Cavalier bounced between a couple of sixty-tonners as the slow lines of traffic snaked around the construction barricades. To my right the surface of the old roadbed had been completely removed; lattices of the reenforcing bars were exposed. They looked like tightly packed nests of vipers—here and there a rusty head stood up prepared to strike.

The turnoff to Lake Shore Drive had been so cleverly disguised that I was parallel with the barrel blocking one of the exit lanes before I realized it. With my sixty-ton pal close on my tail, I couldn't stand on the brakes and swerve around the barrel. I gnashed my teeth and rode down to Thirty-fifth, then took side streets up to Cermak.

Elena's SRO had stood a few doors north of the intersection with Indiana. A niggling doubt I'd had in her story vanished when I pulled up across the street from it. The Indiana Arms Hotel—transients welcome, rates by the day or by the month—had joined the other derelicts on the street in retirement. I parked and went over to look at the skeleton.

When I walked around to the north side of the building, I discovered a man in a sport jacket and hard hat poking around in the rubble. Every now and then he'd pick up some piece of debris with a pair of tongs and stick it into a plastic bag. He'd mark the bag and mutter into a pocket Dictaphone before continuing his exploration. He spotted me when he turned east to poke through a promising tell. He finished picking up an object and marking its container before coming over to me.

"You lose something here?" His tone was pleasant but his brown eyes were wary.

"Just sleep. Someone I know lived here until last night—she showed up at my place early this morning."

He pursed his lips, weighing my story. "In that case, what are you doing here now?"

I hunched a shoulder. "I guess I wanted to see it for myself. See if the place was really gone before I put all my energy into finding her a new home. Come to that, what are you doing here? A suspicious person might think you were making off with valuables."

He laughed and some of the wariness left his face. "They'd be right—in a way I am."

"Are you with the fire department?"

He shook his head. "Insurance company."

"Was it arson?" I'd been so bogged down in the sludge of family relations, I hadn't even wondered how the fire started.

His caution returned. "I'm just collecting things. The lab will give me a diagnosis."

I smiled. "You're right to be careful—you don't know who might come round in the aftermath of a blaze like this. My name's V. I. Warshawski. I'm a private investigator when I'm not looking for emergency housing. And I do projects for Ajax Insurance from time to time." I pulled a card from my bag and handed it to him.

He wiped a sooty hand on a Kleenex and shook mine. "Robin Bessinger. I'm with Ajax's arson and fraud division. I'm surprised I haven't heard your name."

It didn't surprise me. Ajax employed sixty thousand people

around the world—no one could possibly keep track of all of them. I explained that my work for them had been in claims or reinsurance and gave him a few names he'd be likely to recognize. He thawed further and confided that the signs of arson were quite clear.

"I'd show you the places where they poured accelerant but I don't want you in the building if you don't have a hard hat. Chunks of plaster keep falling down."

I showed suitable regret at being denied this treat. "The owner buy a lot of extra insurance lately?"

He shook his head. "I don't know—I haven't seen the policies. They just asked me to get on over before the vandals took too much of the evidence. I hope your friend got all her stuff out—not too much survived this blast."

I'd forgotten to ask Elena if anyone had been badly hurt. Robin told me the police Violent Crimes Unit would have joined the Bomb and Arson Squad in force if anyone had died.

"You wouldn't have been allowed to park without showing good reason for being near the premises—it's a fact of life that torchers like to come back to see if the job got done right. No one was killed, but a good half dozen were ferried to Michael Reese with burns and respiratory problems. Torchers usually like to make sure a building can be cleared—they know an investigation into an old dump like this won't get too much attention if there aren't any murder charges to excite the cops." He looked at his wrist. "I'd better get back to work. Hope your friend finds a new place okay."

I agreed fervently and went off to start my hunt with an easy optimism bred of ignorance. I began at the Emergency Housing Bureau on south Michigan where I joined a long line. There were women with children of all ages, old men muttering to themselves, rolling their eyes wildly, women anxiously clutching suitcases or small appliances—a seemingly endless sea of people left on the streets from some crisis or other yesterday.

The high counters and bare walls made us feel as though we were suppliants at the gates of a Soviet labor camp. There weren't any chairs; I took a number and leaned against the wall to wait my turn.

Next to me a very pregnant woman of about twenty holding a

large infant was struggling with a toddler. I offered to hold the baby or amuse the two-year-old.

"It's all right," she said in a soft slow voice. "Todd just be tired after staying up all night. We couldn't get into the shelter 'cause the one they sent us to don't allow babies. I couldn't get me no bus fare to come back here and get them to find us a different place."

"So what did you do?" I didn't know which was more horrible —her plight or the resigned gentle way she talked about it.

"Oh, we found us a park bench up at Edgewater by the shelter. The baby sleep but Todd just couldn't get comfortable."

"Don't you have any friends or relatives to help you out? What about the baby's father?"

"Oh, he be trying to find us a place," she said listlessly. "But he can't get no job. And my mother, we used to stay with her, but she had to go in the hospital, now it look like she going to be sick a long time and she can't keep up on her rent."

I looked around the room. Dozens of people were waiting ahead of me. Most of them had my neighbor's dragged-out look, bodies stooped over from too much shame. Those who didn't were pugnacious, waiting to take on a system they couldn't possibly beat. Elena's needs—my needs—could certainly take a far backseat to their demands for emergency shelter. Before I took off I asked if Todd and she would like some breakfast—I was going over to the Burger King to get something.

"They don't let you eat in here, but Todd could maybe go with you and get something."

Todd showed a great disinclination to be separated from his mother, even to get some food. Finally I left him whimpering at her side, went to the Burger King, got a dozen breakfast buns with eggs and wrapped the lot in a plastic bag to conceal the fact that it was food. I handed it to the woman and left as fast as I could. My skin was still trembling.

# 3

# Not St. Peter

The kinds of places Elena could afford didn't seem to advertise in the papers. The only residential hotels listed in the classifieds were in Lincoln Park and started at a hundred a week. Elena had paid seventy-five a month for her little room at the Indiana Arms.

I spent four hours futilely pounding the pavements. I combed the Near South Side, covering Cermak Road between Indiana and Halsted. A century ago it housed the Fields, the Searses, and the Armours. When they moved to the North Shore the area collapsed rapidly. Today it consists of vacant lots, auto dealers, public housing, and the occasional SRO. A few years ago someone decided to restore a blockful of the original mansions. They stand like a macabre ghost town, empty opulent shells in the midst of the decay that permeates the neighborhood.

The stilts of the Dan Ryan L running overhead made me feel tiny and useless as I went door to door, asking drunk or indifferent supers about a room for my aunt. I vaguely remembered reading about all the SRO's that came down when Presidential Towers went up, but somehow the impact this had on the street hadn't hit me before. There just wasn't housing available for people with Elena's limited means. The hotels I did find were all full—and victims of last night's fire, savvier than me, had been there at dawn renting the few rooms available. I realized that the fourth time a blowsy manager said, "Sorry, if you'd gotten here first thing this morning when we had something . . ."

At three I called off the search. Panicked at the prospect of housing Elena for some indefinite future, I drove into my Loop office to call my uncle Peter. It was a decision I could make only while panicked.

Peter was the first member of my family to make something substantial of his life. Maybe the only member besides my cousin Boom-Boom. Nine years younger than Elena, Peter had gone to work in the stockyards when he returned from Korea. He quickly realized that the people getting rich in meat packing weren't the Poles hitting cows over the head with hammers. Scraping together a few bucks from friends and relations, he started his own sausage manufacturing firm. The rest was the classic story of the American dream.

He followed the yards to Kansas City when they moved there in the early seventies. Now he lived in a huge house in the tony Mission Hills district, sent his wife to Paris to buy her spring clothes, shipped my cousins off to expensive private schools and summer camps, and drove late-model Nissans. Only in America. Peter also distanced himself as much as possible from the low-budget end of the family.

My office in the Pulteney Building was definitely down market. Most of the Loop expansion in recent years has been to the west. The Pulteney is at the southeast fringe where peep shows and pawn-shops push the rents down. The Wabash L rattles the fourth-floor windows, disturbing the pigeons and dirt that normally roost there.

My furnishings are Spartan gleanings from police auctions and resale shops. I used to hang an engraved sketch of the Uffizi over the filing cabinet, but last year I'd decided its intricate black detail looked too drab with all the olive furniture. In its place I'd put up some splashy posters of paintings by Nell Blaine and Georgia O'Keeffe. They gave the room a little color, but no one would mistake it for the hub of an international business.

Peter had been there once, when he brought his three children to Chicago for a tour several years ago. I had watched him swell visibly as he calculated the gap between our net present values.

Getting hold of him this afternoon took all my powers of persuasion, mixed in with a little bullying. My first worry, that he might be out of the country, or equally inaccessible on some golf course, proved groundless. But he had a phalanx of assistants convinced it was better to handle my business themselves than to disturb the great man. The most difficult skirmish came when I finally reached his personal secretary.

"I'm sorry, Miss Warshawski, but Mr. Warshawski has given me a list of family members who he'll let interrupt him and your name isn't on it." The Kansas twang was polite but unyielding.

I watched the pigeons check themselves for lice. "Could you get a message to him? While I hold? That his sister Elena will be arriving in Kansas City on the six o'clock flight and has cab fare to his house?"

"Does he know she's coming?"

"Nope. That's why I'm trying to get hold of him. To let him know."

Five minutes later—while I paid prime daytime rates to hold—Peter's deep voice was booming in my ear. What the hell did I mean, sending Elena to him unannounced like this. He wasn't having his children exposed to a lush like that, they didn't have guest space, he thought he'd made it clear four years ago that he was never—

"Yes, yes." I finally stanched the flow. "I know. A woman like Elena would just not fit into Mission Hills. The drunks there get manicures every week. I understand."

It wasn't the best opening to a plea for financial aid. After he'd finished shouting his outrage I explained the problem. The news that Elena was still in Chicago did not, as I'd hoped, bring him enough relief to agree to bail her out.

"Absolutely not. I made this totally clear to her the last time I helped her. That was when she foolishly squandered Mother's house in that cockamamie investment scheme. You may remember that I retained a lawyer for her who saw that she was able to salvage something from the sale. That was it—my last involvement in her affairs. It's time you learned the same lesson, Vic. An alkie like Elena will just milk you dry. The sooner you realize it, the easier your life will be."

Hearing some of my own negative thoughts echoed on his pompous lips made me squirm in my chair. "She paid for that lawyer though, Peter, if I remember rightly. She hasn't ever asked you for cash, has she? Anyway, I live in four rooms. I can't have her staying with me. All I want is enough money to make the rent on a decent apartment for a month while I help her find a place she can afford."

He gave a nasty laugh. "That's what your mother said that time Elena showed up at your place in South Chicago. Remember? Not even Tony could stomach having her around. Tony! He could tolerate anything."

"Unlike you," I commented dryly.

"I know you mean that as an insult but I take it as a compliment. What did Tony leave you when he died? That squalid house on Houston and the remains of his pension."

"And a name I'm proud to use," I snapped, thoroughly roused. "And come to that, you wouldn't have gotten your little meatball machine off the ground without his help. So do something for Elena in exchange. I'm sure wherever Tony is now he'd consider it a just quid pro quo."

"I paid Tony back to the nickel," Peter huffed. "And I don't owe him or you shit. And you know damned well it's sausages, not meatballs."

"Yeah, you paid back the nickel. But a share of the profits, even a little interest, wouldn't have killed you, would it?"

"Don't try that sentimental crap on me, Vic. I've been around the block too many times to fall for it."

"Just like a used car," I said bitterly.

The line went dead in my ear. The pleasure of having the exit line didn't compensate for losing the fight. Why in hell were the survivors in my father's family Peter and Elena? Why couldn't Peter have died and Tony been the one to hang around? Although not in the shape he was the last few years of his life. I swallowed bile and tried to shut out the image of my father the last year of his life, his face puffy, his body wrenched by uncontrollable coughing.

Pressing my lips together bitterly, I looked at the stack of unanswered mail and unfiled papers on my desk. Maybe it was time I got into the twentieth century while I still had a decade left to do it in. Make a big enough success of my work that I could at least afford a secretary to do some of the paperwork for me. An assistant who could take on some of the legwork.

I shuffled through the papers impatiently until I finally found the numbers I needed for my upcoming presentation. I called Visible

Treasures to see how late I could bring them in for overnight processing. They told me if I got them there by eight, they would typeset them and create transparencies for me at only double overtime. When I got the price quote I felt a little better—it wasn't going to be quite as bad as I'd feared.

I typed up my drafts on my mother's old Olivetti. If I couldn't afford an assistant, maybe at least I should blow a few thousand on a desktop publishing system. On the other hand, the force it took to use the Olivetti's keyboard kept my wrists strong.

It was a little after six when I finished typing. I dug through my drawers looking for a manila folder to put the charts in. When I didn't find a fresh one I dumped the contents of an insurance file onto the desk and stuck my documents into it. Now the desktop looked like the city landfill right after the trucks drop off their loads. I could see Peter looking at it, his face creasing into little rivulets of suppressed smugness. Maybe being committed to truth, justice, and the American Way didn't have to include working in slum conditions.

I put the insurance material back into its folder and took it over to the filing cabinets, where I found a section on business expenses that seemed close enough. With a glow of virtue I stuck "insurance" in between "Illinois Bell" and "lease." Having gotten that far, I went through the two weeks of mail sitting on the desk, writing a few checks, filing documents, and trashing the circulars. Near the bottom of the stack I found a thick white letter the size of a wedding invitation with "Cook County Women for Open Government" in engraved script on the top left.

I was about to pitch it when I suddenly realized what it was—in a fit of insanity I had agreed to be a sponsor for a political fundraiser. Marissa Duncan and I had worked together in the public defender's office an aeon or two ago. She was one of those people who live and die for politics, whether in the office or on the street, and she chose her issues carefully. She'd been active in our drive to unionize the PD's office, for example, but she'd steered clear of involvement in the politics of abortion—she didn't want anything to drag her down if she decided to run for office.

She'd left the PD a number of years ago to work in Jane Byrne's disastrous second mayoral campaign; she now had a cushy job with a big public relations firm that specialized in selling candidates. She phones me only when she's masterminding some great campaign. When she called four weeks ago I'd just finished a tricky job for a ball-bearing manufacturer in Kankakee. She'd caught me basking in the glow that comes from a display of competence combined with a large check.

"Great news," she'd said enthusiastically, riding over my tepid hello. "Boots Meagher is going to sponsor a fund-raiser for Rosalyn Fuentes."

"I appreciate your letting me know," I said politely. "I won't have to buy the *Star* in the morning."

"You always did have a great sense of humor, Vic." Politicians can't afford to tell you they think you're a pain in the butt. "But this is *really* exciting. It's the first time Boots has ever endorsed a woman in such a public way. He's going to hold a party at his place in Streamwood. It'll be a terrific chance to meet the candidate, get to know some of the people on the County Board. Everyone's going to be there. Rostenkowski and Dixon may even stop by."

"My heart is turning over just at the thought. How much you selling tickets for?"

"Five hundred to sponsor."

"Too rich for my blood. Anyway, I thought you said Meagher was sponsoring her," I objected, just to be obnoxious.

A thread of impatience finally hit her voice. "Vic, you know the drill. Five hundred to be listed in the program as a sponsor. Two-fifty to be a patron. A hundred to get in the front door."

"Sorry, Marissa. Way out of my league. And I ain't that big a fan of Boots anyway." His real name was Donnel—he'd gotten the nickname when the '72 reformers thought they could get Daley's men off the county slate. They'd run some poor earnest wimp whose name I couldn't even remember on the slogan of "Give Meagher the Boot." When Daley muscle got the big guy reelected by a landslide, his supporters at the Bismarck celebration party had screamed "Boots, Boots" when he appeared and he'd never been called anything else since.

Marissa said earnestly, "Vic, we need more women out there. Otherwise it's going to look as though Roz has sold out to Boots and we'll lose a lot of our grass-roots support. And even though you're not with the PD anymore, your name still commands a lot of respect with local women."

Anyway, to make a long story short, she'd used flattery, Fuentes's pro-choice record, and my guilt for having dropped out of political action for so long to get me to agree to be a patron. And I did have a two-thousand-dollar check beaming at me from the desk.

The thick white envelope held the invitation, a copy of the program, and a return envelope for my two hundred and fifty dollars. Marissa had scrawled on the program in her giant, schoolgirl hand, *"Really* looking forward to seeing you again."

I flipped through the booklet, looking at the list of sponsors and patrons. Having agreed to hold the fund-raiser, Boots had gone all out putting the arm on the regular Dems. Or maybe that was Marissa's work. The pages glittered with judges, state reps, state senators, and directors of large corporations. Near the end of the list of patrons was my name. From some ancient yearbook or birth certificate Marissa had dug up my middle name. When I saw the "Iphigenia" jumping out at me, I was tempted to call her and withdraw my support—I try to keep my mother's lunacy in naming me a secret known only to family.

The function was this coming Sunday. I looked at my watch—seven-fifteen. I could call Marissa and still make it to Visible Treasures in time.

Late though it was, she was still in her office. She tried to sound pleased at hearing from me, but couldn't quite carry it off—Marissa likes me better when I'm doing favors for her.

"You all set for Sunday, Vic?"

"You bet," I said enthusiastically. "What are we wearing? Jeans or evening gowns?"

She relaxed. "Oh, it's casual—barbecue, you know. I'll probably wear a dress, but jeans will be fine."

"Rosty coming? You said he might."

"No. But the head of his Chicago office will be there. Cindy Mathiessen."

"Great." I made myself sound like a cheerleader. "I want to talk to her about Presidential Towers."

Caution returned to Marissa's voice at once as she demanded to know why I wanted to discuss the complex.

"The SRO's," I said earnestly. "You know, about eight thousand rooms were lost when they cleared that area to put up the Towers. I've got this aunt, see." I explained about Elena and the fire. "So I'm not feeling too crazy about Boots, or Rosty, or any of the other local Dems since I can't find her a room. But I'm sure if I bring it to— what did you same her name was?—Cindy? If I talk to Cindy about it, she's bound to be able to help me out."

It seemed to me the phone vibrated with the sound of wheels turning in Marissa's brain. Finally she said, "What can your aunt afford?"

"She was paying seventy-five at the Indiana Arms. A month, I mean." It was past sundown now and the room was dark beyond the pool of light my desk lamp shed. I walked over to the wall with the phone to switch on the overheads.

"If I can get her a place, will you promise not to talk about Presidential Towers on Sunday? With anyone? It's a little touchy for people."

For the Dems, she meant. With the spotlight already on the Speaker of the House for ethics questions, they didn't want anything embarrassing said to one of his buddies.

I made a show of reluctance. "Can you do it by tomorrow night?"

"If that's what it'll take, Vic, I'll do it by tomorrow night." She didn't try to keep the snarl from her voice.

I had just twenty minutes to get to Visible Treasures before paying quadruple overtime, but I took the extra minute to write out a check to Cook County Women for Open Government. As I locked the office door behind me I started whistling for the first time all day. Who says blackmailers don't have fun?

# 4

# Auntie Does a Bunk

It was almost nine by the time I got off the Kennedy at California and headed over to Racine. I hadn't had dinner, hadn't had anything since grabbing a Polish at a hole-in-the-wall on Canal at two. I wanted peace and quiet, a hot bath, a drink and a pleasant dinner—I had a veal chop in the freezer I'd been saving for just such a tired evening. Instead I braced myself for a night with Elena.

When I parked across the street and looked up at the third floor, the windows were dark. As I trudged up the stairs I imagined my aunt passed out at the kitchen table. Or on the unmade sofa bed in the living room. Or downstairs seducing Mr. Contreras.

I hadn't given Elena keys or instructions on the two dead bolts. I undid the bottom lock—the one that locks automatically when you shut the door—and switched on the light in the little entryway. It shed a dim glow into the living room. I could see the sofa was restored to its normal upright position.

I went through the dining room to the kitchen and turned on the light there. The kitchen was sparkling. The three days' accumulation of dishes in the sink had been washed and put away. The newspapers were gone, the floor washed, and the tabletop clean and tidy. In the middle sat a sheet torn from one of my yellow pads covered with Elena's sprawling, unsteady writing. She'd written "Vicki," then crossed it out and changed it to "Victoria, Baby."

Thanks a lot for the loan of a bed last night when I needed it. I knew I could count on you in a pinch, you always were a good girl, but I don't mean to hang around and be a burden on you, which I can see I would be, so here's good luck to you kid and I'll be seeing you in the sweet by and by, like they say.

She'd drawn eight big X's and signed her name.

Since three this morning I'd been cursing my aunt for coming to me and wishing I'd return home to find that I'd dreamed the whole episode. I'd gotten my wish, but instead of being elated I felt a little hollow under the diaphragm. Despite her easy camaraderie, Elena didn't have friends. Of course the streets and alleys of Chicago were strewn with her former lovers, but I didn't think any of them would remember Elena if she showed up at their doors. Come to think of it, I'm not sure Elena would remember any of them well enough to know which doors to knock on.

The other unpleasant notion hovering in my mind's back cupboard was prompted by Elena's final sentence. In a high school dramatization of *Tom Sawyer* we'd sung "In the sweet bye-and-bye." It was supposed to be typical of late Victorian hymnology. As I recalled, the sweet bye-and-bye was a syrupy euphemism for life beyond the grave. I had never spent enough time with Elena to know if it was just some catch phrase she used or if she'd gone off to throw herself over the Wacker Drive bridge.

I went carefully through the apartment to see if she'd left any clue to her intentions. The duffel bag was gone, along with the violet nightdress. When I looked in the liquor cabinet I saw nothing was missing except five inches from the open bottle of Johnnie Walker. But from the way she'd been sleeping this morning I kind of thought she'd drunk that before going to bed.

In a way I wished she'd taken the bottle—it would have made me more certain she hadn't any immediate intention of suicide. On the other hand, did someone really spend her whole life drinking and mooching off people and then suddenly have such a strong sense of remorse that at age sixty-six she couldn't take it anymore? On the surface it didn't sound too likely. Lack of sleep and my day among the burned-out buildings of the Near South Side were making me unnaturally morbid.

I debated phoning Lotty Herschel to discuss the matter with her. She's a doctor who sees a fair number of drunks in her storefront clinic on Damen. On the other hand, her day starts at seven with hospital rounds. This was a bit late for a call whose main function was to allay my uneasy conscience.

I put the Black Label back into the cupboard without pouring any. The drink part of my program had lost its appeal when I thought about Elena swallowing five inches and falling into a red-faced stupor. I went into the kitchen, pulled the veal chop from the freezer, and stuck it in my little toaster oven to thaw while I took a bath. Unless I wanted to rouse the police, there was nothing I could do about my aunt tonight.

Somehow soaking in the tub didn't relax me the way it usually did. The image of Elena, her gallant smile a bit lopsided, sitting on a park bench with the family I'd encountered at the Emergency Housing Bureau kept coming between me and rest. I lumbered out of the tub, turned off the little oven, and got dressed again.

Mr. Contreras's living-room light had been on when I came in. I went down the front stairs and knocked on his door. The dog whimpered impatiently as he scrabbled with the locks. When he finally opened the door she leapt up to lick my face. I asked the old man if he'd seen Elena leave.

Of course he had—when he wasn't gardening or checking the races, he was keeping a close eye on the building. We didn't really need a watchdog with him on the premises. Elena had left around two-thirty. No, he couldn't tell me what she was wearing, or if she had any makeup on, what kind of person did I think he was, staring at people and snooping into their private lives. What he could tell me was she'd caught a bus on Diversey on account of he'd gone down to the corner for some milk and seen her climb on. Eastbound, that was right.

"You wasn't expecting her to leave?"

I hunched my shoulders impatiently. "She doesn't have any place to go. Not that I know of."

He clicked his tongue sympathetically and started on a detailed interrogation. My thin stack of patience was about gone when the banker once more opened his door. He was wearing form-fitting Ralph Lauren jeans and a polo shirt.

"Jesus Christ! If I'd known you stood around yelling in the stairwell at all hours, I'd never have bought into this place." His round face puckered up in a scowl.

"And if I'd known what a tight-assed crybaby you were, I'd have blocked your purchase," I responded nastily.

The dog growled deep in her throat.

"You go on up, cookie," Mr. Contreras urged me hastily. "I'll call you if I remember anything else." He pulled the dog into the apartment with him and shut the door. I could hear Peppy whining and snuffling behind it, eager to join in the fight.

"Just what is it you *do* do?" the banker demanded.

I smiled. "Nothing I need a zoning permit for, sugar, so don't wear out your brain worrying about it."

"Well, if you don't stop doing it in the stairwells, I really will call the cops." He slammed his door shut on me.

I stomped back up the stairs. Now he'd have something substantial to tell his girlfriend or his mother or whoever he phoned at night. I live to serve others.

Back in my apartment I turned the little oven on again and started cooking mushrooms and onions in some red wine. Getting the picture of Elena heading east on the Diversey bus made me feel a bit easier. That sounded as though she had a specific destination in mind. In the morning, as a sop to my conscience, I'd talk to one of my police department pals. Maybe they wouldn't mind tracking down the bus driver, find out if he remembered her and where she'd headed when she'd left the bus. Maybe I'd be the first woman on the moon—stranger things have happened.

It was well after ten when I finally sat down with my dinner. The chop was cooked to a turn, just pink inside, and the glazed mushrooms complemented it perfectly. I'd eaten about half of it when the phone rang. I debated letting it go, then thought of Elena. If she'd been trying to sell her ass on Clark Street it could be the cops wanting me to bail her out.

It was a police officer, but he didn't know Elena and he was calling for purely personal reasons. At least partly personal reasons. I'd met Michael Furey when I went to the Mallorys' last New Year's

Day for dinner. His father and Bobby had grown up together in Norwood Park. When Michael joined the police fresh out of junior college, Bobby kept an avuncular eye on him. In Chicago people look after their own, but Bobby is a scrupulously honorable cop—he wouldn't use personal influence to promote a friend's son's career. The boy proved himself on his own, though; after fifteen years Bobby was glad to welcome him into the Violent Crimes Unit at the Central District.

For a while following the transfer Eileen invited the two of us up to dinner on a regular basis. She longed not so much for my second marriage as for my children—she kept trotting the brightest and best of the Chicago police by me in the hopes that one of them would look like good father material to me.

Eileen belonged to the generation that believes a guy with a good set of wheels is more appealing than one who can afford only a Honda. Furey had a little money—his father's life insurance, he said, which he'd been able to invest—and he drove a silver Corvette. He was attractive and cheerful, and I did like driving the Corvette, but we didn't have much except the Mallorys and a love of sports in common. Our relationship settled into an occasional trip to the Stadium or a ball game together. Eileen masked her disappointment but stopped the dinner invitations.

"Vic! Glad I caught you in," Michael boomed cheerfully into my ear.

I finished chewing. "Hiya, Michael. What's up?"

"Just got off shift. Thought I'd check in and see how you're doing."

"Why, Michael," I said with mock sincerity, "how thoughtful of you. How long has it been—a month or so?—and you check in with me at ten P.M.?"

He laughed a little consciously. "Aw, heck, Vic. You know how it is. I got something to ask and I don't want you taking it the wrong way."

"Try me."

"It's—uh, well, just I didn't know you were interested in county politics."

"I'm not especially." I was surprised.

"Ernie told me you're listed as a sponsor for the Fuentes fund-raiser out at Boots's farm on Sunday."

"News sure do travel fast," I said lightly, but I felt myself tensing in reflexive annoyance—I hate having my activities monitored. "How does Ernie know and why does he care?"

Ernie Wunsch and Ron Grasso had grown up with Michael on the northwest side. The odd political jobs they'd done as teenagers and young adults hadn't hurt them any when they decided to join Ernie's dad's general contracting firm after college. Their company wasn't one of the giants, but more and more often you saw cement trucks with Wunsch & Grasso's red and green stripes at construction sites. Their biggest coup had been getting the bid on the Rapelec complex, an office-condo center under construction near the Gold Coast.

"I was afraid you'd take this the wrong way," Michael said plaintively. "Ernie doesn't care. He knows because he and his old man have done a certain amount of work for the county over the years. So of course he gets asked to all the fund-raisers. You know how it is in Chicago, Vic—if you do business with the city or the county, you gotta engage in a little reciprocity."

I knew how it was.

"So of course they got an advance look at the program. And Ernie knows you and I are—well, friends. So he mentioned it. Not something you really need to get hot about."

"No," I agreed meekly. "It just takes me by surprise when two unconnected parts of my life suddenly hook up."

"Know the feeling," he agreed. "I just was wondering if I could go with you. I might attend anyway, since the boys are roping in as many victims as they can. If you're going to be there . . ."

"Let me think about it," I said, after a pause too long to be really polite. "Although—look, I wonder if you could do something for me." I told him about Elena. "I don't know much about her—what her hangouts are. And even though I don't want her living with me, I'm a little worried. I'd kind of like to know she's okay, wherever she is."

"Christ, Vic, you don't want much, do you? You know damned well there's no way I can go to the CTA without a good reason. If I start checking routes and talking to drivers, their union'll be at Uncle Bobby's door within the hour screaming for my butt."

"Maybe I should call Bobby in the morning, talk it over with him." Besides being Michael's godfather, Bobby Mallory had been my own father's protégé and his best friend on the force. He might check up on Elena for Tony's sake—I wouldn't expect him to do it for mine.

"No, don't do that," Michael said hastily. "Tell you what—I'll pass it on to the uniforms on Madison and the Near South Side, ask them to keep an eye out for her and call me if they see her."

"I don't want her being hassled," I warned him.

"Cool your jets, Vic. Discretion is my middle name."

"Yeah, right, and I'm the Queen of Sheba."

He laughed. "So if I look into it, you'll go to Boots's with me on Sunday?"

"Something like that," I admitted, blushing in spite of myself.

"I ought to run you in for trying to bribe a cop." It was a grumble, but the tone was good-natured; he promised to call me tomorrow if he turned anything up. He arranged to meet me at three on Sunday; since he knew the way he offered to drive. I said I'd follow him in my own car—I didn't want to hang around Boots Meagher's farm until midnight while Michael caught up with his old precinct pals.

By the time we hung up my chop had gotten cold and the glazed wine sauce was congealed. I was too tired to heat it up again tonight. Sticking the plate in the refrigerator, I fell into bed and spent the night in uneasy dreams in which I chased Elena across Chicago, always just missing her as she boarded the eastbound Diversey bus.

# 5

# Royal Suite

I worked for the county for five years after passing the bar. During my summers in law school I interned at the Loop's giant firms, and I'd held a lot of weird jobs to finance my college education. The worst was selling books by phone for *Time-Life* from five to nine in the evening. You call people at dinner and they scream at you. Eight or nine times I phoned homes of dead people—once the woman had died only the day before. I extricated myself from her sobbing daughter swiftly and gracelessly.

So I know working for myself beats a whole roster of other employers I can list. Still, being a private investigator is not the romance of the loner knight that Marlowe and Spenser like to pretend—half the time you're doing some kind of tedious surveillance or spending your day in the Daley Center checking backgrounds. And a good chunk of the rest of the time goes to selling people on hiring your services. Often not successfully.

Cartwright & Wheeler, insurance brokers, listened closely to my presentation on the perils and possibilities of filing false claims. They asked a lot of questions, but the nine people in the room didn't feel able to make a decision on hiring me without consulting senior staff. I exuded warmth, professionalism, and a positive mental attitude while trying to force a commitment, but the best I could get was a promise to discuss it at Monday's management meeting.

I went back to my office to stow my five hundred dollars' worth of transparencies in a filing cabinet. Usually I don't get too upset by a lukewarm response, but I was feeling edgy enough about Elena that I slammed drawers and tore up mail to vent my irritation. Larry Bowa liked to destroy toilets after a bad game. We all have our little immature quirks.

When I'd calmed down some I checked in with my answering service. Marissa Duncan had left a message. I called back and spoke with her secretary. Marissa had found a room for Elena in a residential hotel on Kenmore between Wilson and Lawrence. They wanted ninety a month for it. I hesitated a moment. I hated to turn it down —Marissa would be peeved and she had enough connections that I was better off with her feeling good about me. Even worse, what if Elena showed up again at three in the morning?

"She can't move in right away," I said at last. "But I'll stop by and pay for the room on my way home."

"Cash," the secretary said briefly. "And no pets or children."

"Fine." I double-checked the address and hung up. For the first time in my life I found myself wondering what Elena had done for birth control all those years. And I suddenly realized why Gabriella had been so accepting the time she showed up at our house thirty years ago. I couldn't put my finger on exactly what had been said, but Elena had been pregnant. Gabriella helped her find some kind of underground abortion and Elena got drunk.

I sat at my desk, my shoulders slumped, watching the pigeons fight for space on the windowsill. Finally I stretched out a hand to switch on the desk lamp and called Michael Furey at the Central District. He didn't sound enthusiastic at hearing from me, but he said he'd checked the morgue and some of the area hospitals—no gray-haired drunk women had been hauled in since yesterday afternoon.

"Gotta go, Vic, we're hard at it. See you Sunday. . . ."

Normally I would have chafed him about being hard at a poker game, but I hung up without saying anything—I wasn't in the mood for jokes.

I'd noticed too late that one of the pieces of mail I was shredding was from an old client. I rummaged through the scraps on the floor and reconstructed enough of it to see that it was a request for a simple background check. It would keep until Monday—I wasn't in the humor to do that tonight, either. The rest of the paper I scooped up and put into the trash.

Embarrassed by my earlier outburst, I soberly filed the papers remaining on my desk, then went to the ladies' room on the seventh floor for some water to scrub down the surface. That looked so good that I finished by washing the windowsills and filing cabinets too. Clean now in thought, word, and deed, I locked up the office.

En route to the garage I stopped at a cash machine to get the ninety dollars, then joined the slow procession out of the Loop. Everyone leaves work early on Friday in order to maximize the amount of time spent sitting in traffic before starting the weekend.

It was a little before five when I reached the Windsor Arms on Kenmore. The building had gone up when the Duke was in his heyday, enjoying Goering's hospitality and lending his name to residential hotels that hoped to reflect his royal splendor. The Duke of Windsor was dead now, but the hotel hadn't been so lucky. If the facade had been washed since George VI's ascension, it didn't show. Not much more attention had been paid to basic repairs—a number of windows had pieces of cardboard filling in for missing panes.

The inside smelled faintly of boiled cabbage, despite a large poster over the desk that stated emphatically, *"Absolutely* No Cooking in Rooms." Next to the sign Alderman Helen Schiller's face smiled beatifically out at her voters.

No one was behind the desk, but a handful of residents sat in a small lounge watching Vanna White on a tiny TV chained high on the wall. I walked over and asked if anyone knew where the manager was. A middle-aged woman in a sleeveless housedress looked at me suspiciously—people in business suits and nylons who come to residential hotels are usually city inspectors or lawyers threatening action on behalf of the family of a dead resident.

I gave my most trustworthy smile. "I understand you have a room here. For Elena Warshawski."

"What about it?" The woman had the heavy flat drawl of the Irish South Side.

"I'm her niece. She'll be by in a couple of days to move in, but I wanted to pay for a month in advance to hold the room for her."

The woman looked me up and down, her watery gray eyes tight and ungiving. At last she decided my sanctimonious honesty was the real thing. She turned back to the set, waited for a commercial, then heaved herself ponderously out of the vinyl-coated armchair. I followed her out to the desk and behind it into a cubbyhole whose outstanding feature was a large lockbox.

The chatelaine counted my tens twice, wrote out a receipt in a labored hand, then put the money in a sealed envelope and slid it through a slot in the side of the box.

"I don't know how to get into that sucker, so don't think your boyfriend can come around and hold a gun on me to get your money back for you. They come and empty it out twice a week."

"No, ma'am," I agreed helplessly.

"Now I'll show you the room. When your aunt's ready to move in she can come on over. Make sure she brings the receipt with her."

We walked up three flights of stairs, slowly, to accommodate my guide's short, panting breaths, and down an uncarpeted corridor. Empty glass fixtures over the doors were a reminder of the Windsor Arms's grander days—the hall was lighted now by two naked bulbs. The desk clerk stopped at the second door from the end of the left side and unlocked it.

Whoever owned the building apparently owed Marissa Duncan a favor. Either that or hoped Marissa would provide a friendly push up the local political ladder. The window held all four panes, the floor was clean, and the narrow bed made up tidily. A white plastic chest of drawers stood in the corner. A deal table under the window completed the furnishings.

"Bathroom's down the hall. She can lock her stuff in a chest under the bed if she's afraid of junkies. Key comes to me when she's not in the room. And absolutely no cooking in here. The wiring's old. Don't want the place going up in smoke around us."

I agreed soberly and followed her back down the stairs. She returned to *Wheel of Fortune* without another look at me. Once outside I gulped in the air in great mouthfuls.

I never seem to make enough money to put more than a thousand or so into a Keogh plan every year. What was I going to live on when I got too old to hustle clients any longer? The thought of being sixty-six, alone, living in a little room with three plastic drawers to hold my clothes—a shudder swept through me, almost knocking me off balance. A woman with three children in tow yanked them past me—I was just a falling-down drunk for her children to stare at on their way home. I climbed heavily into the Chevy and headed south.

The mixture of guilt and fear the Windsor Arms stirred in me took the edge off my pleasure in the weekend. I went to the grocery Saturday morning and got fruit and yogurt for the week ahead. But when I picked out supplies for a pasta salad I was taking to an impromptu picnic that afternoon I bypassed my usual olive oil for a cheap brand—how could I spend eleven dollars on a pint of olive oil when I couldn't scrape together enough for a third-quarter deposit into my Keogh? I even bought domestic Parmesan. Gabriella would have upbraided me sharply—but then she wouldn't have approved of my buying pasta in a store to begin with.

I got all three morning papers and read them carefully before going over to the park. So far nobody had found any unidentified older women in the river or roaming dementedly about the streets. I had to trust that Furey, or Bobby Mallory himself, would call me if Elena had been arrested. There didn't seem to be anything else for me to do except join my pals at Montrose Harbor and take my aggressions out on a softball.

I couldn't quite shake off my depression, but a game-saving catch I made in the sixth inning cheered me—I hadn't known I could still dive for a ball and come up with it the way I did at twenty. Over Soave and grilled chicken afterwards, I couldn't quite get into the ribald spirits of my friends. I left while the party was still in progress so as to catch the ten o'clock news.

Elena still hadn't surfaced in a dramatic way. I finally decided she was hanging out someplace with Annie Greensleeves and went to bed, torn between disgust with her and irritation with myself.

I'd half been hoping that the gods would blight Boots's party with violent thundershowers, but Sunday dawned with more of the bright, merciless sunshine we'd suffered from all summer. With September drawing to a close, the days were merely warm instead of sweltering, but the Midwest was still suffering from its worst drought in fifty years.

All around the city sidewalks and roadbeds had buckled and collapsed. During the height of the heat wave sparks from the trains had ignited beams holding up the L platforms so that various stations were now closed more or less permanently. Given Chicago's perennial cash shortfall, I didn't expect to see those stops reopen in my lifetime.

I ran Peppy to Belmont Harbor and back, then made my way through the Sunday papers. The *Sun-Times* was the hardest—I've never figured out their organizational scheme and I had to read a lot more than I wanted about home decorating and fall festivals in Wisconsin before stumbling on the metropolitan news.

When I'd finished the *Herald-Star* without finding any word on Elena, it was time to shower and dress for my two-hundred-and-fifty-dollar barbecue. I knew Marissa would probably show up in silk lounging pajamas or something equally exotic, but unless Rosalyn Fuentes had changed dramatically, she would probably wear jeans. It seemed to me good fund-raising etiquette dictated not to upstage the guest of honor. Besides, I didn't want to worry about dry-clean-only clothes at a giant picnic. I put on khaki slacks and a loose-fitting olive shirt. Neat—would camouflage food spills and above all be comfortable for an afternoon in the sun.

Michael arrived a little before three, his black hair and dark eyes set off vividly by a navy blazer and pale blue polo shirt. His normal good spirits had spilled over into exuberance—he liked big parties, he liked getting together with his pals, and he had enough old-fashioned Dem in him to look forward to an afternoon hobnobbing with party bigwigs.

I made a great show of salaams at his elegance. "You sure you want to arrive at Boots's with me? It's really going to tone down your image."

He gave me a mock tap to the nose. "You make me look good, Warshawski. That's why I want you to stay close this afternoon."

"The slum next to the suburb? That's kind of how I feel about the whole affair." Somehow his effervescence made me feel like being disagreeable.

"Aw, come on, Warshawski. Do you really like living in the trash and graffiti? Secretly, down deep, wouldn't you live in the clean open spaces if you could afford it?"

"You stay in Norwood Park," I reminded him.

"Only because those of us who serve and protect you from the graffiti artists have to live in the city. And Chicago crime is more interesting to be around than the stuff in Streamwood."

"Well, that's what I think too. That's why I can't see myself out there." I took my billfold from my handbag and stuffed it in a pants pocket along with my invitation to the party—I didn't want to lug a purse around the picnic all afternoon.

"But you do a lot of investigations in the suburbs," Michael objected as we left my apartment.

"That's why I like city crime better." I turned the double locks. "Someone bonks you on the head and steals your purse. They don't sit in board rooms raving on about the niggers in Chicago while they're sliding a million or two off the top from the company."

"I could introduce you to some muggers," Michael offered when we reached the street. "They need some PR—maybe you're just the gal for them." He sketched a billboard with his hands. "I can kind of see it—clean, honest crime like your granddaddy used to commit."

I laughed in spite of myself. "Okay, okay. Muggers are scum. I just have a chip on my shoulder about the suburbs, that's all. Anyway, I can't afford them. I wouldn't mind knowing what Boots did to finance a move from Division and Central to Streamwood."

Michael framed my face with his hands and kissed me. "Do me a favor, Vic—just don't ask him this afternoon."

I disengaged myself and got into the Chevy. "Don't worry—my mama brought me up to know how to act in public. See you at the ball."

He hopped into the Corvette, flashed his lights at me a few times, and took off toward Belmont with a great screeching of rubber.

# 6

# County Picnic

**O**nce we were on the Kennedy I lost track of Michael. He could afford to do eighty—the highway patrol would give him a professional wink they wouldn't extend to me. He was waiting for me at the exit to the Northwest Tollway; I had him more or less in view as we started winding our way through the hills that swell to the northwest as you leave Chicago.

I'm not sure I would have found Boots's spread if I hadn't been following Michael, at least not on the first go-round. The entrance, which lay on a twisting unlabeled street, was a discreet opening in the hedge separating the road from the gaze of the vulgar. Michael had been going close to sixty around the curves. He braked the Corvette and turned without warning, so that I had to screech to a halt beyond the entrance and find a long enough flat stretch to make a U in. Boys will be boys.

He was waiting for me beside a gate that lay ten feet or so from the hole in the hedge I had turned through. The shrubbery lining the drive partly concealed a ten-foot-high fence connected to the gate. If you tried to breach the ramparts anyway there were a couple of sheriff's deputies to shoot you down.

"Sorry, Vic," Furey said penitently, "I thought the turnoff was up the road another half mile. Shouldn't have been showing off on such a dangerous stretch." When one of the deputies asked me for my invitation, Furey added, "Oh, don't bother her—she's with me."

"Not so's you'd notice it." I fished in my bag for the invitation and held it out, but the guard waved me on without looking at it. This assumption of my relationship to Michael added to my ill humor. I got back into my Chevy while Michael joked with the other men, maneuvered around the Corvette, and drove away with a little spit of gravel. Before the road twisted I could see Furey get back into the Corvette, but I turned a bend and found myself alone on a tree-lined drive.

Whatever damage the summer had done to the corn crop, it hadn't hurt Boots particularly. The trees here showed full, graceful leaves and the grass beyond them was thick and green. In the distance I could make out a stand of corn. I guess if you're chairman of the County Board there are ways to get water to your farm.

I turned another bend and found myself at the party. I'd been hearing music blaring in the distance ever since leaving the front gate. Now I could see a big bandstand beyond the main house with a band in straw boaters and navy blazers going full bore. On the other side of the house smoke hovered lazily over what was presumably the barbecue pit. Boots was sacrificing one of his own cows to Roz's campaign.

A sheriff's deputy, swinging an outsize flashlight, directed me to a crowd of cars in a big yard northeast of the house. Maybe it was a pasture—I remembered seeing one on a Girl Scout outing when I was eleven. Despite the presence of the deputies—or because of them—I carefully locked the Chevy.

Furey caught up with me as I headed toward the bandstand where most of the party was gathered. "Goddamnit, Vic, what's making you so shirty?"

I stopped to look at him. "Michael, I paid two hundred and fifty dollars for the doubtful pleasure of coming to this shindig. I'm not your date, nor yet 'the little woman' whom you can tuck under your arm and hustle past the guards."

His good-humored face tightened into a scowl. "What the hell are you talking about?"

"You treated me like a cipher out there—leaving me standing in the road and then telling the deputies to ignore me because I was your appendage. I don't like it."

He flung up his hands in exasperation. "I was trying to do you a favor, save you a little hassle with the boys at the gate. If I'd known you were going to treat it like a mortal insult I'd of saved my breath."

He strode off toward the crowd. I followed him slowly, irritated as much with myself as with Furey. I didn't like the little trick stunt he'd pulled at the turnoff, but that didn't justify my retaliating in kind. Maybe frustration over Elena's disappearance was making me testy. Or my innate bad humor. Or just being at a Cook County political fund-raiser.

The last time I remembered seeing Boots in the news one of his bodyguards had beaten in the face of a man who had come too close to the boss after a County Board meeting. The man claimed Boots had murdered his daughter—heavy accusations, although he had a long history at Elgin—but breaking someone's nose seemed like an excessive response to insanity. In fairness to Boots, he'd picked up the guy's hospital tab later on—but why did he need bodyguards at all?

That was only the most recent public episode Meagher had been involved in. He also had fingers in dozens of business ventures in the state, the kinds of deals where everybody gets rich if they know which way the tax breaks are going to land. Meagher was a you-scratch-my-back kind of guy—he wouldn't be hosting Rosalyn's fund-raiser if she hadn't made some significant concessions to him.

It wasn't as though Roz were a close pal. She'd been a community organizer in Logan Square when I was with the PD. I'd worked with her on some seminars on law and the community—some ABC's to teach the residents their rights in arenas ranging from housing to immigration officers. Roz was bright, energetic, and a skillful politician. And ambitious. And that meant getting into bed with Boots if she was going to rule a wider sphere than Logan Square. I understood that and I knew it wasn't any of my business, anyway. So why was I getting my tail in a knot?

I skirted my way through the crowd at the bandstand to a bright canopy covering the refreshment arena. Young women in thigh-high minis were threading their way cheerfully through the throng with canapé-laden trays. Just the costume for a feminist activist like Rosalyn, I snarled to myself. I went up to the bar and got a rum and tonic.

Drink in hand, I jostled aimlessly through the crowd. Behind the refreshment tent people were gathered in a thick, noisy clump, loud enough to drown out the band. Beyond that group the throng thinned down rapidly—the land there was hilly and uncultivated, leading into a small wood.

The terrain and lack of chairs notwithstanding, most of the women were wearing nylons and heels. Two of them had come prepared, though—they were sitting on a blanket, stretching their long, tanned legs and taking innocent pleasure in their own beauty. As I passed they cried out to me in an enthusiastic chorus:

"Vic! Ernie told us you might be here. Come sit down. LeAnn's pregnant and we didn't want to spend the afternoon standing in the heat."

I obligingly stopped for a moment. If LeAnn was pregnant it could only be a matter of months before Clara started a new baby as well. The two had been inseparable since childhood and now, adult and married, they lived in adjoining Oak Brook mansions, were in and out of each other's houses all day long to borrow clothes, share a cup of coffee, or entertain their children together. And while Clara's light curls contrasted with LeAnn's straight dark hair, they looked almost indistinguishable in their Anne Klein shorts suits.

"You having a good time?" Clara asked.

"Great. When is the baby due?"

"Not until the end of March. We're only telling friends right now."

I smiled. That included about half the people at the picnic—anyone she knew by name.

I'd met them through Michael Furey. LeAnn was married to Ernie Wunsch and Clara to Ron Grasso. Michael's continued tightness with the pals of his youth never ceased to astound me. Since leaving South Chicago for college I've scarcely seen any of the people I grew up with. But in addition to Ernie and Ron, Michael had seven or eight boyhood friends who got together once a month for poker, went to Eagle River each October to shoot deer, and spent every New Year's Eve together with their wives. The pals were a major reason I'd never really clicked with Michael. Since I had gone out with him, though, LeAnn and Clara now treated me as if I were one of the girls.

I asked politely about the children, two each, and was gladdened to learn how much they loved school, how happy LeAnn was that they were in Oak Brook now and didn't have to worry about the public schools, an interjection from Clara on what a good time they'd had themselves as little girls in Norwood Park, but everything was so *different* now.

"Ron and Ernie here?" I said idly.

"Oh, yes. They went off *hours* ago to get us something to drink. But they know so many people here I'm sure they got waylaid or sidetracked or something."

I offered to bring them something, but they laughed and said they didn't mind waiting. LeAnn put a well-manicured hand on my knee.

"You have such a good heart, Vic. We don't want to interfere, but we know you'd be great for Michael. We were just talking about the two of you when you showed up."

I grinned. "Thanks. I appreciate the testimonial." I pushed myself to my feet, spilling my drink down my pants leg.

LeAnn looked at me anxiously. "I haven't offended you, have I? Ernie's always on my case for saying whatever comes into my head without thinking first." She reached into a large beach bag and pulled out a handful of Kleenex for me.

I dabbed at the khaki. "Nope. Trouble is, Michael's a Sox fan—I just don't think we could ever work things out."

They gave little shrieks of protesting laughter. I left to their chorus of "You *can't* be serious, Vic."

I turned back through the crowd to replace my drink. Near the entrance to the tent I caught sight of Ron and Ernie. They were deep in conversation with Michael and a couple of other men. Their heads were drawn together so that they could talk over the noise. They were so intent that they didn't notice my walking up. I tapped Michael on the arm.

He jumped and swore. When he saw it was me he put an arm around me, but he looked cautiously at the other men, as if to see how they took my entrance. "Hiya, Vic. Enjoying yourself?"

"I'm having a great time. You, too, by the looks of it."

He again looked doubtfully from his companions to me. "We're right in the middle of something now. Can I find you in about ten minutes?"

So much for gestures of reconciliation. I grinned savagely but tried to keep my tone light. "You can try."

I turned on my heel, but Ron Grasso put out an arm. "Vic, honey. Good to see you. Don't mind Furey here—he got out on the wrong side of bed today. . . . No business is more important than a beautiful lady, Mickey. And nothing's more dangerous than keeping one of them waiting."

The other men laughed politely, but Michael looked at me seriously. Maybe he was still pissed. On the other hand, he knows that kind of joke rubs me the wrong way, so maybe he was trying in turn for conciliation. I was barely willing to give him the benefit of the doubt.

Ron introduced me to the two strangers—Luis Schmidt and Carl Martinez, also in construction. And supporters of Rosalyn's campaign.

"Vic's an old friend of Rosalyn's, aren't you?" Ron supplied.

I nodded. "We used to work together in Logan Square."

"You were an organizer?" Schmidt asked.

"I was a lawyer. I used to help out on legal issues—immigration, housing, that kind of thing. I'm a detective now."

"Detective, huh? Like Sergeant Furey here?" That was Schmidt, a short, stocky man with arms the size of sewer pipes straining his jacket sleeves.

They were just interested enough to require an answer. "I work for myself. Kind of the Magnum, P.I. of Chicago."

"Vic looks into fraud cases," Ron put in. "She has quite a track record. Keeps Ernie and me on the straight and narrow, let me tell you."

Everyone laughed politely. His comment seemed so unanswerable that I didn't try. "I ran into LeAnn and Clara behind the tent," I said instead. "They thought you guys were bringing them something to drink."

Ernie hit his forehead. "Mind like cement after pouring it all these years. I'll take care of the girls, Ronnie—why don't you guys wait for me here."

He took my arm and hustled me away to the refreshment tent. "Buy you something, Vic?"

"No, thanks. I'm heading back to the city soon."

He looked at me seriously, eyes dark in a thin, weather-beaten face. "Don't take Mickey too seriously. He's got a lot on his mind."

I nodded solemnly. "I know that, Ernie. And I think this is a good time to leave him alone, let him get it sorted out."

"Could you at least wait until after dinner—go talk to the girls for a while?"

He was hoping I'd take their drinks to them. I smiled gently. "Sorry, Ernie. I know LeAnn would love to see you for a few minutes before you plunge back into it with the boys. She's sitting around back of here with Clara."

"Okay, Vic, okay." He shoved his way to the front of the line. Something in the set of his shoulders told me he was wondering what the hell Mickey saw in me.

# 7

# Speaking in Tongues

**O**n my way toward the parking pasture I saw Marissa standing near the back entrance to Boots's house. She was laughing heartily at some remark of the middle-aged man talking to her. He looked vaguely familiar, but I couldn't place him. Maybe it was just the avid look he was giving Marissa I recognized—with her head thrown back the décolletage of her peach dress sprang into dramatic relief.

Before returning to town I'd let her know I'd done my duty by showing up and that I hadn't laid tales of housing woes on any sensitive ears. I trotted up the path to the house.

Seen up close, her companion was older than I'd thought, perhaps over sixty, with a lot of distinguished gray in his dark hair. Tanned and still muscular, he bore his years gracefully. Probably was wealthy, too, if his camel-hair jacket and Texas boots were any sign. A good haul for Marissa.

"Great party, Marissa—thanks for inviting me."

She hadn't seen me come up. The smile on her dark face dimmed briefly, then glowed again. "Hi, Vic. Glad you could make it."

She didn't really look at me—I should have just let well enough alone. In fact, I should have followed my original impulse and stayed in Chicago. I didn't want to see any of these people and it was abundantly clear that none of them wanted to see me.

"Bye, Marissa. Thanks for letting me participate in this wonderful civic enterprise. Just wanted to let you know I didn't discuss housing with anyone."

At that she did look at me. "You leaving, Vic? Why not stay until after the speeches? I know Rosalyn would love to have a chance to see you again."

My party smile was wearing thin. "She's got a thousand palms to press this afternoon. I'll give her a call at campaign headquarters."

The man in camel hair looked at his watch. "They're talking right now—down around the other side where the pit is. Won't take more than fifteen minutes—Boots promised me he wouldn't go gassing on forever—come along—I should put in an appearance anyway." He held out a well-groomed hand and flashed a bright white smile. "Ralph MacDonald."

While I recited my name I shook his hand appreciatively—it's not often I touch flesh worth several billion dollars. As soon as he'd said his name I knew where I'd seen the face—in the paper a zillion times or so as ground was broken for this or that project he was financing or as he presented a gargantuan check to the symphony. My only question was what he was doing here—I'd kind of assumed he was a Republican.

When I said as much Marissa looked at me with cold disapproval but MacDonald laughed. "Boots and I go back—way back. The boy'd never forgive me if I voted Republican. And he won't forgive me now unless I listen to him blow smoke rings for a while. Marissa?" He held out his left arm. "And—Vic, is it?" He crooked the right.

Who knows, he might like to hear about some of my cases—maybe he needed a few million dollars' worth of investigations and didn't even realize it. Not only that, it would make Marissa steam—in itself a good reason to tag along. I took his arm and let him guide me toward the pit.

The barbecue had been installed on the far side of the house from the refreshment tent. A good-sized crowd was milling around the thick pungent smoke—I couldn't see the poor dead cow through the throng, but assumed she was roasting away.

People were standing in an informal horseshoe around a small platform—really a large tree stump with a few boards nailed to it—

where Boots stood with his left arm around Roz's shoulders. A tall man, Boots has become majestic in late middle age—silver hair swept in leonine waves from his craggy face, broad shoulders usually encased in buckskin, and a deep hearty laugh. His head was tilted back now as he roared in amusement. It was his trademark look, the pose he affected for campaign posters, but even a nonbeliever like me found his laugh infectious, and I didn't know what the joke was.

The crowd near him included men and women of all ages and races. After Boots stopped laughing Rosalyn called out something in Spanish and got a good-natured hand. As I'd expected, she was in faded jeans, her concession to the party a crisp white shirt with a Mexican string tie. She looked just as she used to in Logan Square, her bronze skin clear, her eyes bright. Maybe I was too pessimistic— maybe she was smart enough to figure out how to run with the regular Dems and keep her own agenda intact.

Rosalyn jumped down from a crate she'd been perched on and disappeared from view—she's not much over five feet tall. As she and Boots began pressing hands and exchanging quips, Marissa pulled MacDonald away from me. I smiled to myself. It had to be the first time I'd ever made Marissa downright jealous, and all for a billionaire I didn't have any interest in. At least, not much interest.

Farther back from them I caught sight of the two Hispanic contractors who'd been talking to Michael and the boys. They were watching me narrowly; when they saw me looking at them they smiled guardedly. I sketched a wave and thought maybe the moment had finally come when I could get back to Chicago. Before I could make an escape, though, Rosalyn and Boots materialized near me. Rosalyn caught sight of me and clapped her hands.

"Vic! How wonderful to see you. I was *ecstatic* when I heard you might be here." She hugged me enthusiastically, then turned to present me to Boots. "Vic Warshawski. She used to work for you, Boots, in the public defender's office. But you're working for yourself now, aren't you? They tell me as an investigator?"

I felt like a child prodigy being paraded around for the neighbors. I managed to mumble a species of response.

"What kind of investigator, Vic?" Boots poured his geniality over me.

"Private detective. Primarily financial investigations."

Boots gave his legendary laugh and shook my hand. "I'm sorry the county lost you, Vic—we don't do enough to keep our good people. But I hope your own work is successful."

"Thank you, sir," I said primly. "Good luck on the campaign trail, Roz."

Boots suddenly caught sight of Ralph MacDonald. Genuine pleasure warmed his smile.

"Mac, you old so-and-so. Knew your contribution would double if I didn't see your shining face, huh?" Boots stretched a hand over my head to smack MacDonald's shoulder. "And of course you found Marissa Duncan—you always could pick out the best in show, couldn't you?"

I ducked away from the arm and the hearty bonhomie. Marissa's face was frozen in the mannequin expression most women assume when they're getting the wrong kind of compliment. Reflexively she put a hand to pull the collar ends of her dress together. I even found it in me to feel a little sorry for her.

As I slid away from her I saw Rosalyn ahead of me talking to Schmidt and Martinez. To my surprise they were gesturing toward me. Rosalyn turned her head, saw me looking, and flashed a smile. The stainless-steel front tooth she'd acquired in her poverty-ridden childhood glinted briefly. She spoke earnestly to the contractors, then turned once more to me. She made extravagant signs for me to join her. Making a face to myself I shouldered my way through the eager hands stretched out to her.

"Warshawski! The boys and I were talking about you just now. You've met little Luis, huh? He's my cousin—my mother's sister married a German down in Mexico City and lived to be sorry ever after! You know those old love stories." She laughed gaily. "We could use your help, Warshawski."

"You've got my vote, Roz. You know that."

"More than that, though." Before she could continue, Boots came up with MacDonald in tow. He flashed a perfunctory smile at me and dragged Roz off to confer in the house.

"Wait for me, huh, *gringa*? I'll see you in the porch swing—oh, in an hour," she shouted hoarsely over her shoulder.

I was left glaring at her back. Because I'm a woman in a man's business people think I'm tough, but a truly tough and decisive person would have headed back to town at that point. Instead I felt the tired old tentacles of responsbility drape themselves around me. Lotty Herschel tells me it comes of being the only child of parents I had to look after during painful illnesses. She thinks a few years with a good analyst would enable me to just say no when someone shouts "I need you, Vic."

Perhaps she's right—the sour thought of my parents conjured by her remembered words mingled with the smell of roasting beef and nauseated me. For a moment I felt myself identifying with the dead animal—caught around by people who fed it only to smash its head in with a mallet. I didn't think I could eat any of it. When the head barbecuer suddenly sang out that they were ready to start carving, I hunched my shoulders and left.

I circled the house to find the porch swing Rosalyn had mentioned. What Boots treated as the back of the house had actually been designed as the main entrance when the place was built a hundred years ago or so. A set of shallow steps led to a colonnaded veranda and a pair of doors inlaid with opaque etched glass.

The porch faced a flower bed and a small ornamental pond. It was a peaceful spot; the band and the crowd sounds still reached me, but no one else had strayed this far from the action. I strolled over to the pond and peered into it. Clouds turned rosy by the setting sun made the surface of the water shimmer a silvery blue. A cluster of goldfish swam over to beg for bread.

I glared at them. "Everyone else in this country has a fin stuck out—why should you guys be any different? I just don't have any slush left today."

I felt someone come up behind me and turned as Michael put an arm around my shoulders. I removed it and backed away a few paces.

"Michael, what's going on with you today? Are you peeved because I wanted to drive myself? . . . Is that why you pulled that number on me at the gate and again with your pals back there? You can't muscle me aside and then come caress me back into good humor."

"I'm sorry," he said simply. "I didn't mean it like that. Ron and Ernie introduced me to those two guys—Schmidt and Martinez. They're breaking into construction, just getting a few good jobs, and their work sites are being vandalized. The boys thought they could use some free police advice. When you came up we were in the middle of it. I was afraid you were still mad at me and I didn't know how to handle it and not let them think I wasn't listening to them, either. So I blew it. Can you still talk to me?"

I hunched a shoulder impatiently. "The trouble is, Michael, you belong to a crowd where the girls sit on a blanket waiting for the boys to finish talking business and bring them drinks. I like LeAnn and Clara, but they'll never be good friends of mine—it's not the way I think or act or live or—or anything. I think that style—the segregated way you and Ernie and Ron work—it's too much part of you. I don't see how you and I ever can move along together."

He was quiet for a few minutes while he thought it over. "Maybe you're right," he said reluctantly. "I mean, my mother kept house and hung out with her friends and my dad had his bowling club. I never saw them do anything together—even church, it was always her taking the kids to Mass while he slept it off on Sunday mornings. I guess it was a mistake trying to see you at a function like this." The sun had set but I could see his smile flash briefly, worried, not cocky.

The surface of the pond turned black; behind us the house loomed as a ghostly galleon. It was Michael's ability to think about himself that set him apart from his pals. There was a time when it might have seemed worth the effort to work things out with someone who was willing to stop and think about it. But I'm thirty-seven now and no longer seem able to put the energy into dubious undertakings.

Before I could make up my mind what I wanted to say, Roz whirled up. I hadn't expected to see her—at a function like this she'd have so many demands on her time that a desire to meet with me could easily fade from her mind. Schmidt and Martinez were with her.

"Vic!" Her voice had faded to a hoarse whisper after a long day of talking, but it vibrated with her usual energy. "Thank goodness you waited for me. Can we grab a few minutes on the porch?"

I grunted unenthusiastically.

Schmidt and Martinez were greeting Michael in low-voiced seriousness. I introduced him to Rosalyn. She shook his hand perfunctorily and hustled me across the yard.

The lawn was smoothly trimmed; even at the pace she set we kept our footing in the dark. The porch was outlined by light coming from the other side of the opaque doors. I could see the swing, and Rosalyn's shape when she settled in it, but her face was in too much shadow for me to make out her expression.

I sat on the top of the shallow steps, my back against the pillar, and waited for her to speak. On the lawn behind us I could make out the shapes of Michael and the two contractors as dark splotches. From the other end of the house the band was revving up to a more feverish pitch; the increased volume and the noise of laughter drifted to us.

"If I win the election I'm finally going to be in a position to really help my people," Rosalyn said at last.

"You've already done a great deal."

"No soap tonight, Vic. I don't have time or energy for pats on the back. . . . I'm setting my sights high. Getting Boots to endorse me—it was difficult but necessary. You do understand that?"

I nodded, but she couldn't see that, so I gave an affirmative grunt. Anyway, I did understand it.

"This election is just the first step. I'm aiming for Congress and I want to be in a position for a cabinet post if the Democrats win in eight or twelve years."

I grunted again. The specific shape of her ambition was interesting, but I'd always known she had the ability and the drive to reach for the top. In eight or twelve years maybe the country would even be ready for a Hispanic woman vice president. She must have been born in Mexico, though—that was why she was thinking only of the cabinet.

"Your advice would always be valuable to me."

I had to strain to hear her, her voice had gotten so hoarse. "Thanks for the testimonial, Roz."

"Some people—my cousin—think you might do something to hurt me, but I told him you would never do such a thing."

I couldn't begin to fathom what she might be talking about and said as much. She didn't answer right away, and when she finally did I got the impression she'd chosen her words with great care.

"Because I'm working with Boots. Anyone who knows you knows you've always opposed everything he stands for."

"Not everything," I said. "Just the stuff I know about. Anyway, your cousin doesn't know me. We just met this afternoon."

"He knows about you," she persisted in her raw voice. "You've done a lot of significant work one way and another. People who are connected around town hear your name."

"I don't need soap any more than you do, Roz. I haven't said or done anything to make anyone think I'd stand in your way. Hell! I even paid two-fifty to support your campaign. What does your cousin imagine I'm doing? It may be chicken feed to a contractor, but that's a big outlay for me—I wouldn't do it frivolously."

She put her hand on mine. "I appreciate you coming out for me. I know it took a lot for you to do, both the money and the function." She gave a throaty chuckle. "I've had to swallow a few things, too, to be here—the sidelong looks from the party regulars. I know what they're thinking—Boots is getting a piece of Spanish ass and giving her a spot on the ticket as payment."

"So what is Schmidt worried about? That I'm from the Legion of Decency and I'm going to cook up a sex scandal? I'm *really* offended, Roz. Offended by the thought and by you thinking you had to sound me out over it."

Her callused fingers gripped mine. "No, no, Vic. Don't take it that way. Luis is my little cousin, my little brother, almost, the way he worries about me. Some men he was talking to told him how negative you are to Boots and he got worried on my behalf. I told him I'd talk to you, that's all, *gringa*. Boots has his flaws, after all, I'm not blind to them. But I can use him."

I didn't know if I was hearing the truth or not. Maybe she was sleeping with Boots for the good of the Hispanic community—there was very little Roz wouldn't do to help her people. It would turn my stomach, but I didn't really care. At any rate, prolonging the conversation wasn't going to buy me a copy of her thoughts.

"I don't like you tying your wagon to Boots's star, but I can afford to be picky—I'm self-employed and it's a pretty small operation. And there's certainly something to be said for letting Boots do your dirty work. Pulling the plug on abortions at Cook County the way he did, he owes the women in this town something—why shouldn't it be you."

Roz gave a husky laugh. "I knew I could count on you, Vic."

She summoned enough of her voice to call her cousin. "Hey, Luis, come on, we gotta go get a drink and shake a few more hands."

Luis ambled over to the porch with Michael; Carl Martinez apparently had taken off. "You get everything settled, Roz?" It didn't sound like a casual question.

"Coming up roses. You worry too much, you know—you're just like your mama that way."

We stood up. Roz hugged me. "I may call you yet, Warshawski. Get you to stuff envelopes or hold my hand if I freak."

"Sure, Roz. Whatever you want."

I followed her down the shallow steps. When Luis had hustled her around the side of the house, Furey took my arm.

"Let me meet you back at your place, Vic, get things talked out. I don't want to have matters go completely bust between us without at least saying good-bye in a friendly way."

I was staring at the corner of the house where Roz had disappeared, still trying to figure out what the hell that whole conversation had been about. I was so busy with my thoughts that I found I'd agreed with Furey without even realizing it.

# 8

# A Devoted Mother

It was dark when I pulled up behind Michael's silver Corvette on Racine. I'd expected to be home long ahead of him—he'd run into Ron and Ernie after seeing me into my car. When I pulled out they were still talking. However, relying on superior police knowledge of city routes—and professional courtesy from the traffic cops—he managed to beat me. He climbed out of the Corvette when he saw me behind him and came over to me.

"Vic. This is not destined to be our best day. A call came in on the radio while I was driving over. I'm not supposed to be on duty until tomorrow morning, but Uncle Bobby doesn't care much about official rosters when there's been a triple homicide. Sorry. I'll give you a call tomorrow, okay?"

I tried to muster an appropriate expression of sorrow, but I was just as happy to be on my own tonight. The idea of a nice soak in the tub without having to be pleasant to an outsider had been tantalizing me during the long drive home. I barely waited to wave good-bye before heading up the walk to the front door. And the shattering of my dreams of solitude.

Elena was parked on the first-floor landing, her duffel bag at her feet. Next to her sat a young black woman. Even in the dim hall light I could see she was dressed with a stylishness that highlighted Elena's worn face and bedraggled clothes. When I saw them my guilty worries about my aunt vanished. My stomach knotted and I felt a cowardly impulse to shut the door and head back to Streamwood.

Elena sprang jerkily to her feet and opened her arms in a wide meaningless gesture. "Victoria, sweetie, your nice neighbor let us in so we wouldn't have to wait for you in the lobby. The old gentleman. He's a real gem, you don't find too many as chivalrous as him today. He told us you hadn't left town so I figured we'd just wait for you 'stead of coming back later."

"Hi, Elena," I said weakly. "I found a room for you. Over on Kenmore."

"Oh, Vicki, Victoria, I mean, family's family and I knew you wouldn't let me down. This here is Cerise. She's the daughter of a buddy of mine from the Indiana Arms. Cerise, meet my niece Victoria. Finest niece a woman could ever want. If anyone can help you, she will."

Cerise held out a slim, manicured hand. "Pleased to meet you." Her voice was almost inaudible.

"I can't put her up, Elena," I said grimly. "No amount of sweet-talking is going to make me turn my place into a way station for victims of Wednesday night's fire."

Elena pursed her lips in exaggerated hurt. "No way, sweetie. I wouldn't dream of it. Cerise here needs a detective. When I heard her story I knew you were just the gal for her."

I wanted to pull my hair out by the roots or scream or anything extreme that would keep me from pounding my aunt. Before I could formulate a nonviolent response, the door to one-north opened and the banker popped out again.

"Oh, it's you," he said disagreeably. "I might have known. Well, this time I am calling the cops. I saw your pimp pull off just now in that silver Corvette. What are these—your drug clients?"

"What do you do all day long at work?" I snapped. "Spy on the clerks to see who's taking five minutes too long at her coffee break? You must be one of the most popular guys around if all you do is peer over people's shoulders into their business."

"It's my business if you conduct your sleazy affairs at all hours—"

"No, no, honey," my aunt popped up. "She's a detective. A professional. We've come to consult her on business. You don't want to frown in that angry way—it's just as important for a man to keep his looks these days as it is for a girl, and you'll get terrible wrinkles around your eyes if you keep scowling like that. And you've got very nice eyes."

"Elena, just be quiet, will you? We can discuss Cerise's problem upstairs. Take her on up, okay?" I wasn't going to resolve anything with the guy if Elena was mediating.

Elena protested, hurt, that she was just trying to help me get along better with my neighbors, but she finally agreed to start upstairs. I looked at the banker, debating whether I should say something conciliatory—it's not a great idea to have a vendetta with a neighbor in a six-unit building.

"Be sure to give the cops the Corvette's plates when you call, will you?" I told him. "The fellow who drives it is a detective with the Central District's Violent Crimes Unit. The beat guys'll enjoy razzing him about getting accused of being a pimp. If you didn't catch the plate, it's 'fureous'—that's F-U-R-E-O-U-S." Some days I'm just more conciliatory than others.

He scowled at me with dark angry eyes, trying to decide whether I was bluffing. Hearing the license plate spelled out apparently made him decide I wasn't. He stalked back into his apartment and slammed the door. From the south unit I could hear Peppy's insistent whimpering as she begged to join in the fray. I ran up the stairs two at a time to avoid Mr. Contreras's predictable harangue.

I ushered Elena and Cerise into my apartment. "Can I get you something to drink? Coffee? Soda?"

"I'll take a beer," Cerise said.

"Sorry. I don't have beer. Coffee, milk, or juice. Or I have seltzer and some Coke."

Cerise settled on a Coke while Elena asked for some of that wonderful coffee like my ma used to make. I served up the remains of the pasta salad I'd taken to yesterday's picnic and heated a couple of rolls. Neither woman seemed to have eaten much recently. Beyond Cerise's asking what the queer white things in the salad were, and accepting "calamari" with a wise nod, they both ate rapidly without speaking.

"So what's the problem that needs a detective?" I asked when they'd finished.

Cerise looked at Elena, asking her to speak for her.

"It's her baby," my aunt said.

In the bright light of my living room I could see Cerise wasn't as old as her sophisticated clothes had made her look downstairs. She might have been twenty, but any legitimate bar would card her.

"Yes," I said as encouragingly as possible.

"We think she died in the fire," Elena said.

"Died in the fire?" I repeated stupidly.

"At the Indiana Arms," my aunt said sharply. "Don't gape there like a carp, Vicki. You must remember it."

"Yes, but—you think? Don't you know?"

I'd spoken to Cerise. She shook her head and again turned to Elena. My aunt spoke briskly, using wild hand motions and pursing her lips periodically to underscore a dramatic point.

"The whole point of an SRO, Vicki, is that it's *single* resident occupancy. Single means no one else in the room with you, not even a cockroach, if you get my drift. And certainly no babies. And here's Cerise, trying to get her life together, and she has the sweetest little baby you ever saw, fourteen months old and just starting to toddle, and what's she supposed to do with it while she's out hunting for work?"

Elena paused, as if waiting for an answer, but I didn't try to interrupt the flow.

"So she leaves it with her ma, same as you would if it was you. If Gabriella was still alive, I mean, being as how she always wanted the best for you. And Cerise's ma is just the same. Nothing too good for Cerise and she'll risk getting thrown right out on her rear end"— Elena smacked her own behind to emphasize the point—"if it'd help Cerise here make a decent life for the baby."

When I didn't say anything she repeated her last point sharply.

"Great," I managed.

Elena beamed. "So her ma is kind of a pal of mine. We've knocked back a few beers together, not that I drink, you understand, nor does she, just a few beers now and then in a sociable kind of way." She stared at me defiantly, but I didn't challenge the statement.

"So Zerlina—that's Cerise's ma—is watching the baby while Cerise is out of town Wednesday night when we have the fire. Now

Zerlina's vanished—poof—and poor Cerise can't find out if her dear little baby made it out of the building alive."

She slapped her hands together for effect and watched me expectantly. All I could think was that it was Sunday night, almost four days since the fire—why was Cerise surfacing only now?

"So I told her you'd help," Elena prompted me impatiently.

"Help do what?"

"Well, Vicki—Victoria—she needs to find the poor little thing. She's afraid it'll get her ma in trouble if she goes to the police. You know, for keeping a baby in the room. Maybe she'd never be able to find another place. I said you were just the person for her."

"Why has it taken this long for Cerise to miss the baby?" I demanded.

"I been out of town." It was Cerise's first contribution to the conversation since she'd asked about the calamari. "Otis, he the baby's father, he took me up to the Dells. We trying to work things out, you know, I want him to marry me and make a home for me and Katterina and he don't want to do it. So he promised me a vacation."

I rubbed my forehead, trying to push the more harrowing images of her life out of my brain. "And you just got back today?"

"I went to the hotel," she burst out. "I went straight there. People say I don't love Katterina, leaving her with my mother and all, but I do. I just can't look after her and have my own life too, not twenty-four hours a day. I can't even get a job if I got to stay with her all the time. But I went there first thing, Otis dropped me there, you can ask him, that was yesterday. And I saw about the fire, and I hunted all over for my mama and finally I found Elena this afternoon. But she don't know where Mama is. Except maybe in the hospital where they took the people who was hurt in the fire."

"Maybe the fire fighters found Katterina," I offered. "Maybe she's with DCFS. Have you tried calling them?"

"I can't call them. They just want to take my baby from me, say I'm an unfit mother." She started to cry, her long red earrings bobbing into her shoulders.

"There, there." Elena put a soothing arm around her shoulders. "That's what we need you for, Vicki. We need someone who knows how to talk to all these people, who can handle it without getting Cerise or Zerlina in trouble."

It didn't sound to me as though there was much hope that Katterina had made it through the fire. If a baby had been found there, surely the newspapers would have trumpeted it.

"I'm sorry," I said helplessly to Cerise. "Sorry about Katterina. But you really are the best person to go to the police and to DCFS— you're her mother, you're the only one with a right to ask questions."

She kept crying without looking up at me. I tried explaining that the police were not going to care that Zerlina had had a baby in the room with her, that they couldn't keep her from renting a room ever again, but it washed over both Cerise and Elena like the tide.

I thought of the woman I'd talked to at the Emergency Housing Bureau, the despair she'd shared with the other people in the room, the few rooms and the many people to fill them. If you were that helpless, the police might become another bureaucratic menace, ready to use their power to keep you out of a place to live.

"Okay." I finally said. "I'll make some calls for you tomorrow."

Elena took her hand from Cerise's shoulder and came over to where I was sitting in the armchair. "That's my girl. I knew I could count on you. I knew you was too much your ma's daughter to say no to a fellow human being in trouble."

"Right," I agreed sourly. I looked at the clock on the bookshelves. It was ten. Even if I sent Elena over to the Windsor Arms this late she couldn't take Cerise with her. Gritting my teeth, I pulled out the sofa bed, dug around in my drawers for a long T-shirt for Cerise to sleep in, and locked myself in my bedroom.

# 9

# The Lady Is Indisposed

I woke up early the next morning. My dreams had been of crying babies and fires; I'd jerked awake twice feeling suffocated by flames. When I got out of bed it was again with the feeling that someone had dumped a load of gravel in my head, this time without bothering to crush it too fine.

It was only six. Cerise and Elena were still asleep on the sofa bed, Cerise lying spread-eagled on her stomach, Elena on her back snoring. I felt like a captive in my own home, unable to get to my books or television, but if I woke them, it would be worse. I shut the door softly, put on my jeans, and went down the back stairs. It was too early to wake up Mr. Contreras to take the dog for a run. And even though exercise may be the best cure for a sandy head, running sounded like the last thing I was in the mood for.

I walked the half mile to the Belmont Diner, open twenty-four hours a day, and had the cholesterol special, pancakes with butter and a big order of bacon. I lingered as long as I could, following the saga of the search for the Bears new stadium through all three papers, even taking in every word on the latest zoning scandal to beset the mayor's chief supporters. It's boring to read about zoning scandals because their revelation never has any impact on election results, so I usually skip them.

Around eight I finally trudged back to my apartment. Life was stirring on Racine Avenue as people headed for work. When I got to my building the banker was leaving for the day, his thick brown hair lacquered to his head.

"Hi," I said brightly as we passed. "Just getting off the night shift. Have a good day."

He pretended not to hear me, crossing to the east side of the street as I spoke. Try to be neighborly and you only get stiffed for your pains.

Like LBJ or the Duke of Wellington, Elena could sleep anywhere, anytime. When I opened the kitchen door I could hear her snores oozing from the living room. I also caught my favorite smell, cigarette smoke. Cerise was at the dining-room table, staring moodily at nothing, chain-smoking.

"Good morning," I said as politely as I could. "I know you're really upset about your baby, but please don't smoke in here."

She shot me a hostile look but stubbed her cigarette out in the saucer she'd been using. I took it to the kitchen and tried to scrub the tobacco stains from it. After a few minutes she followed me in and slumped herself at the table. I offered her breakfast but she wanted only coffee. I put water on to boil and got the beans out of the freezer.

"What floor did your mother live on?"

She looked at me blankly and rubbed her bare arms.

"At the Indiana Arms. I'll probably need that information if someone is going to search for Katterina."

"Fifth floor," she answered after another long pause. "Five twenty-two. It was hard on her on account of the elevator didn't work, but she couldn't get nothing lower down."

"When did you leave the baby with your mother?"

Again she stared at me, but this time I thought there was an element of calculation in her gaze. "We did it Wednesday. Before we left town." She rubbed her arms some more. "It's too cold in here. I need to smoke."

It felt warm to me, but I was dressed; she was still in the outsized T-shirt I'd lent her. I went into my bedroom and got a jacket. She put it on but continued to rub her arms.

I ground the beans and poured boiling water through them. "What time Wednesday?"

"You trying to say I saw the fire and shouldn'ta left my baby?" Her tone was sullen but her eyes were still watchful.

I poured more water into the beans and tried to muster some empathy. Her baby was almost certainly dead. She was with a stranger and a white woman at that. She was terrified of the institutions of law and society and I was conversant with them, so to her I was part of them. She wanted to smoke and I wouldn't let her.

Thinking about all this didn't make me feel like running over to embrace her, but it did help me stifle the more extreme expressions of impatience. "Someone set that fire," I said carefully. "Someone hurt your mother and may have hurt your baby. If you were there Wednesday night, you might have seen the arsonist. Maybe he—or she—or they—were hanging around. If you saw someone, we could give the police a description, something to start an investigation with."

She shook her head violently. "I didn't see no one. We go there at three in the afternoon. We give Katterina to my mama. We leave for Wisconsin. Okay?"

"Okay." I poured out coffee for her. "Why are these questions upsetting you so much?"

She was trembling. She took the mug with both hands to steady it. "You acting like I did something bad, like it be my fault my baby's hurt."

"No, Cerise, not at all. I'm really sorry if that's how I sounded. I don't mean that at all." I tried to smile. "I'm a detective, you know. I ask questions for a living. It's a hard habit to break."

She buried her face in the mug and didn't answer me. I gave it up and went into my bedroom. The bed was still unmade. My running clothes had fallen on the floor at the end when I'd kicked the covers off in the night. Untangling my sweats from the bedclothes, I stuffed them into the closet and pulled the covers back up onto the bed. The room wasn't exactly ready for *House Beautiful,* but it was all the housekeeping I was in the humor for.

I lay on the bed and tried to remember the name of the insurance man I'd met at the Indiana Arms on Thursday. It was a bird; that had struck me particularly at the time because his bright-eyed curiosity had made him seem birdlike. I shut my eyes and let my mind drift. Robin. That was it. I couldn't delve the last name from my memory hole, but Robin would get me to him.

I pulled the phone from the bedside table and put it on my stomach to dial. When the Ajax operator connected me with the arson and fraud division, I asked the cheery receptionist for Robin.

"He's right here—I'll put him on for you."

The phone banged in my ear—she must have dropped the receiver—then I got a tenor. "Robin Bessinger here."

Bessinger. Of course. "Robin, it's V. I. Warshawski. I met you at the Indiana Arms last week when you were digging through the rubble there."

"V.I. You the detective?"

"Uh-huh." I sat up and put the phone back on the bedside table. "You said if anybody's been killed, the police would have had a homicide investigation set up. So I assume everybody was rescued?"

"As far as I know." I'd forgotten how cautious he was. A bird making sure the worm wasn't really a rifle barrel. "You know anything to the contrary?"

"A baby was staying there Wednesday night. Staying with its grandmother on the fifth floor." He started to interrupt and I said hastily, "I know, I know. Against the rules. The grandmother has disappeared—maybe one of the smoke victims—so I don't know if they found the baby or not."

"A baby in there. Sweet Jesus, no. . . . I don't know anything about it, but I'll call someone at the police and get back to you. Was it your friend? The one you said had been burned out?"

I'd forgotten referring to Elena as my friend. "No, not her. The grandmother was sort of a friend of hers, though, and the mother just got back into town and found her little girl and her own mama both missing. She's pretty distraught." Or hostile. Or fried.

"Okay." He fumbled around for a moment. "I'm just real sorry. I'll call you back in a couple of minutes."

I gave him my phone number and hung up. I looked distastefully at my bedroom. Because I'm there only to sleep I don't usually pay much attention to it. The queen-size bed takes up a good deal of the available space. Since the closet is large I keep the dresser in there to have enough room to walk around, but it still makes me feel hemmed in to spend much time there during the day. More than ever I resented Elena's snoring presence down the hall, pinning me to one room in my own home.

I paced the short distance from the door to the head of the bed a few times but I kept banging my shin on the bedstead. I couldn't possibly practice my singing in these quarters, especially not with Cerise in the kitchen. Finally I lay on the floor between the window and the bed and did leg lifts. After forty or so with each leg Robin called back. He sounded subdued.

"V. I. Warshawski?" He stumbled a bit on my last name. "I— uh, I've been talking with the police. They say the fire department didn't bring out any children from that place last week. Are you sure the baby was in there?"

I hesitated. "Reasonably sure. I can't swear to it, though, because I don't know any of the people involved."

"They're going to send a team out to comb the rubble, to see if they can find any, well, any remains. They'd like you to be available to come downtown to meet with them, though."

I promised to check in with my answering service every hour if I left my apartment. Slowly hanging up the phone, I wondered what to say to Cerise. As I walked to the door Elena pounded on the other side.

"Yoo-hoo! Vicki! Victoria, I mean. Poor little Cerise isn't feeling too hot. Can you come out and help me settle her upset tummy?"

Poor little Cerise had vomited all over the kitchen table. Elena, at her brightest as she enjoyed the drama, wiped her face with a damp towel while I cleaned up the mess.

"It's the shock, you know," my aunt cooed. "She's worried sick about her baby."

I looked at the younger woman narrowly. She was sick, all right, but I was beginning to think a little more than shock underlay her behavior.

"I think we'll have a doctor take a look at her," I said. "Help me get her dressed and down to my car."

"No doctor," Cerise said thickly. "I'm not seeing no doctor."

"Yes, you are," I snapped. "This isn't a one-woman social agency. You just threw up all over my kitchen and I'm not spending the day nursing you."

"No doctor, no doctor!" Cerise screamed.

"She really doesn't want to go, Vicki," Elena stage-whispered at me.

"I can see she doesn't want to go," I said brittlely. "Just put her clothes on while I hold her arms still. And please don't call me Vicki. It's not a name I care for much."

"I know, I know, sweetie," Elena promised hastily. "It keeps slipping my mind."

Since Gabriella had driven home the point forcefully to Elena all through my childhood—"I didn't name her for Victor Emmanuel to have people talk to her as though she were a silly ingenue"—I didn't see how Elena could have forgotten, but this wasn't the time to argue the point.

Dressing Cerise made me glad I hadn't chosen nursing in a mental hospital as my career. She fought against my hold, screaming and thrashing around in the kitchen chair. I'm in good shape, but she strained my muscles to the utmost. At one point she raked open my left arm with a long fingernail. I somehow managed to hang on to her.

Elena worked with an ineffectuality that brought me close to the screaming point myself. She put Cerise's underpants on backwards and only managed to slide her skirt on after a good fifteen minutes of work.

"Just do her shoes," I panted. "She can wear the T-shirt on top. My keys are in the living room. I left them on the coffee table. Unlock the dead bolts."

I tried to explain which key worked which lock, but gave it up as Elena grew more confused. By some miracle she managed to undo them in less than an hour. Cerise had stopped fighting me by then. She hunched limply over the kitchen table sobbing to herself and offered no resistance as I escorted her out the door. I took the keys from Elena.

"You'd best get your bag. I'm going to drop you off at your new place as soon as Cerise has seen the doctor."

Elena tried to put up a fight of her own, but I was past any feelings of guilt. I kept Cerise propped up against the wall and repeated my demand. My aunt finally shuffled back into my apartment. After an absence long enough that I wondered if she was back at the Black Label, she came out again. She'd taken a shower; her graying hair hung around her head in damp ringlets, but her makeup was complete and, for once, on target. The violet nightgown still hung out the side of the duffel bag. She let it trail along the floor as she followed me down the stairs.

# 10

# A Little Help from My Friends

Lotty Herschel's storefront clinic is about three miles from my apartment, near the corner of Damen and Irving Park. During the short drive Cerise threw up again in the backseat, then started shivering uncontrollably. I thought I might kill Elena, who knelt on the front seat watching Cerise and giving me minute-by-minute updates on what she was doing.

I jerked the car to a stop next to a fireplug in front of the clinic and jogged inside. The small waiting room, painted to look like the African veldt, was packed with the usual assortment of wailing infants and squabbling children. Mrs. Coltrain was keeping order, handling the phone and typing records with her usual calm. I sometimes suggest to Lotty that she found Mrs. Coltrain in a catalog offering to supply offices with old-fashioned grandmothers—not only does she have nine grandchildren, but she wears her silvery hair in a bun.

"Miss Warshawski." She beamed at me. "Good to see you. Do you need to talk to Dr. Herschel?"

"Rather urgently. I have a young woman in my car who's been throwing up and seems now to be going into shock. Can you ask Lotty if she'd see her now if I brought her in, or if I should take her to the hospital?"

Mrs. Coltrain refuses to call Lotty or me by our first names—we gave up urging them on her long ago. She relayed my message to Carol Alvarado, the clinic nurse, and after a couple of minutes Carol came out to help me bring Cerise in. Cerise's skin was cold. It felt thick, like wet plastic, not at all like living tissue. She was conscious enough to walk if we supported her, but her breathing was shallow and her eyes were rolling.

A murmur of resentment swelled around us as we brought Cerise past the waiting room into the examining area—people who've been waiting an hour or more for the doctor don't appreciate line jumpers. Carol got Cerise onto a table and wrapped her in a blanket. Lotty swept in a few minutes later.

"What are you bringing me now, Vic?" She didn't wait for an answer but went straight to Cerise.

I told her what little I knew about the young woman. "Suddenly this morning she started complaining about feeling cold, then she started throwing up. I don't know if it was pregnancy or drugs or some combination, but I didn't feel like dealing with her on my own."

Lotty grunted and pulled back Cerise's eyelids. "She's going to be here for a while. Why don't you come back in a few hours?" She turned to Carol with a request for a medication.

In other words, it was up to me to find out what to do with her when Lotty finished treating her. Not that I'd expected Lotty to do it, but somehow I'd managed to avoid thinking about Cerise's future.

My shoulders sagging, I walked on heavy feet back to the car. I'd forgotten Cerise's eruption, but the smell was a pungent reminder. I returned to the clinic and got some wet rags and a bottle of disinfectant from Mrs. Coltrain. All the time I was cleaning the backseat Elena kept chirping questions about Cerise.

"I don't know," I said wearily as I finally turned the engine on. "I don't know what's wrong with her or what the doctor will do or if she has to go to the hospital. I'll find all that out when I go back at noon and I'll let you know."

Elena put a tremulous hand on my arm. "It's only because her mother and me are pals, Vicki—Victoria. It'd be the same if it was you in trouble and I took you to Zerlina. She'd feel responsible for you because of me, don't you see."

I took my right hand off the wheel to pat her thin, veined fingers. "Sure, Elena. I understand. Your good heart does you credit."

We drove in silence for a while, then I thought of something. "What's Zerlina's last name?"

"Her last name, sweetie? Why do you care?"

"I want to find her. If she's in the hospital, I can't go to the reception desk at Michael Reese and ask for her by her first name. They don't keep track of patients that way."

"If she got hurt in the fire, sweetie, I don't know if she'd be up to seeing you."

"Not up to seeing me?" I tried to keep my tone conversational, but an overlay of a snarl came through anyway. "If you and Cerise want me to do anything more about the baby, she'd damned well better be up to seeing me. And you should do your best to help me find her."

"Language, Victoria," Elena said reprovingly. "Talking dirty isn't going to solve your problems."

"And dancing around the mulberry bush on this one isn't going to solve yours," I snapped. "Tell me her last name or kiss any help from me good-bye."

"When you scrunch up your face like that you look just like your grandmother the last few months I was living with her."

I turned north onto Kenmore and pulled up in front of the Windsor Arms. My poor grandmother. If she'd had a stronger personality, she would have booted Elena out on her rump long before her thirtieth birthday. Instead, except for brief forays, my aunt lived with her until she died.

"Your own family is always the last to appreciate you," I said, turning off the engine. "Now why don't you quit screwing around and tell me Zerlina's last name?"

Elena looked at me craftily. "Is this the new hotel, sweetie? You're an angel to go to so much trouble for me. No, no, don't you go carrying that heavy bag, you're young, you need to save your back."

I took the duffel bag from her and escorted her into the lobby. She fluttered off to the lounge area to talk to some of the residents while I dug in my handbag for the room receipt. The concierge, coming from some basement recess when I tapped the desk bell, clearly remembered me but insisted on getting the receipt before she'd let Elena have the room. For a nerve-straining moment I was afraid I'd stuffed it in my skirt pocket on Friday, but finally found it stuck in the pages of my pocket diary.

I had intended to beard Elena in her room and force Zerlina's surname from her, but was thwarted by the concierge—this was a single-resident hotel and visitors were not permitted in the guest rooms. Elena blew me a kiss with a promise to get back in touch with me.

"And you will let me know what happens to poor Cerise, won't you, sweetheart?"

I forced a glittering smile to my face. "How am I to do that, Elena—by smoke signal?"

"You can leave a message for me at the desk, can't she do that, honey?" she added to the concierge.

"I suppose," the woman said grudgingly. "As long as you don't make a habit of it."

As they disappeared up the echoing stairwell I could hear Elena explaining that I was the smartest, sweetest niece a woman could ever hope to have. I ground my teeth and acknowledged defeat.

The pay phone for residents was in the lounge with the TV. I didn't want to compete with *The Price Is Right;* I walked up Kenmore looking for another phone. After a two-block circuit I decided I'd be better off going back to my apartment.

The super had finally gotten around to putting up the banker's nameplate. I stopped to look at it—Vincent Bottone. I felt vaguely affronted that an Italian could be treating me so rudely—didn't he know that we were compatriots? I glanced at my own nameplate—since my last name was Warshawski, maybe he hadn't been able to guess. I'd have to try speaking to him in Italian and see if that softened him. Or, I realized as I unlocked my apartment door, give me a chance to show him up.

Robin Bessinger was in a meeting, but he'd left word with the receptionist to get him if I called. I tucked the phone under my ear while I waited, and yanked the sheets from the sofa bed. I was just stuffing the mattress back into the sofa frame when Robin came on the line.

"Ms. Warshawski? Robin Bessinger."

"It's Vic," I interrupted him.

"Oh. Vic. I've been wondering what those initials stood for.

Look—the lab says there isn't any trace of a baby's body in the debris. On the other hand, if it got caught in the fiercest part of the blaze, it might have been incinerated. So they've taken samples of the ashes and will get them analyzed, which'll take a few days. But Roland Montgomery—he's with the Bomb and Arson Squad—would like to talk to you, find out firsthand why you think the child was in there."

I wasn't sure I did think Katterina had been in the Indiana Arms. At this point I wasn't sure I believed Cerise had a baby, or even a mother. But I couldn't express any of this to Robin.

"The baby's mother told me," I said. "Where does Montgomery want me to meet him?"

"Can you make it at three in his office? Central District at Eleventh Street." He hesitated for a moment. "I'd like to sit in if you don't mind. A death would affect our insured. Dominic Assuevo will be there from the Office of Fire Investigation."

"Not at all," I said politely. I didn't know Montgomery, but I'd met Assuevo a couple of years ago when my old apartment had been torched. He was a pal of Bobby Mallory's and was inclined to look on me suspiciously by extension.

Before we hung up I asked Robin if he knew Zerlina's last name. He hadn't been given a list of the smoke inhalation victims but promised me he'd get it from Dominic at our meeting this afternoon.

I finished tidying up the sofa bed, then took the sheets down to the washing machine in the basement. I'm not normally so obsessive about cleanliness, but I wanted to get all traces of Cerise—and Elena —out of my apartment. If I washed the sheets, it was a clear commitment to myself that I didn't have to put the younger woman up here when I fetched her back from Lotty's. Although I didn't know what the hell I was going to do with her.

It was possible that Cerise had given Lotty her surname. If she hadn't, I thought Carol might call Michael Reese for me and get them to give her Zerlina's last name. I didn't want to meet with the police until I talked to Zerlina, assuming I could find her at Reese.

When I got to the clinic I learned that a chunk of my schedule had dropped out—Cerise had disappeared. Carol was worried, Lotty angry. Lotty had given her a mild tranquilizer and something to control her nausea. Cerise had slept for about an hour in the examining room. The third time Carol went in to check on her she was gone. Mrs. Coltrain had seen her walk out of the clinic but had no reason to stop her—she'd assumed since Cerise came with me that I had arranged to pay Lotty for her treatment separately.

Of course. I'd forgotten the money. A hundred dollars to pay Cerise's bill and help fund some of the clinic's indigent patients. Lotty, furious with me for interrupting her day with such a case, was in no humor to discount her services. I pulled my checkbook from my handbag and wrote out the check.

"I guess I should have taken her to the hospital," I said wearily, handing it to Mrs. Coltrain. "But she got sick so suddenly and so violently that I was afraid she might be dying on me. I didn't know if she had some neurological disease or was coming down from heroin or what. If something like this happens again, which I hope it doesn't, I won't bother you."

That pulled Lotty up short—she hates having her standard of care impugned. Her tone was a little less abrupt when she responded.

"It was a combination of heroin and pregnancy. If there's to be any hope for that fetus, Cerise needs to get into a drug program today."

"I wouldn't bet the farm on her doing it," I said. "I want to try to get in touch with Cerise's mother."

I explained that Zerlina might be in Michael Reese recovering from the fire but that I didn't have her last name. Carol went off to phone the hospital for me—she felt irrationally responsible for Cerise roaming the streets pregnant and addicted. Getting Zerlina's last name was something active she could do to help.

"Not your problem," I tried to tell her when she returned a few minutes later. "If Cerise is bent on destructing, you can't stop her. You should know that by now."

"Yes, Vic," Carol admitted. "I do know it. But I feel as though we let you down. That's partly why Lotty's so angry, you know. She tries to work at such a high level and then when she fails to save someone she takes it personally. And for it to be someone you brought in."

"Maybe," I said dubiously. The truth was, I was happy that

Cerise had vanished. It was magic. I didn't have to look after her anymore.

"Anyway, the mother's last name is Ramsay." Carol spelled it for me. "She's in room four-twenty-two in the main hospital building. I told the head nurse you were a social worker, so there won't be any problem you getting in to see her."

I made a face as I thanked her. Social worker! It was an apt description of how I'd spent my time since Elena showed up at my door last week. Maybe it was time for me to turn Republican and copy Nancy Reagan. From now on when alcoholic or addicted pregnant strays showed up at my door, I would just say no.

# 11

# Smoking Grandma

**I** climbed into the Chevy and slumped over the wheel. It was only noon, but I was as tired as though I'd been climbing Mount Everest for a week. A faint odor of vomit still hovered in the car, despite the twenty minutes I'd spent scrubbing the backseat. It slowly came to me that I was smelling my own clothes. My jeans were soiled where I'd been kneeling on the car seat—I'd just been too wound up with Elena to notice it earlier. Shuddering violently, I turned on the engine and drove south at a reckless pace, not even bothering to keep an eye out for the blue-and-whites. All I wanted to do was to get home, get my clothes off, get myself scrubbed as clean as I could manage.

I left the Chevy at a wild angle a yard or so from the curb and took the stairs up two at a time. Barely waiting to get inside to strip, I dumped jeans, T-shirt, and panties in a heap in the doorway and headed straight for the bathroom. I stood under the hot water for almost half an hour, washing my hair twice, scrubbing myself thoroughly. Finally I felt cleansed, that addicts and alcoholics were rinsed from my life.

I dressed slowly, taking time to put on makeup and to style my hair with a little gel. A gold cotton dress with big black buttons made me feel elegant and poised. I even burrowed through the hall closet for a black bag to go with my pumps.

On the way out I gathered my discarded clothes and took them to the basement. The sheets were ready for the dryer, but there are limits to my housekeeping fervor—I stuffed my jeans in with the sheets and started the cycle from the beginning.

It was a little after one by now. I wouldn't be able to eat lunch if I wanted to see Zerlina before my meeting with Dominic Assuevo. And I guess I wanted to see her, although my enthusiasm for the Ramsay family was at low tide. I headed over to Lake Shore Drive and joined the flow southward.

Michael Reese Hospital dominates the lakefront for a mile or two at Twenty-seventh Street. I circled the complex a few times until I found someone pulling away from a meter—I was damned if I was going to pay lot fees for this visit. A guard was stationed behind a glass cage in the entryway. She didn't care whether I was a social worker or an ax murderer, so I didn't have to use Carol's cover story to get a pass to the fourth floor.

The distinctive hospital smell—some combination of medication, antiseptic, and the sweat of people in pain—made me flinch involuntarily when I got off the elevator. I had spent too much time in hospitals with my parents when I was younger, and the smell always brings back the misery of those years. My mother died of cancer when I was fifteen, my father from emphysema some ten years later. He was a heavy smoker and there are days when I still get angry about it. Especially today, when I was feeling under siege.

Zerlina Ramsay was in a four-pack. Televisions perched high on facing walls were tuned to conflicting soap operas. Two women glanced indifferently at me when I came in but returned their attention immediately to the screen; the other two didn't even look up. I stood dubiously in the doorway for a moment trying to decide which of the three black women might be Zerlina. None of them bore any overwhelming resemblance to Cerise. Finally I saw a sign attached to one of the beds warning me not to smoke if oxygen was in use. The woman lying there had gauze covering her left arm. Short, her massive build amply displayed by the skimpy hospital robe, she would have been my last choice, but Zerlina had been brought in suffering from smoke inhalation so I supposed she'd needed oxygen. She was attached to what looked like a heart monitor.

I went over to the bed. She turned her gaze toward me reluctantly, her eyes narrowed suspiciously in her jowly face.

"Mrs. Ramsay?" She didn't respond, but she didn't deny it ei-

ther. "My name is V. I. Warshawski. I think you know my aunt
Elena."

Her dark eyes flickered in surprise; she cautiously inspected me.
"You sure about that?" Her voice was husky from disuse and she
cleared her throat discreetly.

"She told me you two hung out together at the Indiana Arms.
Had a few beers together."

"So?"

I gritted my teeth and plowed ahead. "So she was waiting on my
doorstep last night with Cerise."

"Cerise! What planet that girl come down from?"

I glanced around the room. As I'd expected, her companions
were more interested in live theater than TV. They made no effort to
mask their curiosity.

"Can you go out in the hall with that thing?" I gestured at the
monitor. "This is kind of private."

"Those two took money from you, I don't want to hear about it.
I can't even afford me a new place to sleep, let alone pay back all
that girl's bills."

"It doesn't have anything to do with money."

She glowered at me belligerently, but heaved herself to a sitting
position. Her substantial frame gave the impression not of fat but of
a natural monument, maybe a redwood tree that had grown side-
ways but not too tall. She brushed away my hand when I tried to
take her elbow. Grunting to herself, she slid out of bed, sticking her
feet into paper hospital slippers lined up tidily under the edge. The
heart monitor was on wheels. Rolling it in front of her, she made her
way to the door and down the hall like a tidal wave—nurses and
orderlies split to either side when they saw her coming.

She was panting a bit when we got to a small lounge stuck at one
end of the hall. She took her time getting her breath before lowering
herself onto one of the padded chairs. They were covered in cracked
aqua oilcloth that had last been washed when Michael Reese himself
was still alive. I perched gingerly on the edge of the chair at right
angles to Zerlina.

"So Elena is your aunt, huh? Can't say you look too much
like her."

"Glad to hear it. She's thirty years and three thousand bottles ahead of me." I ignored her crack of laughter to add, "I gotta say you don't look too much like Cerise, either."

"That's those thirty years you spoke of," Zerlina said. "I wasn't so bad-looking at her age. And I sure look better than she's going to when she gets to be as old as me, the rate she's going. What kind of story she tell you? She and that aunt of yours."

"Her baby," I said baldly. "Katterina."

Zerlina's face creased in astonishment. For a moment I thought she was going to tell me Cerise didn't have a baby.

"She's picking a funny time to care about that baby, being as how she hasn't paid much attention to it so far to date."

"Katterina wasn't with you Wednesday night when the Indiana Arms burned down?" I couldn't think of a gentle way to ask the question.

"Hm-unh." She shook her jowly head emphatically. "She left the baby with me on Wednesday, all right, but I couldn't keep her with me, not in an SRO, you know. They can be mighty strict about who you got with you, which Cerise knew. But that girl!"

She sat with her hands on her knees, looking broodingly at nothing for a moment. The heart monitor beeped insistently, as though in rhythm with her thoughts. She faced me squarely.

"I might as well tell you the whole story. I don't know why I should. Don't know I can especially trust you. But you don't look like Elena. You don't look like an alkie who'll do the best she can to make money out of your sad news to buy her another bottle."

I felt a little queasy at her words. It's one thing to think of your own aunt turning tricks with the old-age pensioners. It's quite another to imagine her blackmailing people for the price of a drink.

"Not that I haven't had a drink or two in my day, too, and I'll give Elena this, she makes you laugh. You can forget your troubles with her every now and then." She looked away again for a moment, as though her troubles had come too forcefully to mind.

"Well, Cerise had this baby. Last year it was. And this baby had all kinds of problems on account of Cerise is a junkie. She was using heroin all the time she was pregnant. I told her how it would be. She even pretended to be in a program that time they arrested her. She'd been out stealing, her and the boy she was with at the time, and they arrested her. And on account of it was the first time and she was pregnant, they let her go if she promised to go to the program."

She glared at me again, as if daring me to condemn her for having a daughter like that. I made what I hoped was a sympathetic sound and tried to look understanding.

"Then the baby was born—and my, what a time we had! Poor little thing was in the hospital, then Maisie—the other grandmother —took her home. I couldn't, you know. I just live on a little bit of savings I have. I don't have social security—you don't get it for cleaning houses, which is what I did all my life, at least until my heart started giving out on me. But I helped Maisie out as much as I could and by and by we got that baby to sleep at night and even laughing."

"So Cerise never took care of her?"

"Oh, no, she did. Finally she did when she got going with Otis. That was in June. Then suddenly on Wednesday, Cerise comes by saying she can't take it anymore, being home with the baby morning, noon, and night, and I tell her she should be thinking of that before she spreads her legs, you know, not two years later, but she leaves the baby and goes, saying her and Otis is off to the Dells. So I go to the pay phone but I can't find a number for his sister, so I call Maisie and she sends her boy over and gets Katterina. And if you think Cerise is worrying about her, think again, on account of she hasn't come near me here in the hospital."

Maybe it was my imagination, but it seemed to me the heart monitor was beeping faster by the end of her tale. I didn't want to ask her anything that might get her more upset. I also didn't think I had to be the one to let Zerlina know her daughter was pregnant again.

She demanded to know why Cerise had come to see me. When I explained that she was asking me to intervene with the fire department, Zerlina snorted.

"Maybe she does think the baby's dead. Maybe that's why she hasn't been to see me—she's too ashamed. But if her and Elena come to see you together, girl, I advise you to keep your wallet in the bottom of your purse and count all your money before you say good-bye."

I felt an uneasy twinge—I hadn't looked in my billfold before putting it into my black bag. Still, Cerise had been pretty sick, maybe too sick to go hunting for money or credit cards. Before I got up to go I asked Zerlina how long they were keeping her.

She gave a little smile that was half crafty, half embarrassed. "When they brought me in I was unconscious on account of the smoke. And they found my heart was kind of acting up. High blood pressure, high fat in my blood—you name it, I got too much of everything. Except money. So I'm kind of dragging it out, you know, until I can get me a place to stay."

"I see." I'd come across worse crimes in my time. I stood up. "Well, I'm glad the baby's okay, anyway. Cerise disappeared around noon today and I'm not going to put a lot of energy into hunting for her. But if I see her again, I'll let her know her kid is at Maisie's."

She grunted and got slowly to her feet. "Yeah, okay, but I got to call Maisie and tell her Katterina don't go off with Cerise again. You take it easy, girl. What did you say your name was? Vic. And you stay those three thousand bottles behind Elena, you hear me?"

"Got it." I walked slowly down the hall with her to her room door before I said good-bye. Back in the lobby I checked my wallet. The cash was gone and so was my American Express Card. The only thing left was my PI license and that was because it was stuck behind a flap. They'd even lifted my driver's license. I ground my teeth. Cerise might have cleaned me out while I was hiding out in my bedroom this morning. But for all I knew Elena had robbed me when I was struggling with Cerise in the kitchen. I felt my shoulders tighten from futile rage.

I found a pay phone in the lobby and called my credit-card companies to report the cards as stolen. At least I'd memorized my phone card number so I didn't have to stop all my phone calls. I usually keep an emergency twenty in the zip compartment of my purse; when I checked the black bag I found I'd left one in there. On my way out I used it to buy flowers for Zerlina. It wasn't enough, but it was all I could afford.

# 12

# Firing Up
## the Arson Squad

**B**efore leaving the hospital I tried to reach Robin Bessinger at Ajax. I was hoping to cancel our meeting with the Bomb and Arson Squad now that I knew the baby hadn't been in the Indiana Arms, but I was too late—the insurance receptionist told me he'd already left for the police department. I took a deep breath, squared my shoulders, and headed back to Ellis Avenue and my car.

It used to be you could go to Central Police Headquarters anytime day or night and park with ease. Now that development mania has hit the Near South Side, downtown congestion has clogged the area. It took me half an hour to find a place to park. That made me about ten minutes late for the meeting, which scarcely helped my frayed mood.

Roland Montgomery held court in an office the size of my bed. A regulation metal desk crammed with papers took most of the available space, but he squeezed in chairs for me, Bessinger, Assuevo, and a subordinate. Papers were stacked on the windowsill and on top of the metal filing cabinet. Someone should have told him the place was a fire trap.

Montgomery, a tall, thin man with hollow cheeks, gave me a sour look as I came in. He ignored my outstretched hand, pointed to the empty chair in the corner, and asked if I knew Dominic Assuevo.

Assuevo was bull-shaped—thick neck and wide shoulders tapering into narrow hips. His graying sandy hair was cropped close to his head the way the boys used to wear it when I was in third grade. He greeted me with a jovial courtesy not reflected in his eyes.

"Can't stay away from fire, huh, Ms. Warshawski?"

"Good to see you again, too, Commander. Hiya, Robin. I tried to get you a little bit ago but your office told me you were already here." I skirted my way past his long feet to the vacant chair.

Robin Bessinger was sitting in the opposite corner of the tiny room. He seemed a little older than he'd struck me when I first met him, but of course the hard hat had kept me from seeing that his hair had gone gray. He smiled and waved and said hello.

I squeezed in next to the uniformed man and held out a hand. "V. I. Warshawski. I don't think we've met."

He mumbled something that sounded like "firehorse whiskey." I never did learn what his name really was.

"So you think there was a baby in the Indiana Arms, Ms. Warshawski?" Montgomery pulled a folder from the stack in front of him. I had to believe he'd practiced it, that he couldn't know offhand what fire which folder referred to.

"I did when I spoke to Mr. Bessinger this morning. That was before I tracked down the baby's grandmother. I just finished interviewing her in the hospital and she says she had already sent the child to its other grandmother before the fire broke out."

"So we're wasting our time here, is that what you're telling me?" Montgomery's eyebrows rose to his sandy hairline. He made no effort to hide his contempt.

I gave a tight smile. "Guess so, Lieutenant."

"There were no babies in the Indiana Arms when it burned down?" He swung his neck cranelike across the desk at me.

"I can't say that categorically. I only know that the one I'd been told was there—Katterina Ramsay—had left the building earlier in the evening. For all I know there might have been others. You should check with Commander Assuevo here."

The young man next to me had started to write this in his open notebook but stopped at a sign from Montgomery.

"You have something of the reputation of a wit, Ms. Warshawski," the lieutenant said heavily. "Personally, I have never found your sense of humor entertaining. I hope this wasn't your idea of a joke, to turn police and fire department resources loose on a wild-goose chase."

"My comedic talents have always been greatly overrated by Bobby Mallory," I said coolly. I was feeling pretty angry, but it seemed to me Montgomery was provoking me deliberately. I wanted to be the last one to blink.

"Well, the next time you feel an urge to make a joke, call Mallory, not me. Because if you do abuse departmental resources again, Ms. Warshawski, believe me, I will be calling the lieutenant and asking him to give you a good lesson in legalities."

That seemed to be the end of the interview. Short of leaping over the desk and pummeling him with my bare hands, I couldn't think of anything to say or do to express my frustration effectively. I stood up slowly, aligned my belt buckle directly under the black buttons, pulled an imaginary hair from my dress, and shook out the skirt. I beamed happily at Firehorse Whiskey and sketched a wave at Robin Bessinger.

I kept the happy smile on my face all the way down the stairs. Once in the hall I let the waves of anger wash through me. What the hell was eating Montgomery? It could only be his relations with police lieutenant Bobby Mallory. Bobby talks about me one way and thinks about me quite another—he might easily have told the fire commander I was a pain in the butt and a wiseass—his publicly expressed opinion on many occasions. Missing would be Bobby's affection as an old friend of my parents'.

But that didn't excuse the squad commander's behavior. He could have asked me why I had called Robin to begin with. I certainly wasn't going to start piping out self-exculpation when treated to that kind of routine. And Bessinger—why didn't the guy speak up? I made a tight face and headed for the south exit.

"You look like a snake stood up and bit you. Can't you even say hi to your friends?" It was Michael Furey. I hadn't been scanning faces as I hunched my way down the hall.

"Oh, hiya, Michael. Must be sleep deprivation."

"What are you doing here? Helping us keep Chicago safe and legal?" His dark blue eyes teased me.

I forced myself to smile. "Something like that. I've just been meeting with Roland Montgomery about that fire in the Indiana Arms last week."

"The one where your aunt got caught? You oughta stay clear of arson—that's dirty, dirty stuff."

"Dirty work, but someone's got to do it. Since Montgomery doesn't want to, maybe I'll have a crack at it."

"Oh, Monty's not doing the investigation?" His eyebrows shot up and he looked thoughtful.

"Doesn't seem too interested." I kept my tone light.

"Well, in that case—" He broke off. "You don't want me telling you to mind your own business."

I bowed slightly. "Call the boy a mind reader."

He laughed a little, but there was a current of annoyance in it. "I won't, then. But keep it in mind that if Monty isn't touching it, there may be good reasons to stay away from it."

I looked at him steadily. "Like what? Well, it doesn't matter. Just to keep you happy, no one's asked me to look at the arson. But the more people tell me not to touch something, the more I feel like reaching out a hand just to see what's so special about it."

He hunched a shoulder impatiently. "Whatever you say, Vic. I gotta run."

He went on down the hall, greeting uniformed men with his usual good humor. I shook my head and went on outside.

Bessinger caught up with me as I was crossing State. "Slow down, Vic. I'd like to know what was going on between you and Monty in that meeting."

I stopped and faced him squarely. "You tell me. I wondered why you didn't say anything to explain why you thought it worthwhile bothering Montgomery based just on my phone call."

He held up his hands. "I've been around a lot of fires in my time. I don't step in between the accelerant and the kindling. Besides, I did try to talk to him. That's why I stayed after you. But I still can't figure out why he's so angry about this one. Other than manpower shortages, but he's taking it as a personal affront. Why?"

I shook my head. "I can see it would piss him and Assuevo to have the lab sifting through ashes for a nonexistent body. But I only called you in the first place to find out if you knew. When you didn't I took the long route, which meant getting the last name of the baby's mother and tracking down her mother. The grandmother, I mean."

"You didn't know that when you called?" His tone was puzzled, not accusatory.

"I never saw the young woman before—the mother of the baby —until she came to my place late last night. She'd left the kid with her own mother, Zerlina Ramsay, at the Indiana Arms, and she didn't want me talking to Mrs. Ramsay. She said if I knew their last name it would get her mother in trouble, that she'd never find another place to stay. She's a junkie, though—I don't know if that came from drug-related paranoia or real concern about her mother or what."

We were standing on the pavement near the curb. Patrolmen heading up State toward the entrance kept brushing against us. When I stepped aside to avoid a man being decanted from a stretch limo, I ran into a woman trotting down the street toward Dearborn.

"Can't you watch where you're going?" she snapped at me.

I opened my mouth to utter a guerrilla hostility back, then thought maybe I'd done enough fighting for one day and ignored her.

Robin looked at his watch. "I don't need to go back to the office. Want to get a drink someplace? I'm afraid if someone else bumps into us, Monty's going to have us arrested, the mood he's in."

I suddenly felt very tired. I'd been running since eight this morning cleaning up after Elena and Cerise. People as different as Lotty and Roland Montgomery had been chewing me out. A clean well-lighted place and a glass of whiskey sounded like doctor's orders to me.

Robin had taken a cab up from Ajax. He walked back to the Chevy with me and we headed through the early rush-hour traffic to the Golden Glow, a bar I know and love in the south Loop. We left the car at a meter down near Congress and walked the three blocks back to the bar. Sal Barthele, the owner, was alone with a couple of men nursing beers at the mahogany horseshoe counter. She nodded majestically at me when I took Robin over to a small round table in the corner. She waited until we were settled and Robin had exclaimed over the genuine Tiffany lamps to take our orders.

"Your usual, Vic?" Sal asked when Robin had ordered a beer.

My usual is Black Label up. I pictured Elena's flushed, veined face and my missing credit cards. I remembered Zerlina's admonition to keep three thousand bottles behind Elena. Then I thought, hell, I'm thirty-seven years old. If I was going to get drunk every time life threatened me, I would have started in years ago. When I feel like having a whiskey, I'll have a whiskey.

"Yes," I said more vehemently than I'd meant.

"You sure about that, girl?" Sal mocked me gently, then went to the bar to fill our order. Sal's a shrewd businesswoman. The Glow is only one of her investments and she could easily afford to turn it over to a manager. But it also was her first venture and she likes to preside over it in person.

Robin took a swallow of his draft and opened his eyes in appreciation. "I've probably walked by here a hundred times going to the Insurance Exchange. How could I have missed this stuff?"

Sal's draft is made for her privately by a small brewer in Steven's Point. I'm not a beer lover, but my pals who are think it's pretty hot stuff.

I told Robin a little about Sal and her operations, then steered the talk back to the Indiana Arms. "You ever find any evidence that the owner was trying to sell the place?"

Robin shook his head. "Too early to tell. His limits aren't out of line, but that doesn't matter. It's really more a question of what's going on with the building and him and his finances. We haven't got that far yet."

"What does Montgomery say?"

Robin frowned and finished his beer before answering. "Nothing. He's not going to dedicate any more resources into investigating the arson."

"And you don't agree?" I drank a glass of water, then swallowed the rest of my scotch. The warmth spread slowly from my stomach to my arms and some of the tension the day had put into my shoulders disappeared.

"We never pay a claim when arson is involved. I mean, not unless we're a hundred percent sure the insured didn't engineer it."

He held up his glass to Sal and she brought over another draft.

She had the Black Label bottle with her but I shook my head over the idea of seconds. Elena must have been affecting me after all.

"I just don't understand Montgomery, though. I've worked with him before. He's not an easy guy—not much looseness there—but I've never seen him as nasty as he was to you this afternoon."

"Must be my charm," I said lightly. "It hits some men that way." I didn't think it was worth explaining my theory about Montgomery and Bobby Mallory to a stranger.

Robin refused to laugh. "It's something about this fire. Why else would he tell me the file was closed? He said they'd only reopened it because you thought there might be a body in there. Now they want to put their manpower where it's more urgently needed."

"I've never worked with the Bomb and Arson unit, but I assume they're not too different from the rest of the police—too few people, too many crimes. It doesn't seem so unbelievable to me that Montgomery would abandon an investigation into an underinsured mausoleum in one of the city's tackier districts. The fire fighters and police may serve and protect everyone, but they're human—they'll respond to the neighborhoods with more political clout first."

Robin made an impatient gesture. "Maybe you're right. Insurance companies have to be more allergic to arson. Montgomery may want to concentrate on the Gold Coast, but we can't be so picky. Even if he's abandoning the Indiana Arms, we won't. At least not for the time being."

Or at least not until his boss also got his sense of priorities reorganized. But I kept that last unkind thought to myself and let the talk drift to the joys of home ownership. Robin had just bought a two-flat in Albany Park; he was renting out the ground floor while living on top and trying to rehab the whole place in his spare time on weekends. Stripping varnish and putting up drywall are not my idea of a good time, but I'm perfectly ready to applaud anyone else who wants to do it.

After his third beer it seemed natural to think about moving on to food. We agreed on I Popoli, a seafood restaurant near Clark and Howard. After that it seemed natural to drive up to Albany Park with him to inspect the rehab work. One thing kind of led to another, but I left before they drifted too far—I hadn't packed any equipment when I left my apartment for the day. Anyway, AIDS is making me more cautious. I like to see a guy more than once before doing anything irrevocable. Still, it's nice to get an outside opinion of one's attractions. I went home at midnight in a far better mood than I would have thought possible when I got up twenty hours ago.

# 13

# Washing Up

I slept late the next morning. Usually as soon as I wake up I get out of bed and get going—I'm not a napper or a snoozer. But today I felt a catlike languor envelop me, a sense of well-being that came from knowing I had my castle to myself. The street noises were subdued—the nine-to-fivers were long gone about their business—and I felt suspended in a little bubble of privacy.

By and by I padded into the kitchen to make some coffee. The remains of yesterday's shambles made a slight dent in my euphoria, enough to decide me not to skip my run two days in a row. I had cleaned up after Cerise, but the dirty rags were still in the sink, giving off a faint smell of Clorox mixed with old vomit. I needed to throw them in the wash and might as well do it at the start of my run.

Down in the basement after doing my stretches, my good mood deteriorated further on finding that someone had dumped my laundry on the floor—wet. A note scribbled in angry haste lay on top: "You don't own the basement too!" I knew Mr. Contreras would never have done such a thing. The second-floor tenants were Korean; their English didn't seem up to the pointedness of the message. My third-floor neighbor was a quiet older Norwegian woman who almost never appeared. That left the banker, good old Vincent Bottone.

I put the clothes back in the washer, added the rags, poured in a double measure of soap and a good cup of Clorox, and left Westinghouse to do my dirty work. I stopped on the first floor for the dog, who was more than usually eager to see me—it had been several days since she'd had a good workout. Mr. Contreras was disposed to question me about my aunt and Cerise, but the dog was whimpering so loudly I was able to make my escape in fairly short order.

As I jogged up to Belmont and across to the harbor, my mind kept shifting to Vincent Bottone, trying to come up with some fitting response to his desecration of my laundry. Of course I shouldn't have gone off and left it all day, but did he really have to dump it on the floor and add a hostile note? My best idea was to break into his apartment some weekend when he was out and steal his briefcase for Peppy to chew to bits. But then he might poison the dog—he was just the type.

By the time Peppy and I got back home my early euphoria had evaporated completely. I turned the dog back to Mr. Contreras and pleaded a heavy work load to escape a second barrage of questions. Halfway up the stairs I remembered my laundry and stomped back to the basement to shift it to the dryer.

The washer was still in its final spin cycle. Propping my elbows on the vibrating machine, I tried to resolve on an action plan for the day. I had to get my driver's license replaced, which meant trekking up Elston by bus—I shouldn't even have been driving last night without it. After that—I wondered if it was worthwhile trying to confront Elena about my missing stuff. If she knew, she wouldn't admit it; anyway, the thought of dealing with her coy evasions nauseated me. If it was Cerise who had robbed me, I didn't have any desire to find her, even if I knew where to look.

Since I wasn't going to mess with those two anymore, there was nothing to stop my getting back to paying—and waiting—clients. I repeated some pretty stern orders to myself about going upstairs, getting dressed, and heading for the Loop, but something kept me planted in front of the washing machine.

The rhythm of the spin cycle was soothing. My mind relaxed while I stared at the dials. The niggling questions buried by Cerise and Elena's exigent needs came fluttering back to the surface of my brain.

Rosalyn. Why had she gratuitously sought me out at Boots's

party? With a thousand people to meet—lots of them with lots of bucks—did she really want to assure herself that I was on her side?

I wished I could believe it. I just couldn't. She could see I'd shelled out for her; that should have been guarantee enough for someone who wasn't particularly close to her. Despite her and Marissa's soap, my public support wasn't particularly useful to her. I haven't been politically active for a long time. My name is getting better known in the financial world, but it doesn't count for anything in county politics. In fact, knowing I backed Roz—or any other candidate—could just as likely make people who know me from my PD days vote against her as for her.

I couldn't help believing she thought I knew something that might damage her. She had some secret and her cousin was worried I knew about it. It was after he'd pointed at me that she'd come back and asked me to meet her at the swing. She'd sought me out to scout the lay of the land.

"It doesn't matter, Vic," I said aloud. "So she's got a secret. So who doesn't? None of your business."

Grunting, I moved the heavy wet clothes from the machine to the dryer. I slammed the door shut and scowled at the knobs. The trouble was, she'd made it my business by seeking me out in that strange way. If she and Marissa were making a patsy out of me between them—I bit off the thought in mid-sentence and headed for the stairs. I was halfway up when I realized I hadn't turned on the dryer. I stomped back to the basement and set the wheel in motion.

I put on my newest jeans so I'd look tidy and respectable for the driver's license people. With it I wore a rose-colored blouse so I'd photograph decently.

All during the slow bus ride up Elston and the long wait while state employees processed applicants at a pace just short of total morbidity, I toyed with different ways of getting a fix on Roz's situation. My first thought had been to head to the Daley Center to see if she was being sued. But if someone were on her case, the papers would have the story—the first thing the eager reporters do when someone runs for office is check the public record on them.

With a start I realized my turn had come. I filled out the forms, handed over my three pieces of identification, waited some more, agreed to give away my kidneys and eyeballs if some cokehead totaled me, and finally got my picture taken. My care in dressing had been to no avail—I still looked like an escapee from the psycho ward at Cook County. Maybe I should lose this license, too, and try again.

I trudged back onto the Number 41 bus and endured the long trek south. The sight of my demented-looking photograph did make me think of someone who might know what Roz was up to. Velma Riter was a photographer whom I'd met when she was with the *Herald-Star*. She'd been assigned enough times to cover stories I'd been involved in that we got to know each other, at least by sight. Shortly before leaving the paper to go into business for herself, she'd done a big photo-essay for a special issue on "Fifty Women Who Move Chicago." I'd been included, as had Roz.

The artist was at home. She'd evidently been expecting some other call because she answered the phone eagerly on the first ring but seemed startled at hearing it was me.

"V. I. Warshawski," she repeated slowly, drawing out the syllables. "Well, well. To what do I owe the pleasure?"

"I just had my driver's license redone. I was wishing you could doctor the photo for me."

"Forged passports are my real specialty," she said dryly. "What are you up to these days?"

"Not much. I saw Roz Fuentes on Sunday, though, out at a big shindig Boots Meagher was throwing for her."

"I knew about it—she wanted me there, but I'm getting ready for a show. I wouldn't even have answered your call if I hadn't been expecting to hear from my agent."

I made appropriate noises of congratulation, wrote down the gallery name and opening date, and apologized for disturbing her work. "You keep up with Roz?"

"I'm doing some work for the campaign." A thread of impatience hit Velma's voice. "Vic, I really don't have time for a chat right now."

"I wouldn't be bothering you if I knew someone else to interrupt. Roz got me kind of worried, though. I wondered if she was digging herself into some kind of pit her pals ought to know about."

"Just what did she say to make you think that?"

"Not so much what she said but what she did." I told her about

Roz breaking away from the crowd just to sound out how much I cared about her alliance with Boots.

"You worry too much about other people's business, Warshawski. Some people even think you're a pain in the butt. Go catch some real criminals and leave Roz's business alone. She's cool."

Her closing words made my cheeks flame. I hung up without even trying to reply. I had an ugly vision of myself as a crank and a busybody.

"She still shouldn't have come around asking if I was going to do anything to hurt her," I muttered aggrievedly to myself.

Hunching my shoulders, I went back outside. I was flat and I didn't have a cash card. The rest of the afternoon was taken up with errands to replace my missing credit—to the bank to cash a check and apply for a new card. To the grocery to get some food and a new check-writing card. At four I finally took some time to go to the Daley Center and dig around a little on a background check for an old client. Velma's words still stung so much I didn't even try looking Roz up.

The documents library closed at four-thirty. I walked across town to my office to see what new bills had come in since Friday, stopping at a deli to pick up a giant chocolate-chip cookie and a cup of bitter coffee.

While I finished the cookie I switched on the desk lamp and called my answering service. Both Michael Furey and Robin Bessinger had phoned. And one of the managers from Cartwright & Wheeler, the insurance brokers where I'd made my presentation last Friday.

I sat down heavily. A potential client. A paying client. And I had completely forgotten to make a follow-up phone call. After spending five hundred dollars and two days on a presentation to them.

Maybe this showed the beginning of senile dementia. They say the short-term memory is the first thing to go. Harassed though I'd been yesterday by dealing with Cerise and Roland Montgomery, I still should have remembered to make a phone call that important. I looked at my pocket diary—there it was. Call Cartwright & Wheeler. I'd even put in the number and the name of the contact person.

When I phoned it was to get bad news—they'd decided they didn't need my help at this time. Of course once they'd put off the decision the odds were against their choosing to hire me. But Velma was right—I spent so much time worrying about other people's business, I couldn't even keep track of my own. The vision of myself as a grotesque busybody returned. The outcome might not have been different if I'd remembered to call yesterday, but at least I'd feel like a professional instead of a fool.

# 14

# Caught
# in the Act

I returned Furey's and Robin Bessinger's phone calls, more for
something to do to stop my self-flagellation than from any real enthusiasm to talk to either. Furey wanted to apologize for his comments to me at the department yesterday and arrange a final trip to
the Sox, who like the Cubs had long since faded into the sunset.

"I didn't mean to criticize you," he added. "It's hard for us
born-and-bred chauvinists to reform."

"That's okay," I assured him with what goodwill I could muster. "I wasn't at my best, anyway—Lieutenant Montgomery was
jumping on my ass for the wrong reasons and it didn't leave me
feeling very friendly."

After we'd talked a little about the meeting, and he'd given me
some tips on the best way to handle Monty, he inquired about Elena.

I'd forgotten asking him to do a search for her. More dementia.
More repellent busybodiedness. "Oh, nuts. I'm sorry—I should have
told you—she showed up Sunday night safe and sound. With a truly
hideous protégée."

"Sounds bad," he said with ready sympathy. "What was the
protégée? Someone from the Indiana Arms?"

"Daughter." I gave him a thumbnail sketch of Cerise. "Now
she's vanished into the woodwork, pregnant, addicted and all."

"Want to give me her name and description? I could ask the
boys to keep an eye out for her."

"Ugh." The last thing I wanted was for someone to drop Cerise on my doorstep again. On the other hand, for the sake of the fetus she was working on, someone ought to try to get her into a drug program. Why not the cops? I gave Michael the details.

"I don't think this week is a good time for me to set a play date —I've been letting too many things slide and it's starting to get me down. I'll call next Monday or Tuesday, okay?"

"Yeah, Vic. Fine." He hung up.

Furey was fundamentally good-natured. Caring enough to look out for a pregnant junkie he'd never seen. Eileen Mallory was right —he was good father material. I just wasn't looking for a father. At least not for my unborn children.

I called Robin next. The lab they used had reported on the samples from the Indiana Arms. They'd confirmed his initial hunch on the accelerant—it had been paraffin.

I tried to force my mind to care about what he was saying. "Is it hard to buy?"

"It's common," he responded. "Easy to get hold of, even in large quantities, so I don't think we can trace the user by looking for a purchaser. What's interesting was the timing device they used to set the thing off. A hot plate had been plugged into it in the night man's quarters."

"So maybe the watchman had something to do with it." Hard to think he didn't if a timer was wired to his own appliance.

"The owner says he had only a night man at the desk, that he didn't think the building warranted a watchman. We haven't been able to locate the guy, though. . . . Vic, you've done a lot of work for Ajax in the past. Successful work. I wondered—I talked to my boss—could we hire you on this one?"

"To do what?" I asked cautiously. "I don't know a thing about arson—I couldn't tell an accelerant from a match."

He didn't respond directly. "Even though the building was underinsured, we're reserving over a million dollars. People were injured, and that means liability claims on top of the property loss. The police may not care, but it'd be worth it to us to invest several thousand in a professional investigation if we could save the big money. We'd like you to try to find the arsonist."

I watched the windowpanes vibrate at the continuous stream of rush-hour L's running just underneath. A little dirt shook loose, but not as much as whirled up to add to the glass's gray opacity. It wasn't a scene to bolster my low sense of competence.

"My fan club at Ajax doesn't exactly include a unanimous chorus of senior staff. Does your boss have the authority to hire me without a lot of other people getting involved in the approval process?"

"Oh, yeah. That's easy. We budget for outside investigators— they don't have to be approved on a case-by-case basis." He paused. "Could I interest you in dinner tonight? Try to help you make up your mind?"

I could picture his head tilted birdlike to one side as he watched to see if the worm would pop out of the ground. The image made me feel like smiling for the first time since finding my laundry on the floor this morning. "Dinner would be great."

He suggested Calliope, a lively place on north Lincoln that served Greek-style seafood. They didn't take reservations, but people could dance in the adjoining cabaret while waiting for their tables.

After hanging up I shut my office for the day. Another couple of inquiries had come in that I ought to deal with, but I didn't have the emotional energy for work this afternoon.

By the time I walked back to the north end of the Loop for my car and picked my way through the rush-hour traffic home, I just had time for a long bath before dressing for dinner. I lay in the tub a good forty-five minutes, letting my mind float to nowhere, letting the water wash away the sharpest edge of self-doubt.

When I finally got out and started dressing, the late-summer twilight was turning the evening air a grayish-purple. I watched Mr. Contreras working in the backyard. The tomato season was ending but he was cultivating a few pumpkins with tender care. He liked to do Halloween in style for the local kids. In the dim light I could just make out Peppy lying on the grass, her nose on her forepaws, gloomily waiting for activity that might include her.

I went down the back way to bid him and the dog good night. The old man was on his dignity, miffed at my shortness with him this morning, but the dog was ecstatic. I had to work hard to keep her from transferring leaf loam or manure or whatever Mr. Contreras was piling on the pumpkins to my black silk trousers.

He refused to be mollified by my light remarks. I felt myself on the verge of apologizing and bit back the words in annoyance—there was no reason for him to know every detail of my life. If I wanted to keep a few small segments private, I shouldn't have to say I was sorry. I gave him a cool farewell and slid through the back gate so that the dog couldn't follow. Her frustrated whimpering accompanied me down the alley.

I walked the short mile to the restaurant. Stepping around a wide hole in the concrete I slipped on a discarded hot dog. Just one more of the joys of city life. I dusted my trouser knees. The fabric was bruised slightly but not torn. Not enough damage to justify a move to Streamwood.

Robin was waiting for me outside the restaurant door, looking elegant in gray flannel slacks and a navy blazer. He had come early to sign up for a table and the manager was just calling his name when we walked in. Perfect. If you're born lucky, you don't have to be good. Robin ordered a beer while I had a rum and tonic and some of the cod roe mousse the Calliope was famous for.

"How did you become a detective?" he asked after we'd given our dinner orders.

"I used to be with the public defender." I spread some of the mousse on a piece of toast. "Trial division. It's hideous work—you often get briefed on your client only five minutes before the trial begins. You always have more cases than time to work them effectively. And sometimes you're pleading heart and soul for goons you hope will never see the light of day again."

"So why didn't you just go into private practice?" He scooped up some of the mousse. "This is good," he mumbled, his mouth full. "I never tried it before."

It was good—just salty enough to go down well with beer or rum. I ate some more and finished my drink before answering.

"I'd spent five years in the PD's office—I didn't want to have to start again at the beginning in a private practice. Anyway, I'd solved a case for a friend and realized it was work I could do well and get genuine satisfaction from. Plus, I can be my own boss." I should have given that as my first reason—it continues to be the most important with me. Maybe from being an only child, used to getting my own way? Or just my mother's fierce independence seeping into my DNA along with her olive skin.

After the waiter brought salads and a bottle of wine, I asked Robin how he ended up as an arson specialist. He grimaced.

"I don't know anyone whose first choice is insurance, except maybe the kids whose fathers own agencies. I majored in art history. There wasn't money to send me to graduate school. So I started work at Ajax. They had me designing policy forms—trying to make use of my artistic background"—he grinned briefly—"but I got out of that as fast as I could."

During dinner he asked me about some of the earlier work I'd done for Ajax. It was my turn to make a face—the company didn't know if it loved or hated me for fingering their claims vice president as the mastermind of a workers' comp fraud scam. Robin was fascinated—he said there'd always been a lot of gossip circulating, but that no one had ever told the lower-downs what their vice president had really been up to.

Over Greek-style bouillabaisse he spent a little time persuading me to go back into the Ajax trenches once again. I knew I needed a major job, not just the nickel-and-dime stuff that had come over the transom the last few days. I knew I didn't feel up to hustling for new clients right now. I knew I was going to say yes, but I asked him to call me at my office in the morning with some details.

"It's been a roughish day," I explained. "Tonight I just want to forget the detecting business and unwind."

He didn't seem to mind. The talk drifted to baseball and childhood while we finished eating. Dancing in the back room afterwards, we didn't talk much at all. Around midnight we decided the time had come to move the few blocks north to my place. Robin said he'd leave his car at the restaurant and pick it up in the morning—we'd both had too much to drink to drive, and anyway, it was a beautiful late-summer night.

We turned the six blocks into a half-hour trek, moving slowly with our arms locked, stopping every few houses for a long kiss. When we finally got to my place I whispered urgent warnings of silence on Robin—I didn't want Mr. Contreras or Vinnie the banker descending on us. While Robin stood behind me with his arms wrapped around my waist, I fumbled in my bag for my keys.

A car door slammed in front of the house. We moved to one side as footsteps came up the walk. A car searchlight pinned us against the apartment entrance.

"That you, Vicki? Sorry to interrupt, but we need to have a chat." The voice, laden with heavy irony, was almost as familiar to me as my own father's. It belonged to Lieutenant Robert Mallory, head of the Violent Crimes Unit at the Chicago Police's Central District. I could feel my cheeks flame in the dark—no matter how cool you are, it unsettles you when your father's oldest friend surprises you in a passionate embrace.

"I'm flattered, of course, Bobby. Two and a half million souls in the city, including your seven grandchildren, and when you have insomnia you come to me."

Bobby ignored me. "Say good night to your friend here—we're going for a ride."

Robin made a creditable effort to intervene. I grabbed his arm. "They'll put you in Cook County with the muggers and the buggers if you hit him—it's a police lieutenant. Bobby—Robin Bessinger, Ajax Insurance. Robin—Bobby Mallory, Chicago's finest."

In the searchlight Bobby's red face looked grayish-white; lines I didn't usually notice sprang into craggy relief. He was coming up on his sixtieth birthday, after all. I'd even been invited to the surprise party his wife was planning for him in early October, but I hadn't thought of the milestone as meaning he might be getting old. I pushed aside the stab of queasiness the idea of his aging gave me and said more loudly than I'd intended, "Where are we riding to and why, Bobby?"

I could see him wrestle with the desire to grab me and drag me forcibly to the waiting car. Most people don't know that if you're not under arrest you don't have to go off with a policeman just because he tells you to. And most people won't fight it even if they know it. Even a good cop like Bobby starts taking it for granted; a citizen like me helps him keep his powers in perspective.

"Tell your friend to take a hike." He jerked his head at Robin.

If I obeyed him on that one, he'd play by the rules. It wasn't a great compromise, but it was a compromise. I grudgingly asked Robin to leave. He agreed on condition that I call him as soon as the police were done with me, but when he got to the end of the walk, he stood to watch. I was touched.

"Okay, he's gone. What do you need to talk about?"

Bobby frowned and pressed his lips together. Just a reflex of annoyance. "Night watchman found a body near a construction site around nine-thirty. She had something on her linking her to you."

I had a sudden image of my aunt, dead drunk, getting hit by a car and left to die. I put a hand on the side of the building to steady myself. "Elena?" I asked foolishly.

"Elena?" Bobby was momentarily blank. "Oh, Tony's sister. Not unless she shed fifty years and had her skin dyed for the occasion."

It took me a minute to work out what he meant. A young black woman. Cerise. She wasn't the only young black woman I know, but I couldn't imagine any of the others dead near a construction site. "Who was it?"

"We want you to tell us."

"What did you find that made you connect her with me?"

Bobby pressed his lips together again. He just didn't want to tell me—old habits die hard. I thought he was about to speak when the door opened behind me and Vinnie the banker erupted into the night.

"This is it, Warshawski. This is the last time you get me up in the middle of the night. Just so you know it, the cops are on their way over. Don't your *friends* ever think—shining a light straight into a window where people are sleeping? And talking at the top of their lungs? Or are you trying to lure people inside?"

He had changed out of his pajamas into jeans and a white button shirt. His thick brown hair was combed carefully from his face. He might even have taken the extra time to shampoo and blow-dry it before dialing 911.

"I'm glad you phoned them, Vinnie—they'll be real happy when they get here. And so will the rest of the block when the squad cars cruise in with those new strobes of theirs painting the nighttime blue."

Bobby looked at Vinnie. "You call the cops, son?"

The banker stuck his chin out pugnaciously. "Yes, I did. They'll be here any minute. If you're her pimp, you've got about two minutes to disappear."

Bobby kept his tone avuncular. "Who you talk to, son—the precinct or the emergency number?"

Vinnie bristled. "I'm not your son. Don't think you can buy *me* off too."

Bobby looked at me, his lips twitching. "You been trying to sell him nickel bags, Vicki?"

He turned back to Vinnie, showing his badge. "I know Miss Warshawski isn't the easiest neighbor in the world—I'm about to take her off your hands. But I need to know if you called 911 or the precinct so I can cancel the squad cars—I don't want to waste any more city money tonight pulling patrol officers away from work they ought to be doing because you have a beef with your neighbors."

Vinnie bunched up his lips, not wanting to back down but knowing he had to. "911," he muttered, then said more defiantly, "And it's about time someone took her in."

Bobby looked toward the street and bellowed, "Furey!"

Michael climbed out of the car and trotted over. Just what I needed to complete the transformation of romance into farce—Michael must have seen me in a clinch with Robin at the door.

"This kid here called 911 when he heard me talking to Vicki—get on the radio and find out who's coming and cancel them, okay? And turn off the light. Guy needs his beauty sleep."

Michael, at his most wooden, ignored me completely and headed back to the car. Vinnie tried asking for Bobby's badge number so he could lodge a complaint with the watch commander—"your boss" as he put it—but Bobby put a heavy hand on his shoulder and assured him that everyone had better things to do with their time, and if Vinnie had to be at the office in the morning, maybe it was time he turned back in.

"Well, at least get this woman to stop conducting her business in the front hall in the middle of the night," Vinnie demanded petulantly as he opened the front door.

"Is that what you do, Vicki?" Bobby asked. "Lose your lease downtown?"

I gritted my teeth but didn't try to fight it as he took my arm and ushered me down the walk—Mr. Contreras would doubtless be out next with the dog if we stayed any longer.

"Elena," I said shortly. "She's come around a few times in the last week. Always after midnight, of course."

"I haven't seen her since Tony's funeral. Didn't even know whether she was still in town."

"I wish I hadn't seen her since then, either. She got burned out of her place last Wednesday—you know that SRO fire near McCormick Place?"

Bobby grunted. "So she came to you. Underneath it all you're not that different from your folks, I guess."

That left me speechless for the remainder of the short walk. Bobby opened the back door for me. I waved at Robin and climbed inside.

Michael was sitting in the front seat, John McGonnigal—the sergeant Bobby most preferred to work with—in the back. I said hello to both of them. They kept up an animated conversation about police business all the way to the morgue. Even if I'd wanted to, I couldn't have joined in.

# 15

# At the Rue Morgue

**S**ome practical bureaucrat put the county morgue on the Near West Side, the area with Chicago's highest murder rate—it saves wear and tear on the meatwagons having to cart corpses only a few short blocks. Even during the day the concrete cube looks like a bunker in the middle of a war zone; at midnight it's the most depressing place in town.

As we walked up to the sliding metal doors marked "Deliveries," Furey began a series of morbid one-liners, a kind of defense against his own mortality I suppose, but still unpleasant. At least McGonnigal didn't join in. I moved out of earshot, into the entryway—a small box of reenforced glass whose inner door was locked. A knot of clerks at the reception counter inside looked me over and went back to an animated conversation. When Bobby materialized behind my left shoulder, the party broke up and someone unlocked the door.

I pushed it open when the buzzer sounded and held it for Bobby and the boys. Furey still wouldn't look at me, not even when I went out of my way to be superpolite. Last time I'd go to a political fundraiser with him, that's for sure.

For the public brought in to identify their nearest and dearest, the county provides a small furnished waiting room—you can even look at a video screen instead of directly at the body. Bobby didn't think I needed such amenities. He pushed open the double doors to the autopsy room. I followed, trying to walk nonchalantly.

It was a utilitarian room, with sinks and equipment for four pathologists to work at once. In the middle of the night the only person present was an attendant, a middle-aged man in jeans with a green surgical gown thrown loosely around his shoulders. He was hunched over a car-and-track magazine. The Sox were on a seven-inch screen on the chair in front of him. He looked at us indifferently, taking his time to get up when Bobby identified himself and told him what we wanted. He sauntered to the thick double doors leading to the cooler.

Inside were hundreds of bodies arranged in rows. Their torsos were partially draped in black plastic, but the heads were exposed, arcing back, the mouths open in surprise at death. I could feel the blood drain from my brain. I hoped I wasn't turning green—it would put the cap to my night if I got sick in front of Furey and McGonnigal. At least Furey had shut up, that was one good thing.

The attendant consulted a list in his pocket and went over to one of the bodies. He checked a tag on the foot against his list and prepared to wheel the gurney into the autopsy room.

"That's okay," Bobby said easily. "We'll look at her in here."

Bobby took me to the gurney and pulled the plastic wrapping away so that the whole body was exposed. Cerise stared up at me. Stripped of clothes, she looked pathetically thin. Her ribs jutted ominously below her breasts; her pregnancy hadn't yet given any roundness to her sunken stomach. Her carefully beaded braids lay tousled on the table—I stuck a hand out involuntarily to smooth them for her.

Bobby was watching me closely. "You know who she is, don't you?"

I shook my head. "She looks like a couple of different women I've met briefly. What did she have that made you think I knew her?"

He compressed his lips again—he wanted to yell at me but he belongs to a generation that doesn't swear at women. "Don't play games with me, Vicki. If you know who it is, tell us so we can get moving on tracking down her associates."

"How did she die?" I asked.

"We don't know yet; they won't do a postmortem until Friday.

Probably a heroin overdose. That help you distinguish her from the others?" Bobby's sarcasm is always heavy.

"What do you care, anyway? Dead junkies must be a dime a dozen around here. And here are three crack guys from the Violent Crimes Unit only three hours after she was found."

Bobby's eyes glittered. "You ain't running the department, Vicki. I don't account to you how I decide to spend my time."

The intensity of his anger surprised me; it also spelled in large block letters that he hadn't chosen to be here. I stared at Cerise thoughtfully. What about her life or death could bring heat from the top down to the Central Division in such a short stretch?

"Where was she found?" I asked abruptly.

"On the big construction project going up near Navy Pier." That was McGonnigal. "Watchman found her in the elevator shaft when he was making his rounds, called us. She hadn't been dead too long when the squad car got there."

"Rapelec Towers, right? What made him look down the shaft?"

McGonnigal shook his head. "One of those things. Why she was on the site we'll probably never know, either. Nice secluded place at night if you want to shoot up in peace, but awfully far from where you'd expect to find her."

"So what did she have that made you think of me?"

Bobby nodded at Furey, who produced a transparent evidence bag. Inside was a plastic square. My photograph was glued in the left corner, looking just as demented as the one I'd had taken this morning.

"Hmm," I said after I'd looked at it. "Looks like my driver's license."

Bobby smiled savagely. "This isn't Second City, Victoria, and nobody's rolling in the aisles. You know this girl or not?"

I nodded reluctantly. Like Bobby, I hate giving information across police barricades. "Cerise Ramsay."

"How'd she get that license?"

"She stole it from me yesterday morning." I crossed my arms in front of me.

"Did you report it? Report the theft?"

I shook my head without answering.

Bobby slammed his hand against the side of the cart hard enough that the metal rattled. "Why the *hell* not?"

He really was pissed. I looked at him squarely. "I thought Elena might have taken it."

"Oh." The fire went out of his face. He jerked his head at Furey and McGonnigal. "Why don't you boys wait for me in the car?"

When they'd left he said in quiet, fatherly tones, "Okay, Vicki, let's have the whole story. And not just the sections you think I'll find out anyway. You know Tony would say the same thing if he was here."

Indeed I did. It's just that I was too old to do things because my daddy told me to. I didn't have a client to protect, though. There wasn't any reason not to tell him the pathetic little I knew about Cerise, just as long as we didn't do it surrounded by cold bodies.

Bobby got the attendant to show us to a tiny cubicle where the ME's drink coffee or whiskey or something in between dissections. And I told him everything I knew about Cerise, including Katterina and Zerlina. "I can sign the papers if you want. Her mother's got a bad heart—I don't think it would do her any good to come down here."

Bobby nodded. "We'll see about that. What were you doing at Eleventh Street that rattled Roland Montgomery's cage so bad?"

The shift in topic was casual and expert, but it didn't make me jump. "Nothing," I said earnestly. "I don't understand it myself."

"He came to see me with a full head of steam and demanded I run you in if you showed up anywhere near the Indiana Arms."

Bobby's tone was neutral—he wasn't criticizing, just offering me information, telling me he couldn't protect me if I got powerful people mad at me. At the same time he'd make a stab at it if I gave him the inside track on why the Indiana Arms was a hot topic. Unfortunately I couldn't help, and in the end he got angry—he couldn't see that I wasn't being obstructive, that I was well and truly ignorant. He thinks I take on clients and cases just to thumb my nose at him, that I'm having a late-life adolescent fit. He's waiting for me to grow out of it the way his six children all did.

It was two when Furey, driving recklessly and wordlessly, dropped me at my apartment. I didn't make any attempt to be conciliating—I could understand why he was pissed, but at the same time it was just the luck of the draw that he'd seen me with Robin. It was farce, not tragedy—I wasn't about to pretend to be Desdemona.

I waited inside the front door until his car had screeched its way up Racine to Belmont. My Chevy was parked across the street. I climbed in, made a U, and headed south through the empty streets toward Navy Pier.

The Rapelec complex was a monster. It wasn't actually on Navy Pier of course—no development has been approved there because the aldermen can't figure out how to divide up the zoning payoff pie. The site was on the west side of Lake Shore Drive facing the pier, a strip of decaying warehouses and office buildings that has suddenly become development heaven.

The construction site took up the whole section between the river and Illinois Street. The foundations had been poured last May. They were up about twenty stories now in the towers, but the office/retail complex was going more slowly. The sketches in the papers had made it look like a giant high school auditorium. They were taking their time with the support structure.

Bare light bulbs slung around the top of the skeleton outlined its iron bones. I shuddered. I'm not exactly afraid of heights, but the thought of perching up there without walls around—not so much the height, but the nakedness of the building frightened me. Even at ground level it seemed menacing, with black holes where windows should be and wooden ramps that led only to fathomless pits.

By now my skin was crawling. I had to fight an impulse to run back to the Chevy and head for home. Concentrate on putting one step in front of you, Vic, and curse yourself for a fool for leaving your party clothes on, instead of changing to sneaks and jeans.

I circled the site from the outside. The blue-and-whites had long gone, leaving behind a crime-scene barricade but no guard. There were at least a dozen ways into the grounds in the dark. Looking nervously above me, I selected an entrance lined with lights that didn't seem to have any steel beams poised to drop on it. My pumps made a soft *thwick* on the plank.

The boards ended at the third story. I stepped off onto a cement slab. Ahead of me and to the right shadows engulfed the floor and the beams, but the lights continued on the left where more wood had been dropped to make a crude floor cover. My palms were sweating and my toes felt ticklish when I forced myself down the corridor.

The lower floors were enclosed at this point, but no inner walls had been built. The only light came from the naked bulbs strung along the structural beams. I could see dimly into the recesses of the building. Steel beams stuck shadowy fingers upward to support the deck above. Inky splotches might be holes in the floor or maybe just some piece of machinery. I thought of Cerise coming here alone to die and the skin at the base of my neck prickled uncontrollably.

"Hello!" I cupped my hands and yelled.

My voice echoed faintly, bouncing from the steel beams. No one answered. Sweat now dropped from my neck inside my cotton sweater. A faint night breeze dried it, leaving me shivering.

The rough flooring suddenly ended in a nest of plywood cubicles. The door to the one on my right stood open. I went in. The room was dimly lit by the bulbs from the hall outside. I hunted around for a switch, finally finding a likely candidate in a thick cable. I touched it nervously, afraid I might be electrocuting myself, but the room lights came on.

Two large drafting tables were set up against one wall. Cradles holding books that looked like giant wallpaper samples covered the other three. I pulled one out. It was very heavy and didn't handle easily. Straining, I laid it across the cradle and flipped it open. It held blueprints. They were hard to follow, but it seemed to me I was looking at a corner of the twenty-third floor. In fact, this whole volume seemed to be devoted to the twenty-third floor. I shut it and slid it back into its nest.

A couple of hard hats stood on one of the drafting tables. Underneath them lay a stack of work logs. These documents were much easier to interpret—the leftmost column listed subcontractors. Next to them were slots to fill in billable hours for every day of the week. I studied the log idly, wondering if I'd see any familiar names.

Wunsch and Grasso figured prominently as the lead contractor in the joint venture that was building the complex. Hurlihey and Frain, architects, also had put in a bunch of hours. I didn't realize architects kept working on a project after construction started.

One name struck me as rather humorous—Farmworks, Inc. I wondered what agricultural needs a building like this had.

Farmworks put in a lot of time too—they were submitting over five hundred hours for the week just ending.

A heavy step sounded on the wood flooring outside. I dropped the papers, my heart jumping wildly.

"Hello?" My voice came out in a quaver. Furious with myself for being so nervous, I took a deep breath and went out into the corridor.

A thickset black man in coveralls and a hard hat scowled at me. He held a flashlight. The other hand rested on the butt of a gun strapped to his waist.

"Who are you and what the hell are you doing up here?" His baritone was heavy and uncompromising.

"My name's Warshawski. I'm a detective and I'm here with some follow-up questions about the dead girl you found."

"Police left hours ago." He moved his hand away from the gun, but his hard eyes didn't relax.

"I just came from the morgue where I met with Sergeant McGonnigal and Lieutenant Mallory. They forgot to ask a couple of things I need to know. Also, since I'm here, I'd like to see where you found her."

For a tense moment I thought he was going to demand some police identification, but my fluency with the right names apparently satisfied him.

"I can't take you down to where I found her unless you have a hard hat."

I picked up one of the Hurlihey and Frain hats from the drafting table. "Why don't I just borrow this one?"

His cold eyes weighed me some more, not wanting to let me do it, but he seemed to be a man of logic and he couldn't argue himself into sending me back to Mallory empty. "If you people did your homework you wouldn't have to waste so much of my time. Come on. I'm not going to wait while you trip around in those ridiculous shoes of yours—our liability policy doesn't pay for police who don't dress right for the job."

I picked up the hard hat and followed him meekly back into the shadowy maze.

# 16

# Tender Site

**A**s I stumbled behind him in the dark I persuaded him to tell me his name—Leon Garrison. He was a night security man, head of a team working the Rapelec site. His firm, LockStep, specialized in guarding construction projects. It seemed to me part of his anger toward me was hurt pride that someone had climbed onto the premises to die without his knowing about it. He was further annoyed that I'd managed to come in undetected as well. When I explained I'd shouted a couple of times to try to rouse someone it didn't cheer him any.

He took me down to the bottom in a hoist that ran along the outside of the building, moving the levers with a morose efficiency. When we got off he shone the flashlight in swift arcs in front of him, uncovering coils of wire, boards, loose chunks of concrete. By staying half a step behind him I could see the obstacles in time to avoid them. I had a feeling that disappointed him.

He stopped abruptly in front of a deep square pit. "You know anything about construction?" he demanded.

"Nope."

That improved his mood, enough that he explained they put the elevators in last, after the shafts were built up to the height of the building and the machinery installed on top. The cradles they rest in go down a good way—they have to be able to cushion the elevators if the cables break or some other ghastly accident occurs.

This building had four banks of eight elevators each. Garrison

moved along to the hole where he'd discovered Cerise's body, looking in each one to make sure no more unwelcome surprises awaited
him. When we got to the right one he pointed the flashlight up so I
could see the platform supporting the crane some twenty stories
overhead. The crane took up the space that the elevators would fill
once the place was finished.

Between the depth of the pit and the crane platform swaying
gently overhead, I felt a rush of nausea. As I stepped back from the
edge I thought I caught a little smirk on Garrison's face—he'd been
trying to upset me.

"Why did you look in here, anyway?" I tried to sound forceful,
not as though I was on the brink of throwing up.

"We had a fire in one of the cradles last week. Guys like to dump
trash in here on account of it's an open hole. Someone flipped a butt
in and things started burning. I just check to see what kind of rub-
bish we're piling up."

I asked him to shine the flash down into the pit again. A rough-
hewn set of slats had been nailed down the side so that you could
climb in and out if you wanted to, but it wasn't at all easy to get into.
It was hard to believe Cerise, or any addict, would go to all that
work just to find a private place to shoot up.

"How often do you check them?"

"Just once a night, usually. That was near the start of my shift.
Since the fire I look in the pits first."

"And you saw her and called 911?"

He scratched the back of his head behind the hard hat. "Strictly
speaking I called August Cray first. He's in charge of the site at
night. He came down here, took a look, and told me to call the
police. Then he called the contractor."

"Wunsch and Grasso?"

"You'd have to ask Cray—this project's got a bunch of contractors working on it. They need to know if anything special is happening on the site, and I guess you could call a dead body pretty
special."

He seemed to be smirking again, although it was kind of hard to
tell in the dark. I wondered where this Cray person had been when I
was calling out on the third floor. Anyway, he phoned someone at
Wunsch and Grasso, maybe Ernie himself. Then Ernie buzzed his

boyhood pal Furey and told him to make sure the building site was clean, that they didn't get any adverse publicity or any liability suits. That was plausible, even likely, but it didn't explain why Bobby had been called in and why he was ticked about it.

Unless the boys had used their connection to Boots to get county heat on the investigation? But that didn't make any sense—they would want to keep the thing as quiet as possible, and getting Boots and the county involved would have the opposite effect. I prodded Garrison as best I could, but he didn't know whom Cray had called or why the city had sent the head of their Violent Crimes Unit in.

"You see everything you need?" Garrison asked roughly. "I don't want another relay coming from the cops tonight telling me they forgot one last diddle-shit question. There's plenty of work to do here."

"This should do it," I said. "I think you can feel safe from the police for at least twelve hours."

"I'd better be." He snapped off the flash and headed back toward the hoist. "I guess I'd better tell Cray you've been here—he likes to know who's on the site at night."

We rode back to the third floor. "You're dressed kind of funny for a cop, aren't you?" he said when we got off.

"I'm dressed funny for a construction site," I corrected. "Even detectives have private lives. Cerise Ramsay's death interrupted mine." The memory of Bobby shining his spotlight on Robin and me popped into my head. It seemed funnier now than it had at the time. I bit back a laugh as Garrison knocked on the door to one of the little cubicles.

Cray turned out to be a heavy white man in his late fifties. He eyed me suspiciously as Garrison outlined the reason for my visit.

"You didn't hear her when she came up here?" the security man asked.

"I was in the john," Cray answered briefly. "You get what you need here? Next time, call ahead."

I smiled brightly. "Next time I sure will. Who did you call— Ernie or Ron?—after Garrison told you about the body?"

Cray's frown deepened. "Does it matter?"

"It kind of does. A dead junkie shouldn't bring down a senior cop and I'm trying to figure out why."

"Why not ask your boss that?" He kept a heavy, unpleasant edge to his voice.

"Lieutenant Mallory? I did ask him—he wasn't saying. Just for the record, he's not my boss."

"Just a minute here." Cray got to his feet. "Let's see some ID from you."

I pulled out my wallet and took out the laminated miniature of my PI license to show him.

"You're not with the police? We went through all that for you and you're not a cop? Goddamn you, I ought to get your ass arrested."

I smiled at him again. "I can give you Lieutenant Mallory's home number if you want to ask him to do it. But I never said I was with the city. I told Mr. Garrison I was a detective. He could have asked for my ID up front. I know Ernie and Ron—I can phone up tomorrow and see who you called."

"Then do that. Get off my building. Fast. Before someone has an accident and drops a load of steel on your cute little head."

He was breathing hard. I didn't see any reason to be so excited, but it seemed to me that the prudent course was to vacate the premises. There are just so many dead bodies a construction site can absorb in one night.

Back in the Chevy I suddenly felt a wave of exhaustion wash over me. My feet were sore; they throbbed inside my pumps. It had really been stupid to subject the poor things to so much rough terrain. I slipped out of them and drove home in my nylons. The cold accelerator pedal felt good against my hot soles.

At the apartment I resisted the temptation to ring Vinnie's bell. Not out of any nobility of character—I wanted to sleep in and he'd be bound to retaliate in some awful way if I woke him now.

Peppy whimpered behind Mr. Contreras's door when she heard me go by but thankfully she didn't start barking. The old man was just deaf enough that he'd sleep through her crying, but not her barking. Upstairs I started shedding clothes as soon as I got inside. By the time I reached my bedroom I was naked. I climbed into bed and was asleep almost immediately.

I slept deeply, but my dreams were filled with Elena and Cerise chasing me through miles of steel beams. I'd think I was in the clear and then suddenly a giant elevator pit would open in front of me. Just as I was backing away Cerise would be there staring at me, naked as she'd been at the morgue, her braids tangled, stretching her arms out and begging me to save her. In the background Velma Riter's voice echoed against the steel, saying, Mind your own business, Vic, a lot of people think you're a pain in the butt.

When the ringing phone woke me at ten I came to heavily. I fumbled with the phone before getting the mouthpiece the right way up. " 'Lo," I mumbled heavily.

"May I speak to Victoria Warshawski, please."

It was the efficient voice of a professional secretary. I managed to get the idea across that it was me. When she put me on hold I sat up to grapple with a sweatshirt—in case it was a client I didn't want to be seen naked.

"Vic? Ernie Wunsch. Hope I'm not disturbing you—my girl said she thought she woke you up."

When he'd dated LeAnn she'd been his girl; now she was his wife and his secretary had become his girl. It was too confusing a concept to put across with my mind so heavy from sleep so I only grunted.

"I had a message a few minutes ago from the Rapelec site saying you'd stopped by there in the middle of the night."

I grunted again.

"Something wrong we can help you with, Vic? It gets me kind of pissed to think you were going on my site behind my back."

"Hang on a minute, Ernie, I'll be right with you." I put the phone down and went to the bathroom. I didn't hurry things and on my way back I stopped in the kitchen for a glass of water. By the time I picked the phone up again Ernie was well and truly pissed but my head felt a bit clearer.

"Sorry, Ernie—I was right in the middle of something when you called. You know a young woman was found dead at the site last night."

"Some black junkie. What business was it of yours?"

"She was a protégée of mine, Ernie. I promised her mother I would look after her and I failed pretty miserably." I could see Zerlina Ramsay's strong, anguished face in my mind's eye and it didn't cheer me any.

"So?"

"So when I heard she'd died at the Rapelec site I thought I'd better go check it out, see if I could learn any reason she might have gone there."

"You ever want to talk to my people again, Vic, you check it out with me first. Cray was damned angry that you came there impersonating a police officer. He was all for having you arrested. If I hadn't known it would embarrass the hell out of Mickey, I would have done it too. You want to play at detective you go do it someplace else." He sounded downright ugly.

"While I'm playing at detective, Ernie, there is one thing you can tell me—why was it so important to you that somebody really senior come and investigate? If you'd left it with the beat people, they'd have just reported a dead junkie and I probably never even would have heard about it."

Even as I asked the question, part of the answer came to me. Ernie called Furey because he was a pal and he was with the cops. Furey got Bobby involved. No, that didn't make sense—Furey would have wanted Mallory to stay far away, to minimize any fuss at the Rapelec site. Well, maybe he'd botched it and hadn't been able to keep it from Bobby. But that didn't make sense, because Bobby was pissed at being called in—someone had ordered him to go there when he hadn't wanted to.

While all this was spinning through my head Ernie said heavily, "Just learn to mind your own business, Vic. Everyone will like you better."

I was getting kind of peeved at this message. "Oh, go make ugly faces at someone who's scared of you, Ernie. You don't impress me any."

As he hung up I thought I heard him mutter, "I still don't see what Mickey sees in you."

And I couldn't see what a sweetie like LeAnn saw in him. What did she do when he started rattling his chains at her? Probably giggled and said, "Oh, Ernie, don't be such a crybaby."

I stumbled into the kitchen for some coffee, my feet tender and swollen from last night's escapade. Was Ernie angry because he felt I'd undermined his control of his project site? Or was there something specific about Cerise's death that was bugging him? I couldn't imagine what, but I couldn't come up with any reason why Bobby had been dragged unwillingly into the investigation. My brain was still woolly and remote, though, not churning ideas with any facility.

I resisted the temptation to take my coffee to the bathroom and while away the morning soaking my sore toes in the tub. I know that however unappetizing it seems, running is the best antidote to a thick head. Anyway, a big dog like Peppy depends on running for her mental health—it wasn't fair to leave her to the sedate walks Mr. Contreras could manage.

I grumbled my way to the living room to do my stretches. They took longer than usual. Even so I didn't feel fully fit when I pulled on my sweats and stomped down the back stairs.

Peppy heard me coming and raced up to greet me. She was always ready to move from deep sleep to intense action without taking time between to loosen up. Recognizing my sweats, she whipped herself into a frenzy, dancing around me several times, rushing to the bottom of the stairs, then darting back up to check my progress. Mr. Contreras came to his back door as we passed.

"Just taking Her Serene Doggedness out for a spin," I said.

He nodded without speaking and retreated into the kitchen. Still feeling wounded. I gritted my teeth, but didn't try calling to him. I wasn't ready to kiss and make up.

I moved up the alley to Belmont at a slow gait, calling Peppy back to me at the intersections, trying to avoid pulling a muscle. At the harbor I finally felt loose enough to actually run full out for the better part of a mile, but I kept it to a jog again as I started back.

I picked Peppy up at her usual spot by the lagoon. She'd found a family of ducks and was diving after them hopefully. Until they finally took off toward the lake she pretended not to hear me calling —a fit response for ignoring her the last couple of days. Then she came loping up to me, tongue out, grinning wickedly—I knew you were calling me all along, but you'll never be able to prove it.

My head felt a lot cleaner on the way home. Back at the apartment I even felt good enough to make up with Mr. Contreras. I knocked on his kitchen door, told him I'd been up till four on a case, and asked if he had any coffee ready. That made me feel totally virtuous—his coffee is foul, overcooked stuff, and it would be faster for me to brew a fresh pot than to chew the fat with him.

He allowed as how he had some left over from breakfast and opened the door, looking sternly from the dog to me. "Why'd you let the princess go in the water? Let alone it's only sixty degrees out, the water in that lagoon hasn't been clean since 1850."

Characteristic. In order to be forgiven I had to be scolded. I bared my teeth in the semblance of a smile. "I know, I know. I begged and pleaded with her, but you know how it is—lady wants to do something, she does it without taking advice from anyone."

He gave me a sharp look. "Seems to me I've known ladies like that, uh-huh. And then you got to just ride it out until they're ready to listen to you again."

I smiled significantly. "That's right. That's it exactly. Now, how about some coffee."

# 17

# An Aunt's House Is Her Castle

**M**r. Contreras gets vicarious pleasure from my thrills. He'd heard the excitement last night when Bobby had accosted Robin and me, but he'd still been on his dignity—"I know you like to keep your own business to yourself, doll" was how he put it—and so he'd kept the slavering Peppy inside. And I hadn't thought I had blessings to count. By the time I'd stepped him through the morgue and the late-night tour of Rapelec Towers, he was palpably jealous.

"Should have taken me with you, doll. They threaten to dump a load of steel on you, I'd of known how to handle it."

"Indeed you would," I agreed, blenching slightly. The time or two he'd come to my defense with a pipe wrench still haunts my nightmares. "Thanks for the coffee. I've gotta go now—need to see a man about a dog and all that stuff."

Or a woman about the hair of the dog, I thought grimly as I ran up the stairs to my own place. Time to nail Elena down to some approximation of the truth. I took a perfunctory shower, patted myself dry while pulling on my jeans, tucked my rose silk shirt into the waistband, and headed for the door.

I was just starting to lock it when the phone rang. I sprinted back inside. It was Robin. Robin. I'd forgotten to call him, but he didn't seem to be bothered by it.

"Everything go okay last night?"

"Depends on what you mean. They wanted me to ID a kid whose body they'd found at a construction site."

He made sympathetic sounds. "Did you?"

"Yeah. She was black, poor, and an addict, so the odds were against a happy ending, but it was still a shocker."

"The cops could've acted a bit more human to you under the circumstances."

"I suppose under the circumstances they were trying to jolt me into telling the truth."

He hesitated a moment. "I don't want to be a pest, especially after you've had a bad night, but have you thought any more about taking on the Indiana Arms investigation? We need to get going."

I felt a warm little glow under my rib cage. Someone thought I was a competent human being, not a pain in the butt who should mind her own business. Even though I'd made up my mind last night to do the job, it just felt good to have someone—some man— call up and think first that I should be working, not that I should stay home and play with dolls.

"The only trouble is, I don't know anything about fires. And I don't think I can educate myself fast enough to do a technical investigation."

"We don't need you doing any of the engineering work—we hire a lab to handle that. What you can do is a financial check on the owner, see if he had any kind of motive to set the fire himself. What I hear, you're about the best for that kind of work."

The glow expanded from my ribs to my cheeks. "Fine." I took the owner's name and address: Saul Seligman on north Estes. He was in his seventies and semiretired, but he went into his office on Irving Park Road most afternoons. I conscientiously wrote down the phone number there as well.

"Could we try dinner again?" Robin asked. "Someplace near my house so the cops don't arrest you halfway through the evening?"

I laughed. "How about Friday? I'm pretty beat and I have a lot of work the next few days."

"Great. I'll call Friday morning to pick a place. Thanks a lot for taking on the case."

"Yeah, sure." I hung up.

It was past noon now. If my aunt was still the woman she used to be, she'd just be getting up. I drove with a reckless nervousness, covering the four miles in under ten minutes, and screeched to a halt across from the Windsor Arms. A couple was sitting on the side-walk, their backs against the building, deep in an argument over whose fault it was that Biffy disappeared. I paused long enough to figure out that Biffy was a cat. The pair didn't spare me a glance.

I didn't get much more attention in the lobby. The chatelaine was watching TV in the lounge, her back to me. The five or six people with her were absorbed by the intensity of feeling pounding out of the high-perched screen. One of them looked up but went back to the show as I started up the stairs.

I took them two at a time and jogged down to Elena's room at a good trot. The door was shut. I tried the knob, then pounded loudly. No answer. I pounded again but didn't call out—if she recognized me, she'd play possum for the next twenty-four hours.

Finally she yelled in a sleep-thickened voice, "Go away. I've got a right to my beauty sleep same as you, you cloth-headed bitch."

I pounded some more, keeping it up steadily until she yanked the door open under my hand. She tried shutting it in my face as soon as she saw me but I followed her into the room.

"Sorry to break into your beauty rest, Auntie," I said, smiling gently. "Isn't it a little risky to call the manager a cloth-headed bitch?"

"Victoria, sweetie. What are you doing here?"

"I came to see you, Elena. I've got some bad news about Cerise."

The violet nightdress still hadn't been laundered. The mixture of stale beer and sweat it gave off was overpowering. I moved to the window and tried to open it, but it had been painted shut with a lavish hand. I sat on the bed. The mattress was about an inch thick; the springs underneath creaked and a little tendril of iron poked through into my buttock.

"Cerise, sweetie?" She blinked in the dim light. "What about her?"

I looked at her solemnly. "I'm afraid she's dead. The police came and got me at midnight last night to identify her body."

"Dead?" she repeated. Her face changed rapidly as she tried to decide how to react, moving from blankness to outrage. It seemed to me that one of the intermediate phases was cunning. Finally a few tears coursed down her veined cheeks.

"You shouldn't break news to people like this, it's really wrong of you. I hope you didn't go pounding your way into Zerlina's hospital room, waking her up and telling her terrible things about her daughter. Gabriella would be ashamed if she knew what you'd done. *Really* ashamed. Anyway, I thought you were keeping an eye on that poor little girl. Why did you let her run off and get herself killed?" She was clearly working hard to build up some anger.

"She kind of did it on her own. By the time I got back to Dr. Herschel's Monday afternoon she'd taken off. I called the cops and asked them to keep a lookout for her, but there's a lot of city and not enough boys in blue to patrol it. So she died of an overdose in the bottom of an elevator shaft at a construction site."

Elena shook her head, lips pursed together. "That's terrible, sweetie, terrible. I can't take news like that sprung on me so suddenly. Why don't you go away and let me digest it on my own? I'll have to see Zerlina, and what I'll ever say to her—you go on, now, Vicki. You were a good girl to come and tell me but I need to be alone."

I kept the gentle smile on my face and looked up at her earnestly. "I will, Elena. I'll go real soon. But first I need you to tell me what little scam you and Cerise had decided to run."

She pulled herself up and gave me a look of outraged dignity. "Scam, Victoria? That's a very ungenteel word."

"But it describes the process to a tee. What money-making scheme had the two of you fixed on?"

"The poor girl isn't even cold and you come here sullying her memory. I don't know what Gabriella would say." She plucked nervously at her gown.

The thought of my mother brought me a smile of pure amusement. "She'd say 'Tell the truth, Elena—it will hurt coming up but then you'll feel healthy again.' " Gabriella had held a firm belief in the value of purging.

"Well, irregardless, I don't know what you're talking about."

I shook my head. "Not good enough, Auntie. You and Cerise showed up on my doorstep full of fear over the fate of poor Katterina. Somehow overnight that evaporated—Cerise pulled a disappearing act and you were playing mighty coy yourself. If either of you had been that worried, you would have figured out some way to get back in touch with me."

"Cerise probably didn't have your phone number. She probably couldn't even remember your last name."

I nodded. "That wouldn't surprise me. But all she had to do was wait at Dr. Herschel's clinic and there I'd be ready—loyal, conscientious, and industrious, or whatever the Scout motto says. No. The two of you had something in mind. Or else you wouldn't have been so reluctant to tell me Zerlina's last name."

"I just didn't think you should go badgering her—"

"Un-unh. You told Zerlina last Wednesday she couldn't keep the baby at the Indiana Arms. What'd you do—blackmail her for the price of a bottle? Ugly stuff, Elena, but it saved the kid's life. You knew when you saw me on Sunday that Zerlina had sent the baby away. I want to know what the *hell* you were doing, and why you dragged me into it." The intensity of my feeling brought me to my feet; I glared down at my aunt.

The ready tears filled her eyes. "You get out of here, Victoria Iphigenia. You just leave. I'm sorry I ever even came to you after the fire. You're just a damned snot-nosed buttinski who can't show any respect to her elders. You may think you own Chicago but this is my room and I can call the police if you don't leave."

I looked around the room and my anger faded, replaced by shame and a wave of hopelessness. Elena couldn't back up her threat—she didn't even have a phone. All she had was her duffel bag and her sweaty filthy nightgown. I blinked back tears of my own and left. As I walked away under the empty light fixtures, I could hear her scrabble the key in the lock.

Out front the couple had stopped arguing and were making up over a bottle of Ripple. I walked slowly to my car and sat hunched over the steering wheel. Sometimes life seems so painful it hurts even to move my arms.

# 18

# Not Donald Trump

**W**hat I wanted was to decamp for some remote corner of the globe where human misery didn't take such naked forms. Lacking funds for that, I could retire to my bed for a month. But then my mortgage bill would come and go without payment and eventually the bank would kick me out and then I'd have some naked misery of my own, sitting in front of my building with a bottle of Ripple to keep it all out of my head. I started the engine and drove north to Saul Seligman's office on Foster.

It was a shabby little storefront. The windows were boarded across the bottom; on the top right side "Seligman Property Management" was lettered on the pane in peeling gold scroll. Between the boarding and the grime on the glass, I couldn't see inside, but I thought a light was on.

The door moved heavily under my hand; it had caught on a piece of loose linoleum that worked as an effective wedge. When I got inside I tried to tamp it down but it curled up as soon as I took my foot away. I gave up and moved to the high, scarred barricade separating Saul from the world beyond. If he was rolling in loot, he wasn't putting any of it into the front office.

The back area held five desks, but only one was inhabited. A woman of about sixty was reading a library copy of Judith Krantz. Her faded blond hair was carefully sculpted in a series of waves. Her lips moved slightly as she slid one pudgy, ring-encrusted finger down the page. She didn't look up, though she must have heard me working on the linoleum. Maybe the book was due today—she still had about half to read.

"I can tell you how it comes out," I offered.

She put Judith down reluctantly. "Did you want something, honey?"

"Mr. Seligman," I said in my brightest, most professional tone.

"He's not in, dear." Her hand strayed for the book.

"When do you expect him?"

"He's not on a regular schedule now he's retired."

I found the latch on the inside of the gate in the barricade. "Maybe you can help me. Are you the office manager?"

She swelled a bit. "You can't come barging in here, honey. This is private. Public out front."

I shut the gate behind me. "I'm an investigator, ma'am. Ajax Insurance hired me to look into the fire that destroyed one of the Seligman properties last week. The Indiana Arms."

"Oh." She toyed with a wedding band that cut deep into her finger. "Is there some kind of problem?"

"Arson's always a problem." I perched on the corner of the desk adjacent to hers. "The company won't pay the claim until they're convinced Mr. Seligman didn't have anything to do with setting the fire."

She pulled herself up in her seat; her pale blue eyes darted fire at me behind her glasses. "That is an outrageous suggestion. The very idea! Mr. Seligman would no more . . . Do you have any proof to back this up?"

I shook my head. "I'm not accusing him of setting the fire. I just need to make sure that he didn't."

"He didn't. I can promise you that."

"Great. That means the inquiry will be short and sweet. How many properties does he own—besides the Indiana Arms, I mean."

"Mr. Seligman is the sweetest, most honest—look, he's a Jew, okay, and I'm a Catholic. Do you think that ever bothered him? When my husband left me and I had my two girls to look after, who paid their tuition bills so they could stay on at St. Inanna's? And the Christmas presents he gave them, not to mention me, if I said it once I said it a hundred times, he'd better not let Fanny see the kinds of presents he gave me, not if he wanted to stay happily married, which he was until she died three years ago. He hasn't been the same since, lost interest in the business, but if you think he would have burned down a building, you're the one who's crazy."

When she finished she was flushed and panting a little. Only a beast would have persisted.

"Do you collect the rents in here, Mrs. . . ."

"Donnelly," she snapped. "The building managers do that. Look. You'd better show me some kind of authorization if you're going to come barging in asking questions."

I dug my license out of my billfold and handed it to her with one of my cards: V. I. Warshawski, Financial Investigations. She looked them over suspiciously, studying the photo, comparing it to me. For some reason my face had come out a kind of lobster hue in the picture. It always fools people.

"And how do I know you're with the insurance company?" It was a halfhearted snipe but a valid one.

"You can call the company and ask for Robin Bessinger in the arson division. He'll vouch for me." I'd have to get something in writing from them—I'd better walk a copy of my contract for services over tomorrow and pick up a letter of authorization.

Her eye strayed to the phone, but she seemed to decide it was too much trouble to fight me any further. "Okay. Ask what you want, but you'll never find any proof connecting Mr. Seligman to that fire."

"What's your position with the company, Mrs. Donnelly?"

"I'm the office manager." Her face was braced in fierce lines to deflect any attack on Mr. Seligman.

"And that means you . . . ?"

"People call in with complaints, I get the building super to check them out, or the property manager, whoever is in charge. I arrange for bids if any work has to get done, that kind of thing. Detectives come in asking questions, I talk to them."

It was an unexpected flash of humor; I grinned appreciatively. "How many properties are there?"

She ticked them off on her fingers—the one on Ashland, the one on Forty-seventh, and so on, seven altogether, ending with the Indiana Arms. I noted the addresses so I could drive by them, but judging by the locations, none of them was a big money-maker.

No, rents weren't down any. Yes, they used to have a lot more people in the office, that was when Mr. Seligman was younger—he used to buy and sell properties all the time and he needed more staff to do that. Now it was just her and him, a team like they'd always been, and you wouldn't find a warmer-hearted person, not if you looked through the suburbs as well as the city.

"Great." I got up from the edge of the desk and rubbed the sore spot where the metal had cut into my thigh. "By the way, where do you bank—not you personally, Seligman Properties?"

The wary look returned to her face but she answered readily enough—the Edgewater National.

As I was opening the gate something else occurred to me. "Who will take over the business for Mr. Seligman? Does he have any children involved in it?"

She glared at me again. "I wouldn't dream of prying into such a personal matter. And don't go bothering him—he's never really recovered from Fanny's death."

I let the gate click behind me. Wouldn't dream of it, indeed. She probably knew every thought Seligman had had for twenty years, even more so now his wife was dead. As I urged the door over the loose linoleum, I wondered idly about Mrs. Donnelly's own children, whom the old man had so generously educated.

Before getting into the car I found a phone on the corner to call Robin. He was in a meeting—the perennial location of insurance managers—but his secretary promised to have a letter of authorization waiting for me in the morning.

The afternoon was wearing on; I hadn't had a proper meal all day, just some toast with Mr. Contreras's foul coffee. It's hard to think when you're hungry—the demands of the stomach become paramount. I found a storefront Polish restaurant where they gave me a bowl of thick cabbage soup and a plate of homemade rye bread. That was so good that I had some raspberry cake and a cup of overbaked coffee before moving farther north to find Mr. Seligman.

Estes is a quiet residential street in Rogers Park. Seligman lived in an unprepossessing brick house east of Ridge. The small front yard hadn't been much tended during the long hot summer; large clumps of crabgrass and weeds had taken over the straggly grass.

The walk was badly broken, not the ideal path for an elderly person, especially when the Chicago winter set in.

The stairs weren't in much better shape—I sidestepped a major hole on the third riser just in time to keep from twisting my ankle. A threadbare mat lay in front of the door. I skidded on its shiny surface when I rang the bell.

I could hear the bell echoing dully behind the heavy front door. Nothing happened. I waited a few minutes and rang again. After another wait I began to wonder if I'd passed Seligman somewhere on Ridge. Just as I was getting ready to leave, though, I heard the rasp of bolts sliding back. It was a clumsy, laborious process. When the final lock came apart the door opened slowly inward and an old man blinked at me across the threshold.

He must have been about Mr. Contreras's age, but where my neighbor had a vitality and curiosity that kept him fit, Mr. Seligman seemed to have retreated from life. His face had slipped into a series of soft, downward creases that slid into the high collar of his faded beige turtleneck. Over that he wore a torn cardigan, one side of which was partly tucked into his pajama pants. He did not look like the mastermind of an arson and fraud ring.

"Yes?" His voice was soft and husky.

I forced a smile to my lips and explained my errand.

"You're with the police, young lady?"

"I'm a private investigator. Your insurance company has hired me to investigate the fire."

"The insurance? My insurance is all paid, I'm sure of that, but you'd have to check with Rita." As he shook his head, bewildered, I caught a glimpse of a hearing aid in his left ear.

I raised my voice and tried to speak clearly. "I know your insurance is paid. The company hired me. Ajax wants me to find out who burned down your hotel."

"Oh. Who burned it down." He nodded five or six times. "I have no idea. It was a great shock, a very great shock. I've been expecting the police or the fire department to come talk to me, but we pay our taxes for nothing these days. Let it burn to the ground and don't do nothing to stop it, then don't do nothing to catch the people who did it."

"I agree," I put in. "That's why Ajax hired me to investigate it for them. I wonder if we could go inside and talk it over."

He studied me carefully, decided I didn't look like a major menace, and invited me in. As soon as he'd shut the door behind me and fastened one of the five locks, I began to wish I'd finished the conversation on the stoop. The smell, combined of must, unwashed dishes, and stale grease, seemed to seep from the walls and furniture. I didn't know life could exist in such air.

The living room where he took me was dark and chilly. I tried not to curse when I ran into a low table, but as I backed away from it I caught my left leg on some heavy metal object and couldn't help swearing.

"Careful, there, young lady, these were all Fanny's things and I don't want them damaged."

"No, sir," I said meekly, waiting for him to finish fumbling with a light before trying to move any farther. When the heavily fringed lamp sprang into life, I saw that I'd tripped on a set of fire irons mysteriously placed in the middle of the room. As there was no fireplace perhaps that was the ideal spot for them. I threaded my way past the rest of the obstacles and sat gingerly on the edge of an overstuffed armchair. My rear sank deep within its soft, dusty upholstery.

Mr. Seligman sat on a matching couch that was close by, if you discounted an empty brass birdcage hanging between us. "Now what is it you want, young lady?"

He was hard of hearing and depressed but clearly not mentally impaired. When he took in the gist of my remarks his sagging cheeks mottled with color.

"My insurance company thinks I burned down my own building? What do I pay rates for? I pay my taxes and the police don't help me, I pay my insurance and my company insults me—"

"Mr. Seligman," I cut in, "you've lived in Chicago a long time, right? Your whole life? Well, me too. You know as well as I do that people here torch their own property every day just to collect on the insurance. I'm happy to think you're not one of them, but you can't blame the company for wanting to make sure."

The angry flush died from his cheeks but he continued muttering under his breath about robbers who took your money without giving you anything in return. He calmed down enough to answer routine questions on where he'd been last Wednesday night—home in bed, what did I think he was, a Don Juan at his age to be gallivanting around town all night?

"Can you think of any reason anyone would want to burn down the Indiana Arms?"

He held up his hands in exasperation. "It was an old building, no good to anybody, even me. You pay the taxes, you pay the insurance, you pay the utilities, and when the rent comes in you don't have enough to pay for the paint. I know the wiring was old but I couldn't afford to put in new, you've got to believe me on that, young lady."

"Why didn't you just tear it down if it was costing you so much?"

"You're like everyone today, just considering a dollar and not people's hearts. People come to me, it seems like every day, thinking I'm a stupid old man who will just sell them my heart and let them tear it down. Now here you are, another one."

He shook his head slowly, depressed over the perfidy of the younger generation. "It was the first building I owned. I put together the money slowly, slowly in the Depression. You wouldn't understand. I worked on a delivery truck for years and saved every penny, every dime, and when Fanny and I got married everything went into the Indiana Arms."

He was talking more to himself now than to me, his husky voice so soft I had to lean forward to hear him. "You should have seen it in those days, it used to be a beautiful hotel. We made deliveries there in the morning and even the kitchens seemed wonderful to me —I grew up in two rooms, eight of us in two rooms, with no kitchen, all the water hauled in by hand. When the owners went bankrupt— everybody went under in those days—I scraped together the money and bought it."

His faded eyes clouded. "Then the war came and the colored came pouring in and Fanny and I, we moved up here, we had a family then anyway, you couldn't raise children in a residential hotel, even if the neighborhood was decent. But I never could bring myself to sell it. Now it's gone, maybe it's just as well."

Out of respect for his memories I waited before speaking again, looking around the room to give him a little privacy. On the low table nearest me was a studio portrait of a solemn young man and a shyly smiling young woman in bridal dress.

"That was Fanny and me," he said, catching my glance. "It's hard to believe, isn't it?"

I took him gently through the routine—who worked for him, what did he know about the night man at the Indiana Arms, who would inherit the business, who would profit by the fire. He answered readily enough, but he couldn't really think ill of someone who worked for him, nor of his children, who would get the business when he died.

"Not that it's much to leave them. You start out, you think you'll end up like Rubloff, but all I've got to show for all my years is seven worn-out buildings." He gave me his children's names and addresses and said he'd tell Rita to let me have a list of employees— the building managers and watchmen and maintenance crews.

"I suppose someone could burn down a building if you paid him enough. It's true I don't pay them much, but look at me, look how I live, I'm not Donald Trump after all—I pay what I can afford."

He saw me to the front door, going over it again and again, how he paid his taxes and got nothing and had nothing, but paid his employees, and would they turn on him anyway? As I walked down the front steps I could hear the locks slowly closing behind me.

# 19

# Gentleman Caller

There was an errand I couldn't put off before going home. I squared my shoulders and drove south through the rush-hour traffic to Michael Reese. Zerlina was still in her four-pack, but one of the beds was empty and the other two held new inmates who looked at me with vacant faces before returning to *Wheel of Fortune*.

Zerlina turned her head away when she saw me. I hesitated at the foot of her bed—it would be easier to take her rejection at face value and go home than to talk to her about her daughter. "Quitters never win and winners never quit," I encouraged myself, and went to squat near her head.

"You've heard about Cerise, Mrs. Ramsay."

The black eyes stared at me unblinkingly, but at length she gave a grudging nod.

"I'm very sorry—I had to identify her early this morning. She looked terribly young."

She scowled horribly in an effort to hold back tears. "What did you do to her, you and that aunt of yours, to drive her to take her own life?"

"I'm sorry, Mrs. Ramsay," I repeated. "Maybe I should have tried to find her on Monday. But she left the clinic where I'd brought her and I didn't have any idea where she might go. I tried talking to Elena this morning; if she knew anything, she was keeping it to herself."

I stayed another five minutes or so, but she wouldn't say anything else, nor did her face relent. When I got back in the car I sat for a long time rubbing my tight shoulder muscles and trying to imagine a place I could go to find some peace. Not my apartment—I didn't want to confront either Mr. Contreras or Vinnie tonight. I was too tired, though, to drive out to the country, too tired to deal with the noise and distraction of a restaurant. What I needed was a club of the kind Peter Wimsey used to retire to—discreet, solicitous servants leaving me in total peace yet willing to spring into immediate action at my slightest whim.

I put the Chevy into gear and started north, going by side streets, dawdling at lights, finally hitting Racine from Belmont and coasting to a halt in front of my building. On my way in I stopped in the basement for my laundry. Some kind soul had taken it from the dryer and left it on the floor. My limbs heavy and slow, I picked it up one item at a time and put it back into the washer. I stayed in the dimly lit basement while the machine ran, sitting cross-legged on a newspaper on the floor, staring at nothing, thinking of nothing. When the washer clanked to a halt I stood up to dump my things once more into the dryer. Easily the equivalent of an evening at the Marlborough Club.

It was only when I got upstairs that I remembered giving the servants the day off, so there was no dinner ready. I sent out for a pizza and watched a *Magnum* rerun. Before going to bed I returned to the basement for my clothes. By a miracle I arrived before one of my neighbors had time to dirty them again.

Thursday morning I brought a contract down to Ajax, got a letter of authorization from them, and proceeded on my investigation. I spent Thursday and Friday tracking down Seligman's children—both in their forties—and talking to the different night watchmen, janitors, and building managers who made up the Seligman work team. Mrs. Donnelly—Rita to Seligman—even grudgingly let me look at the books. By the end of Friday I was reasonably certain that the old man had had no role in the fire.

His children didn't take any active part in the business. One daughter was married to an appliance dealer and didn't work herself. The other, a marketing manager with a Schaumburg wholesaler, had been in Brazil on business when the fire took place. That didn't mean she couldn't have masterminded it, but it was hard to see why. The two stood to inherit the business, and it was possible that they were going to torch the properties for their insurance money to increase the value of the estate, but it was a slow way to dubious wealth. I didn't write them off, but I wasn't enthusiastic about them as candidates, either.

My talks with Mrs. Donnelly left me scratching my head. She seemed loyal to the old man, but I couldn't help thinking she knew something she wasn't telling. It wasn't so much what she said as the sly look I got when the talk drifted to her children and what their expectations of Mr. Seligman might be. If it hadn't been for that occasional smirk, I would have given Seligman a complete pass to Ajax.

On Saturday I finally found the night man from the Indiana Arms. He was holed up with a brother on the South Side, trying to avoid any inquiry into his activities on the night of the fire. We had a long and difficult conversation. At first he assured me he hadn't left the premises for a minute. Then he came around to the idea that he'd heard a noise outside and gone to investigate.

Finally a combination of threats and bribes brought forth the information that he'd gotten a list of the races at Sportsman Park along with fifty dollars in betting money. They'd come in Wednesday's mail, he didn't know who from, he certainly hadn't kept the envelope. He didn't think it would matter if he left for an hour or two; when he got back late—after a snort with his buddies—the hotel was burning beautifully. He took one look at the fire trucks and headed for his brother's house on Sangamon.

It was clear that someone had cared enough about burning down the building to study the night man, find out he bet the races, and know he couldn't resist a free night at the track. But that someone wasn't Saul Seligman. I put it all together in a report for Ajax, wrote out a bill, and asked whether they wanted me to pursue the matter further.

If your primary goal is to find the arsonist, then I will try to discover who sent the money. Since no envelope exists and Mr. Tancredi claims never to have seen any strangers regularly lurking around the premises, finding who sent the money will be a long and expensive job. If all you want is a strong probability that your insured did not burn his own property, we can stop at this point: I believe Mr. Seligman and his subordinates are innocent of arson.

After putting it in the mail I walked the ten blocks to Wrigley Field and watched the Cubs die a painful death at the hands of the Expos. Although my hapless heroes were twenty games below five hundred the ballpark was packed; I was lucky to get a seat in the upper deck. Even if I could have gotten a bleacher ticket, I don't sit there anymore—NBC made such a cult of the Bleacher Bums when the Cubs were in the '84 playoffs that drunk yuppies who don't know the game now find it the trendy place to sit.

It was after five when I got home. A late-model black Chevrolet bristling with antennae was parked illegally next to the hydrant in front of my building. I looked at it with the usual curiosity you give an unmarked police car when it's next to your home. The windows were rolled up and I couldn't see through the smoky glass, but when the door opened I saw Bobby Mallory had been driving himself.

I was surprised to see him—it was the first time he'd ever come to my apartment without a formal escort. I hurried to the curb to greet him.

"Bobby! Good to see you. Nothing's wrong, is it?"

He ran a hand through my hair, a rare gesture of affection since I graduated from high school. "Just thought I'd come by and see you, Vicki, make sure you're not playing with some kind of fire that's likely to burn you."

"I see." I tried to keep my tone light while a wall of caution shut down part of my mind. "Is that something you can do in one sentence out here on the sidewalk or do you want to come up for some coffee?"

"Oh, let's go inside, be comfortable. If you've got decaf, that is— I can't take coffee late in the day anymore. I'm almost sixty, you know."

"Yeah, I know." I wondered if he was trying to pump me obliquely for word on what Eileen had planned for the big day, but I didn't think he'd treat me to such an elaborate routine for that. I politely held the door for him and let him precede me up the three flights.

Bobby, still on his good behavior, ignored the untidy heap of papers in the living room. I tried not to feel embarrassed at being caught in such chaos by an old friend of my parents and went to scrounge in my kitchen.

"I'm afraid I'm out of decaf," I apologized a few minutes later. "I can give you some juice or a Coke or wine. No beer, though."

He took a Coke. One of Bobby's fetishes, in addition to not swearing in front of me, is not to drink with me—he can't get over the idea that he'd be encouraging me in immorality. He drank a little, ate a handful of crackers, gestured at the piano, and asked if I was still working at my singing. My mother had been an accomplished musician, an aspiring operatic soprano whose career had been cut short when her family shipped her to America to escape fascism. One of Bobby's unexpected traits was to share her love of opera; she used to sing Puccini for him. He would be a happy cop if I'd fulfilled her dream and become a concert singer instead of aping my dad and turning into a detective.

I had to admit my voice was a little rusty. "Seen any rare birds lately?"

Another unexpected hobby of Bobby's was photographing birds. As he discoursed on taking his two oldest grandchildren to the forest preserve last weekend, I wondered how long we were going to pretend that this was just a social call.

"Mickey's coming out with us tomorrow," he said. "He's a good boy. Young man, I should say, but I've known him since he was born."

"Yes, he's told me you're his godfather." I sipped some Coke and watched him over the rim of the glass.

"Eileen and I were both hoping you two would hit it off, but she keeps telling me you can't force these things."

"He's a Sox fan. It would never work out."

"Even though you like sports and race around playing police, you want a guy who's more artistic."

I didn't know whether to jump down his throat for calling my work "playing police" or be amazed that he put so much thought into my character. "Maybe I just don't want to be married. Michael hangs out with a crowd where the wife is the little woman who stays home and has kiddies. That may be your dream for me but it's not my style, never has been and never will be."

" 'Never' is a long time, Vicki." He held up a hand as the blood rushed to my face. "Hold your fire. I'm not saying you're wrong. Just don't get yourself out on a limb where you'll saw yourself off rather than admit you changed your mind. But that's not what I came to say to you."

It made me downright mad to think of him and Eileen sitting at dinner, planning my marriage to his godson—"Maybe truelove will get her mind off wanting to be a boy and play boys' games with guns and baseballs"—as though my life and my choices were of no account. I bit back a diatribe. Yelling at Bobby could only put me at a severe disadvantage.

"I haven't asked Mickey anything about you," he went on. "I figure it's his business. But he's been like a cat on a hot stove since he saw you clinched with that kid the other night."

"I can't call up and apologize for being found necking at my own front door."

"Just go easy on him, will you, Vicki? I'm fond of the boy. I don't want an explosion on my staff because you're turning them on and off like faucets. I know there's been something between you and John, even though neither of you admits it; I don't want a blowup between him and Mickey. Or Mickey and you. You may not believe it, but I'm fond of you too."

My cheeks flamed again, this time with embarrassment. "There's never been anything between McGonnigal and me. He gave me a lift home last winter in the middle of the night. I was beat, he thought I looked cute when vulnerable, we had one kiss and both knew we couldn't cross that line again. Since then it's been like I was Cleopatra's asp. And I'm damned if I'm going to apologize to him for that."

"Don't swear, Vicki, it's not nearly as attractive as you modern young women think." He put his glass down on the magazines covering the coffee table and got up. "I was talking to Monty yesterday afternoon—Roland Montgomery, Bomb and Arson Squad—he knows I know you. He says you're poking around in that Indiana Arms fire we asked you not to touch."

I gave a tight little smile. "Just playing police, Bobby—I wouldn't worry about it since it's only a game, not the real stuff."

He put a large hand on my shoulder. "I know you think you're a big girl—what are you now, thirty-five? Thirty-six? But your parents are both dead and they were my close friends. No one's so big they don't need someone else looking out for them. If Monty said to keep away from that fire, you keep away. Arson's about the nastiest thing on this planet. I don't want to see you messed up in it."

I closed my lips in a tight ball to keep my ugly words in. He'd touched about ten raw nerves in five minutes and I was too angry to give any kind of coherent response. I saw him to the door without telling him good-bye.

When I heard his car start I sat at the piano and vented my feelings in a series of crashing, dissonant chords. Yeah, I ought to practice, ought to keep my voice limber before I got too old and my vocal cords lost their flexibility. I ought to be everyone's good little girl. But for my own self-respect I needed to solve the arson.

I got up from the piano and jotted a second note to Robin:

> I sent you a report this morning, but as I've thought over the case during the day I believe it is critical to locate the person who sent Jim Tancredi the money for the track.

It was only when I'd mailed it that I calmed down enough to wonder why Bobby had come to see me—to talk to me about Michael Furey? Or to warn me off the Indiana Arms investigation?

# 20

# Heavy Warning

Bobby's visit left such a bad taste in my mouth that I wanted to tell Eileen I couldn't make it to her party. But Bobby was right about one thing—you shouldn't saw off the limb you're sitting on just to salve your pride.

I called a couple of friends to see if anyone wanted to take in a movie but everyone was out. I left messages on various machines and stomped off to the kitchen to scramble some eggs. Normally sitting home alone on Saturday doesn't trouble me, but Bobby's visit made me wonder if I was doomed for an old age of crabby isolation.

I turned on the TV and moodily changed channels. You'd think Saturday night they could offer something enticing for the stay-at-homes, but the networks thought all America was out dancing. When the phone rang I turned off the set eagerly, thinking maybe someone was returning one of my messages. I was startled to hear Roz Fuentes's husky voice.

She didn't even say hello before she started lambasting me for butting my nose into her business. "What are you trying to do to me, Warshawski?" Her voice had recovered its usual rich, throaty timbre; the vibration through the phone made my ear tingle.

"I'm not doing anything to you, Roz. Don't you have a campaign to run? Why are you picking on me?"

Her rich chuckle came, but it lacked mirth. "Velma called me. She said you were trying to get her to spill some dirt on me, that she put you in your place but she thought I ought to know. What kind of dirt are you looking for, anyway?"

I bared my teeth at the phone. "Hey, Roz—Velma put me in my place. Relax."

"Vic, I gotta know." She spoke softly, urgently—it was like listening to the Chicago Symphony string section. "This campaign means *everything* to me and my people. I told you that last weekend. I can't afford to have someone lying in the bushes waiting for me with a shotgun."

It had been too long a day for me to make any great display of subtlety. "Roz, I don't care if you've been sleeping with Boots and the whole county board to get yourself on the ticket. What bugs me is you going out of your way to ask me if I was sandbagging you. What would even make you *think* such a thing unless you're getting me to sign on to something I'm going to be very sorry about later? I'm thin-skinned, Roz; it gets me itzy if someone is trying to make a monkey out of me."

"I came to you as a show of respect for our old relationship," she said indignantly. "Now you are twisting my friendship into something evil. Velma was right. I should know better than to turn to a white girl with my concerns."

"A white boy is okay, though?" I was thoroughly riled. "Boots can be your ally but I can't? Go save the Chicago Hispanics, Roz, but leave me out of it."

We hung up on that fractured note. I was mad enough to call Velma to demand chapter and verse on not trusting me just because I was white, but a conversation like that can go nowhere constructive.

Sunday morning I got a further indication that the Fuentes-Meagher pot had something cooking in it when Marissa invited me to stop by for drinks that evening. Something spontaneous and casual, was how she put it, for people she hadn't spent enough time with at Roz's campaign. I told her I was truly overwhelmed to be remembered by her and that the thought of such an evening was irresistible. Marissa had herself well in hand, though, and refused to be ruffled.

At five I set out for her Lincoln Park town house, one of those three-story jobs on Cleveland where every brick has been sandblasted and the woodwork refinished so it glows warmly. Marissa rented out the ground floor and lived in the upper two.

When I got to the top of the first flight she met me in the landing to escort me into what she called her drawing room. As usual Marissa looked great, her idea of casual being bulky red silk trousers, a matching pajama-style top, and lots of silver jewelry. I hadn't worn jeans, but I couldn't help feeling she'd dressed with the intention of making me look dowdy.

The drawing room, which had once been the two front bedrooms, ran the width of the building, its row of mullioned windows looking out on Cleveland. Whatever negative thoughts I had about Marissa didn't include her taste—the room was simply but beautifully furnished, a high-Victorian look predominating, complete with red Turkish rugs scattered at strategic places. An exotic array of plants gave the whole scene warmth.

When I complimented her she laughed and said it was all due to her sister, who owned a plant rental business and rotated fresh shrubbery for her every few weeks. "Let me introduce you to some of the folks, Vic."

Some fifteen or twenty people were chattering with the ease of familiarity. As she led me toward the nearest group the doorbell rang again. She excused herself, telling me to help myself to a drink and see if I knew anyone.

I'd half expected to see Roz, or even the Wunsch and Grasso contingent, but the only person I recognized was Ralph MacDonald. I tipped my hat to Marissa—she must be even better connected than I'd realized for the great man to spend a Sunday evening at such a low-profile function as this.

He was talking to a couple of banker-looking types who'd dressed down for the weekend in open-necked shirts and sport jackets. Two women in their little group were talking sotto voce to each other so as not to disturb the boys. This sample of good wifely conduct made me gladder than ever I hadn't stood by my own man, a lawyer who now lived in palatial splendor in Oak Brook.

The bar, set in the far corner behind one of the trees, had just about anything one's heart could desire, including a bottle of indifferent champagne. The whiskey was J&B, a brand I can take or leave, so I poured myself a glass of the chardonnay. It made me feel too much like a Lincoln Park native for comfort, but it wasn't a bad wine.

I took it over to an armchair and watched Marissa return with the newcomers, a thirty-something couple I also didn't recognize. She brought them to a clump not too far from me where they were greeted enthusiastically as Todd and Meryl. Marissa, the perfect hostess, stayed to chat, then moved to the MacDonald group before responding again to the buzzer.

By and by two women in black slacks and white blouses came in with trays of hot hors d'oeuvres. Ralph MacDonald moved over with the two women from his huddle just as I was helping myself to a couple of spinach triangles.

"Vic? I'm Ralph MacDonald—we met at Boots's shindig last weekend."

"I remember you, of course—but I'm surprised you know me." I tried to sound suave while hastily swallowing the last of my pastry.

"Don't be modest, Vic—you're a pretty memorable gal."

The comment was innocuous but the tone seemed charged. Before I could question him he introduced me to the two women, who obviously were as enthusiastic at meeting me as I them. They filled small plates with a sample of treats and retired to the bankers as Marissa brought another unaccompanied man over to us. She introduced him as Clarence Hinton; he and MacDonald clearly knew each other reasonably well.

"You remember Vic from last Sunday, Ralph," Marissa stated.

"I was just telling her not to undersell herself." He turned to me. "Actually I probably wouldn't have remembered you if I hadn't run into Clarence here after you left."

I shook my head.

"Clarence and I were both friends of Edward Purcell."

I flushed against my will. Purcell had been chairman of Transicon and the mastermind of a major fraud I'd uncovered in my first big investigation. It wasn't my fault he'd committed suicide the day before the federal marshals were coming to pick him up, but I had to fight back a defensive retort.

I forced myself to ask Clarence in a neutral voice if he was a developer too.

"Oh, I play around with putting projects together. I don't have

MacDonald's energy for that kind of thing. Ralph, I want a drink and the lady here needs a refill. I'll be back in a minute."

"Mine's bourbon on the rocks," MacDonald said as Hinton turned to the bar. To me he added, "I'm glad you came, Vic—I've been hoping to have a chance to talk to you."

I raised my eyebrows. "About Edward Purcell? It's been almost ten years."

"Oh, I've always felt sort of disappointed with Teddy for that. There's no lick so hard you can't fight it in court."

"Especially in this town," I said dryly.

He flashed a smile to let me know he got the joke without finding it particularly funny. "I don't hold Teddy against you. No, I wanted to talk to you about something more contemporary."

Maybe this was going to be my big break—detective to the stars. My chance to fund an international enterprise that would make my uncle Peter swoon with envy. Before I could ask, Clarence returned with the drinks and Ralph shepherded us down the hall to a small back room. It had probably been a maid's room in the old days of the house, but Marissa had decorated it in white on white and used it for watching TV.

I sat in one of the hard-upholstered chairs and smoothed my challis skirt over my knees. MacDonald stood across from me, his foot on the rung of the couch, while Hinton leaned against the door. There was no special menace in their faces but the poses were meant to intimidate. I sipped a little wine and waited.

When it was clear I wasn't going to say anything, MacDonald began. "Donnel Meagher has been chairman of the Cook County Board for a lot of years."

"And you think the time has come for him to pack it in?" I asked.

MacDonald shook his head. "Far from it. He's developed a political savvy in that time that no one else in this area can match. I expect you don't agree with all his positions, but I'm sure you respect his judgment."

"If I respected his judgment I'd agree with his positions," I objected.

"His political judgments." MacDonald smiled thinly. "After

Clarence pointed out who you were I asked around about you. The consensus is, you consider yourself a wit."

"But with good judgment," I couldn't help saying.

He declined the gambit. "Boots picked Rosalyn Fuentes for the county slate based strictly on her political merits. That's the kind of decision I understand you may have a hard time with."

In my secret heart I hadn't really expected he wanted to hire me, but it was still a letdown to think he only wished to warn me off Roz. "I don't have any trouble with that kind of decision. Boots is clearly a political mastermind, and if Roz can get his backing, her future looks golden."

"So you're not trying to sandbag her campaign?" That was Hinton's first contribution to the discussion.

"You guys are making me awful, awful curious," I said. "Marissa put the arm on me to go to Roz's fund-raiser in the name of a decade-old solidarity. I shelled out more money than I've ever given a candidate, was bored out of my head, and was getting ready to leave when Roz talked to me just to make sure I wasn't going to do anything to hurt her. Now you two lock me in a little room to pick my brain. I don't know anything about Roz's secrets and I wouldn't care what they were if people weren't going out of their way to make me wonder."

"It really would be better if you minded your own business this time around," Hinton said in a toneless voice more ominous than a shout.

MacDonald shook his head. "She's not going to listen to threats, Clarence—her whole history makes that clear. . . . Look, Vic— Roz needs Boots's support if she's going to win her first county-wide contest. But Boots needs her too—the Hispanic wards pretty much vote the way she tells them to."

That wasn't news to me so I didn't say anything.

"Roz committed a major indiscretion in her youth. She confessed it all to Boots when they were talking over the slate and his opinion was that it wouldn't hurt her if it came out in five years, when she had a big base, but that it could be pretty damaging to her home support if they learned about it now. So someone said something to her at the barbecue that made her think you were probing and she was trying to assure herself that you weren't."

"And what was that youthful indiscretion?"

MacDonald shook his head. "Even if I knew, I couldn't tell you —Boots is an old political hand and he doesn't share secrets with people who don't need to know them."

"Well, you know my reputation—I don't care if she was screwing the village goat, but I don't sign on for fraud."

MacDonald laughed. "You see, Vic, everyone has a different notion of morality. There are plenty more people in Humboldt Park who would care about the goat than any money she'd siphoned off a public works project. So don't set up your own standards to run the county by, okay?"

I smiled sweetly. "Just as long as no one is making *me* the goat. That's probably what I most care about."

He came over and helped me to my feet. "It would take a smarter crew than us to do that. Let's go back to the party—I want some of those little salmon things before the ignorant mob gets them all."

When we returned to the drawing room Marissa caught Ralph's eye anxiously. He nodded fractionally to telegraph all's well, that I'd been convinced. But of what?

# 21

# Auntie's Turning Tricks Again

**W**hen I got home the sun had just set and the air was still softly lit. I went slowly upstairs to my living room and stood at the window looking out. Vinnie the banker emerged from our building and climbed into his car, a late-model Mazda. A gaggle of teenage boys headed south, yelling raucous slogans and dumping their potato-chip bags onto the sidewalk.

I let the curtain fall and went to sit in my armchair. I didn't want to learn something awful about Roz. I really didn't. I wanted strong women in public office and she was better than most. So why did she keep rubbing my face in it?

I hadn't turned on any lamps. In the twilight the room seemed ghostly, a place where no living creatures moved. The image of Cerise's dead face came into my mind and I felt an unbearable sadness for the waste that had been her life. And again, unwanted, came the nagging question about what Bobby was doing at the site within hours of her body being discovered. And what was he doing coming to see me yesterday? Off and on all day I'd worried over it like a sore tooth, but couldn't put it to rest.

I had one client, Ajax, to look into one issue—had Saul Seligman burned down his own building. As a host of people from Bobby Mallory to Velma Riter and Ralph MacDonald kept reminding me, neither Cerise nor Roz was any of my business. Of course the cops thought the Indiana Arms wasn't any of my business, either.

By and by I got stiffly to my feet and went down to Mr. Contreras's apartment to borrow the dog. Sometimes he has enough sensitivity to spare me an intrusive barrage. Tonight, mercifully, was such a time. He handed Peppy over to me with a stern adjuration not to feed her cheese or anything else dangerous to her delicate GI tract and returned to the tube.

I walked Peppy around the block before returning to my own apartment. She thought that was a pretty miserable excuse for a workout, but when I fixed her a plate of spaghettini with dried tomatoes and mushrooms to go with my own, she cheered up. She wolfed it down and came to lie on my feet while I turned to the phone.

Murray Ryerson was Chicago's leading crime reporter. He'd been with the *Herald-Star* for almost eleven years, moving from covering the city wire stories to nickel-and-dime stabbings to now where he was a leading authority on the frequent intersection of crime and politics in town.

He didn't show any particular enthusiasm at hearing from me. At times we've been friendly enough to be lovers, but both of us covering the same scene and having strong personalities make it hard to avoid conflict. After the latest clash between our jobs Murray had been furious. He still hadn't warmed up. He believed I'd held back significant chunks of a story until it was too late to use them. Actually I'd held back significant chunks that he never even knew about, so he probably had a right to a grievance.

Tonight he told me astringently that he was very busy and if it was business it could wait until he was in the office tomorrow.

"Does she have a name?" I asked hopefully.

"Make it snappy, Warshawski. I'm not in the mood."

It was easy to be brief since I didn't have much to say. "Roz Fuentes. She's on the county ticket and she thinks I think she's hiding something. Is she?"

"God, Vic, I don't know. If you had to bother me at home to ask me that—"

"I wouldn't have," I interrupted him. "Do you know who Ralph MacDonald is?"

"You're wasting my time, Warshawski. Everyone knows MacDonald. He's the leading contender to put together the package for the new stadium-retail-housing complex."

I hadn't heard that. Murray told me loftily I didn't know everything, that it was just county scuttlebutt because of Boots being tight with MacDonald.

"And I don't need you calling me at home catechizing me to remember what an inside track Ralph MacDonald has in county building projects. He and Boots grew up together. They got big together. Everyone knows that. So come to the point or hang up."

I scowled at the phone but plowed ahead in my best Girl Scout style. "Ralph is hanging out with a lady I sort of know—Marissa Duncan. She's kind of a political PR woman, fund-raiser, that type of thing. She trotted him out for me tonight at her Lincoln Park town house to tell me to lay off Roz."

"Yeah, I know Marissa. She's at all the right events. If she and Ralph want you to leave them alone, it's not news—they must know what a pain in the ass you are. It still could have waited until morning."

When I didn't say anything he grudgingly allowed that he didn't know of anything about Roz that the paper was holding back. They do that more often than the trusting public likes to think—they don't run a juicy story because it will stub an important advertiser or religious figure's toe. Or even worse, they want to wait and drop it like a stink bomb when it will hurt the most people.

"But you'll check tomorrow for me?" I persisted.

"Only if I get an exclusive on your obituary, Warshawski."

I made a face at the phone. "The number of french fries you eat I'm bound to outlive you, Murray. . . . Did you see anything about a dead junkie picked up at the Rapelec construction site?"

I could feel him trying to figure it out on the phone—which was the real reason I'd called, Roz or the junkie. "I missed that one," he said cautiously. "Friend of yours?"

"In a way." Peppy got up and started sniffing around the corners. "I ID'd her. It just seemed strange to me that some of the city's top cops were there—thought you might know about it. Well, sorry to have bothered you at home—I'll talk to you at the paper tomorrow."

"Warshawski—oh, the hell with you. Go find someone else to run your errands." He hung up with a bang.

Peppy had found some dust balls behind the piano that she was bent on eating. I retrieved them from her mouth and hunted around for a tennis ball to play a little indoor fetch with her. She likes to sit on her haunches and catch the ball without letting it bounce. The hitch is, I have to go scampering after it if she doesn't make it. I was lying on my back pulling it from under the piano when the phone rang. I clambered upright to answer the phone and bounced the ball to Peppy. She watched it go by her with a look of pure disgust and slumped dejectedly onto her forepaws.

It was Michael Furey. I stiffened at once, thinking Bobby must have given him a little godfatherly advice on the best way to handle stubborn women.

Furey was ill at ease. I didn't do anything to make him relax. "Sorry to bother you so late in the day. Do you have a minute? I need to talk to you about something. Can I come over?"

"Is this Bobby's idea?" I demanded.

"Well, yes, I mean not that I come over, but—"

"You can tell him from me to butt out of my business. Or I'll tell him myself."

"Don't make this harder for me than it already is, Vic. She's not just your private business, even if you wish she was."

I held the receiver away from my face and looked at it for a minute. "You're not calling about—about Tuesday night?" I asked stupidly.

"No. No, nothing like that. Though I admit I owe you an apology. This—it's about your aunt and it's not real easy talking about it on the phone."

My heart squeezed shut. "Is she dead?"

"No, oh no, it's just—look, I hate being the one to do this to you, but Uncle Bobby—the lieutenant—he thought you and I were, well, since we'd been friends it would come better from me than anyone else."

Wild thoughts of Elena's somehow being responsible for the fire at the Indiana Arms clashed with the fear of a drunken stupor turned to disaster. I sat on the piano bench and demanded to know what Michael was talking about.

"There's no easy way to say this. But she's been spotted a couple of times soliciting in Uptown, mostly old guys, but a couple of times young ones who were pretty affronted."

Relief that it was so trivial made me laugh—that and the image of Elena taking on someone like Vinnie the banker or Furey himself. I hooted so loudly that Peppy came over to see what the trouble was.

"It's not as funny as all that, Vic—the only reason she hasn't been arrested is because of the connection between your family and the police. I was hoping you could go talk to her, ask her to stop."

"I'll do my best," I promised, gasping for breath, "but she's never paid much attention to anything anybody said to her." I couldn't help it, but started laughing again.

"If I came along?" he suggested tentatively. "Uncle Bobby thought it might make more of an impact if someone from the force was there to back you up."

"Tell me the truth—he was too chicken to confront her, wasn't he?"

Michael hedged on that one—he wasn't about to slander his commander, even if Bobby was his godfather. Instead he asked, even more hesitantly, if I might be free to do it tonight. I looked at my watch. It was only eight-thirty; might as well get it over with.

"If she's in, she's probably drunk," I warned him.

"She won't be the first one I've seen. I'll pick you up in twenty minutes."

I still had on the red rayon challis skirt I'd worn to Marissa's party. I changed it for jeans—I didn't want Furey to think I was dressing up for him. When he rang the buzzer, right on time, I took Peppy back down to Mr. Contreras. She was totally miffed—no run, no games, and now she had to stay inside when I was setting out on an adventure that would doubtless include chasing a lot of squirrels and ducks.

Michael had recovered a certain amount of his breeziness. He greeted me jauntily, asked if I'd gotten over the shock of identifying Cerise, and solicitously held the door of the Corvette open for me. I gathered my legs together and swung them over the side, the only possible way to get into that kind of car—I've always wondered how Magnum leapt in and out of that Ferrari.

"Where does she live?" he asked, starting the car with a great roar.

I told him the address of the Windsor Arms but left him to find his own way. You never have to give a Chicago policeman street directions. Maybe we should require a year of patrol duty for all would-be cabdrivers.

Michael used police privilege to block the hydrant in front of the hotel. A couple of drunks came over to inspect the Corvette but slid into the night when Furey casually let them see his gun. When he got inside no one was at the desk. I had headed toward the stairs, Michael behind me, when a voice shouted from the lounge, "Hey! No one up those stairs but residents."

We turned to see a man in green work clothes push himself out of a chair and head toward us. Behind him some mindless sitcom was blaring from the high-perched TV. In his youth the man had been muscular, maybe played high school football, but now he was just big and sloppy, his belly straining the buttons on his green work shirt.

Michael flashed his white teeth. "Police, buddy. We need to talk to one of the inmates."

"You got some ID? Anyone can come in here saying they're police."

He might be three-quarters drunk and run to seed, but he had some spunk. Michael seemed to debate playing a police heavy, but when he caught me watching him he pulled his badge from his pants pocket and showed it briefly.

"Who you after?" the night man demanded.

"Elena Warshawski," I said, before Michael could put out the police none-of-your-business line. "Do you know if she's in?"

"She ain't here."

"How about if we go upstairs and see for ourselves," Michael said.

The man shook his head. "Wouldn't do you any good. She took off three days ago. Packed up all her stuff and took off into the night."

"Thursday?" I asked.

He thought for a minute, counting backward. "Yeah, that'd be right. She in some kind of trouble?"

"She's my aunt," I said. "She gets lonesome and tries to find people to keep her company. I want to make sure she's okay. You know where she went?"

He shook his head. "I was setting in there, watching the two

A.M. movie, and seen her sneaking down the stairs. 'Hey, sis, ain't no law against you coming downstairs in the middle of the night. You can walk upright,' I calls to her. She gives a gasp and asks me to go outside to see if the coast is clear. None of my business what business people get up to, so I goes out and watches her head over to Broadway. No one was bothering her so I come back inside. And that's the last I seen her."

That was an unsettling scenario. Something had rattled her badly enough to make her scoot from a secure bed, badly enough to keep her from landing at my door.

"Can I go up and look at her room?" I asked abruptly. "Maybe she left something behind, some sign of why she bolted."

The night man scrutinized me through drink-softened eyes. After asking for a look at my driver's license, he decided I passed whatever internal test he was running. We went back to the stairs and followed him as he trudged heavily to the third floor. Michael asked me in an urgent whisper if I had any idea where she might have gone.

"Hm-umh." I shook my head impatiently. "Probably the only friend she had from the Indiana Arms is in the hospital still and doesn't have a place to stay anyway."

The night man laboriously fiddled with the keys at his belt until he found one to unlock Elena's room. He flipped a switch that turned on the naked bulb overhead. The room was bare. Elena had left the nylon bedding jumbled. It hung over the end, trailing on the floor, exposing the thin pad of a mattress as a tawdry indictment of the whole room.

I shook out the bedding. The only thing concealed in it was a bra turned gray and shapeless with age. Elena had emptied the plastic chest. Nothing remained in the box under the bed. Since the night man had a master key it was always possible he'd been there already to clean it out, but as far as I knew Elena didn't have any valuables to leave. The bra seemed like such a forlorn relic that I folded it and stuffed it in my shoulder bag.

I shook my head uselessly. "Maybe I could talk to some of the other residents. See if any of them know why she might have left."

The night man rubbed his big hands along the sides of his pants. "You can, of course, but when they see your boyfriend here is a cop, they probably won't want to talk to you. Besides, I don't think your aunt knew anyone here that good."

When she was drunk she might have said anything to anyone, even people she'd never seen before in her life. Someone she'd shared a bottle with three or four days would seem like a lifelong friend. I asked the night man when he came on—he would be easier to work with than the daytime chatelaine.

"Six. I'm off tomorrow and Tuesday."

So if I wanted to question the residents, I should do it tonight. My shoulders slumped dejectedly.

Michael was watching me sympathetically. "Look, Vic. Why don't you put together a good description. I'll get it out to the uniforms. If we're looking for her hard, we have a good chance of turning her up and it'll save some wear and tear on you."

"Thanks." I smiled gratefully. It was that kind of concerned gesture that had always been his most attractive trait.

We followed the night man back downstairs. Before we left I decided to secure Elena's room for her through October. The night man—I finally got his name—Fred Cameron—took my money and wrote out a receipt in a large clumsy hand.

Back in Michael's Corvette, I gave a careful description of Elena, including what I could recall of her wardrobe. He relayed it through the radio, underscoring the urgency of finding her, and asking that any sighting be reported directly to him.

As we turned south I asked when Elena had been seen soliciting. "If she's been seen since Thursday, the places she's been spotted are probably close to where she's hanging out."

"Good point. I'll check the reports when I get back to the station." He swooped around a car in an intersection and speeded into the southbound Broadway traffic. It's that kind of maneuver I've always liked least in him.

"You don't have any idea why she would have taken off like that, do you?" he asked.

"No. Something must have scared her, but I don't know what. She was kind of friendly with the young woman who died at the Rapelec site. I know she was shaken when I told her about it, but she didn't take off until late the night after I told her. I don't have a clue. I suppose I will have to talk to some of the residents."

He pulled up in front of my building and gunned the engine a bit. "Despite what that guy Cameron said, Vic, I think people will talk to me. Why don't you let me handle it—you're too close to the situation and that always makes for a bad interrogation."

I agreed readily, even willingly. After a pause I asked if they'd turned up anything on Cerise to explain why she'd chosen the Rapelec site to shoot up.

"Nope. We only came out because Boots has some money in the project and he wanted to make sure there wasn't anything funny about a dead body there. He's sensitive to scandals around election time. Uncle Bobby was plenty mad about being dragged into it, I can tell you. And Ernie was pissed that you came around afterwards."

"I know—he called and told me."

Michael fiddled with the ignition key. "Look, Vic—I'm sorry I acted so dumb that night. It was just jealousy seeing you with another guy when you told me you were too busy to go out last week."

"He was a potential client. One thing kind of led to another."

Vinnie's Mazda pulled up in front of us. He got out with another man, a tall, loosely knit fellow who seemed to be on pretty friendly terms with him. Well, well. Who would have thought it.

"I was wondering if I could come in with you, sort of patch things up."

"No," I said as gently as possible. "We've been spinning around too much this last week, Michael. I can't put it all back together right now."

"So you'll be off screwing this other guy, this client," he said bitterly.

"None of your business, Michael—you know that."

He slapped the steering wheel but didn't say anything. "Ah, hell, Vic. If I make another scene now, you'll never give me the time of day again. I'll let you know when we run your aunt to earth."

I got out of the car. I'd barely shut the door when he was off down Racine with a great roar from the engine.

# 22

# Tearing Up the Ryan

I slept badly, my dreams again haunted by Elena. I was searching for her through the barren corridors of midnight Chicago. I could hear her whining "Vicki, sweetie, where are you when I need you?" but I never actually saw her. Michael Furey stood nearby shaking his head: "I can't help you, Vic, because you wouldn't let me inside."

I got up around seven, my neck stiff from my restless sleep. I moved sluggishly through my morning routine, wondering if I should have invited Michael up last night. Would he still question Elena's hotel mates as thoroughly since I'd sent him packing? Should I try to do it myself? Did I even care where my aunt had gone, let alone why? Even as the last bitter thought went through my head I felt ashamed. Who else did she have to care about her, if not me?

Maybe Zerlina Ramsay. I considered her. Of course relations between the two were a bit peculiar, but she might be someone Elena would consider a friend. I drank a second cup of coffee, then took Peppy on a hurried mini-run to the lake. By the time I showered and changed into a respectable pair of trousers, a cotton-ramie beige sweater and a good jacket, it was still just shy of nine.

The penalty for rising and shining early is lolling in traffic. If I'd had a proper breakfast instead of toast while I dressed, I'd have gotten to the hospital just as fast. As it was I only met with disappointment—Zerlina had checked out on Friday. No, the hospital didn't know where she'd gone, and even if they did, they really couldn't tell me.

I stomped back to the Chevy in annoyance. How the hell would I ever find her? All I knew about her was that her granddaughter's other grandmother was called Maisie. Cerise's boyfriend's first name was Otis. That gave me a great starting point—comb every apartment in Chicago asking for Otis or Maisie and when people answered to those names find out if they knew someone named Zerlina.

Zerlina's knowing anything was a long shot, anyway. I'd only gone zooming down to the hospital because it was something to do. Otherwise I was better off leaving the search for Elena to the police. They had the resources; Michael had broadcast her description. Someone would find her.

I drove back north to the Loop, parking my car in the underground garage. Until Ajax asked me to proceed I couldn't justify any further work on the Indiana Arms. It was time to do some of my bread-and-butter financial work and to send out query letters to small or midsize firms who could use my expert advice. After going to my office to pick up the client letters with the names of their would-be executives, I headed to the Daley Center.

Somehow, though, instead of looking up John Doe and Jane Roe, I found myself checking on Rosalyn Fuentes and her cousin Luis Schmidt. No one was after Roz, but Luis had started several actions a couple of years back. He'd sued the city for turning down his bid to repave the parking lot at the Humboldt Park Community Service Center. He claimed that they had discriminated against him as a Hispanic in favor of a black contractor who was a crony of the mayor's. That action went back to 1985. More recently, in 1987, he had sued the county on similar charges, this time for not getting the job to build a new court building in Deerfield. His partner, Carl Martinez, had been a party to both suits. He'd withdrawn the complaints about six months ago without a settlement. That sounded as though someone had slipped him a few bucks to soothe his hurt feelings.

I shrugged. If it had happened that way it wasn't savory, but it was just too common to be the kind of dynamite that would cost Roz an election. If Chicago has one law that everyone obeys, it's "Look out for your own." Still, thinking back over Boots's party, it seemed to me it was Luis who had warned Roz about me—it was only after he'd been talking to her, pointing at me, that she'd come back and sought me out.

I went upstairs to look at partnership and corporation filings. Roz owned a minority interest in Alma Mejicana, her cousin's contracting business, but no one could conceivably imagine that as even a venial sin. If Ralph MacDonald had been telling the truth and Roz was hiding a youthful indiscretion, then maybe something had happened in her Mexican childhood. If so, I didn't give a damn and I didn't see why she would expect me to.

"None of your business, Vic," I said aloud. "Remember—some people think you're a pain in the butt."

A man using the microfiche reader next to me looked up, affronted. I stared intently at the screen in front of me, pursed my lips, scribbled a note, and pretended I hadn't heard—or said—anything.

It really was time to get to my clients. Still, I made a genuine note, writing down Schmidt's name, Alma Mejicana, and the address on south Ashland. Maybe there was a way to get a look at his sales figures. Or I could go over to the county side and see if any contracts had been going to Schmidt recently.

That turned out to be a fruitless idea. They did keep a list of contracts, of course, but I had to know the project name to find out who'd gotten the bid. They were not going to let me go through the myriad files looking for one contractor. I sucked on my teeth. Now it was *really* time to get to work.

As I turned to leave, the door at the end of the corridor opened and Boots came in, a handful of men listening as he made a forceful point. He caught sight of me and gave the legendary smile and a wave on his way into his office. He hadn't remembered me personally, but knew he knew me. It was a strange sensation—against my volition I felt myself warmed by his recognition and smiling eagerly in return.

Perhaps to dispel the hold his magic had on me I butted one step further into Roz's business. I called Alma Mejicana, said I was with OSHA, and wanted to know where they were pouring today. The man who answered the phone, speaking minimal English in a heavy accent, couldn't understand my question. After a few fruitless exchanges he put the phone down and went to fetch someone else.

I'd met Luis Schmidt only once, but it seemed to me that the suspicion-laden voice belonged to him. Just in case he had an acute aural memory, I sharpened my tone to the nasality of the South Side and repeated my pitch.

He cut me off before I could get my whole spiel out. "We have no problems; we don't need anybody coming to watch us, especially not OSHA spies."

"I'm not suggesting you do have problems." It was hard to be glib and nasal at the same time. "We've been told that minority contractors in Chicago are allowed sloppier safety practices than white-owned enterprises. We're doing a random spot check to make sure that isn't the case."

"That is racism," he said hotly. "I do not allow racists to look at my work. Period. Now disappear before I sue you for slander."

"I'm trying to help you out—" I started with nasal righteousness, but he hung up before I could finish the sentence.

Okay. Alma Mejicana didn't want OSHA hanging around their construction sites. Nothing bizarre about that. A lot of businesses don't want OSHA crews. So leave it alone, Vic. Get back to projects for people who are paying you.

It was that sage advice that took me over to the University of Illinois library to look up Alma Mejicana in the computer index to the *Herald-Star*. And to my joy they had gotten part the Dan Ryan reconstruction. In a February 2 story the paper listed all the minority- and women-owned businesses participating in the project. The suits Luis had filed must have made an impression on the feds when they handed out the Ryan contracts. I remembered the protest from black groups over the small number of minority contractors involved; given Chicago's racio-ethnic isolationism, I didn't suppose they were appeased to see Alma Mejicana eating part of the pie.

With a certain amount of self-deception I could make myself believe that I would pass the Ryan construction anyway on my way back to the Loop. It wouldn't really count as an additional detour from my legitimate business to check out Luis.

I went on down Halsted to Cermak, then snaked around underneath the expressway's legs looking for a way to get at the construction zone. Cars and trucks were parked near the Lake Shore Drive access ramp. I pulled the Chevy off the road into the rutted ground below the main lanes of traffic and left it next to a late-model Buick.

Once again I was badly dressed for a construction site, although my linen-weave slacks weren't quite as inappropriate as my dress silk pants had been. I picked my way through the deep holes, around pieces of convulsed rebars that had fallen down, past the debris of ten thousand sack lunches, and hiked up the closed southbound ramp.

As I got close to the top the noise of machinery became appalling. Monsters with huge spiked arms were assaulting concrete, driving cracks ten feet long in their wake. Behind them came an array of automated air hammers, smashing the roadway to bits. And in their wake rumbled trucks to haul off the remains. Hundreds of men and even a few women were doing other things by hand.

I surveyed the carnage doubtfully from the edge of the ramp, wondering how I could ever get anyone's attention, let alone find one small contractor in the melee. Now that I was here I hated to just give up without trying, but I should have worn work boots and earmuffs in addition to a hard hat. Dressed as I was, I couldn't possibly climb around the machinery and the gaping holes in the expressway floor.

When I moved tentatively toward the lip of the ramp, a small man made rotund by a layer of work clothes detached himself from the nearest crew and came over to me.

"Hard-hat area, miss." His tone was abrupt and dismissive.

"Are you the foreman?" I asked.

He shook his head. "Dozens of foremen around here. Who you looking for?"

"Someone who can point out the Alma Mejicana crew to me." I was having to cup my mouth with my hands and yell directly into his ear. As it was he needed me to repeat the request twice.

He gave the look of pained resignation common to men when ignorant women interrupt their specialized work. "There're hundreds of contractors here. I don't know them all."

"That's why I want the foreman," I screeched at him.

"Talk to the project manager." He pointed to a semi trailer rigged with electric lines parked beyond the edge of the road. "And next time don't come around here without a hard hat."

Turning on his heel, he marched back to his crew before I could thank him. I staggered across the exposed rebars to the verge. Like the area underneath the expressway, this had become a quag of mud, broken concrete, and trash. My progress to the trailer was necessarily slow and accompanied by a number of catcalls. I grimaced to myself and ignored them.

Inside the trailer I found chaos on a smaller scale. Phone and power lines were coiled over every inch of exposed floor. The rest held tables covered with blueprints, phones, computer screens—all the paraphernalia of a big engineering firm consolidated into a small space.

At least a dozen people were crammed in with the equipment, talking to each other or—based on shouted snatches I caught—to the crews in the field. No one paid any attention to me. I waited until the man nearest me put down his phone and went up to him before he could dial again.

"I need to find the Alma Mejicana crew. Who can tell me where they're working?"

He was a burly white man close to sixty with a ruddy face and small gray eyes. "You shouldn't be on the site without a hard hat."

"I realize that," I said. "If you can just tell me where they're working, I'll get a hard hat before I go out to talk to them."

"You got any special reason for wanting them?" His small eyes gave away nothing.

"Are you the project manager?"

He hesitated, as if debating whether to claim the title, then said he was an assistant manager. "Who are you?"

It was my turn to hesitate. If I came up with my OSHA story or a similar one I'd have to produce credentials. I didn't want Luis to know I'd been poking around his business, but it couldn't be helped.

"V. I. Warshawski," I said. "I'm a detective. Some questions have come up about Alma Mejicana's work practices."

He wasn't going to field that one on his own. He got up from his table and threaded his way to the back of the trailer where a tiny cubicle had been partitioned off. His bulky body filled the entrance. I could see his shoulders move as he waved his arms beyond my field of sight.

Eventually he returned with a slender black man. "I'm Jeff Collins, one of the project managers. What is it you want?"

"V. I. Warshawski." I shook his proffered hand and repeated my request.

"Work practices are my responsibility. I haven't heard anything to make me question what they're doing. You have a specific allegation I could respond to?" He wasn't hostile, just asserting his authority.

Since I didn't know anything about construction practices I could scarcely talk about their equipment. My brain raced in search of an idea. "I do financial investigations," I said, putting it together as I spoke. "My client thinks Alma's way overleveraged, that they've taken on projects they can't handle just so they can claim they're eating at the same table with the big boys. He's worried about his investment. I wanted to look at their equipment to see if they own it or lease it."

It sounded woefully thin to me, but at least Collins didn't seem to find it bizarre. "You can't go on the site looking for that kind of thing. I've got several thousand men out there. Everything they're doing is carefully coordinated. I just can't allow unauthorized civilians out there."

I was going to argue my case, but he frowned in thought. "Chuck," he said abruptly to the ruddy white man, "call down there and ask about their trucks. Give the lady the report." To me he added, "That's the best I can do for you and it's more than I should."

"I appreciate it," I said with what sincerity I could muster. It actually didn't satisfy me at all—I wanted to *see* Alma at work, see if anything strange jumped out at me just by looking at them. But I had no choice. The Dan Ryan construction zone was not a location I could infiltrate.

Collins returned to his office and Chuck got on the phone again. After ten or fifteen minutes of shouted conversation with a variety of people, he beckoned me to his table.

"I thought they were in sector fifty-nine but they'd been moved to a hunnert and twenty-one. I don't think you have to worry about them paying for their trucks—all the stuff they have on site belongs to Wunsch and Grasso."

When I looked at him blankly he repeated the information in a louder voice. I pulled myself together, gave him my sweetest smile, and thanked him as best I could.

# 23

# Stonewalled

**B**y the time I got back to the Loop it was too late to use any of the Daley Center reference rooms. I parked illegally in front of the Pulteney so I could check my messages. When I got into the elevator it took a few minutes for me to realize it wasn't moving, so lost in thought was I. As I climbed the four flights I kept turning it over in my mind.

How strange was it really for Luis to be using Wunsch and Grasso machinery? It had hit me like a bolt at the trailer, but it might not mean that much. Luis and his partner knew Ernie and Ron, that was clear from their close confab at Boots's party. If Alma Mejicana was struggling to find a toehold in the Chicago construction business, they might well lease equipment from a bigger firm.

"Mind your own business, Vic," I chanted out loud as I unlocked my office. "If Roz is hiding dirt from her girlhood, it's not your affair."

I turned on the lights and checked in with my answering service. Robin had called, as had Darrough Graham, wanting to know where in hell his report was. I called Graham first, since he was a promptly paying customer, told him I'd been away for a few days and that I'd get the job done tomorrow. He wasn't happy but we've been working together a long time—he wasn't going to break up over this. Still, I could not continue ignoring my good clients.

While I waited for the receptionist to hunt down Robin—he'd asked to be interrupted for my call—I pulled a pad of newsprint out from behind my filing cabinet. Using a thick Magic Marker, I drew up a list, with time lines, of all my current assignments. Still propping the receiver under my ear, I took the sheet and taped it to the wall facing my desk.

"That's your work," I lectured myself sternly. "Do not do anything else until all those tasks are accomplished."

"Vic?" Robin's voice cut into my lecture. "Are you there?"

"Oh, hi, Robin. Just thinking aloud. When you work by yourself you can't tell the difference between speech and thought."

"Oh. I wonder if isolation is too big a price for working alone." We chatted for a few minutes, about that, and about whether I'd like some company for dinner. When I agreed he switched to business.

"Your report came in today—your two reports. I went over them with my boss—we decided we want you to do some more checking. I'm not questioning your assessment of the old man's character, but somebody got that night watchman out of the way. It was clearly someone who knew his habits, so it had to be either a resident or a person in the Seligman operation."

"Or an outside party who was watching him," I put in.

"Yeah, I suppose. The trouble is, the only person who really benefits from the fire is the old man—or his children if he dies. Before we pay the claim I want to make sure Seligman didn't send the guy money for the track. Can you give us another week?"

I looked at my time lines. If I did Graham's project tomorrow morning, I could stretch the rest of my work around the Ajax job and still get it all done by the end of Friday—as long as I didn't take any more time to worry about Roz, about why my call to Velma had prompted her to sic Ralph MacDonald on me, and all the rest of it.

"You still there, Vic?"

"Yup. Yeah, I guess I can give you guys another week. Are you going to pay my current bill or do you want me to give you a new one with all my hours after I finish this next stint?"

"We've already sent that one through for payment—you'll get a check in ten days or so. . . . You say Seligman's not losing money but he's not making much, either."

I drew a circle on the newsprint with my Magic Marker. "I don't think he cares that much. I can try to find his old books, see how profits compare with fifteen or twenty years ago, but he just doesn't strike me as a guy pining over his lost billions."

"Well, do some more hunting, see what you can find. I know you won't let your bias for the guy cloud the way you look at the evidence. . . . See you at seven-thirty, right?"

"Right." It was couched as a compliment, but it was really a warning. Impetuosity is the detective's worst enemy.

I added eyes and a nose to the circle and gave it some whiskers. Despite Robin's warning, I couldn't believe in the old man's guilt, not unless he had some personality aberration that hadn't come through the two times I'd spoken with him. Robin was right, though, Seligman had the glaring financial motive. Of course his children would inherit the estate and maybe they were savvy enough to torch the building now so that they wouldn't come under suspicion when he died.

I gave the face a floppy suit and a hand held out asking for money. Someone at the Indiana Arms might have seen something she was too circumspect to come forward with—when you live in the margins you learn not to make yourself conspicuous. If I could locate any of these former residents, maybe I could persuade them to talk to me. Maybe I should get photos of the younger Seligmans from the old man and show those—although of course they could easily have hired someone to do the legwork. It didn't matter that the daughter had been in Brazil—she still could have engineered the fire.

The problem with this plan was that even if Rita Donnelly would give names of any of the old inhabitants, it would take an army to find out where they'd moved after the fire. Of course I had two residents—Zerlina Ramsay and my aunt. I didn't know where either of them was, but that was a trifling problem for an intelligent investigator.

It dawned on me that I might find Zerlina through the morgue. If she had collected Cerise's body, they would have a record of her address. What I needed was someone who could get that for me. A police officer could do it, but I could hardly call Furey for help and then deny him the chance to spend personal time with me. Bobby would rather see me dead than help me with an investigation. At least he'd rather see me in jail. John McGonnigal was acting kind of aloof to me these days.

There was someone on Bobby's staff who didn't feel particularly hostile toward me. Terry Finchley. I wouldn't say we were friends, but all our interactions in the past had been pleasant. And once a few years ago he'd told me he liked the way I stood up for my friends. It was worth a try.

By a miracle Finchley was at the station. He expressed cautious pleasure at hearing from me.

"I need a favor," I said abruptly.

"I know that, Miss Warshawski. You wouldn't have called otherwise. It's not about Furey, is it?" He had a light pleasant tenor with a hint of humor in it.

"No, no," I assured him. Of course everyone in Bobby's unit would be aware of the ups and downs of Michael's and my relationship. I told him about Cerise and my wanting to find Zerlina.

When he answered again his voice was cold as he said he didn't think that was an appropriate use of his time.

"It probably isn't. But I think they'd respond to a query from you where they wouldn't from me."

"Ask Furey. Or McGonnigal." He spoke with finality.

"Detective," I said quickly, before he could hang up, "I called you because I didn't feel able to call them. I know I know them better than you, that we don't know each other that well, but I thought you wouldn't mind. It's not a—a menial task, it's one the police can do and I can't. I need to find Mrs. Ramsay to see if she saw anything . . ." When he didn't respond my voice trailed away in a tangle of hopeless syntax. "I'm sorry. I won't bother you another time."

"You say you didn't feel able to call Furey or McGonnigal. Why?"

I was starting to get annoyed myself. "It's not really your business, Detective. It's totally personal and I know personal business is a happy topic for public discussion in the squad room."

"I see." He was silent for a minute, thinking, then he said abruptly, "It's not because I'm black?"

"Oh." I felt my cheeks flame. "Because Mrs. Ramsay is? No. I wasn't thinking about that. I'm sorry. It didn't occur to me it would look that way."

"I forgive you," he said with a return to his easier tone. "This time, anyway. Next time look before you leap. And go easy on Furey —he's not a bad guy, just rough around the edges. What's your number?"

I gave it to him and he hung up. I went to the window and watched the L cart commuters past. I couldn't make up my mind whether I'd been out of line or whether Finchley overreacted. The problem was, he probably got so many slights so many hours of the week that it didn't matter what my intentions were—they came out sounding like the crap he was used to hearing.

I looked at the pigeons checking each other for lice regardless of the color of their plumage. On the surface the animal kingdom looked healthier than us humanoids. But one day last summer when a gull had joined them on the ledge the pigeons had pecked and squawked at it until it left, its neck bloody.

I went back to my desk and read the junk mail that had come in the last few days. Seminars on how to manage my office better, seminars on improving surveillance techniques, special offers on weapons and bullets. I swept it all into the garbage impatiently. Finally, irritated with myself for neglecting my business too much the last few weeks, I went through my file of potential customers and started typing query letters.

I'd done three when the phone rang. It wasn't Finchley but someone from the morgue—he'd asked her to call me directly. Cerise's body had been released to Otis Armbruster at an address on Christiana.

I thanked the woman and pulled out my city map. Sixteen hundred south Christiana is not in the happiest part of town. It's not a great place for any woman to be alone at night, especially a white one. I considered putting it off until the morning, then my discomfort over my talk with Finchley returned. If Cerise or Zerlina navigated those streets, I could too.

Just as I was turning out the lights Furey called. I tensed at first, thinking Finchley might have been discussing our conversation with him, but he was calling about Elena.

"You haven't heard from her, have you?" he asked. "Because we got another soliciting complaint last night—from a bar in Uptown that's trying to cater to yuppies—and it sounded like it might have been her."

I rubbed the back of my neck, trying to ease out some of the stiffness. "I haven't heard from her, but I'm leaving now to see a woman she knew pretty well at the Indiana Arms. I'll see if Elena's checked in with her."

"You want me to come along?" He tried unsuccessfully to cloak his eagerness.

"No, thanks. She's not going to be real eager to talk to me to begin with. The sight of a police officer will cause a total shutdown."

"Give me a call later, okay? Let me know if you learn anything?"

"Sure." I stood up again. "I've got to go. Bye."

I hung up before he could ask anything more, like Zerlina's name and address, and left quickly to avoid any more calls. I took the stairs down two at a time—when going on an unpleasant errand do it as fast as possible.

The Chevy had a parking ticket stuck under the wipers. Crime does not pay in Chicago, especially for Loop parking offenders.

I went down Van Buren, took a look at the slow line of cars on the Congress, and elected to go by side streets. Wabash to Twenty-second Street was a good run. Once I was clear of the expressway interchanges the westbound traffic also moved well. It was only a few minutes after six when I turned north onto Christiana.

At this point I was about seven miles southwest of the Rapelec complex on Navy Pier. If Cerise had been living here, why had she gone all that way to find a quiet place to shoot up? I couldn't make sense of it.

Vacant lots interspersed with gray stone three-flats made up the street. Their broken or boarded windows showed the buildings tottering on the edge of collapse. During the day it looked like Beirut. Now the purple twilight softened the worst outcroppings of rubble in the lots, muting the abandoned cars into soft dark shapes.

The only businesses seemed to be the taverns sprinkled liberally on every corner. There were few cars out. Someone rode on my tail from Cermak to Seventeenth, making me rather nervous, but when I finally slowed and moved to the right, he darted around me with a great blaring of horn. It was a ghost town, seemingly uninhabited except for the occasional knot of young men arguing or joking in front of the bars.

I pulled up across from the Armbruster apartment. It was another stone three-flat. Lights shone yellow through the sheets covering the first- and second-story windows. The third floor was boarded up. As I walked up the crumbled sidewalk I could hear a radio blaring loudly.

Inside the entryway a strong scent of Pine-Sol showed someone making an effort to overcome the urine. It was almost successful, but the stench still lingered underneath, turning my stomach. Presumably the same hand had screwed a grate over the sprung mailboxes. The postman could get letters through, but you had to unlock the grate to get them out.

The Armbrusters were on the second floor. No stairwell lights existed. I picked my way slowly in the dark, testing each stair before putting weight on it. Twice a major portion of the tread was missing and my heart lurched as nothing but air met my foot.

At the second-floor door an infant's howling mixed in with the radio. I pounded on the door with the side of my closed fist. On the second try a deep-voiced woman demanded to know who was there.

"It's V. I. Warshawski," I yelled. "I've come to see Mrs. Ramsay."

The door held a peephole; I positioned myself so that my clean honest face would be visible from the other side. For a while nothing happened. Then the radio and the baby stopped almost simultaneously; I could hear someone undoing a series of locks.

When the door opened a thin middle-aged woman faced me holding a baby. The child's soft cheeks were still wet with tears. She turned her head away when she saw me watching her and buried her chubby hands in the thin woman's tight bun. Something about the immovable tidiness of the woman's hair and the severe ironing of her dress made me think she was responsible for the Pine-Sol in the lobby.

Zerlina stood behind her, overshadowing her both in girth and in the rich blackness of her skin. I presumed the other woman was Maisie and that she held Katterina.

"How did you find me?" Zerlina demanded.

"The morgue gave me the address of the person who took Cerise's body. It was just a guess that you'd be here, but you'd talked about Otis and about Katterina's other grandmother, so I thought you might all be together."

All the light was behind them. I had to squint to see their faces, but I thought it would be better if I waited to be invited in. No one seemed in a hurry to do so.

"You can't come around hounding people in the privacy of their homes," Maisie growled, jiggling the baby to let her know the anger wasn't for her.

I rubbed my face tiredly. "Someone burned down a big hotel two weeks ago. No one died but a lot of people were hurt, including Mrs. Ramsay. She's the only person I know who might be able to give me some help in finding out who did it."

"I'm not the only person you know, little white girl, as you're well aware," Zerlina said. "Ask that precious aunt of yours."

"The last time I talked to Elena I told her about Cerise. That scared her so much she ran away from home. She's been hiding on the streets ever since. I figure you're made of sterner stuff."

Her strong face set into stubborn lines. "You figure what you want to. Between the two of you, that aunt of yours and you got my daughter dead. I don't have *nothing* more to say to you."

Before Maisie could slam the door in my face I pulled out a card and gave it to Zerlina. "If you change your mind, you can call me at that number. Someone takes messages twenty-four hours a day."

Before she'd bolted the first lock the radio started again. The insistent beat of the rap music followed me down the stairs and into the night.

# 24

# Asleep in a Basement Room

I spent the night at Robin's. He was a sweet and thoughtful lover, but he couldn't wipe the decay of north Lawndale from my mind. Falling into a fitful sleep around one, I was jerked awake by a dream in which I was walking up Christiana while a car trailed me. I woke up just before it ran over me.

I fumbled around on the night table for my watch. Squinting in the dark, I could just make out the hands: four-ten. I lay down again and tried to go back to sleep. In a strange bed, though, with the memory of a bad dream lingering, I couldn't relax. Finally, a little after five, I gave it up and tiptoed into the bathroom with my clothes.

In the kitchen I found a spiral notebook next to the phone. I tore out a page and scribbled a note to Robin, explaining why I was taking off, and slipped out quietly.

At five-thirty the city was barely coming to life. Lights burned in a number of apartment windows—this was a neighborhood of hard workers who started the day early—but I was alone on the road until I hit a main artery.

When I got to my own place I felt tired enough to go back to bed. This time I managed to sleep until eight. When I got up again I felt groggy and disoriented. I pulled on a sweatshirt and a pair of underpants and sat in the kitchen reading the paper and drinking coffee until past nine when Furey called.

"I thought you were going to phone me last night, Vic."

I didn't like the angry impatience in his tone. "I thought so, too, Michael, but it slipped my mind. If I'd had anything to report, I might have remembered, but the woman wouldn't even let me in the front door."

"Why don't you give me her name and I'll give it a try?" He dropped the anger for indulgent coaxing.

"Why don't you give it a rest, Furey? Elena isn't doing anyone any harm out there. You must have a godzillian murders and rapes and stuff to keep you happy. She'll turn up in due course, drunk and repentant, and in the meantime I don't think she needs all this city money lavished on her."

"The only reason we're doing it is because Uncle Bobby wanted to save you the embarrassment of bailing her out of women's court," he said stiffly. "If I had any say in the matter, I wouldn't be wasting time looking for her."

"Then I'll call Bobby and tell him I don't care." I caught sight of the clock and suddenly remembered my time lines. *Damn* it all. I should have been at Daley Center twenty minutes ago to get a jump on Darrough Graham's project.

"Sorry, Michael—I've got to run."

"Wait, Vic," he said urgently. "Don't tell the lieutenant. He'd take a stripe off my butt if he knew I'd been complaining to you."

"Okay," I agreed, irritated, "but in that case, stop riding me. The second I see her or hear from her I'll let you know. Good-bye."

I slammed down the receiver and ran into my bedroom. As I was zipping my jeans the phone rang again. I let it go at first, thinking it was probably Furey, then gave in to the pressure of the bell.

"I want Victoria Warshawski." The accented voice belonged to the man I'd spoken to yesterday at Alma Mejicana.

He pronounced it "Warchassy." After saying it correctly I asked who wanted her.

"This is Luis Schmidt, Warchassy. A little bird told me you been prying into my work crew down at the Ryan. I'm calling to tell you to mind your own business."

"I think you have the wrong number." I took the phone from my ear while I pulled a yellow cotton sweater over my head. "There's no one here named Warchassy."

"This ain't Victoria Warchassy? The private dick?" he demanded angrily.

"I'm a private investigator, but my last name is 'Warshawski.'" I kept my tone affable.

"That's what I been saying, bitch. I'm talking to you. If you know what's good for you, keep your damned nose out of other people's business."

"Oh, Looey, Looey, you just said the magic word. I purely hate it when strange men call me a bitch. You just bought yourself a whole lot of interest in what Alma Mejicana is doing down at the Ryan."

"I'm warning you, Warchassy, to butt out of what don't concern you. Or you could be very, very sorry." The phone slammed in my ear.

I tied my running shoes and took the stairs two at a time. Behind Mr. Contreras's door I could hear Peppy whining. She recognized my step and wanted to come with me. It wasn't fair to make her hang out with Mr. Contreras all day—he couldn't run her properly. But I just couldn't stop for her.

I felt close to screaming at the pressure of all the demands on me. The dog. Furey. Elena herself. Graham. My other clients. And now my bravado to Luis Schmidt. Well, damn him anyway for calling up with stupid threats.

If only I could get a few bucks ahead of the game, I'd take some time off, just get clean out of this town for six months. I ground my teeth at the futility of the idea and savagely jerked the Chevy into gear.

By three o'clock I had finished an exhaustive search into the life and loves of Graham's prospective marketing vice president. In the report I included the fact that the guy had a steady girlfriend along with his wife and infant son—not that Graham would care. It would make me run ten miles in the opposite direction, but Graham didn't think what happened below the belt had any bearing on job performance.

Not until I had typed up the report and sent it across the Loop by messenger did I break for lunch. By then hunger had given me a nagging headache, although I felt better mentally for being able to cross a major task off my time chart.

I went to a vegetarian café around the corner for soup and a bowl of yogurt. That took care of the hunger, but my headache grew more intense. I tried ignoring it, tried to make myself think about Luis Schmidt and his anger at my visit to the Ryan construction site. My head hurt too much for logic. When I retrieved the Chevy from the underground garage, I wanted just to drive home and go back to bed, but all the time I'd wasted lately was still haunting me. I slogged north to Saul Seligman's house.

He wasn't happy to see me. Nor did he want to let me have pictures of his children. It took every ounce of energy I had to keep being gentle and persuasive through the blinding pain thudding in front of my eyes.

"In your place I'd be angry too. You have a right to expect service for the premiums you pay. Unfortunately, there are just too many dishonest people out there and the good guys get stuck as a result."

We went on like that for forty-five minutes. Finally Seligman made an angry gesture. He moved to a massive secretary in one corner and opened its rollaway top. A pile of papers cascaded to the floor. He ignored those and pawed through a drawer behind the remaining papers until he found a couple of photos.

"I suppose you'd stay here until dawn if I didn't give you these. I want a receipt. Then go, leave me alone. Don't come back unless you're telling me you've cleared my name."

The pictures were both group shots, taken at some kind of family party. His daughters stood in the middle, on either side of his wife, while Rita Donnelly and two other young women flanked them. Those two were presumably her daughters, but I didn't much care at this point—I was having too much trouble seeing.

I pulled a small memo pad from my bag to write out the date and a description of the pictures for Seligman. The letters danced around the page as I wrote; I wasn't sure my note made sense. Seligman stuck it in the secretary, rolled the top back down, and hustled me out the door.

I drove home more by luck than skill. By the time I got there I was shivering and sweating. I managed somehow to make it upstairs to my bathroom before being sick. I felt a little better after that, but crept off to bed, putting on a heavy sweatshirt and socks before crawling under the blankets. As I got warm my tense neck and arm muscles relaxed and I drifted into a deep, drugged sleep.

The ringing phone brought me slowly back to life. I was buried so far down in sleep that it took some time to connect the noise with something outside me. After a long spell of weaving the ringing in with my dreams, my mind finally swam lazily back to consciousness. I felt newly born, the way you do when an intense pain has been washed out of your system, but the insistent bell wouldn't let me enjoy it. Finally I stuck out an arm and picked up the receiver.

"H'lo?" My voice was thick and slurred.

"Vicki? Vicki, is that you?"

It was Elena, crying extravagantly. I looked at the clock readout in resignation: one-ten. Only Elena would rouse me at this godawful time.

"Yes, Auntie, it's me. Calm down, stop crying, and tell me what the trouble is."

"I—oh, Vicki, I need you, you've got to come and help me."

She was well and truly panicked. I sat up and started pulling on the jeans I'd left on the foot of the bed. "Tell me where you are and what kind of trouble you've got."

"I—oh . . ." She started sobbing heavily, then her voice disappeared.

For a moment I thought I'd lost the connection, but then I realized she was covering up the mouthpiece. Or someone else had covered it. She'd been running away and her pursuers had caught up with her? I waited in an agony of indecision, thinking I should hang up and summon Furey, not wanting to hang up until I was sure I'd lost her. Since I had no idea where to send police resources I waited, and after a couple of heart-wrenching minutes she came back.

"I ran away," she sniffed dolefully. "Poor little Elena got scared and ran."

So she hadn't been in mortal terror, just rehearsing her act. I kept my voice light with an effort. "I know you ran away, Auntie. But where did you run to?"

"I've been living in one of the old buildings near the Indiana Arms, it's been abandoned for months but some of the rooms are still in real good shape, you can sleep here and no one will see you.

But now they've found me. Vicki, they'll kill me, you've got to come help me."

"Are you in the building now?"

"There's a phone at the corner," she hiccoughed. "They'll kill me if they see me. I couldn't go outside in the daylight. You've got to *come,* Vicki—they *can't* find me here."

"Who will kill you, Elena?" I wished I could see her face instead of just hearing her—it was impossible to sort out how much truth she was spouting along with the rest of it.

"The people who've been after me," she screamed. "Just *come,* Vicki, stop asking so many goddamn questions, you're like a goddamn tax collector."

"Okay, okay," I said in the soothing voice one uses with infants. "Tell me where the building is and I'll be there in thirty minutes."

"Just kitty-corner to the Indiana Arms." She calmed down to a quavering sob.

"On Indiana or Cermak?" I tied my running shoes.

"In-Indiana. Are you coming?"

"I'm on my way. Just stay where you are by the phone. Call 911 if you think someone really is coming."

I turned on the bedside lamp. Dialing Furey's home number, I carried the phone over to my closet. It rang fifteen times before I gave up and tried the station. The night man said Michael wasn't in. Neither were Bobby, Finchley, or McGonnigal.

I hesitated, undoing the safe in the back of my closet where I keep my Smith & Wesson. Finally I explained that Bobby wanted Elena found and that Michael had been assigned to look for her.

"She just called me from an abandoned building on Indiana. She says she's in trouble—I don't know if she is or not, but I'm on my way down there to get her. I'd like Furey and the lieutenant to know."

He promised to put out a call on the radio to Michael for me with the address. I set the phone on the closet floor while I checked the clip. It was full and the ninth bullet was chambered. I carefully made sure the safety was on, put a shoulder holster over my sweatshirt, and left.

When I got to the bottom Peppy started barking anxiously behind Mr. Contreras's door. She hadn't seen me all day, she'd missed her run, and she was determined I wasn't going to leave without her. Her barking followed me down the walk to the street.

As I was getting into the Chevy, Vinnie stuck his head out his front window. He yelled something, but I was already rolling and didn't hear him.

I headed for Lake Shore Drive. The Dan Ryan would decant me closer to the site, but I wasn't up to dealing with the construction and detours in the dark. For the same reason I left the Drive at Congress and went down Michigan Avenue instead of negotiating the spaghetti behind McCormick Place.

The moon was nearly full. Once I'd slid past the streetlamps onto south Michigan its cold light created black-and-white stills: objects highlighted with unnatural clarity, their shadows pitch black. I was feeling a little weak still, from being sick and from having eaten only once in the last twenty-four hours, but my mind was wonderfully clear. I could make out every drunk on the benches in Grant Park, and when I turned onto Cermak and up onto Prairie, I could even see the rats slithering through the vacant lots.

In the moonlight the Near South Side looked like postwar Berlin. The lifeless shells of warehouses and factories were surrounded by mountains of brick-filled rubble. When I got out at Twenty-first and Prairie, I was shivering from the desolation of the scene. I took a flashlight from the trunk and stuck it in my jacket pocket.

I took the Smith & Wesson from my shoulder holster and crept along the shadows on Twenty-first, holding it in my right hand. The cold metal brought me little comfort. I was wound up enough to take aim at a passing alley cat. It snarled at me, its eyes glinting in the moonlight as it passed.

Even as my heart pounded I wondered how much of Elena's panic to believe in. I remembered all the times she'd gotten Tony out of bed with urgent alarms, only to have them dissolve—revealed as the phantasms of her drinking. This might easily turn into another such evening—maybe I shouldn't even have roused Furey.

My lingering doubts didn't make me careless. When I got to Indiana I stayed awhile in the shadow of an abandoned auto parts dealer, straining my eyes and ears for any kind of movement. I'd worried about finding Elena's hideout from her vague directions, but there was only one hotel on the street besides the Indiana Arms. The moonlight picked out the dead neon lights of the Prairie Shores Hotel, halfway down the block on my side of the road.

I heard a rustling across the street and knelt, the gun cocked again, but it was a large plastic bag dragged loose from the rest of the garbage by the ubiquitous rats. Against my will I saw their yellow teeth tearing my exposed hands; they felt tingly and uncontrolled and I hugged them under my armpits, the gun digging into my left breast. I gritted my teeth and headed down Indiana.

Across from me loomed the burned-out hull of the Indiana Arms. The sharp night air carried the acrid scent of its charred beams to me and I fought back a sneeze. When I got to the corner I could see the pay phone but not my aunt. I prowled around the street for a few minutes, tempted to return to my bed. Finally I squared my shoulders and went over to the Prairie Shores Hotel.

Its front was boarded shut; I cautiously circled around to the back. The door there was heavily chained, but on the north side a broken window provided an easy entrance.

I shone my flashlight through the missing panes. I was looking at part of the pantry for the old kitchen. I trained the light around as much as I could see of the interior. No one was there, but a rustling and the sudden darkening of shadows along the top of the broken cabinets told me my yellow-toothed pals were.

I wished I'd worn a cap. I tried not to think of the red eyes watching me as I climbed carefully over the bent metal frame. A glass shard caught in the crotch of my jeans. I stopped to loosen the fabric and listened some more before moving again. Still no human sounds.

Once inside I picked my way carefully from the pantry to the kitchen. The old smells of grease still hung heavily there; no wonder the rats were so interested. I got lost in a maze of service rooms but came at length to a door that opened on a flight of steep stairs.

Before starting down I stopped to listen again. I shone the light on each step, not wanting to tumble through the rotten boards. Every few treads I called out softly to my aunt. I couldn't hear her.

A hall led from the bottom of the stairs to another rabbit warren. I checked each of the rooms whose door opened but saw nothing except decayed furnishings. At the end of the hall another corridor led to the right. When I stuck my hand out to steady myself as I peered around the corner, I clawed at open air. I gulped and jumped back, but the light showed me nothing more menacing than a dumb waiter.

I called to Elena again but still got no reply. I turned out the light to make my ears work harder. I could hear nothing except the scrabbling and squealing of the rodents.

Tiptoeing, straining my ears, I moved down this side corridor. A series of rooms lined it. I tried each in turn, shining the light around, calling softly to my aunt. Some were empty, but most were stacked with rotting refuse from the old hotel—abandoned sofas with stuffing sticking out at all angles, mattresses, old iron springs. Every now and then I'd catch a movement, but when I stopped to look all I saw was red eyes glaring back.

Finally I reached the far end of the corridor, where a lifeless phone hung. It was an old black model with a dial face lined with letters, not numbers. When I replaced the receiver and lifted it again, no dial tone came. It was as dead as the building.

Anger gripped me. How *dare* she do this to me, call me out on a bootless errand to a rat-infested shell? I turned and began marching at a good clip back up the corridor. Suddenly I thought I heard my name. I stopped in my tracks and strained to listen.

"Vic!"

It was a hoarse whisper, coming from a room on my left. I thought I'd looked in there but I couldn't be sure. Flinging the door open, I shone the flash around the heap of old furniture. A large mass lay on a sofa wedged in the corner. I'd missed it on my first cursory scan of the room.

"Elena!" I called sharply. "Are you there?"

I knelt next to the couch. My aunt was lying on her side, wrapped in a filthy blanket. Her duffel bag leaned against the wall, the violet nightdress still poking from one side. Relief and anger swept through me in equal measures. How *could* she pass out after calling for me in such a way?

I shook her roughly. "Elena! Wake up. We've got to go."

She didn't respond. Her head lolled lifelessly as I shook her. My stomach churning, I laid her gently down. She was still breathing in short shallow snorts. I felt her head. Along the back was a tender swollen mass. A blow—from a fall or from a person?

I heard someone move behind me. Panicking, I pulled the gun from my holster again. Before I could get to my feet the night around me broke into a thousand points of light and I fell into blackness.

# 25

# The Lady's Not for Burning

**M**y headache had returned full force. I tried desperately to be sick. My empty stomach could produce only a little bile, which left me more nauseated than ever. I was so sick I didn't want to move, but I knew I would feel better if I went to the kitchen and put some compresses on my aching head and drank some Coke. My mother had always spoon-fed me Coke for a stomachache. It was a miracle cure.

I sat up and got so fierce a stab of pain that I cried out. And realized beneath the pain that I wasn't home in bed—I had been lying on a couch, one that smelled so bad I couldn't lie back down even with my aching head.

I sat with my head on my knees. I was on a couch with no cushions. When I stuck out a gingerly hand I could feel the tufts of padding spring out. My groping hand came on a leg. I recoiled so fast that the lights danced in front of my eyes again and I retched. When the spasm subsided I reached out tentatively and felt it again. A thin bony knob of a kneecap, the hem of a thin cotton housedress.

Elena. She'd called me, gotten me to the burned-out shell of the Indiana Arms. And then? How had I come to be unconscious? It hurt my head to think. I stuck up a hand and touched the locus of the pain. A nice lump, the consistency of raw liver and about as appealing. I'd been hit? Or had I fallen? I couldn't remember and it was too much work trying.

But Elena was hurt too. Or maybe passed out. I fumbled in the dark to find her chest. I could feel her heart beneath the thin fabric. It kept up a shallow, irregular beat. And she had a head injury. She'd been hit, someone had called my name so I'd think it was she calling, and all the while she was lying in here unconscious. And then he (she? that hoarse whisper had sounded like Elena) had knocked me out.

I was so pleased with remembering the evening's events that I sat for a bit without moving. My memory wasn't quite right, though. I hadn't come to the Indiana Arms but an abandoned hotel across the street from it. It was only the acrid smell of smoke that made me think I was in Elena's old building.

I leaned against the foul remains of upholstery to rest my eyes. The acrid smell didn't diminish. I hadn't thought the wind was so strong tonight as to blow ash across the street, and anyway, how intense would the fire smell be a week later? Something else was burning, some other part of the Near South Side going up in smoke. Not my problem. My problem was to feel well enough to get out of here.

I'd brought a flashlight with me. Pushing back my nausea, I got down on my hands and knees to hunt for it. Crawling on the malodorous floor, I stumbled against a piece of hard metal. My gun, I realized after a moment or two of blind groping. I picked up the Smith & Wesson. In the dark my fingers automatically checked the safety before fumbling it into my shoulder holster.

I couldn't find the flashlight, only pieces of chewed-up cushion. When I touched a warm little body I couldn't keep back a scream. I stumbled upright, my head spinning. I couldn't force myself to get back down on the floor to hunt further. We'd have to make our way out in the dark.

I blundered around the room, tripping on nameless forms, running into some bedsprings with enough force to jolt my ribs and make tears stream down my face. Good. That's good, V.I. The pain in your side will keep you from harping on your stupid head. It's doing you no good so just disregard it. Better still, unscrew it and leave it on the couch.

When I finally found the door I couldn't open it. I pulled with all my might but couldn't get it to budge. Maybe I had it wrong, maybe it opened outwards. But all my shoving didn't move it. I was locked inside.

I wanted to sit on the floor and cry in frustration, but the thought of the warm little fur balls kept me on my feet. It's okay, Vic, it's a fixable problem. You're just feeling sorry for yourself because your head hurts.

I pulled the Smith & Wesson from my holster, turned off the safety, held it against the keyhole, and fired. The recoil went up my arm, jarring my shoulder. The sound in the small room echoed frenziedly in my sore head, making spirals cartwheel in front of my closed eyes.

When I tried the door again it shook but didn't open. "Come on, dodo brain, think," I urged aloud. If blowing the keyhole didn't open the door, it was because it was nailed shut, not locked. I was too tired to figure out how to find where the nails were and shoot around them. I plowed four shots into the hinges where they attached to the wall, bracing myself each time for the recoil, for the sound. By the last shot the air was so smoky and my head ringing so badly that I had to go down on my knees. I vomited more bile and rested, gasping for air, trying to force my vibrating head to stillness.

When I finally got back to my feet I pushed against the door. I was so feeble at this point that I couldn't put much into my thrust, but I felt the paneling give a little. I tucked the gun back into my holster, sucked in a deep breath, and flung my right shoulder against the edge of the door. Something splintered on the other side. I pushed again and felt the whole thing give. I put out an arm to explore and found that the rotted wood had fractured, leaving a large jagged opening.

Leaning against the jamb to catch my breath and steady my head, I thought the smoke seemed more intense in the hall than in the room. It wasn't gun smoke, but fire.

The reason I'd been smelling smoke since I came to was because the damned building was on fire. Not left over from the Indiana Arms. Fresh, new fire created just for me. The building I was in was on fire. Someone had knocked me out, locked me in a room, and set fire to the place. The Prairie Shores Hotel, that was its name. In my mind's eye I saw the dead neon sign swaying a little in the night air.

That's so helpful, your last thought can be congratulations on dragging the name from your slug brain. Instead of that, maybe try to do a little work. Otherwise, Robin Bessinger is going to be picking through debris for your charred bones in the morning.

I went back to my aunt, trying to figure out a way to move her. My whole head hurt from the effort of thinking. I had to fight an overpowering impulse to lie back down and rest, to take my chances on waking up again in time.

Elena didn't weigh much, but even if I'd been totally myself, I couldn't have carried her far. I was afraid dragging her might jar her too much in her injured state and finish her off, but what other choice did I have? If I left her on the mattress, though . . . It might be more awkward, but the mattress would make a good barrier if we had to go through fire.

It had handles on the sides but not along the narrow end. I took my keys from my pants pocket and made some gashes in the cover. If they didn't rip off completely, they'd be good enough. I stumbled over to Elena's duffel bag and ripped the strap free. Even that much effort made me pant and brought another wave of pain crashing across my brain to the front of my head. I had to lean against the wall until it receded enough that I could walk.

I ran the strap through the gashes I'd made in the mattress cover. Before starting to haul it, I knelt again to feel Elena's heart. It maintained its erratic beat.

I slipped the duffel strap over my head and shoulders and pulled the ends around my waist. Stooping slightly against the weight behind me, I began dragging it toward the door. When I got that far I put the strap down and gently maneuvered the mattress by hand out to the hall—I didn't want to bang Elena's head into the splintered door.

Once in the corridor I began a nightmare journey. Around us in the dark the rats were twittering, unnerved by the fire and trying to delve deep into the bowels of the building. They kept running over my feet. I knew they had to be crawling around the mattress, crawling on my aunt's body. That thought made me shudder and start to black out.

I leaned a hand against the wall and forced my mind to clear, forced the thought of what was happening behind me out of my head, forced the swells of pain to the back of my brain. Smoke was starting to drift toward me down the hall, further fogging me. I wanted to sit but was too scared of the rodents clamoring for air on the floor to be able to.

I was almost at the basement stairs. If the smoke was getting thicker, it meant the fire was at the top of the stairs and I wouldn't be able to make it through the maze to an exit.

My eyes were streaming. My throat was raw and I could feel a searing tightness in my chest when I tried to inhale. I might have been able to run up on my own with my sweatshirt around my head, but if I tried it with Elena, we'd both die.

So move, Vic. Don't stand there, go back, put your harness back on, that's a good cow, turn around and pull. A door stood open at the bottom of the stairs. I had just enough sense to heave it shut before taking up my burden again and heading back down the hall.

My arms were beginning to tremble from overexertion. I couldn't remember any real poems so I started chanting jumping-rope rhymes to give some rhythm to my movements and take my mind from my fatigued body.

"Dance, girl, dance, girl, hop on one foot." But hop to where? I didn't remember any other doors in the section of basement we were trapped in. Then, at the intersection of the two corridors, I thought of the dumbwaiter I'd inadvertently found.

I stuck a hand in and explored it. It was a large space, originally used for hauling furnishings from the basement. When the hotel had been built it stood in Chicago's most exclusive neighborhood. They'd needed lots of linens and things, and before a widespread use of electricity this made an ideal passageway.

If the fire was inside the building, the shaft would also be an ideal conduit for flames. But if it had been started on the outside and was working inward, we might have a grace period. It was possible, of course, that rats had long since chewed through the cables. Anything is possible, Warshawski, my old Latin teacher used to say. I want to know what *is*.

I slipped Elena from the mat and hoisted her, straining, over one aching shoulder. "Up we go, Auntie. Just relax and breathe normally."

I slid her into the box. It was high enough that she could have sat up, but I laid her on her side. I looked at where the mattress lay.

Travel light or keep my only tool? I hoisted it up and folded it into an awkward bundle next to my aunt, checking to make sure she had breathing room. Finally I stuck a foot into the box and hiked up to the top.

It was covered with greasy dust and little things that were probably rat droppings. "But there are no rats here, Auntie, because they've all been clever enough to burrow underneath the building. We will rise above it all."

I fumbled in the dark for the cables, found one and tugged. It creaked ominously but the box didn't move. There was tension on the line, though—it was still connected somewhere. I pulled again and felt the box sway a little. Maybe I had the wrong cord. I held on to it with my left hand and waved my right around in the dark air. Finally I found another rope on the other side of the shaft.

I shifted my weight across the box and tugged with both hands. The dumbwaiter jerked underneath me and started to move. It was slow, tedious work. The rope burned my bare palms. My biceps had pretty much turned to water by now and strongly resisted the idea of more exercise. "You're at the wall now, Vic—go for the burn," I mocked myself, then returned to rope chants.

I'd been through my repertoire twice when we finally came to the opening onto the ground floor. The door was shut. When I put a hand on it, it was scalding to the touch. A poor exit choice. I tried looking up but it was a futile exercise. Even adjusted to the dark, my eyes could make out nothing.

I started hauling again, sticking a hand up every few pulls to see if I was going to run into ceiling. The pain in my head had passed beyond agony to some light, remote feeling, as though the top of my head were floating some miles from my body. Every time I stopped working to feel about, though, it came crashing down with a pounding thud. Was this what it was like to use heroin? Was this what Cerise had crawled off to the Rapelec site to feel—her head buoyant above her body?

"Last night and the night before, twenty-four robbers came knocking at my door. Asked them what they wanted, this is what they said"—the words kept spilling out, against my volition, long after I couldn't stand the sound of them. In the dark I was seeing pinwheels spinning through the elevator shaft, flashing strobes of light from my burned-out retinas. Future and past disappeared into an endless present, presence of rope, of muscles beyond fatigue, of hand over raw hand, and the unbearable sound of my own voice spewing out childhood chants.

The rope abruptly stopped moving. For a few seconds I kept tugging at it, frustrated at breaking my liquid crystal movements. Then I realized we were at the end of the line. If we couldn't get out here, we were—well, at the end of our rope.

I sat down on the box. My knees were stiff from the long haul upward and gave me little protesting stabs at my abrupt bending. I leaned down and felt for the dumbwaiter door. It was cool to the touch. I turned around, climbed down the front of the box, and twisted around to sit against the bulk of the mattress.

The door was stiff but not locked, as I'd first feared. I leaned against the mattress and pushed as hard as I could with my wobbly legs. The door creaked. I drew my knees to my chest, ignoring their throbbing, and kicked hard. The door popped out of its frame.

I slid out and turned around for my aunt. Years of abusing her body had given it great resilience—she remained unconscious, but her shallow uncertain breaths still came snorting out.

I propped her against the wall and forced my tired legs down the hall. Now that we were above ground, faint light from the full moon and streetlamps gave a pale glow to the walls, enough that I could walk without feeling my way. In the distance I could hear the deep excited honking of fire engines. All I had to do was find a window where they could see me.

"Love will find a way," I sang softly to myself. "Night or day, love will find a way." I was skating, moving so smoothly I was almost floating. My cousin Boom-Boom and I were on the forbidden frozen lagoon, circling round and round until we slid dizzily onto the ice. We weren't supposed to be there, no one knew how thick the ice was, if it gave way, we'd drown for sure because no one would rescue us. The first one to give up was a chicken and I wasn't going to be a chicken to my cousin. He was a better skater than me but he wasn't tougher.

He was near me someplace, I knew that, but I couldn't quite find him. On and on I skated, calling his name, opening every door but not seeing him. I got to a window and stared through it at a metal platform. I thought Boom-Boom was behind me, but when I turned he was gone. When I looked back at the window all I found was my own reflection. Beyond the glass lay a fire escape.

I struggled with the window but it was painted shut. I looked around the room for a tool, but it was completely bare. I lifted my trembling right leg and kicked as hard as I could. The ancient glass shivered and cracked. I kicked again and the whole bottom pane gave way.

I looked down. Below me the building was burning steadily and fire was licking upward. We'd come up three stories and we'd better get back down them fast. The fire escape was at the back. Whatever firepower belonged to the distant engines was around the other side of the building.

I lurched back down the miles of corridors I'd traveled until I came to Elena, still snorting away under the dumbwaiter. I pulled her pallet from the box and got her settled on it again. At some point my body must surely give out, no longer respond to the senseless commands of an imperial brain. I flogged myself onward, a good warhorse, old and near collapse but responding to one last call to arms.

Back at the fire escape I wrapped my sweatshirt around my right arm and knocked out the remaining shards. Then I slid Elena to the floor, moved her pallet to the fire escape, and lifted her again, my hamstrings and back shrieking in dismay, and laid her out on the mattress.

"You'll have to wait here for me, Auntie. I'll be back, just breathe deeply and don't be afraid. I've got to get help, I can't carry you on my own."

Slowly, each leg weighing a thousand pounds, I dragged myself down the stairs, down through the cloud of smoke, past the point of feeling, to the place where breath and sight were collapsed into one solid pinpoint of agony, finding the end of the escape, swinging down, feeling the bottom flight fall loose and my feet dragging on the ground.

I rolled through the smoke and staggered around the side of the building. A multitude was there. Firemen, onlookers, cops, and a man in uniform who came to me and told me sternly the building was dangerous, no one was allowed beyond the police barricades.

"My aunt," I gasped. "She's up on the fire escape around the side. We were in the basement when the fire started. You've got to get her."

He didn't understand me and I turned to a fireman helping guide a heavy hose. I tugged on his sleeve until he turned in annoyance. I pointed and gasped until someone understood and a little troop jogged off into the smoke.

# 26

# Doctor's Orders

"**W**hat are you doing with your clothes on?" Lotty Herschel was sharp to the point of unfriendliness.

"I'm going home." Getting dressed with both hands taped in gauze had been a chore. "You know I hate hospitals—it's where they send people to die."

"Someone should have burned those," Lotty said coldly. "They smell so bad, I can hardly stand to be in the same room with you."

"It's the blood and the smoke," I explained. "And I guess stale sweat—I worked up a pretty good meltdown hoisting myself up those ropes."

Lotty's nostrils curled in distaste. "All the more reason to remove them. Dr. Homerin cannot possibly examine you with that stench coming from you."

I'd noticed a slender middle-aged man standing patiently behind Lotty and assumed he was another resident seeking education at my feet. At my head, actually.

"I don't need another goddamn examination. Twenty-four hours here and I feel like a pot roast every housewife in Chicago has taken a poke at."

"Mez Homerin is a neurologist. You got a nasty blow to the head. I want to make sure that that thick Polish skull of yours hasn't taken any irremediable harm."

"I'm fine," I said fiercely. "I don't have double vision, I can tie my shoes with my eyes closed, even with these baseball mitts covering my fingers, and if he sticks pins in my feet, I'll know about it."

Lotty came over to stand next to me, her black eyes blazing. "Victoria, I don't even know why I bother. This is the third time you've been hit hard enough to knock you out. I don't wish to spend my old age treating you for Parkinson's or Alzheimer's—which is exactly where you're heading with your know-it-all reckless attitude. If you don't get your clothes back off this minute—this instant—you may be sure of one thing—I will *never* treat you again. Do you understand?"

Her anger was so intense it made my knees wobble. I sat back on the bed. I was pretty angry myself, enough that my head started pounding savagely as I spoke.

"Did I send for you? This is Michael Reese, not Beth Israel— you came barging in without so much as a by-your-leave, at least not a by-my-leave. Someone tried to murder both my aunt and me. Getting out of that building was one of the most harrowing experiences of my life and you scream at me about my clothes and Alzheimer's disease. If that's your attitude, leave with my blessing—I don't need your kind of medical care."

Dr. Homerin coughed. "Miss Warshawski. I can understand your being upset—it's a natural side effect of concussion and the other experiences you went through last night. But as long as I'm here, I think I might as well examine you. And it would be easier to do if you could take your clothes off and put on your hospital gown."

I glowered at him. He turned to Lotty and said apologetically, "Dr. Herschel?"

"Oh, very well," she snapped. She whirled on her heel with the precision of a figure skater and swept out of the room.

Dr. Homerin pulled the curtain around my bed. "I'll wait out here—give me a call when you're ready."

I could go ahead and leave, but it would make me feel incredibly stupid. Angrily I kicked my running shoes off. With thick clumsy fingers I unfastened the buttons of my shirt and unzipped my jeans. I took as much time as I possibly could before sullenly calling out that I was ready.

Dr. Homerin sat on the chair next to the bed. "Tell me a little about your injury—what happened?"

"I was hit on the head," I muttered churlishly.

He refused to acknowledge my ill humor. "Do you know who hit you or what was used?"

I shook my head and saw black circles swirl around. "No. He was hiding in the room. I was looking at my aunt, who was drunk." I frowned. "No. I thought she was drunk, but it turned out she had been coshed. That's right, I realized someone had hit her and that he might still be there and as I was jumping up to protect myself I got hit from behind."

He nodded, like a professor at a promising pupil. "It's very good that you have so much recall—very often the memory immediately before such an incident is blocked out by what we call protective amnesia."

I rubbed the tender spot on the back of my head. "What I don't remember is what happened afterwards. I know I was climbing a rope in an elevator shaft but I can't remember how I got Elena up with me. And then we came out. The fire fighters had to bring my aunt, but I think I got out on my own?"

My voice trailed off as I tried to focus the blur of memory. Mallory had shown up along with Furey when I was in the emergency room, but someone had been in the crowd around the fire who didn't belong there. I remembered a faint inflection of surprise mixed in with a sense of my imminent death as the paramedics carried me through the barricades. The face swam on the edge of my consciousness. Tears of frustration pricked my eyelids when my aching head refused to concentrate.

"I can't remember," I said helplessly.

"Do you have any idea of why this happened?"

His gray eyes looked harmlessly genial behind their thick lenses but I stiffened at once. "Did Bobby—Lieutenant Mallory—tell you to ask that?"

There'd been quite a scene in the emergency room, with Bobby roaring at me like a bull elephant on a rampage. Dominic Assuevo and Roland Montgomery from the Bomb and Arson Squad had joined him, but it was only because I kept passing out that the resident on call finally threw them out of the examining area.

Homerin shook his head. "The police haven't spoken to me at all. I'm just checking your ability to answer logical questions."

In the intervals between sleeping and tossing in pain I'd been testing that skill myself, without any happy answer. Maybe someone arriving to torch the building had seen Elena come out. He followed her, heard her phone me, then when she went back inside he knocked her out and waited to get me, too, before setting the place on fire. It could have happened that way, but it seemed awfully elaborate: Why not just torch the place while she was out of the way? Maybe she'd seen him clearly enough to recognize him again, so he felt she had to die. But then why go for me too? My head was starting to disintegrate. I couldn't figure it all out. I wanted to go home and I was starting to feel too helpless even to get out of bed again.

Seeing my fatigue and frustration, Homerin switched to a general interrogation—did I know who the President was, the mayor, people like that? I wished I didn't but rattled off the names. After that we went through the pins-in-the-feet routine and he banged on my knees and elbows and felt my head—all the usual medical stuff that lets the doctor know all your pieces are still attached to your aching body.

When he finished looking at my eyes and rotating my head around a few times, he sat back in the visitor's chair. "I know you want to leave, Miss Warshawski, but it would be better if you stayed another day."

"I don't want to." I was close to breaking down and sobbing.

"You live alone, don't you? I just don't think you're up to looking after yourself right now. There's nothing wrong with you that I can see, barring the side effects of concussion. They did a CAT scan of your head in the emergency room Wednesday morning and nothing alarming showed up. But you'll manage better if you let us look after you another day."

"I hate being looked after, I can't stand it." I didn't want to be like Tony, reduced to such helplessness he couldn't even breathe on his own at the end. The sound of his harsh wheezing breathing cut through my brain and against my will I found myself crying.

Homerin waited patiently for me to dry my eyes and blow my nose. He asked if there was something specific I wanted to talk about, but the memories of my dying parents were too painful to mention to a stranger.

Instead I blurted out, "Is Lotty right? Am I going to get Alzheimer's disease?"

A smile twitched at the corner of his mouth. "She's worried about you—that's why she dragged me down here and got the house staff to agree to let me see you. I'm not a prophet, but three blows in seven years—it's more than you need, but you're not taking the regular pounding that a boxer does. I'd worry more about feeling better now. And give me a call if you have any unusual symptoms."

He fished a card from his wallet and handed it to me: Mez Homerin, boy neurologist, with an address on north Michigan and another in Edgewater. "What kind of symptoms?" I asked suspiciously.

"Oh, blurred vision, trouble with your memory, any tingling in your fingers or toes. Don't lie aound worrying about them—I'll be startled if you have any. Concentrate on getting your strength back. But please call me if you want to talk about any concerns."

He put a gentle stress on "any" and I stupidly felt like crying again. "There is my aunt," I said as assertively as I could. "Do you know how she's doing?"

"Your aunt? Oh, the woman you rescued. . . . She'd been hit on the head, right? Do you know if she's here?"

I didn't, but he said he'd find out and get a progress report for me. I'd been planning on getting up and dressing as soon as he left, but my crying bout had put the finishing touches to my fatigue. I was asleep almost before his hospital coat disappeared behind the curtain.

# 27

# We Serve
# and Protect

It was Saturday before the pounding in my head receded completely. I'd gone home on Friday, admitting—only to myself—that Mez Homerin had been right: I was better off for the extra day of people waiting on me. As it was, Friday involved so many difficult encounters that by the time I went to bed I was wishing I'd stayed in the hospital. The worst was with the police—Homerin had shielded me from Roland Montgomery of the Bomb and Arson Squad.

Of course the cops were most anxious to speak with me. Montgomery had been in the emergency room with Mallory and Furey early Wednesday morning and he'd sent a subordinate to Reese both Wednesday and Thursday. Since I'd slept through most of Wednesday I only learned about the subordinate's visit on Thursday. When Mez left me he encountered the detective in the hall. Their altercation led to a big red notice on my chart proclaiming "No visitors" and a lot of excitement among the orderlies and nurses who reported the episode to me in dramatic detail later.

I took a cab from the hospital to my car, which started with a reproachful groan that it kept up all the way to my apartment. Mr. Contreras saw me pull up a bit after noon. While I was sponging myself off as best I could without soaking my gauze mitts, he came to the door laden down with food.

"You shoulda let me know when you was coming home, doll. I could've come and got you—you shouldn't be driving with your hands all wrapped up like that."

"I just wanted to be by myself for a while. In the hospital you're a twenty-four-hour-a-day freak show for every medical student in the city."

"You shouldn't try to do so much on your own, cookie. No shame in asking for help every now and then. And I know darn well you wouldn't eat *nothing* this afternoon if I didn't bring it to you, so you want to be alone, you say the word and the princess here and I'll go, but not till we see you eat something."

I gave up trying to hint him away, but made him wait in the living room while I finished washing and changing. Peppy, feeling no inhibitions, stayed next to me until I was done.

Lotty'd been right about one thing—my clothes stank so badly I could scarcely stand being in the same room with them, let alone the same body. I didn't even want to wash them. Although it was my newest pair of jeans I stuffed them into a bag and put it outside my back door to cart down to the garbage.

Finally clean from my bra to my socks, I joined the old man. He'd prepared a special feast, much more food than I could deal with in my sickly state, but he was miffed that he'd had to hear all my news secondhand.

"If you was going off into danger like that, you might of notified me," he grumbled. " 'Stead the first thing *I* know about it is the morning paper. That oversize teenager Ryerson putting in a story about 'Chicago's most troublesome private eye' and I start reading and of course there you are, rescuing bodies from burning buildings, hit on the head, and not even a phone call to me from the hospital. I says to the princess here, I says, 'You could be an orphan and you'd be the last to know.' "

Peppy thumped her tail to corroborate his story. Her liquid amber eyes gazed at me with unwavering intensity as I slowly chewed a piece of steak.

"Ever since my aunt came prancing into my life two weeks ago you've been riding me for getting you up in the middle of the night. I figured if I woke you up to tell you where I was going, I'd just get another lecture."

"That's not fair." He was hurt and astonished that I could think such a thing. On top of that he was pretty darned tired of me leaving him standing on the sidelines while I went out and had all kinds of fabulous life-threatening adventures.

"It's not the first time, doll. You forget how I helped you and Dr. Lotty out that time her clinic was attacked. You don't remember how I took on them guys trying to break into your place. I may be seventy-seven but I'm in good shape, I'm still a good man in a fight."

It was precisely because I *had* remembered his assistance that I tried never to involve him in the livelier aspects of my work. If I told him that, though, it would be just too painful for him. I skated around it, saying Elena was so prone to drunken fables, I hadn't taken her claims of endangerment seriously. By the time I finished he was nodding portentously.

"I know just what you mean, doll. I used to work with a guy like that. Of course he was a danger to the whole shop, showing up drunk most days, and the ones he arrived sober he didn't stay like that past lunchtime. There was the day he didn't turn off the surface grinder, and Jake—you remember Jake—lost most of the little finger on his left hand, but Crenshaw—Crenshaw was the drunk—he claimed it was me using the machine when I wasn't supposed to . . ."

His good humor restored, Mr. Contreras went on in this vein at some length. The happy drone of his voice, the weight of the meat in my stomach, the warm pleasure I felt at being back in my own home, sent me drowsing in my armchair. I held my hand down and let the dog lick my fingers while I nodded sleepily in tune to the old man's speech.

The shrill burr of the phone startled me awake. I stretched an arm out to the piano and picked up the receiver.

"Tried to write your obit for you, Warshawski, but you made it through one more time. How many lives you got left, anyway? Three?"

It was Murray, with more vibrant energy than my head could handle. "I hear you called me the most troublesome detective in Chicago."

"Private eye," he corrected. "Nothing libelous in that—I checked with the legal department. You can sue me only if it's not true. What I want to know is, who did it? Did it come out of Roz Fuentes's camp or your dead junkie, Cerise?"

"Ask the cops—the city pays them to investigate arson and attempted murder."

"And you're just going to stay home and watch TV while they sort it out?" He guffawed. "Between us ace investigators, what were you doing down there?"

Black spots were starting to dance in front of me from the resonance of his voice. I moved the earpiece away from my head. "Performing feats of derring-do. I understand it was in all the papers."

"C'mon, Warshawski," he said, trying to wheedle. "I do lots of stuff for you. Just a few little words."

He was right—if I wanted help from him, I had to throw him the occasional quote. I told him everything from the moment Elena called me to my drop from the fire escape.

"Now it's your turn—what was the fire department doing there so pat?"

Mr. Contreras looked at me as intently as the dog, miffed I was telling my tale to Murray but wanting all the juice. I took the phone over to the couch where I'd dumped my bag and pulled out my memo pad. "Anonymous phone call," I scribbled on it for Mr. Contreras as Murray boomed the news at me. Someone had called 911 from a pay phone at the corner of Cermak and Michigan. The police didn't have a clue as to who phoned, except for its having been a man.

"So you think it was someone after your aunt?" Murray asked. "How is she, by the way?"

"I don't think anything right now. My head hurts like all the cement trucks on the Ryan just ran over it. And my aunt, who has the system of a goat, sat up and took nourishment yesterday. She refused to talk to me, though, when I started asking her pointed questions, and is acting sick enough that the docs are stonewalling the cops for her. You can call Reese and see if the medicine men will let her talk to you, but don't set your hopes too high. Now you know everything I do. I'm going to bed. Good-bye."

I hung up before he could say anything else and ignored the phone when it started ringing again. Mr. Contreras solicitously offered to fix me up with pillows and a blanket on the couch, to leave me the dog, to make me tea, to do a thousand things that made the black spots grow into giant spirals.

"I need to be alone in my own bed. I can't take any more people now. I know you mean well, I know you're helping like mad, but I'm going to faint or scream or both if you don't take the dog and leave."

He was a little hurt but he'd seen concussion cases before, he knew it took time before you really felt yourself, and in the meantime the smallest things got you down—sure, doll, sure, he'd leave me alone, sleep was the best thing for me right now. He gathered up the dishes, clicking over the small amount of steak I'd eaten—gotta get your strength back up, doll, you look like you lost ten pounds the last few days—finally collecting the dog and heading down the stairs. I locked the triple dead bolts and stumbled to my bedroom.

The spirals receded back to spots as I thrashed around in an uneasy doze. The image of Elena, her face sunk into deep canyons, drips in her malnourished arms, kept swarming into my half sleep. She was a pain in the ass but someone had tried to kill her; I couldn't just abandon her at this point.

I'd tried talking to her before I left this morning but she'd pretended to sleep. "It's no good playing possum, Auntie—you're going to have to talk to me sometime," I'd warned her.

Mez Homerin interrupted my lecture to her, taking me by the arm and hustling me from the room.

"She's had a severe shock to a system that wasn't in the best shape to begin with. She needs to be completely free from any kind of stress or harassment if she's to recover. I've forbidden the police to question her. Do you want me to bar you from the room too? She needs your support, not your abuse."

"Bar me from her life," I'd snapped at him. "Keep her from calling to demand that I help her one last time—write it on her hospital forms. Make sure she doesn't put my address in as her own or list me as the guarantor of her bill. Do all those things and you can keep me out of her room with all the righteousness you want."

Homerin looked at me steadily during my outburst and then said in a gentle voice that he thought I ought to consider bringing her home to convalesce when she was a little stronger. That was when

I'd left the hospital—before I gave in to my urge to take his stethoscope and strangle him with it.

Now, though, tossing restlessly, I was tormented wondering how much I owed my aunt. Would my uncle Peter thrash in guilt for saying no? Of course not. I hadn't even called to ask him—my tired brain wasn't up to rebutting his smugness. Did I have a duty to Elena that overrode all considerations of myself, my work, my own longing for wholeness?

I'd held glasses of water for Gabriella when her arms were too weak to lift them herself, emptied wheelchair pots for Tony when he could no longer move from chair to toilet. I've done enough, I kept repeating, I've done enough. But I couldn't quite convince myself.

Such unquiet sleep as I achieved was broken up for good at four when the police came, represented by Roland Montgomery and Terry Finchley. Montgomery kept a finger on the bell until I couldn't ignore it, and then said through the intercom that if I didn't let them up to talk, they'd get a warrant and take me downtown. It was Montgomery who did all the bullying. Terry Finchley, sent by Bobby to represent Violent Crimes, was clearly unhappy with Montgomery's approach but was too junior to protest very forcefully.

I shuffled into the living room with a blanket wrapped around me. I'd been sweating heavily in my uneasy dozing and felt a chill run through me when I got out of bed. The black spots had gone away but my head was thick, as though someone had stuffed it with wool. I sat on the couch with my legs curled up underneath me.

"Let's have the whole story, Warshawski. What were you doing in that building? How did it come to catch fire while you were there?"

"The force of my fiery personality," I mumbled, my tongue thick.

"What was that?" Montgomery demanded angrily. Finchley shook his head slightly, trying to warn me without the arson expert seeing.

"I called Furey," I said, suddenly remembering. "He wanted to know where my aunt was and I left a message with the night man saying where I was going. Did he get it? Is that why he and Bobby were at the fire?"

"I'm asking the questions," Montgomery snapped. "Why did you call the station?"

"Get the chip off your shoulder, Lieutenant, and listen to me. I just explained why I called the station. Did Detective Furey get my message?"

Finchley spoke swiftly, before Montgomery could bellow at me. "Furey was at a poker game; he left his beeper in his coat pocket and didn't get the message until he went over to get a cigar and found the thing vibrating away. Then he called the station, got your message, and went roaring down to the Near South Side. By that time, though, someone had already reported the fire. Lieutenant Mallory gave the night operator a pretty good going-over for not notifying someone else in the unit, but you hadn't said anything about an emergency."

"So Furey and Bobby stormed the hospital. How come you're here now?"

*"Miss* Warshawski," Montgomery interrupted frostily, "Detective Finchley is here to help with an investigation. Why the department sent him is none of your business."

I wanted to make a grandiose statement about how the police worked for the citizens and how I was one, and therefore one of Montgomery's bosses, but I felt too sick to fight. I just wrapped the blanket closer about me and continued to shiver. And when Montgomery asked me I went back through all the tired old details. About Elena disappearing, about Furey coming around hunting for her, her early morning phone call, and on and on.

"So why did someone want to leave the two of you there to die?" Montgomery asked.

"You're the bomb-and-arson whiz, Lieutenant. You tell me. All I know is, she called up scared, I found her on a pallet in the basement barely breathing, got knocked out myself, and am lucky to be here enjoying this scintillating conversation with some shred of my wits intact."

Finchley started a sentence, then changed his mind and made an industrious note in his pocket diary. In the dim lamplight his closely cut hair merged with the black smoothness of his face.

Montgomery scowled at me but only said, "The Prairie Shores

Hotel is across the street from that fire you were so excited about last week."

I gave the thread of a smile. "Amazing."

"I'm wondering if you set the fire yourself, to try to get the department to respond to your demands for an investigation into the Indiana Arms."

I felt a jolt, the way you do when the earth goes on hurtling through space and you haven't quite moved with it. Finchley's jaw dropped. He clearly hadn't been privy to Montgomery's theories. "I didn't know we were considering that possibility, Monty," he said softly.

"And I would never have suspected you of so extravagant an imagination," I put in. "Sounds like you read too much Tom Clancy on your days off."

Finchley hid a smile so fast I wasn't sure I'd seen it. "Monty, what evidence do we have that points to Miss Warshawski?"

Montgomery ignored him. "You tried to waste police resources last week, claiming there had been a baby in the Indiana Arms that was never there. It's one of the hallmarks of arsonists that they can't stand to have their handiwork ignored."

"Hunh-unh." I shook my head. "You go away and do some real work on this problem before you bother me again. You find out about the accelerant and who had access to it, and you come up with a reason for me knocking myself out and then setting the fire and then scrambling to get away. Then we'll talk some more."

"Accomplice," Montgomery said smugly. "You must have run afoul of your partner in this."

I leaned back in the corner of my couch and shut my eyes. "Good-bye, Lieutenant. The door will lock automatically behind you."

He started shouting at me. When I didn't respond he got up and shook my shoulder until my head throbbed in earnest.

"You're one step away from a complaint of police brutality," I said coldly. "Unless you have a warrant with my name on it, you get the hell out of my place now."

If Finchley hadn't been there, I think Montgomery would have slugged me, but he could see whose side the detective was on—he wasn't nearly as dumb as he looked.

"Just watch your ass, Warshawski. I'm going to be sticking to you like your underpants. If you're up to something, next time we'll catch you red-handed."

"Thanks for the warning, Lieutenant. It's a help to know who your enemies are before you hit the streets."

When the door shut behind them I did up all the bolts again and checked the back door for good measure. I was too tired to think about what it all meant, too tired even to call Bobby and chew his ear off about it. I staggered back to my bedroom and fell back into a deep, unrestful sleep.

# 28

# A Few Kind Words from a Friend

**R**obin phoned later that evening, concerned that he hadn't been allowed to see me in the hospital and glad I was still in one piece. He was eager to drive down for a convalescent visit. I was too worn out for more company but said he could stop by on Saturday if I felt better.

Before he hung up I remembered a question. "By the way, did Ajax insure the Prairie Shores Hotel—the place I was in?"

"No. It was the first thing I looked at, but of course we don't cover abandoned buildings. And if it's any comfort to you, it wasn't owned by your pal Saul Seligman. So it's either a vendetta against that block of Indiana or someone with a grudge against the War-shawski family."

The last comment was meant as a joke, but it reminded me again of Elena, her red-veined face slack and empty. I muttered something to Robin about feeling too feeble for jokes and hung up. I did not have to be a Victorian angel and go sit with her. I didn't, didn't, didn't.

I stumbled into the dining room and dug around in the cupboards hunting for stationery. It had been so long since I'd written any personal letters that the box had landed behind the fondue set and silver salad servers left over from my brief marriage. I stared at the pieces in bewilderment: Why had I carted those particular items all over Chicago with me for the eleven years since my divorce?

I wasn't up to making a decision about them today; I thrust

them back into the cupboard and sat down with the yellowed stationery to write my uncle Peter. It was a difficult letter—I had to overcome my dislike of him enough to plead Elena's case with conviction. I described the accident, made much of my own decrepitude and the fact that I'd saved her life, and concluded with a plea that he either take her in himself or put her up in a convalescent facility. In the morning I'd express it to Mission Hills. It was the best I could do for Elena.

In the bathroom mirror my face looked sunken, nothing left but cheekbones and eyes, their gray looking almost black against the pallor of my skin. No wonder Mr. Contreras had been eager to fill me with steak. I stepped on the scale. My weight had fallen below a hundred and thirty pounds. I couldn't afford to be that light if I wanted to have the energy to do my job. I wasn't hungry but I'd better eat something.

I wandered moodily to the kitchen. After all this time any resemblance between the stuff in my refrigerator and human food was purely coincidental. I smelled the yogurt. It was still okay, but the vegetables and fruit had passed the point of no return while the orange juice smelled both rotten and fermented.

I took a bag of fettucini from the freezer and sawed off a hunk with my big butcher knife. While it boiled I ate the yogurt directly from the carton, trying to put some order into the chaos that enveloped me.

Several people had been annoyed with me the last week or two. Ralph MacDonald had descended from his throne to hint me away from Roz Fuentes's affairs. Saul Seligman was upset that Ajax wouldn't honor his claim. Zerlina Ramsay blamed me and Elena for her daughter's death. It was quite a list, but I didn't know that any of them would express their annoyance by leaving both Elena and me to die by fire. Of course Lotty was angry with me, too, but she preferred to do her scorching directly.

Then there was Luis Schmidt. He'd called me a bitch on Tuesday and told me not to ask any more questions about Alma Mejicana or he'd make me sorry. I'd flipped back some good macha retort and he'd hung up on me. So if I was going to go pawing around any of these people, Luis was the place to start.

The hissing of water on gas startled me back to the present—the fettucini had boiled over, extinguishing the pilot. Of course I couldn't find a box of matches among the jumble on the stove. I started slamming doors open and shut. I just couldn't take this life anymore, living alone, no one to pet me when I came home from the wars, nothing to eat, no matches, no money in the bank. I grabbed a handful of spoons and spatulas and flung them as hard as I could at the kitchen door.

When the clatter died down the grate over the door vibrated in a mournful bass for a few seconds. My shoulders sagged in defeat. I shuffled over to the door to collect my utensils. A wooden spoon had landed on the refrigerator. When I reached up for it I knocked a box of matches down. Okay, good. Have fits. They get results. I stuffed the implements back into a drawer and relit the stove.

Besides Luis and the possible problems of Alma Mejicana, I had to consider my aunt's affairs. I didn't want to think about her any-more—and not just because I didn't want Victoria the Victorian Angel nudging me to look after her. Her tales of woe had sucked me into a series of hideous events lately, starting with my hunt for her new home and culminating in my near death. I couldn't take much more probing into her life.

I still wasn't hungry, but I was starting to feel light-headed from lack of food. I drained the pasta and grated some rock-hard cheddar onto it. It was slow work with my padded hands. My arm muscles were still sore enough that I gave it up, panting, with only a few teaspoons of cheese for my effort. My right palm stung so violently I was afraid I might have rubbed the scab off through my mitt.

I carried the plate in my left hand into the living room. After forcing several mouthfuls down I leaned back in my armchair and made myself think about my aunt. Elena ran away when she learned about Cerise's death. It's possible something else had frightened her —I didn't know much about her day-to-day life. With her character she could easily have stubbed more than one toe.

But I had to start somewhere. Linking her flight to Cerise's death made sense. It would take a strong compulsion to force her from a secure berth. Since losing the Norwood Park bungalow she'd lived precariously on the small annuity scraped out of the remains of the sale. Even though the Windsor Arms was a desolate place, she'd had too much experience of hand-to-mouth living to turn her back on it lightly.

She and Cerise had been working some scam together. When I told Elena that Cerise was dead she'd been both crafty and uneasy. So she'd gone to their mark. That made sense too—twenty-four hours had lapsed between my telling her about Cerise and Elena's disappearance. She'd had time to talk to their target and find out . . .

My thought trailed away. She'd found out that Cerise had been murdered? Was that possible? What else could frighten her into running away, though? Someone saying, Look what we did to your friend. The same thing could happen to you. A quart of whiskey inside you and death by exposure on Navy Pier and who'd be the wiser.

I rubbed my aching head. Romance, Victoria. You need facts. Just say for starters that Cerise and Elena had a tiger by the tail. To find out what it was I needed Elena to start talking. Or Zerlina Ramsay—it was remotely possible that Cerise had confided in her mother.

My phone books were buried under a stack of music on the piano; I'd been singing more recently than I'd been looking up numbers. No Armbrusters were listed on south Christiana. I called directory assistance to make sure. So I'd have to make another trip to north Lawndale. I gritted my teeth in anticipation of this treat. And after that I should find out where everyone on my list of annoyed patrons had been early Wednesday morning. Although if Ralph MacDonald or Roz's cousins had tried torching me, they'd probably hired someone else to do it. Still, it would be worth finding out where they'd been. It wasn't exactly a job for a convalescent. Maybe I could wait until Sunday to start working on it.

My eyes were too sore for television or reading. My body ached too much for anything else. After I force-fed myself the plateful of fettucini I went back to bed. Lotty capped my wonderful day by phoning at eight-thirty to see if I was still alive.

"I'm doing okay," I said cautiously. If I told her I hurt like hell, I'd only get a lecture on my just deserts.

"Mez told me he'd released you today. He didn't think you were ready to go home, but I assured him you had an iron constitution and would be ready to do something else life-threatening next week."

"Thank you, Lotty." I lay down in the dark with the phone propped on a pillow next to my mouth. "If I turned my back on people who came to me in need, I can imagine how loudly you'd cheer. And if I avoided all risks—stayed home watching the soaps or something—you'd really be leading the applause meter."

"You don't think you could find some point of balance between doing nothing and putting your head in the noose?" she burst out. "Do you know how I feel every time I see your body come in on a stretcher not knowing if you're alive or dead, not knowing if this time your brain is ruined, your limbs paralyzed? Do you think you could manage your affairs so that you stopped a few feet short of the point of death, maybe even ask the police to take those risks?"

"So someone else's friend or lover can do the worrying, you mean?" I wasn't angry, only very lonely. "It will happen inevitably, Lotty. I won't be able to jump through hoops or climb up ropes forever. Someone else will have to take over. But it won't be the police. Not when I have to fight them every inch of the way to look into arson and they still won't do it. Or when their only answer to my near death is to accuse me—"

I broke off. Maybe Cerise and Elena had seen who set fire to the Indiana Arms and were going after him. Or her. Or them. Still, if that was so, it could be the arsonist was disposing of her by his favorite means. And maybe assumed she'd confided in me so I had to go too? And—but had they murdered Cerise? The police said it was an overdose, pure and simple.

"I know I shouldn't be losing my temper with you. It's only my fear of losing you, that's all." Lotty said.

"I know," I said wearily. "But it just puts that much more pressure on me, Lotty. Some days I have to fight a hundred people just to be able to do my job. When you're the hundred and first I feel like all I want to do is lie down and die."

She didn't say anything for a long moment. "So to help you I have to support you doing things that are a torment to me? I'll have to think about that one, Victoria. . . . One thing I don't support, though. That you dedicate your life to your aunt. Mez mentioned that part of your conversation to me. I suggested that if you were a man, he would never even have raised the topic with you except to ask if you had a wife to do the job."

"What did he say?"

"What could he say? He hemmed and said he still thought it was a good idea. But there's a limit to how much of yourself you have to immolate for people, Victoria. You almost killed yourself for Elena. You don't have to sacrifice your mind as well."

"Okay, Doctor," I muttered. I blinked back tears—I was so weak that one little sentence of support made me feel like crying.

"You're exhausted," she said curtly. "You're in bed? Good. Get some sleep. Good night."

When she hung up I switched my phone over to the answering service. I fumbled around with the switch in the dark to turn off the bell. When my thick ungainly hands had managed that I finally fell into a deep clear sleep.

# 29

# **Heavy Flowers**

**W**hen I woke up on Saturday it was past nine-thirty. I'd slept more than thirteen hours and for the first time in a week I felt rested for my time in bed. I let myself come to slowly, not wanting to bring on black spots by jerking my head.

In the bathroom I unwrapped my hands. The palms had turned an orangey-yellow. I flinched in nausea—their swollen discoloration made a sickening wake-up call. When I gently pushed the blood blisters lining my hands like railroad tracks, they seemed to be healing. I tried to remember that injuries always look their worst when they're on the mend, but the squishy mass still made my stomach turn. I also wasn't sure I could wrap them back up again myself. The hospital had given me a salve and some dressing but hadn't included a manual on how to apply them with my teeth.

Still, if I kept my hands on the edge of the tub, I could take a proper bath. I turned on the water, threw in some milk bath, and toddled off to the kitchen to make coffee. Since I could use only my fingertips to handle the kettle, it was a slow and tiresome experience. By the time I had a cup poured the bath was close to overflowing. I climbed in carefully, holding the coffee in my fingers. When I sank down cross-legged a great wave swept over the side of the tub but my hands stayed dry.

I lay soaking until the water became tepid, thinking of nothing at first, then going back to my painful headwork of the previous night. I still couldn't understand why Cerise's death had terrified

Elena into flight, unless someone had pumped Cerise full of heroin and left her to die. I couldn't move on that idea, though. I didn't have any evidence—it was just the only explanation that I could come up with. And how had Elena known? She'd found it out in the twenty-four hours between my visit to her and her panicky exit in the middle of the night. While she was lying mute behind a protective barricade of doctors and nurses I didn't have any way of finding out. I'd have to drop it for now.

What I could do was take a look at Alma Mejicana. I put the coffee cup up on the windowsill and looked at my palms again, grimacing. Tomorrow would be the ideal time to slide into their offices, but I didn't think I'd be much more healed by then than I was this morning.

I soaped down and pulled myself cautiously from the tub. Drying off presented more difficulties. It's only when you can't use them that you realize how much you need your hands. The third time I dropped the towel I left it on the floor and climbed back into bed to finish drying.

The front doorbell rang just as I was trying to hoist jeans over my still-damp rump. I'd forgotten Robin was coming. I slid my arms through a zip-up jacket and managed to have it closed by the time he got to the third-floor landing.

"Vic! Good to see you in one piece." He looked me over critically. "You don't seem nearly as battered as I figured from the news reports. How you feeling?"

"Better than I did a few days ago. My head's clear, that's the main thing."

He held out a bunch of late-summer flowers picked from his own tiny, carefully tended plot. I got him to carry them into the kitchen and fill a pitcher for me. Something about the bright gold daisies on the table suddenly gave me an enormous appetite. I wanted pancakes, eggs, bacon, a whole farmer's breakfast.

Even though he'd eaten several hours ago, Robin obligingly agreed to go to the corner diner with me. He even overcame his own nausea to dress my hands for me. I thought with my palms padded I could manage a bra, but the hooks still were too much for me. It was one thing to get my hands dressed, another to need help with a bra. I put on an outsize sweatshirt and headed downstairs without one.

Mr. Contreras and the dog were coming in the front door as we left. He looked Robin over with critical jealousy. Peppy jumped up on me and started licking my face. I played with her ears and introduced the two of them to Robin.

"Where you off to, doll?"

"Breakfast. I haven't had a proper meal since Monday night."

"I told you yesterday you was looking peaked. The princess and me would have brought you breakfast if you'd asked, saved you a trip out. I only didn't come up because I figured you was still asleep."

"I need the exercise," I said. "Robin here will make sure I don't overdo it."

"Well, you call me if you need help. You be sure and give him my number, doll. You pass out or something in the restaurant, I don't want to see it in the papers first."

I gave him my solemn word that he would have the honor of providing me smelling salts if needed. He scowled at us but went on inside with Peppy.

"Who is he?" Robin demanded when we were out of earshot. "Your grandfather?"

"He's just my downstairs neighbor. He's retired and I'm his hobby."

"Why's he so rattled about you going out to eat?"

"It's not breakfast—it's breakfast with you. If he was twenty years younger, he'd be beating up any guy who came visiting me. It's tiresome, but he's essentially so good-hearted I can't bring myself to punch him down."

The four blocks to the Belmont Diner wore me out. I've been through convalescence before. I know the early part is slow and then your strength comes back pretty fast, but it still was frustrating. I had to work to get the tension in my stomach to subside.

Most of the waitresses at the diner know me—I probably catch at least one meal a week there and sometimes more. They'd all read about my misadventures and crowded around the table to find out how I was doing and who the talent I'd come in with was. Barbara, whose section I was in, shooed the others away when they started offering juice and rolls. When I ordered a cheese omelet, potatoes, bacon, toast, and a side of fruit with yogurt, she shook her head.

"You're not going to eat all that, Vic—it's twice what you get when you've just run five miles."

I insisted, but she was right. I got through half the omelet and the potatoes but couldn't even make a pro forma effort with the fruit. My stomach strained uncomfortably; all I felt up to was napping, but I forced myself to talk a little shop with Robin.

"You know anything about the fire at the Prairie Shores? What kind of accelerant they used, whether things looked the same as at the Indiana Arms?"

He shook his head. "The Indiana Arms job was more sophisticated because there were people on the premises. It looks as though they put a fuse in the wires in the night man's quarters when they'd gotten him off to the track. They had a trailer going down to a stock of paraffin in the basement and a timer so they didn't have to be anywhere near the place. The fire you were in they didn't have to be that careful—they just dumped gasoline in the kitchen and at the doors to the basement, set the thing off, and took off." He looked at me soberly. "You were lucky, V.I. *Damned* lucky."

"That's what gets the job done. Napoleon wanted lucky generals, not theoretical whizzes." It gets me edgy when people lecture me on a narrow escape. I *had* been lucky, but all the luck in the world wouldn't have helped if I didn't also keep myself in top physical and mental shape. Why didn't my skill count for anything?

"Yeah, but he was beaten in a big way in the end. . . . Do you have any idea who did this to you? My management is concerned that it came out of your investigation into the Indiana Arms—that you're sitting on information you haven't shared with us."

I tried to keep my temper even. "I don't know who did it. It's possible it's connected to your claim, but the only person who can tell me is lying doggo. If I had that kind of information, I wouldn't be so unprofessional as to keep it to myself."

He hesitated, toying with the salt shaker. "I'm just wondering—my boss and I were talking yesterday—we work with a lot of investigators. Maybe we should bring someone else in on the Seligman case."

I sat stiffly in my booth. "I realize I don't have the results you want, but I've done the financial checks and a pretty good rundown on the organization. If you want someone else to talk to the night

watchman or explore what Seligman's children may have been doing, that's your call, of course."

"It's not your competence, Vic, but—well, this assault on you
just has people questioning your judgment."

I tried to relax. "I went down there because I got an SOS from
my aunt. Since she has a strong proclivity for alcoholic histrionics I
wanted to see her myself first rather than share that part of my
family life with outsiders. If I'd had any serious inkling of danger, I
would have handled things differently. But I am really, really fed up
with being chewed out by everyone from doctors to the police to you
for saving her and escaping from danger with my own life intact."

By the time I finished I was panting. I leaned back in my chair
with my eyes shut, trying to head off the incipient pain in my head.

"Vic, I'm sorry. I'm glad you're alive. You've been doing a mar-
velous job. But we wonder whether someone else could bring a different perspective. Just the fact that your aunt *is* involved may be
affecting your detachment."

"That's your right," I repeated stiffly. "But if you bring someone
else in, I will not work in a subordinate capacity to him. Or her. I'll
be glad to share my notes and my ideas, but I won't continue working for Ajax."

"Well, maybe we don't have to hire someone else at this point.
There is a city Bomb and Arson Squad . . ." Robin offered tentatively.

"Who wouldn't even look at the Indiana Arms for you. Don't
put your faith in them just because I've gotten some licks—it'd take
more than that to get Roland Montgomery to look at the case seriously. He's even spinning a little story about me setting the fires
myself."

Robin looked startled. "You're joking!"

When I told him about my meeting yesterday with Montgomery, he made a sour face. "What the hell is with that guy? He hates
outsiders horning in on arson inquiries—I know—we've clashed before—but this is outrageous even for him."

His mention of outsiders brought the elusive memory of a face at
the fire swimming back to my mind, but I couldn't place it. "You
don't know who called in the alarm, do you? If the fire trucks hadn't
been there, I don't think my aunt would have made it out."

Robin shook his head again. "I have pals in the fire department who let me see everything they have on both fires, but the call to 911 was anonymous."

I ran my fork around in the congealed grease on my plate, trying to come up with questions I should ask about the fire. Did the police have a list of the onlookers, for example, or had anything been left behind at the site that might point to the arsonist?

My heart wasn't in it, though. The questioning of my professional judgment wounded me as few other criticisms could. At the same time I saw myself in a shameful light, clattering off to the Prairie Shores Hotel like a giant elephant thundering through the veldt. If I'd called the cops—of course, I had called Furey. Still, a full police battalion might have saved both Elena and me a knock on the head. But the truth was, if it happened again tonight, I would do it the same way all over again. I couldn't expose Elena to the ribald indifference of the police. I have to solve my private problems privately. I don't even know if it's a strength or weakness. It just is.

I paid my bill and we set off silently for my apartment, neither of us pretending the conversation hadn't occurred. Outside my building Robin played with the bandages on my right hand, choosing his words.

"Vic, I think we'll let the Seligman investigation go on the back burner for a few days. We'll get someone to talk to the night watchman in more depth, but we won't ask him to take over the case. Next week, when you're feeling better, we'll see what he's turned up and you can decide how you feel about going ahead with the rest of it."

That seemed fair to me. It didn't stop me feeling depressed as I slowly hiked upstairs, but it did ease the tight knot between my shoulder blades.

As I was unlocking my door Mr. Contreras and the dog came bounding upstairs. When they reached the second landing I could hear him scolding her gently—he couldn't see where he was going; did she have to keep racing back and forth under his feet? Trip him up and then where would she be with me gone all the time. I felt the knot come back to my neck and faced them without a welcoming smile.

Mr. Contreras was hidden behind a giant parcel wrapped in the striped paper florists use. "This came while you was out, doll," he panted. "I thought I might as well accept it for you so they didn't bring it by when you was asleep or something."

"Thanks," I said with what politeness I could muster—I just wanted to go into my own cave and hibernate. Alone.

"It's okay, doll, I'm happy to help. What happened to your friend? He leave you high and dry?" He set the parcel down gently and wiped his forehead.

"He knew I wanted to rest," I said pointedly.

"Sure, cookie, sure. I understand. You want some time by yourself. You need me to do anything for you?"

I was about to utter a firm denial when I thought of the letter I wanted to express to my uncle Peter. I needed to sleep so badly I couldn't get to the post office before their early Saturday closing.

Mr. Contreras was more than pleased to mail it for me. He was ecstatic that I'd chosen him for the errand. He was so thrilled I wished I'd fought back my fatigue and taken the damned thing myself.

When he bustled off with the letter—"Don't give me no money now, doll, I'll settle with you later"—I dragged the flowers inside. It was a magnificent bouquet, reds and golds and purples so exotic I hadn't seen them before. They were arranged in a handsome wooden bowl lined with plastic. I fished around among the foliage for a card.

"Glad you're out of the hospital," ran the round unformed writing of the florist. "Next time try to pick quieter work."

It was signed "R.M." I was so tired I didn't even want to try to decide if it was a good-natured gibe or a warning. I locked all the bolts, turned off both phones, and stumbled into bed.

# 30

# Preparing for the High Jump

**W**hen I got up on Sunday I knew I'd turned the critical corner toward recovery. I wasn't back to my full strength, but I felt clear-headed and energetic. The lingering depression from my breakfast with Robin resolved itself to a manageable problem—my ability to handle the Seligman investigation was in doubt, not my entire career and personality. Even my hands were better. I didn't take off the gauze, but I could do simple household chores without feeling that the skin was splitting open to the bone.

The early detective gets the worm. Although it was unlikely that anyone would come into the Alma Mejicana offices at all on Sunday, they were less likely to do so first thing in the morning.

Before taking off I went into the living room to do a modified version of my exercises—I wasn't ready to start running yet, but I needed to keep limber. Ralph MacDonald's flowers dominated the room. I'd forgotten them. As I stretched my quads and tightened my glutes, I eyed the tropical rain forest balefully. Whether meant as a threat or a humorous compliment, they were overwhelming, too big a gesture from a man who scarcely knew me.

When I finished my leg lifts—twenty-five with each leg instead of my usual hundred left me breathless—I scrambled into my jeans and a sweatshirt. Straining, I carried the flowers down to my car. I drove over to Broadway and picked up a bagel, an apple, and some milk at one of the delis.

My attempts to eat and drive at the same time showed the state of my healing—two-handed, the steering wheel was manageable. With one hand my palms started smarting and my wrist ached. I pulled over at the corner of Diversey and Pine Grove to eat. The tropical flowers stained the car with their heavy scent, making it hard to eat without queasiness. I rolled the window all the way down, but the smell was still heady. Finally I gulped down the milk and started south without finishing the bagel.

Sunday morning is the best time to drive in Chicago, because there isn't any traffic out. I made the nine miles to Michael Reese in fifteen minutes without pushing the speed limit.

Getting the massive bouquet up to the fourth floor taxed my healing palms and shoulders almost beyond endurance. When I got off the elevator a sympathetic orderly offered to take it from me.

"These are gorgeous. What room you want them in?"

I gave him Elena's room number. He carried the pot as easily as if it were a football—as easily as I could have done a week ago. I followed him down the hall and into Elena's room. A woman about my own age in a yellow nylon gown was sitting in Elena's bed reading the *Tribune*.

My jaw dropped slightly, the way it does when you're taken unawares. "My aunt," I said foolishly. "She was here on Friday."

"Maybe she checked out," the orderly suggested.

"She wasn't in very good shape. Maybe they moved her." I scurried back to the nursing station.

A middle-aged woman was making elaborate notes in a chart. I tried interrupting but she held up a warning hand and continued writing.

Finally she looked at me. "Yes?"

"I'm V. I. Warshawski," I said. "My aunt, Elena Warshawski, was here—she'd been hit on the head and was unconscious for a day or so. Did they move her or what?"

The nurse shook her head majestically. "She left yesterday."

"Left?" I echoed, staggered. "But—they told me she was in bad shape, that she ought to have a month or so of convalescent care. How could they just let her go?"

"They didn't. She took off on her own. Stole the clothes belonging to the lady she shared a room with and disappeared."

My head started spinning again. I gripped the countertop to

steady myself. "When did this happen? Why didn't someone call me?"

The nurse disclaimed all knowledge of the particulars. "The hospital called whoever was listed on her forms as next of kin. They may not have felt you needed to know."

"I am her next of kin." Maybe she'd given Peter's name, though —I shouldn't push my rights as her nearest and dearest too hard. "Can you tell me when she took off?"

She snapped her pencil down in exasperation. "Ask the police. They sent an officer over yesterday afternoon. He was pretty annoyed and got all the details."

I was close to screaming from frustration and confusion. "Give me the guy's name and I'll talk to him with pleasure."

She sighed audibly and went into the records room behind the counter. The orderly had been standing behind me all this time holding the flowers.

"You want to take these, miss?" he asked while I waited.

"Oh, give them to the person who's been here longest without any visitors," I said shortly.

The nurse came back out with a file. "Michael Furey, detective," she read without looking up. She went back to the chart she'd been working on when I interrupted. The interview was clearly over.

Back in my car my arms trembled—carrying Ralph MacDonald's flowers in had overstrained them. So Elena'd done another bunk. Should I care? The police knew about it. Presumably they'd keep an eye out for her. I had better things to do.

Instead of driving over to the Alma Mejicana offices on south Ashland, I took the Chevy back to the Prairie Shores Hotel. It started groaning again as I turned onto Indiana.

"You think *you* feel bad," I grumbled. "I don't want to be here, either. And my hands hurt."

The palms were sore under my mitts. They throbbed against the hard steering wheel. Next car I got would have power steering.

The Prairie Shores made a fitting neighbor now for the Indiana Arms. The two blackened shells leered at each other across the street. Not even Elena could be hiding out in one of them. But there were other abandoned buildings on the block—an old warehouse, a boarded-up school, the remains of a nursing home. She could be in any of them. I didn't have the energy to hunt through them all. Let the police do it.

I headed down Cermak at fifty, weaving in and out of traffic, sliding through red lights. I was just plain pissed. What kind of cute little game was she playing, anyway? And how much time did I have to spend playing it with her? She'd gotten someone rattled enough to try to kill her. And instead of talking to me about it she was skulking around town thinking she was a smart enough drunk to keep out of his way. Or her way, I amended conscientiously.

I turned left on Halsted in front of a madly honking, braking semi. That cooled me down pretty fast. The worst thing in the world to do with a car is use it when you're angry. Tony had told me that, as close to angry himself as he ever got, when he took my keys away from me for a month. I'd been seventeen and it was the worst punishment I'd ever endured. It should have cured me of this kind of outburst.

I kept up a sober, alert pace the three miles to the Amphitheater. Alma Mejicana's offices were behind it on Ashland. Tony used to take me to horse and dog shows there, but it had been a good twenty-five years since I'd been in that part of town. I'd forgotten the maze of dead-end streets between Ashland and Halsted. Even having to double back to Thirty-ninth and make my way on the main streets brought me to the contracting company in twenty minutes.

I drove slowly past their drab brick building. The door was padlocked shut. The high-set dirty windows reflected the gray morning air—no lights were on behind them. I made a careful circuit down the alley behind the building. The rear metal doors had a heavy chain slung through their handles clamped together with a businesslike American Master padlock.

I drove on through the alley and went up Ashland again to Forty-fourth. I left the Chevy at the corner, across from a handkerchief park where an old man was walking a lethargic terrier. Neither of them paid any attention to me. I walked down the alley with my head up, purposeful, I belonged there. When a Dumpster lid clattered shut behind a nearby gate, I didn't jump, at least not very high.

With an American Master you need either an acetylene torch, a high-quality saw, or the key. I didn't have any of those. I studied the chain regretfully. It was bigger than me too. After a complete circuit of the building I didn't think I could get to the windows without a ladder. That left the roof, which also meant coming back and doing it at night.

Down the alley a telephone pole stood close enough to a building that I could shinny up and make my way across to Alma Mejicana. I stretched my arms up against it. The first spikes were about four feet out of reach. Still, some kind of footstool should make the climb possible.

Three flat-topped cubes of varying height lay between the pole and my target. I paced the distance. I'd only have to manage five feet at the widest jump. Even in my feeble state I ought to be able to do that in the dark.

I looked for a landmark that would let me know I'd reached Alma. The buildings facing the alley were lined with undifferentiated high wood fencing, but a garage had been built into the wall catty-corner to the contractor. I should be able to spot that with my flashlight.

The old man and the terrier were sitting on a bench reading the morning paper when I got back to the Chevy. Neither of them looked up even when I slammed the car door shut. I headed over to the Ryan at a brisk clip. The Chevy started its hideous grinding when I pushed it to sixty on the expressway but quieted down at forty. I made it home in time to catch the Bears' opening kickoff against the unbeaten Bills. Like all good Chicagoans, I turned the TV sound off and caught the radio commentary—we like Dick Butkus's knowledge and his partisanship.

With the Bears cruising at halftime, I looked at the Sunday papers. I was flipping idly through the *Star*'s "Chicago Beat" section when the Seligman name jumped up at me. The company offices on Montrose had been burgled. Mrs. Rita Donnelly, fifty-seven, a thirty-year employee, had been killed.

Behind me Jim Hart and Butkus were carrying on about the fine points of Dan Hampton's first-half play. I switched the radio off and read the story slowly.

The *Star* had only given it five inches. I went through the *Tribune* and the *Sun-Times* and finally found enough detail to let me know the time the police thought it had happened—late Friday afternoon—the mailman's discovery of her body on Saturday when he went in through the unlocked front door with a registered letter, and Mr. Seligman's shock. Mrs. Donnelly had left two daughters, Shannon Casey (thirty-two) and Star Wentzel (twenty-nine), both married, and three grandchildren. Mass would be at St. Inanna's parish Tuesday afternoon; visitation at the Callahan Funeral Home Monday evening. In lieu of flowers money should be sent to the St. Inanna scholarship fund.

The Bears and Bills were stacked in a violent heap on the silent TV screen—the second half had started without me. I switched off the set and went to the window to look out. It could have been random violence—money came into the office. Someone knew that, staked it out, killed her before she could get to the bank.

"Just don't forget that's possible," I lectured myself out loud. "Don't get so wound up in your favorite theories that you ignore the amount of random ugly violence in this town." How could it have been random, though, with Cerise dead, the attack on Elena and me, the two fires. It all connected someplace. The murderer had ransacked the files, but no money had been taken, either from the office or from Mrs. Donnelly's own bag.

Mrs. Donnelly's death made me do something I had felt too churlish to do earlier—call Furey to see what he knew about Elena.

He sounded pleased enough to hear from me, although I could tell by the background noise I'd interrupted a party. "You got us all kind of worried, Vic. You doing okay?"

"I was feeling better until I went to the hospital this morning to visit my aunt. They told me you'd come around to talk to her and that they gave you all the details."

"Yeah. I tried calling you a few times but just got your answering service. I was hoping you might have some idea where she went. She's our only real lead on Wednesday's fire."

"Besides me." I told him about Montgomery's theory.

"Oh, Monty—he gets a little off balance sometimes. Don't pay any attention to him. What about your aunt? I checked that hotel on Kenmore, but she hasn't been back there since she skipped ten days ago."

I suggested the abandoned buildings on the Near South Side and he promised to get a patrol unit to check them out. The pals had all come over to watch the game—he kind of wanted to get back to it, but he'd talk to me later in the week.

The phone rang as soon as I'd hung up. It was my uncle Peter, frothing because of my letter: What did I think he was, some cretin that he'd expose his children to someone like Elena?

"It's okay, Peter—she's vanished. No one's going to ask anything of you." Actually I was planning on calling Reese tomorrow to make sure they had his name and address as Elena's financial guarantor, but I didn't see it would help him any to learn that this afternoon.

The news didn't mollify him. "Just get this through your head, Vic—if I'd wanted to stay tied to a bunch of losers, I wouldn't have moved away from Chicago. If that offends you, I'm sorry, but I want more for my children than Tony wanted for you."

I was about to launch a full-scale counterattack on how Tony wouldn't have wanted sleaze for me, but even as I started it I realized the futility of saying anything. Peter and I had been around this track together a good many times. Neither of us was going to change. I hung up without saying good-bye.

I went back to the window and looked down at the drab bungalows facing my building. Maybe Tony would have wanted a mansion in Winnetka for me, but he'd only known bungalows and walk-ups —he wouldn't think they were any disgrace for me.

My fight with Peter had exhausted me more than carrying around that tropical rain forest had this morning. If I wanted to prance around the rooftops tonight, I needed some rest. I switched off the phones and fell into my bed.

# 31

# House Calls

It was six when I woke up again. My shoulder muscles had stiffened from the aftermath of carrying Ralph MacDonald's flowers up to Elena. I wanted to soak them under a hot shower. That was impossible with my gauze mitts. Anyway, I needed to keep my hands protected for my upcoming labors.

Although I'd had a little peanut butter while watching the Bears, I hadn't eaten a proper meal yet today. I still didn't have any real food in the house. I'd planned to ask Robin to drive me to the store yesterday, but after his squib about taking me off the case it had gone out of my mind. I didn't think I could do my Santa Claus imitation without dinner.

I pulled on the top to my long underwear and put a black cotton sweater on over that. It might be cool on the rooftops and I didn't want anything as bulky—or as visible—as a jacket. Jeans and my black basketball high-tops completed the ensemble that the well-dressed burglar was wearing this year. I also needed some kind of dark cap or scarf to keep light from reflecting from my face or hair. I rummaged through my drawers and came up with a soft black linen square Eileen Mallory had given me last Christmas. I didn't think the green and blue design woven into it would show up at night.

If I'm carrying my gun I usually wear a shoulder holster. Since I wanted to bring a few tools with me tonight, I dug out an old police-style belt with a holster and holes for slinging handcuffs or a truncheon.

My best flashlight was buried in the Prairie Shores rubble, but I had another one someplace. After rooting through the dining-room cupboard and the hall closet, I found it at the back of the refrigerator top. Although a little greasy to the touch, its battery still worked. I strung some twine through the hook on its end and tied it to my belt. A small hammer, a screwdriver, and a dark hand towel completed my supplies. I used to have a set of picklocks given to me by a grateful client in my PD days, but the police had confiscated those several years ago. I picked up my rolling footstool from behind the refrigerator and headed out.

I managed to slink out of the apartment without rousing Mr. Contreras, Peppy, or even Vinnie the banker. The fall twilight had set in, purply-gray and changing quickly to black. No passerby could make out my equipment belt. I stuck it in the Chevy's trunk with the footstool and drove the four blocks to the Belmont Diner for dinner. After a bowl of hearty cabbage soup and a plate of roast chicken with mashed potatoes, I felt too stuffed to move.

Gluttony is a terrible enemy of the private detective. I'd have to wait a good hour before starting my trek, maybe even longer. You're disgusting, I admonished myself privately as I paid the bill. Peter Wimsey and Philip Marlowe never had this kind of problem.

Back in the Chevy I drummed my fingers on the steering wheel. If I returned to my apartment, the chances were good I'd run into the old man. If his jealous sixth sense warned him I was setting out on an adventure, I might not be able to get away without him. I didn't want to go to a movie. I didn't want to sit in my office with a novel.

I put the car into gear and went north, up to Estes. The Chevy seemed to be behaving itself again—maybe I'd been imagining the groan in its engine.

It was only eight when I got to Saul Seligman's house, not too late for visiting even an old man. I could see a dim glow of light behind the heavily draped windows. A late-model Chrysler stood immediately in front of the house. I parked just behind it and went up the walk to ring the bell.

After a long wait the locks turned back. Seligman's elder daughter, Barbara Feldman, answered the door. She was close to fifty, well groomed without being fashionable, her reddish hair dyed and carefully set, her sweater and slacks tailored but comfortable.

She looked at me vaguely, not remembering me from the visit I'd paid to her Northbrook home.

"I'm V. I. Warshawski," I said loudly enough to penetrate the glass. "The private investigator who came to see you last week about the fire at the Indiana Arms."

Mrs. Feldman cracked the door so she could speak without shouting back at me. "My father isn't well this evening. He's not up to seeing anyone."

I nodded sympathetically. "Mrs. Donnelly's death must have upset him terribly. That's why I've come. If he's really ill I won't stay long, but it's possible he knows something that would help me get a line on her killer."

She frowned. "The police have already been here. He doesn't know anything."

"They may not have known the right questions to ask. I think I do."

She thought it over, sucking on her upper lip, then shut the door. At least she didn't rebolt the myriad locks. While I waited for her to come back I did some gentle quad stretches. I didn't want to face a five-foot jump and miss because I hadn't loosened up. A couple passing by with a small dog on a leash eyed me curiously but didn't say anything.

Mrs. Feldman came back after about five minutes. "My father says you can't help, that all you do is bring trouble. He thinks you caused Auntie Rita's death."

There's always something unsettling about a grown person using childhood names to discuss friends and relations—as if the world around her is so kaleidoscoped that Auntie Rita or Mummy or Daddy means the same thing to everyone listening to her.

"No," I said patiently, "I didn't do that. It's possible, though, that Mrs. Donnelly knew something the person who torched your father's hotel didn't want disclosed. She may not even have known it was a terrible secret. If I talk to Mr. Seligman, maybe we can find out what they'd discussed the last time they were together. That might give me a lead on why she was killed. And that can help us figure out who killed her."

Mrs. Donnelly had known something. I was sure of that. I hadn't thought it had anything to do with the arson—more about her children, it had seemed, in some way that had made me wonder vaguely if Mr. Seligman might have been their father. I hadn't thought it concerned either me or Ajax, but now it seemed I'd been mistaken.

Mrs. Feldman trundled back into the recesses of the house with my message. I felt a little absurd communicating this way, as though she were the wall and I was Thisbe. After a shorter wait she returned to tell me her father would see me.

"He says you're like one of the plagues and if he doesn't talk to you now, you'll just hound him until he does. I don't think he should, but he never listens to me anyway."

I followed her into the stale hallway. We went down to the end of the passage into the kitchen, a room even more cramped and dingy than the musty living room where I had seen the old man before. He was huddled at the Formica table in a shabby plaid dressing gown, a mug of tea in front of him. Under the dim ceiling bulb his skin looked like a moldy orange. He kept his eyes on the tea when we came in, stirring it relentlessly.

"I'm sorry to bother you, Mr. Seligman," I began, but he interrupted me with a snarl.

"The hell with that. If you were sorry to bother me, intrude on me, make my life miserable, why do you keep coming around?" He didn't lift his eyes from the mug.

I sat down across from him, banging my shin against the refrigerator as I pulled one of the grimy chairs away from the table. "I suppose it does look as though I'm the one assaulting your life, since I'm the only stranger you see. But someone out there doesn't like Seligman Property Management. They torched the Indiana Arms and they killed Mrs. Donnelly. I'd kind of like to see they get stopped before they do anything else, such as come after you."

"I just want to stop you coming after me," he muttered sullenly.

I held up my gauze mitts and spoke harshly. "Someone tried to do that last Tuesday, tried to burn me to death so I'd never go after anyone again. Was that your idea?"

He finally looked up at me. "Anyone can wrap bandages around their hands." The words were truculent but he couldn't hide the little hiss of breath when he saw the gauze.

I unwrapped the left hand without speaking. Now that the palm was healing it looked worse than before, yellow pustules surrounding the angry red line down the middle. He glanced at it, then looked away, scowling. He couldn't keep his eyes from sliding back to it. Mrs. Feldman made an uneasy noise in the background but didn't speak. Finally I put the palm down on my lap.

"After I came by here on Tuesday did you *see* Mrs. Donnelly or just talk to her on the phone?"

When Mr. Seligman hesitated his daughter answered. "She came by most evenings, didn't she, Pop? Now that you've stopped going into the office every day."

"So she came by after I was here? And what did you talk about?"

"My business. Which is none of your business, young lady."

"When you told her I'd asked for a photograph, why did it upset her?" I kept my body completely still, my voice monotonous.

"If you know so much about it why are you asking me?" He muttered the snipe to his tea mug.

"Was it your children or her children she was worried about? Or is that the same thing?"

Behind me Mrs. Feldman gasped. "What are you trying to say? What's wrong with you, anyway, to come around badgering him when he's had such a shock."

I ignored her. "How many daughters do you have, Mr. Seligman?"

I was way off target. I could tell by his look of outraged disgust. "I'm just glad Fanny didn't have to live to hear this kind of garbage in her own kitchen."

"So why did it bother her that you gave me the picture?"

"I don't know." It was a sudden, frustrated explosion. "She came by, we talked, I told her you'd been around, hounding me, still not letting me have my money, but you wanted a picture of Barbara and Connie. Then, when I told her I let you have the one taken at our fortieth anniversary, Fanny's and mine, she got all excited. She wanted to know which picture it was. Of course I only gave you one I had a copy of, I don't expect someone like you to return something sentimental, that's why I picked that one. I told her all that and she started carrying on about how I was desecrating Fanny's memory letting you have something from such a personal time."

By the time he finished his orangey cheeks were spotted with red and he was panting. "Now are you happy? Can you leave me in peace?"

"I think so. Probably. When is the service for Mrs. Donnelly? Tuesday afternoon?"

"Don't you go barging in destroying her funeral. I still think it's all because of those questions of yours she's dead."

I met his angry glare sadly. I had an uneasy feeling he was right. I got to my feet, wadding the discarded gauze from my left hand into a tight ball.

"I'll give you back your picture, Mr. Seligman, but it won't be for a few more days. I won't come back here again, but I would like to get into your office. Can you arrange that for me?"

"You want the keys? Or you want to just break in like those hoodlums that killed Rita?"

I raised my eyebrows. "I didn't read about a break-in. I thought the door was open for normal business and they walked in."

"Well, it's locked now and you can't have the keys. You'll just have to do your grave robbing someplace else."

Fatigue was starting to hit me. I didn't have any more energy to give to arguing with him. I stuffed the wadded gauze into my jeans pocket and turned without speaking.

Mrs. Feldman bustled me down the hall. "I hope you can leave him alone now. I shouldn't have let you in in the first place, but he's never listened to me. If my sister'd been here—she looks just like Mother. Don't come back again. Not unless you have his check for the Indiana Arms. It's just a fire to you, but it meant something special to him."

I started to say something about my own warm and wonderful character but broke it off—she wouldn't care. I'd barely stepped across the threshold when she began snapping the locks shut.

# 32

# A Leap in the Dark

I didn't feel like an overstuffed goose anymore, that was one good thing. At the same time, my bravado had cost me the dressing to my left hand. I tested it gingerly against the steering wheel. The blisters rolled and squished a bit.

I got out and opened the trunk and pulled out the towel I'd stuck in my equipment belt. I wrapped it around my left hand, using my teeth to hold it in place while I tucked the ends inside. It made a slippery glove, but I could manage driving now.

As I drove across Touhy to the Edens, I was so tired and depressed that I wondered if I should abandon my project at Alma Mejicana. Often when I feel like quitting I hear my mother's voice in my head, exhorting me. Her fierce energy was tireless—the worst thing I could ever do in her eyes was to give up. Tonight, though, I heard no echoes in my head. I was alone in the dark city with my sore palms and bruised shoulders.

If you're going to sink into self-pity, go home to bed, I scolded myself. Otherwise, your mission is bound to fail. For acrobatic derring-do you need to be at the peak of self-confidence, not down in a well.

I didn't want to dwell on the scene in Seligman's musty kitchen, but I forced myself at least to think about what he'd told me. Rita Donnelly had been sitting on something. I should have probed her harder about her daughters at the time, but it had seemed so purely personal. If it wasn't their paternity she'd been hiding, what was it about them she didn't want people to know?

The light at McCormick stayed red so long I was only roused from my musings by the violent honking behind me. Startled, I leapt forward through the intersection, barely clearing it on the yellow and getting a finger from an irate driver accelerating past me.

Going sixty on the Edens, I found managing the steering so difficult with my towel-wrapped hand that I couldn't think about anything except the car and the traffic. I moved into the right-hand lane and slowed to fifty. As I maneuvered past the construction zone at Roosevelt, the damned engine started grinding again. I had to slow to forty before the noise subsided.

I drove straight to Ashland without mishap and once more circled the Alma Mejicana building through the alley. No lights showed. This time I parked on Forty-fifth near the mouth of the alley in case I needed to get to my car quickly.

I tied Eileen's scarf around my head and pulled the equipment belt from the trunk to strap around my waist. With the weight I'd lost recently it hung a little low; the flashlight and hammer banged unpleasantly into my thighs when I walked. I hugged the footstool close to my chest. It was an unpleasant sign of my weakened state that a weight I would normally find negligible slowed me down tonight.

Even though the night air was pleasantly cool the streets were empty. Most of the buildings on the east side of the alley were commercial; the residents behind the fence on the west side probably hung out on the street behind.

It was just after nine-thirty when I reached the telephone pole down the alley from Alma Mejicana. I looked up at it dubiously in the starlight. Behind their wrappings my palms tingled. I undid the towel on my left hand and stuck it in my waistband at the small of my back. On the footstool my outstretched fingertips were just shy of the first set of spikes. I planted my feet firmly on the stool, bent my knees, and jumped.

The first time I was too scared about slicing open my left palm and didn't hang on. The clatter I made knocking the footstool across the alley woke the neighborhood dogs. I lay in the shadow of the fence, rubbing my thigh where the hammer had dug in when I crashed, waiting for angry householders to appear.

When no one came I picked up the rolling stair and carried it back to the pole. The dogs were thoroughly roused now; I could hear various shouts at them to shut up. Their unified chorus apparently made the owners think they were barking at each other.

Back on top of my stool I took some diaphragm breaths, leaning my head against the pole. The pole is an extension of my arms. It welcomes me as a sister. It will not fight me as an intruder.

I repeated this litany a few times, bent my knees, and jumped without waiting to think it out. This time I grabbed hold of the spikes and wrapped my thighs around the pole, ignoring the sharp bite of the hammer and the twinge in my shoulder blades. I moved fast, still not thinking about my hands, shinnying up the rough wood until I could reach the second row of spikes and hoist myself up standing.

Once I'd done that it was easy to climb the remaining ten feet so I was level with the building top. When I stepped onto the roof I felt exhilarated with my achievement, so much so that pain and fatigue lay shielded behind a wall in my head. I ran lightly across the rooftop, judged the three-foot gap, and jumped it easily. The next break was wider, and upward, but confidence was now carrying me in an easy tide. I turned off my mind and made the jump, my left foot scraping the side of the wall but the right landing clear on the asphalt.

I went to the edge facing the alley and cautiously shone my flash. My garage marker lay in front of the next building; Alma Mejicana was the one beyond that. The jump this time was the five-footer, but downward. The building where I landed was close enough to my target that they almost shared a common wall.

I stepped across and explored the surface. Sure enough, a trapdoor lay behind the vent pipes. I pried at it gently with the claw end of the hammer. As I'd hoped, they didn't bother locking it; it came up heavily. I laid my towel on the asphalt behind it and hoisted it slowly open, my shoulders sending out little white-hot sparks of pain that I tried to ignore. I had to strain to get the door to a balance point and then drop it softly on the towel beneath.

I lay down next to it, catching my breath and making sure no alarms sounded. The moon was in its dark phase. The stars were chips of cold glass in the black sky. Despite my exertions and my long underwear, I shivered.

Before the night demons could approach me I sat up and shone my flashlight into the building. Opening the trap had released a set of hanging stairs. I climbed softly down in my black high-tops. I was in a small attic where the heating and cooling apparatus was set up. Some rough stairs, wide enough to handle equipment, led to the main part of the building.

Even though the streets were empty I didn't want to risk rousing someone by turning on the building lights. Stuffing the scarf in my back pocket I started exploring the interior. A frugal use of my flashlight showed that the two floors of the building had been divided into a series of offices. For the most part they were bare of furniture. One was set up with a metal desk and an Apollo computer.

On the ground floor Schmidt and Martinez had separate offices equipped with a certain degree of luxury. Schmidt liked the sleek Milan style while Martinez favored a heavier baroque Spanish look. Because the ground-floor rooms were windowless, I could turn on their office lights and explore to my heart's content.

I whistled a little under my breath as I opened and shut desk drawers and filing cabinets. I didn't have time to go through all their papers. I just wanted some obvious clue left out on a desktop, something like "Kill V. I. Warshawski and her aunt Elena tonight by torching the Prairie Shores Hotel."

Someplace they should have a big chart showing all of Alma Mejicana's projects. Even after going through the premises twice I didn't find any obvious sign of work in progress. It could be that it was all stored on the Apollo, but that meant any time someone wanted to check their commitments to see if they could bid on a new job, they'd have to crank up the machine and get a printout.

Maybe they were such a small operation they could work on only one project at a time. If that was so, how had they been able to get part of the Ryan contract? Even if they were leasing equipment from Wunsch and Grasso, they couldn't get involved in projects that size without substantial resources.

I made a face and started hunting for ledgers. Maybe all the bookkeeping was done on the computer upstairs, but they still had to have some kind of hard copy of their transactions. Anyway, I didn't believe they used that machine: the room it was in was completely empty except for the metal desk it sat on—it held none of the papers and manuals you expect to find around a machine in active use.

It was midnight when I finally located the books in the bottom drawer of a filing cabinet. By then my eyelids had started to swell with fatigue. One thing I hadn't thought to bring was a flask of coffee, but I found an electric machine and a can of Mexican coffee in the storeroom and recklessly helped myself to a pot. I carried the ledgers into Luis's office and sat at his glossy black desk with my coffee. It was the heat more than the caffeine that kept me going.

The books were perfectly straightforward. Payments were received from various project owners, such as the U.S. government in the case of the Dan Ryan, and payments were made for heat, cement, and other necessities of contracting life. But the biggest consistent payees were not suppliers. They were Wunsch and Grasso and Farmworks, Inc.

I shut my swollen eyes, trying to remember why I knew that name. When I woke up it was three o'clock. My neck was stiff from where I'd slumped over in Luis's chair and my heart raced uncomfortably—I could have slept until morning and been surprised in here by the Alma Mejicana employees.

When I glanced back down at the ledgers, though, I remembered Farmworks, Inc. perfectly—that was the bizarre name I'd seen on the time sheets at the Rapelec site the night Cerise was found dead there. I rifled through Luis's desk drawers for a pad of paper. Not finding any, I ripped a blank sheet from the back of the ledger and jotted some of the numbers down. I had an inkling of what they meant, but with morning near I didn't have time to think, just to copy and get going.

I put the ledgers back in the drawer where I'd found them, cleaned the coffeepot, and tiptoed back upstairs to shut the trapdoor to the roof, pulling my towel in first. The front door could be unlocked from the inside. I wouldn't be able to lock it again, but they would just think they'd forgotten to shut it properly on Friday night.

Even if they suspected a break-in, I hadn't left any personal signs behind. Anyway, I was far too beat to go back the way I'd come.

I undid the bolts and stepped out onto Ashland. I was about ten feet from the door when the alarms went. I'd been going to circle through the alley for my footstool, but this seemed like a good time to buy a new one. I moved up the street at a brisk walk—never let anyone see you running when an alarm sounds.

A car heading up Ashland to Forty-fifth slowed. I fished in my back pocket for the scarf—I should have put it on before I left the building. It wasn't there. I dug in my jacket pockets, my waistband, my belt, but somewhere in the recesses of Alma Mejicana I'd lost it.

My hands trembled and my legs turned rubbery. I made myself walk naturally. If the police or Luis Schmidt found it, who was going to know it was mine? Bobby Mallory probably didn't keep track of the presents his wife handed out and it was most unlikely he'd ever be shown this evidence.

Reciting this high-level logic didn't calm me, but it occupied enough of the front of my mind to keep me from total panic. It helped that the passing driver, while still going slowly, didn't stop. For all I knew he wasn't concerned about the alarm but was debating whether to try to assault a woman carrying as much weaponry as I had strapped to me. I kept facing straight ahead, trying to make him invisible. When I turned left at the corner he continued north.

My control broke; I jogged the remaining half block to my car and headed for the Ryan without waiting to see if anyone responded to the alarm.

# 33

# Dressing for Work

"**F**or she's a jolly good sister, Though her hands are a giant blister," I sang in the bath. It was eleven Monday morning; I had risen from a sleep as sound as if I were one of the just, instead of a moderately successful burglar.

The morning papers contained no news of my break-in. Of course they'd probably been at the printer as I was driving home, but I didn't think an alarm at a small business on the South Side would get a mention when they couldn't find any signs of damage. My late-night panic had vanished. I'd left a piece of evidence behind, it was true, but that scarf was sold by the dozen at various Irish import shops around the city each week. It was only my own guilty fears that had made me think it could be traced to me. The one thing I should *not* do was call Furey or Finchley or any of my other police pals to inquire about Alma Mejicana.

I'd unwrapped my right hand before climbing into the tub. The blisters on the left had broken and reshut with a lot of oozing. They stung sharply when I cautiously put my hand in the water. The right, protected behind its gauze shielding, was starting to look like real skin. Nothing makes you heal faster than good genes. Good work, V.I., good choice of parental chromosomes.

Even though my shoulders were stiff and my neck sore, I felt pretty happy. "Music is the voice of love," I crooned, soaping my armpits.

I didn't know what Farmworks, Inc. was. I hadn't found proof that Luis Schmidt had tried to murder me. I wasn't any closer to knowing whether Cerise had been killed, or why Elena had run scared, but my successful burglary proved better than a tonic.

I bounded out of the bath, did a more vigorous exercise routine than I'd managed yesterday, and put on my jeans and a shirt to borrow the dog from the old man. Peppy had set up a barking when I came in last night, but neither Mr. Contreras nor Vinnie the banker had popped out to see me so I'd hoped I'd gotten home free.

Mr. Contreras's suspicious scrutiny when he answered my knock made me wonder, but I didn't volunteer anything—when I was a public defender I was always having to caution my clients against boasting out of euphoria. The easiest way to get caught is to pull off a slick job, then feel so full of yourself that you have to brag about it. Then one of your pals gets pissed at you and squeals, and there you are at Twenty-sixth and California talking to the PD.

"You musta been tired, cookie, to sleep this late," Mr. Contreras said severely.

"Yeah, but I'm much better this morning. I'm going to take her royal heinie out for a walk." I showed him my healing palms and got grudging consent to take the dog. It would have been cruel to turn me down, considering that she was practically wriggling out of her skin in her eagerness.

I wasn't up to running her, but I drove her over to the lake and threw sticks into the water for her. A pair of winter gloves seemed to provide enough protection for my hands. Since golden retrievers are born knowing the backstroke, my only difficulty came in persuading Peppy to get back into the car when my shoulders grew too sore to throw anymore.

I parked the car illegally by the hydrant in front of our apartment and ran in to drop her off with Mr. Contreras. He refuses to believe that lake water won't ruin her delicate constitution, but before he could get well into the body of his complaints I smiled and said good-bye.

"You'll be able to remember it all to tell me later," I assured him as he glared at me in the doorway.

I ran upstairs to my own place and dug my hiking boots out of the hall closet. I pulled my gun from the belt where I'd draped it on a chair early this morning and stuck it in my waistband. The phone began ringing as I was shutting the front door but I let it go. Despite my sense of urgency, I took the time to lock all three dead bolts—someone had wanted to kill me, after all, and there was no reason to invite an ambush.

I pulled my gloves back on and headed for Lake Shore Drive. Although the grass in the lakefront parks was brown and sere, the soft air and sparkling water eased the memory of the harsh summer. As I drove south I sang "We're on the way to Grandma's farm" and other selections from childhood.

The underground garages were full, but even having to park in one of the pricey Wabash Avenue lots didn't seriously dampen my spirits. I whistled under my breath as I took the feeble Pulteney elevator to the fourth floor.

Our building management doesn't believe in such unnecessary expenses as hallway lights. Only the emergency bulbs at either end of the corridors provide a faint illumination, enough to fumble your keys into your lock. As I got off the elevator I could see a dim shape outlined against the wall across from my office. I don't get much walk-in business—most of my corporate clients prefer that I come to them. It's one of the reasons I can run my business from such dismal surroundings.

If someone wanted to shoot me, this was the perfect opportunity. I thought about racing for the stairwell and fetching help, but Tom Czarnik, the building super, was waiting for a chance to prove me an unfit tenant. And getting the cops would take so much time that my visitor would probably be long gone before they got there.

And the real truth, V.I., is that you can't stand asking people for help. This cold thought came to me even as I was trotting down the hall, moving from side to side and hunching my shoulders to minimize my size. When I came up to the shadowy figure I gave a little gasp of laughter, release from my fears—Zerlina Ramsay was waiting for me.

"I didn't know if you was ever coming in here, girl. I've been here since eight this morning." It was a comment more than a complaint.

"I've been under the weather," I said, wrestling clumsily with the keys in my gloved hands. When I finally turned the right one in the lock the door opened slowly—a week's accumulation of mail was blocking it. I scooped it up and held the door open for Mrs. Ramsay.

"You could have called me at home if you needed me—I'd have been happy to go see you."

Under my office lights her skin color looked healthier than when she'd been in the hospital. Her dour hostess apparently was looking after her well.

"Didn't want to do that. I didn't know who you lived with, whether they'd let you talk to me." She lowered herself carefully into my utilitarian guest chair. "Anyway, I didn't want Maisie to hear me on the phone to you."

I dumped the mail on my desk and swiveled in the desk chair to face her. My desk faces the window with the guest chairs behind it so that a steel barrier won't intimidate visitors.

"I heard on the news you'd been hurt in that fire last week. Across from the Indiana Arms, wasn't it?" She nodded to herself and I waited patiently for her to continue. "Maisie says leave you to yourself—you got Cerise in trouble, leastways your aunt did, let you get yourself out by yourself."

I didn't feel responsible for Cerise's death, but I also didn't see what purpose arguing about it with her would serve. Anyway, she could well be right about Elena, at least partially right.

"It seemed to me the two of them had some scheme going," I ventured. "I thought maybe they wanted to pretend Katterina had died so they could collect a big award from the insurance company."

"You could be right." She sighed unhappily. "You could be right. Blaming you doesn't take away the pain of having a child like that, one that uses heroin and crack and God knows what-all else, and steals and lies. It's just easier to blame you than lie in bed asking myself what I should of done different."

"Elena's no prize, either," I offered. "But my dad was her brother and they didn't make 'em any better than him."

"Yeah, but you didn't bring her up. If I hadn't a had to work so hard, be gone all the time—" She broke herself off. "No use talking about it now. It's not why I came up here. Took me three buses too."

After a brooding silence in which her full lips disappeared into a narrow slit in her face, she said, "It's no news to you that that aunt of yours, that Elena, likes to tell a story or two."

She waited for my agreement before continuing. "So she claims she saw someone talking to Jim Tancredi a few weeks before the fire, and then she came over to my room the night the place burned down telling me he'd been there again."

She smiled in embarrassment. "You gotta understand, the kind of life we lead, any new face is excitement. Maybe you wouldn't of been interested, but I was. And that was when she saw I had my little granddaughter with me, Cerise and Otis dropped her off, you know, and she gets real righteous about how no children can be in the building and she'll talk to Tancredi about it, so I give her the price of a bottle and she goes off, but I figure I'd better get our little princess over to Maisie. With an alkie like Elena you can't trust her to keep her mouth shut just because she *says* she will."

When she looked at me defensively I grunted agreement—I knew that chapter and verse on Elena too well to argue the point. "What did she say about the man she'd seen? Black, white, young, old?"

She shook her head regretfully. "He was white, I'm pretty sure of that, even though she didn't say it in so many words. But she said he had the most gorgeous eyes, that was her expression, and I can't see her using it about a black man."

That was really helpful—Elena thought every man under eighty-five had the most gorgeous eyes. Still, she'd used it in my hearing. The night of the fire. Vinnie the banker, he came to chew me out and she told me not to upset a boy with such gorgeous eyes.

That memory brought the elusive face in the crowd at the Prairie Shores to the forefront of my mind. Vinnie. Vinnie, who shouldn't have been within fifteen miles of the Near South Side. I'd opened my eyes as the paramedics were carrying me through the crowd and seen him looking down at me. It was a slide shown so briefly on my retina that I only now remembered opening my eyes for that brief flash.

I came slowly back to the room. At first I thought I'd have to revise my agenda for the day and go racing off to see him. But as the rushing in my head subsided and reason returned, I remembered I didn't know which bank he worked for.

"You okay?" Zerlina asked anxiously.

"I'm fine. I think it's just possible I may know who she was talking about." Although would Elena have hidden the fact that she'd seen Vinnie before? Wouldn't it be more in keeping with her to issue sly hints? There hadn't been time, though—we'd been fighting about whether she could stay. That could have driven Vinnie from her mind. And then that night she and Cerise showed up together, they started with a story about Katterina, but after they were in bed together Elena suggested blackmailing Vinnie as a better idea. At that point of course she wouldn't say anything about him to me.

"Elena's disappeared again," I said abruptly. "Took off from her hospital bed Saturday morning. She'd taken a pretty good blow to the head and shouldn't have been walking, let alone running."

"They didn't say nothing about her on TV, just you on account of you being a detective. And that you'd rescued your aunt, which I was pretty sure had to be Elena. I didn't come here today because of her, but I'm sorry for her. She's not an evil person, you know, nor Cerise wasn't, either. Just weak, both of them."

She brooded over it in silence for a bit. When it was clear there wasn't anything else she wanted to say, I asked if I could give her a lift.

"Um-unh. I show up in some white girl's car everyone on the street's going to be up telling Maisie about it. No, I'll just go back the way I came. It doesn't matter, taking three buses, you know—I don't have anything else to do with my time these days."

The rush of excitement I'd felt over remembering seeing Vinnie at the fire died away after Zerlina left, and with it much of my earlier euphoria. It was hard to think about her life and that of Elena and maintain a great flow of good cheer. Then, too, the more I considered Vinnie as an arsonist the less sense it made. Maybe he was a pyromaniac sociopath, but it seemed too incredible a coincidence that he would move in below me and then turn out to be torching my aunt's building. Of course even sociopaths have to live someplace, and he couldn't have known that my aunt lived in one of his target buildings. And that might explain his being awake and irritable so soon after the fire.

My mind kept churning futilely. Finally I willed myself to turn it off. I flipped quickly through the mail. Two checks, goodie, and a handful of get-well cards from corporate clients. The obvious junk mail I pitched. The bills could certainly wait, but the incoming money would defray my expenses this afternoon.

I stopped at a cash machine to deposit the money and withdraw a couple of hundred. Armed with that I walked west on Van Buren, hunting for a place that carried work clothes. The systematic mowing down of the Loop to make room for glitzy high rises has driven most of the low-rent business away. Van Buren used to be jammed with army surplus outlets, hardware shops, and the like, but only the peep shows and liquor stores have kept a tenacious hold on the area. They would probably go last.

I had to walk the better part of a mile before I found what I was looking for. I bought a hard hat and a heavy set of coveralls and work gloves. At five-eight I'm tall for a woman, but I still fit easily into a man's small.

Everything looked too new to convince anyone I was a seasoned construction worker. Back in my office I laid the coveralls on the floor and scooted across them in my desk chair several times. Now they looked new but covered with grease.

I keep a set of tools in my filing cabinet to work on the women's toilet, which goes out an average of twice a month. Since Tom Czarnik would like to get rid of all women tenants, not just me, I've learned to do plumbing basics over the years. I took out the wrench and pounded my hard hat a few times. It still looked too new, but I was able to add a few artistic dents and scratches to it. It would have to do.

I pulled the coveralls on over my jeans, moving the gun to one of the deep side pockets, and added my small supply of office tools to the others. Useless on the Ryan, but I thought they gave me a touch of authenticity. I emptied the contents of my handbag into various other pockets and shut off the office lights. I'd left my hiking boots in the car. I wouldn't put them on until I got to the Ryan—they were too hard to drive in. Tucking the hard hat under my arm, I took off again. This time it was my office phone that I ignored as I locked the dead bolt.

The elevator, which had been running with great difficulty when I got back with my work clothes, had given out completely. I squared my shoulders and headed for the stairs.

# 34

# **Heat from the Top**

**I** laced up my boots and hiked up the broken on ramp I'd slid across in my street shoes last week. A good set of boots with treads made a big difference; I moved at a good clip to the top. In my hard hat and coveralls I fit in well enough that no one spared me a glance.

As I tramped along the shoulder I realized I shouldn't have worried about how new my clothes looked—concrete dust soon enveloped them. I pulled my sunglasses out of one of the front pockets to protect my eyes but I didn't have any way to keep the dust out of my lungs. Still, my hacking cough gave me an added touch of authenticity. The only thing I lacked was a bandanna at the throat—in red or yellow it could be pulled up over the mouth when one was actually bent over an air hammer.

Actually I was missing something else—a union card. Even if I'd wanted to risk recognition by the men in the trailer, I couldn't go asking for the Alma Mejicana site without showing I belonged to the fraternity. I kept trudging along, looking for the bright red and green Wunsch and Grasso logo.

I was stronger than I'd been two days ago, but the longer the hike became, the less enthusiasm I felt for my project. I realized, too, that the compleat construction worker ought to have strapped a water jar to her belt loops. It was cooler today than it had been for a while, but walking along in heavy overalls, lugging my wrenches, breathing the dust, turned my face hot and my throat scratchy. My shoulders sent up sympathetic warning shouts.

Earplugs would have been a help too—the noise was staggering. Air hammers, giant earth movers, cement trucks, bulldozer-like things with evil-looking spikes attached to a front claw, combined with the shouting of several thousand men to raise a discordant chorus. Few of the genuine workers wore earplugs—it's better to go deaf than display an unmanly weakness.

I was walking south along the west side of the road. To my untutored eye this was the most complex part of the project, since they were adding a whole new lane for traffic merging south from the Eisenhower. I scanned that part of the construction, then strained to see around the traffic using the middle four lanes to make sure I didn't miss the Wunsch and Grasso logo on the northbound side.

I was almost at the I-55 turnoff before I found their equipment, mercifully on my side of the expressway. I hoisted myself up onto the guardrail to wait for my second wind while I surveyed the territory. The Alma Mejicana part of the operation involved about a half-dozen machines and perhaps twenty or thirty men.

Their contingent wasn't pouring concrete. Instead, as nearly as I could figure out, they were readying the roadbed, using giant rollers to mash rock into tiny pieces, then coming along after with another machine to smooth it down. The men not operating the machines were walking alongside them with picks and shovels, correcting flaws at the edges. Several stood by surveying the work.

It was a busy, industrious scene, and despite the modern machinery, one that harked to an earlier era. None of the crew was black, and as far as I could tell none of them was Hispanic, either. Most of their hard hats were decorated with the Wunsch and Grasso logo. It's one thing to borrow someone's equipment, but even a small firm ought to be able to spring for their own hard hats.

I hopped down from the fence and went up to one of the men surveying the work. Close to the rock crushers the noise was so intense that it took some effort to get the surveyor's attention.

When he finally looked up at me I bawled in his ear, "Luis Schmidt here today?"

"Who?" he bellowed back.

"Luis Schmidt!"

"Don't know him."

He turned back to the road, signaling to one of the men. I thought he was going to pass my inquiry on, but instead he wanted to point out something that had to be done to the roadbed. I tapped his arm.

He jerked around impatiently. "You still here?"

"Is this the Alma Mejicana site?"

He rolled his eyes—dumb broad. He pointed at the machine nearest him. "What do *you* think?"

"I think you're with Alma Mejicana and leasing equipment from Wunsch and Grasso."

He was beginning a scathing put-down when another one of the surveyors came over. "What's going on here?" he demanded, silencing the first man with a commanding arm wave.

"I'm looking for the Alma Mejicana crew," I bawled. "I was told they were using Wunsch and Grasso equipment."

The second man dragged the first off to the side. They had an animated conversation that I couldn't hear, but it involved a lot of gesturing—at the roadbed and at me. Finally the first man went on down the road another ten yards while the second came back to me.

"Rudy's new on the site. The crew are A-M men, but the foremen and the equipment are all from Grasso. He didn't know that. What do you need here?"

He thrust his weather-beaten face close to mine so I could hear him. Maybe I was being fanciful, but behind the film of white dust his expression seemed cold, almost menacing.

"I'm looking for Luis Schmidt." It was the only line I had so I stuck to it.

"He's not on the site. I'll take a message for him."

I shook my head. "I don't mind waiting."

"He won't be here today, lady. Or tomorrow. So if you have a message, let me have it. If you don't, get off the site."

He looked at a couple of men with picks and jerked his head. When they ambled over he said, "Lady got on the site by mistake. You want to see she gets off and stays off."

I held up my hands placatingly. "It's okay, big guy—I can find my own way out. Anyway, I got what I came for."

I trotted northward at a good clip. The pick bearers trotted along next to me, keeping up a line of small talk that I fortunately couldn't make out. No one could possibly attack me right here on the Dan Ryan with two thousand men to witness it. Assuming my screams penetrated the sound of the machinery, or they didn't think I was a scab and join in mauling what was left of my body.

About a half mile up the road, when I thought I might throw up from exertion, they decided they'd fulfilled their mission. One of them poked me playfully in the side with his pick. The other told me he guessed I'd learned my lesson but they could really make it *stick* —ha, ha—if I came back.

I nodded without speaking and staggered clear of the roadbed to collapse on the slope rising up on its west side. I lay there for half an hour, sucking in great mouthfuls of chalky air. They couldn't have known who I was. If there was some red alert out on me, they could easily have knocked me accidentally under one of the rock crushers. But they must have some general cautionary warning against anyone prying around about Alma Mejicana.

What if I'd been with the feds? Would the second foreman still have behaved so precipitously? Massive bribe-taking doesn't seem to have penetrated federal bureaucrats yet, but maybe Roz—through Boots—had some other source of protection for her cousin's firm.

From where I was lying the Sears Tower dominated the near horizon. The sun was low enough in the sky to turn its windows a fiery copper. It was too late for me to go to the Daley Center to look for any background on Farmworks, Inc. I lay there watching the fire on the tower mute into soft oranges, then darken.

Finally I got to my feet and began the long trek back to my car. My legs were a bit wobbly—too much exertion too soon, I told myself sternly. Nothing to do with the surge of fear over the guys with the pickaxes.

Day crews were starting to pack it in. Night shifts hadn't started yet. There was a lull in the noise and a general relaxation in the work frenzy. The machines were still moving doggedly, but the ground crews were standing around laughing, drinking longnecks that they somehow spirited onto the site.

It took over half an hour to move the mile to my car. By then most of the other vehicles parked around it had left. Alone among the detritus under the giant stilts of the expressway, I shivered. When I got in the car I carefully locked the doors before starting.

It was after five-thirty. I turned up Halsted instead of joining the packed throngs on the expressway or the drive. No one on the site knew who I was, but I didn't take the hard hat off until I was north of Congress.

When I got home I dumped the overalls and the hard hat in the hall closet and headed straight for the tub. I longed for sleep but I still had several errands to run. I tried to convince my wobbly legs and sore shoulders that a long bath would do them as much good as twelve hours of sleep. More good. It might have worked when I was twenty, but when you're closer to forty than thirty there are some myths the body won't believe.

Carbohydrate packing was my next great idea. Although there was no fruit or meat in the house I still had onions, garlic, and frozen pasta. Just the kind of dish my mother thought adequate for a Saturday dinner, while my father, who could never bring himself to criticize her, longed privately for chicken and dumplings.

I found a can of tomatoes in the back of my cupboard. I couldn't remember buying this brand and studied the label dubiously, trying to figure out if they were still any good. I opened the can and sniffed. How do you tell if something is full of botulism? I shrugged and dumped them in with the onions. It would be fairly entertaining if I escaped the ravages of mad killers only to die of food poisoning in my own kitchen.

If the tomatoes were poisoned they didn't affect me immediately. In fact, the bath and the dinner did make me feel better—not as good as if I'd had my sleep, but good enough to go on for a bit. I was even whistling a little under my breath when I went into the bedroom to change.

My only lightweight black dress has big silver buttons down the front. With black stockings and pumps I looked more as though I were on my way to the theater than a funeral, but I thought white stockings wouldn't be much of an improvement. It would have to do.

While I was looking up the Callahan Funeral Home, the phone rang. It was Terry Finchley from the Violent Crimes Unit.

"Miss Warshawski! I've been trying to reach you the last few days. Did you get my message?"

I thought of all the ringing phones I'd let go lately and realized I hadn't checked in with my answering service for some time. "Sorry, Detective. What's up? Any new evidence linking me to the Prairie Shores or Indiana Arms fires?"

I thought I heard him sigh. "Don't make my life harder than it is, Vic, okay?"

"Okay, Terry," I agreed meekly. "To what do I owe the pleasure of hearing from you?"

"I—uh—discussed our interview with the lieutenant. You know, the talk Lieutenant Montgomery and I—"

"Yes, I remember that particular conversation." I had sat on the piano bench with the phone book in my lap, but I stopped searching the Callahans.

"He, the lieutenant, Lieutenant Mallory, I mean, was—uh—quite astonished that Montgomery would suggest such a thing—linking you with the arson, you know—and he went and had a talk with him. I just thought you'd like to know that you probably won't be hearing from him again."

"Thank you." I was pleased and surprised, both at Bobby's going to bat for me and at Finchley's taking the time to phone me about it. That took a little extra courage.

"Well, check in with your service in the future—don't leave me sweating it out for three days. See you Saturday."

Saturday. Oh, right. Bobby's sixtieth birthday. Yet another item on my burgeoning to-do list—a present for him. I rubbed my tired eyes and forced myself back to the phone book. The Callahan Funeral Home was on north Harlem. I dug around in the accumulated papers on the coffee table for my city map. The address put it just north of the expressway there; it should be a pretty easy run across town.

I was packing up my good handbag when the phone rang again. I was going to let it go, but it might be someone else who'd been leaving messages for three days.

"Miss Warshawski. Glad I caught you in."

"Mr. MacDonald." I sat back down on the piano bench in astonishment. "What a surprise. I'm sorry I haven't sent you a note yet for the flowers—I'm moving a little slowly with my convalescence."

"That's not what I hear, young lady—I hear you barely rose

from your sickbed before you started prancing around town prying into business that's no concern of yours."

"And what business is that, old man?" I just cannot stand being called "young lady."

"I thought we had an agreement that you'd leave Roz Fuentes alone."

I put the receiver in my lap and stared at it hard. It could only be my invasion of Alma Mejicana that he was referring to. But he couldn't know about that—my only link to them was a scarf that could scarcely be traced to me—no one had ever seen me wear it because I never did. So it was my trip to the construction site. But what was his connection with Alma Mejicana that he'd know about that so fast?

"Are you there?" His voice came scratchily from my lap.

I put the receiver back to my face. "Yeah, I'm here but I'm not with you. I don't know what I've done that you think is harassing Roz. And I don't know why you're so protective of her, anyway."

He laughed a little. "Come, come, young la—Miss Warshawski. You can't go blundering all over the Ryan without people hearing about it. Construction's a small community—word gets around fast. Roz is hurt that you're looking at her cousin's business behind her back. She mentioned it to Boots—he asked me to take the time to give you a call."

"So all this stuff is going on at Boots's command? You work for him or something, Ralph? Somehow I thought he and the whole county were in *your* back pocket."

"All what stuff, young lady?" he demanded sharply.

I waved a vague hand. "Oh, arson, murder, attempted murder, that kind of thing. Boots says—go git me a dead alkie and you say, yessir, Chairman Meagher. And you find you someone to do it? Is that what's been going on around town lately?"

"That would be offensive if it weren't so ludicrous. Boots and I go way back. We're involved in a lot of projects together. Over the years the press has decided on a prolonged smear campaign about our relationship and business methods that *you* apparently have bought into. I'm disappointed in you, Vic—you seemed like a sharp young lady to me."

"Gosh, thanks, Ralph. And did you mastermind the fire that

almost killed me last week? Was that how you and Boots decided to respond to Roz's hurt feelings?"

His breath came in a little hiss in my ear. "For your information, not that I owe you a *damned* thing, the report in the *Star* was the first I knew about that fire. And I'd go on oath with that. But if you've been treating other people around town the way you've been behaving toward Roz, it wouldn't surprise me that one of them tried to put you out."

"That sounds strangely like a threat to me, Ralph. You're sure, you're absolutely positive, that you didn't order that arson last week?"

"I said 'on oath,' " he snapped. "But if I were you, I'd watch my step, young lady—you were lucky to get out of that alive, weren't you?"

"No, I wasn't, old goat," I yelled, fear disguising itself as anger. "I was skilled. So go tell Roz or Boots or whoever is yanking your chain that I rely on my wits, not my luck, and that I'm still trucking."

" 'Bulldozing' would be a better word, young—Miss Warshawski. You don't know what you're doing, and you're liable to cause a major mess if you don't stop blundering around in the middle of things that don't concern you." He spoke in a crisp, no-nonsense tone that no doubt ended debate with subordinates.

"Is that supposed to make me snap a salute and shriek 'Yessir, Mr. M.'? I'm going to the papers with what I've learned so far. If I don't know what I'm doing, they've got the resources to look into it in a lot more detail." I wasn't going to tell him I'd noticed a striking absence of any minority workers at the Alma site—they could ship in a few dozen before Murray showed up with a photographer.

MacDonald thought this one over for a few minutes—it obviously hadn't been in the script when he called. "Maybe we can change your mind on that one. What would it take?"

"Not money, I can assure you." Or a new car, despite the ominous noises the Chevy was making. "But a complete story on Alma and Roz and what you all are so jumpy about could persuade me that you're right—that I don't know what I'm doing there."

There was another long pause. Then MacDonald said slowly,

"We might be able to arrange that. Just don't go to the papers until we've talked again."

I ground my teeth. "I'll give you a day, Ralph. After that all bets are off."

"I don't like threats any better than you do." He gave a humorless chuckle. "And I'm not scampering around to meet your timetable. You'll wait until I have something to say and like it. And if you think you can go off to your friends at the *Star* or the *Tribune* in righteous indignation, just remember that both publishers are personal friends. It's time someone in this town had the guts to stand up to you."

"And you're just the man to tame the wild mare, Ralph? Maybe it's time someone taught you that playing Monopoly on Michigan Avenue doesn't mean you own the world." I slammed the receiver down hard enough to make my palm tingle.

# 35

# Daughters in Mourning

**O**ne good thing about MacDonald's call—getting angry had given me an adrenaline rush. I felt charged with energy as I drove up the street to Belmont.

It was past eight now. The September sky was completely dark, and in the dark, chilly. I should have picked up a jacket on my way out, but I'd been too annoyed to think properly. Should have brought my gun, too, although I didn't think Vinnie would follow me around hoping to ambush me.

I made it to the funeral home by a quarter to the hour. It was a small stone building, with a discreet sign identifying it as a chapel. A few cars still dotted the parking lot when I pulled in. I jogged to the front entrance in my pumps in case they were going to shut down the viewing at nine sharp.

The door shut with a faint whoosh. Beyond a small vestibule with a place for coats and umbrellas lay a larger reception area paved in thick lilac pile. Dark paneled walls hung with a few pious prints created an atmosphere of heavy Victorian mourning. I found myself walking on tiptoe even though my shoes made no sound on the dense lilac. No one came out to greet me, but they couldn't have heard me come in.

A small square card behind a glass at the end of the reception room told me that the Donnelly visitation was in Chapel C. A hall to the right led to a series of rooms. I didn't check their labels, but went to the one door where light was showing.

A handful of women were sitting on folding chairs near the door talking, but softly, out of deference to the open coffin along the far wall. They looked at me, decided they didn't know me, and went back to their conversation. I recognized Mrs. Donnelly's daughters from the picture Mr. Seligman had given me, although I didn't know which was Shannon and which Star.

A man materialized from one of the corners. "Are you here for the Donnelly viewing, miss?"

He was short, and his plump bald head made him look about fifty. Close up, though, I saw he must be younger than I. I nodded, and he took me over to look at Rita Donnelly. They had put her in a two-piece dress, white with a tasteful pattern of blues and greens on it, and her face was as carefully made up as she'd done it herself the times I'd spoken with her. Dressing the dead for burial, from brassiere to panty hose, robs them of dignity. The makeup, including shadow and eyeliner on her closed lids, made it impossible for me to think of her as anything but a china doll on display.

I shook my head, which the young man took as a sign of respect. He led me back to the front of the room and asked me to sign the guest register. At this point one of Mrs. Donnelly's daughters detached herself from the chatting group and came over to shake my hand.

"Did you know my mother?" She spoke softly, but her voice had the unmistakable nasality of Chicago's neighborhoods.

"We were business acquaintances. She talked a great deal about you and your sister—she was very proud of you. Of course I know Barbara Feldman."

"Oh. Uncle Saul's daughter." Her blue eyes, slightly protuberant like her mother's, looked at me with greater interest. "She was too much older than us to play with when we were little. We knew Connie better."

Her sister, seeing us talking at some length, got up to join us. Even with them standing side by side I couldn't tell which was the elder—at thirty a year or two either way doesn't show the way it does when you're three.

I held out my hand. "I'm V. I. Warshawski, a business friend of your mother's."

She shook my hand without volunteering her name. The boorish manners of the younger generation.

"She knows Uncle Saul, too, Star."

That solved the name problem—I'd been talking to the elder, Shannon. "I know your mother hoped to get you involved in Mr. Seligman's business. Do you think you might want to now that she's —gone?"

I'd started to say dead, the real word, but remembered in time that most people don't like to use it. The two sisters exchanged glances that were part amused, part conspiratorial.

"Uncle Saul's been very good to us," Shannon said, "but his business is really too small these days. Mother only stayed on there out of affection for him. There really wasn't even enough for her to do."

I wasn't sure what I was after, but something had made Mrs. Donnelly not want me to show pictures of her daughters to anyone connected with the Indiana Arms arson. I couldn't ask them outright if they knew Vinnie Bottone, or if they were involved in arson for hire.

I tried a delicate probe. "But she got you interested in real estate, I understand."

"Are you a buyer?" Shannon asked. "Is that how you knew Mother?"

"Really more of a seller," I said. "Do you work for a firm that might be interested in buying?"

"I don't, but Star might."

Star blinked her blue eyes rapidly. "I don't really work for a real estate firm, Shannon, you know that. It's just a holding company."

"Farmworks, Inc?" I asked casually.

Star stared open-mouthed at me. "Mother must have really liked you if she told you that, but I don't remember ever hearing her mention your name."

"Word gets around," I said vaguely. "Was it through you that Farmworks hooked up with Seligman?"

"I don't think it's respectful to discuss business here at Mother's viewing." Star looked pointedly at Mrs. Donnelly's open casket. "You can come by the office if you want, but I don't think we do anything that you'd be interested in."

"Thanks very much." I shook hands with both sisters. "I'm sorry about your mother's death. Call me if I can do something to help."

I turned around as I left the chapel, hoping for signs of consternation, but the two had rejoined their small circle of friends. As I was wading through the lilac pile the bald young man caught up with me.

"You didn't sign the register, Miss—the family would appreciate knowing who was here."

I took the proffered pen. In a spirit of malice I signed "V. Bottone" in a large dark hand. The young man thanked me in a soft sober voice. I left him standing under a print of a Pietà.

It was ten by the time I got back to my own building. The Chevy behaved itself as long as I kept below fifty. Maybe nothing major was wrong.

It was kind of late for neighborly visits, but the lights were still on in Vinnie's living room. I ran up the stairs two at a time, changing quickly into jeans before racing back down again. On my way out I thought of my gun. If Vinnie really was a pyromaniac, it might be a good idea not to talk to him unarmed. I dashed back in, stuck it in my waistband, and took off again.

I was panting by the time I got to the bottom, but fortunately it took Vinnie several minutes to answer my knocking. I was on my way to the lobby to ring his bell when I finally heard the lock turning back. He was in sandals and jeans with a Grateful Dead T-shirt —I hadn't known he could dress for comfort.

When he saw me his round smooth face puckered up in a frown. "I might have known it could only be you disturbing me this late in the evening. If you're trying to sell some coke or crack, or whatever you deal in, I'm not interested."

"I'm buying, not selling." I stuck my right leg between the jamb and the door in time to keep him from slamming it shut. "And you'd better have something very good to give me or the next people here will be police detectives."

"I don't know what you're talking about," he said angrily.

From the living room behind him a man called out, asking who was at the door.

"If you don't want your friend to listen to our conversation, you can come up to my place," I offered. "But we're going to keep talking until you explain why you were at the Prairie Shores Hotel last Wednesday."

He tried shoving the door against my leg. I pushed back and slid into the vestibule. He glared at me, his brown eyes tiny specks of fury.

"Get out of my apartment before I call the cops!" he hissed at me.

A tall young man came out of the living room to stand behind Vinnie, topping him by a good four or five inches. It was the same guy I'd seen getting out of the RX7 with Vinnie a week or so ago.

"I'm V. I. Warshawski," I said, holding out my hand. "I live upstairs, but I haven't had a chance to get to know Mr. Bottone very well—we keep pretty different hours."

"Don't talk to her, Rick," Vinnie said. "She pushed her way in and I want her to leave. She's the one we—the one who conducts her *business* in the stairwells at three in the morning."

Rick looked at me interestedly. "Oh! *She's* the one we—"

Vinnie cut him off. "I don't know what she's doing butting in here, but if she doesn't leave in ten seconds, I want you to call the cops."

"Do that," I urged with savage cordiality. "Only make it the Central District, not the local station. I want some of the guys who were at the Prairie Shores fire last week to come by and make an ID. Your friend Vinnie was there and I bet someone will recognize him."

"You're making this up," Vinnie snapped.

I knew I was right, though—the anger had gone out of his face and he was looking worried.

I pushed my advantage. "In fact, I bet they could match his voice with the one on the tape calling the fire into 911."

"You're lying," he blurted. "They don't make tapes of those calls."

"Sure they do, Vinnie. You gotta learn a few police procedures if you want a life of crime. What did you do—force Elena to phone me, then knock her out and wait for me in the dark? You call my name when I didn't see her right off?"

"No!"

"Don't lie to me, Vinnie—I can put you at that fire. The police have got you on tape. And Elena recognized you. She's run away again, but she described you to a friend when she saw you hanging out at the Indiana Arms."

"I don't know who this Elena is!" he bellowed.

"You know, Vinnie, I think you ought to tell her what happened." Rick looked at me. "Vinnie thinks you've been harassing him. If you two are going to be neighbors the best thing you can do is clear the air between you."

"Whose side are you on, anyway?" Vinnie muttered, but he didn't offer any resistance when his friend took his arm and gently propelled him back to the living room.

I followed. His apartment was pretty much a copy of mine in terms of layout, but his style—and budget—were way out of my league. The living room was done in textured contrasting whites. The long wall backing onto the stairwell was covered by an abstract oil in different blues and greens. That was the only color in the room —the bookshelves and coffee table were a clear glass or acrylic or something.

I lowered myself carefully into one of the low-slung nubby armchairs, hoping that my jeans wouldn't leave any telltale dirt streaks behind. Vinnie sat as far from me as he could get, in a matching chair near the front window, while Rick leaned against the wall near him.

"So tell me what happened," I invited.

When Vinnie didn't show any inclination to answer, Rick spoke for him. "This was a week ago tomorrow night, right? We were asleep—" He broke off to look at me guardedly, to see if I was going to scream and yell at this revelation. When he saw I wasn't reacting he went on.

"The dog was barking her head off—that woke us up. The bedroom is next to the hall, you know."

In my place it was on the outside and the kitchen was next to the hall, but they were reversed on the first floor because of the way the back stairs came down—I knew from all the times I'd been in Mr. Contreras's kitchen picking up the dog.

"We got up and saw you leaving. And Vinnie said it was the last time you'd wake him up in the middle of the night. He said you did something illegal and had the cops paid off but he was going to track you down, catch you in the act, and go to the police with hard evidence that would make them arrest you." He cocked his head on one side. "Just out of curiosity, what is it you do? You don't look like a dealer or a hooker."

I couldn't help smiling. "I'm a private investigator, but that doesn't have anything to do with why I've been waking him up. Actually it's an aunt of mine—she got burned out of her home and came to me for late-night assistance a few times. But Vinnie reacted so violently I couldn't bring myself to confide in him. So what did you do when you saw me leave?"

"We got in the Mazda and followed you."

Rick had a cool poise that made me wonder what he saw in Vinnie. Still, it wasn't the first ill-matched couple I'd ever met. I thought back to my cautious approach down Indiana to the Prairie Shores. I didn't think I'd been followed.

"We waited on Cermak," Rick explained. Neither of us was paying any attention to Vinnie, who sat hunched inside his Dead T-shirt. "If you were really meeting a drug dealer, I didn't want to be caught in the middle. And that was the eeriest street I've ever seen. We drove up and down Cermak a few times; we saw you come down Indiana and disappear behind that building, the one that burned. So we turned up the street and watched and after about twenty minutes we saw the place start up in flames and some guy running off. That really freaked us, but we thought we'd better call 911. Is it true that they tape the calls?"

I nodded abstractedly. Of course this could be a romance cooked up to appease me, but it had the ring of truth to it. Vinnie looked too sulky, for one thing, and the bit about not wanting to leave Cermak Road sounded authentic.

"Could you describe the man you saw running away from the building?"

Rick shook his head. "It was dark and he was dressed in dark clothes. I think he had a leather jacket on, but I was too nervous to pay much attention. I'm pretty sure he was white; I think I saw the lamplight reflect off his cheekbones, but I'm not sure if I really remember that."

"Then you stayed around to see if someone came to put out the fire?"

He looked a little ashamed. "I know we should have rushed into the burning building to save you, but we didn't know what you'd been up to—whether you'd set the fire yourself, maybe you'd gotten out however you came in. And the fire got going fast."

"Because of the accelerant," I said absently. "But Elena told Mrs.—told someone that she'd seen the man who torched the Indiana Arms and that he had the most gorgeous eyes. And that's what she said when she saw Vinnie the first night she woke him up. So I thought maybe she'd recognized him and had been blackmailing him."

My voice trailed off as Rick began to laugh. "This is pure Restoration, Vinnie. Come on, lighten up! You think she's running a crack house upstairs all the time she's tracking you down as a pyromaniac. I want you two to shake hands and have a drink together."

Vinnie didn't want to and I wasn't much in the humor for it, either, but Rick went off to the kitchen and came back with a bottle of Georges Goulet. It seemed churlish not to have at least one glass. In the end Rick and I drank that bottle and part of another one while Vinnie stomped angrily off to bed.

# 36

# Treasure Hunt

I didn't have a clear memory of getting back to my own apartment. Ten hours later I wished I didn't have a clear sense of waking up, either. Someone was running an artificial surf machine inside my head. It swooshed and swirled when I tried standing. Even if I hadn't drunk the champagne, I would have felt awful—my hike around the Ryan had stiffened up my legs. My shoulders felt as though I'd spent the night on a circular saw. With the better part of a bottle swelling my cytoplasm, I wished I could spend the next twelve hours unconscious.

Instead I staggered into the kitchen looking for orange juice. The maid or wife or whoever looked after these things hadn't been to the store yet. I thought about going out myself, but the idea of being in direct sunlight made me feel so ill that I had to sit down. When the spasm passed I went into the bathroom, located the Tylenol, and took four, extra-strength, with a couple of glasses of cold water. After a long soak in the tub with the water as hot as I could tolerate, I shuffled back to bed.

When I woke up again it was past noon. I didn't feel like running a mile but I thought I could manage getting dressed and going to the grocery. When you feel really lousy, puppy therapy is indicated. I stopped at Mr. Contreras's to pick up Peppy.

"You look terrible, doll. You doing okay?" He was wearing a red shirt so brilliant it hurt my eyes.

"I feel like death. But I'm going to get better. I just want to borrow the dog for a while."

His faded brown eyes were bright with worry. "You sure you even oughta be dressed? Why don't you go back to bed and I'll fix you something to eat. You shouldn't of got out of the hospital so soon. I don't know what Dr. Lotty would say if she could see you."

I swayed slightly and caught hold of the doorjamb. Peppy came over to lick my hands. "She'd say I got what was coming to me. This is just cork flu—it doesn't have anything to do with my injuries, or at least not much."

"Cork flu?" He cocked his head to one side. "Oh. You been drinking too much. Don't do that, doll. It's no way to solve your problems."

"No, of course it isn't. Who should know that better than you? I'll bring Peppy back later."

I wobbled off with the dog while he was squawking righteously about how knocking back a few with the boys was not the same as me drowning my sorrows in whiskey, I should know by now it was bad for my system. Peppy was totally uninterested in these fine points of ethics, or the different morality prevailing for men who drink than for women. She was staggered that we weren't going running. She kept looking up at me to see if I was watching her, then looking very pointedly to the east to say we should be going that way.

When she saw it wasn't going to happen she took it like a lady, waiting sedately outside the grocery on Diversey and staying fairly close going home. She'd run half a block ahead of me, come back to see if I was still there, tree a squirrel a few yards back, then move ahead again. Back at my apartment she placed herself on the kitchen floor between the stove and the table. In my stupefied condition I kept stepping on her tail but she didn't move—what if some food fell?—she wanted to be able to get to it before I tripped on it. That's what a guard dog is for.

I squeezed some orange juice and fried hamburgers for the two of us, hers without rye or lettuce. The hamburger raised my blood sugar to the point that I thought I might even manage to live another few days.

I'd intended to go back to the Recorder of Deeds office to look up Farmworks; if it wasn't a partnership, I'd have to drive to Springfield to see whether they'd been incorporated. Halfway through the second bottle last night, though, as Rick described in hilarious detail the collapse of a set he'd designed for the *La Brea Tarpit Wars,* I'd remembered the Lexis system. If you had a pal who subscribed to it, you could find out who the officers of a closely held company were as long as it had filed to do business in Illinois.

I wasn't up to taking the first step, visiting the Recorder's office in the old county building, but I went to the living room to call Freeman Carter. He's my attorney, not exactly a pal, and he wouldn't get me the information for nothing, but it still beat driving to Springfield.

Freeman expressed himself pleased at hearing from me—his secretary had brought in the news clips about my near death. He'd been waiting for me to feel better before seeing if I wanted to start a civil action against anyone.

"You mean the way you have to do if the Klan murders your kid?" I asked. "What is it you do—sue for being deprived of your civil right to life?"

"Something like that." He laughed. "How are you feeling?"

"I'm coming along, but I was too ambitious yesterday—I'm not going out today. I was wondering if you'd do something for me."

"Maybe, if it relates to my proper professional role in your life and if it is very clearly marked 'legal.' "

"When have I ever asked you to do something illegal?" I demanded, stung.

He responded more promptly than I really enjoyed. "There was the time you asked me to give you financial details on one of Crawford, Meade's other clients. That's not only illegal but highly unethical. Then when you wanted me to get a restraining order against Dick you could hardly stand it when I turned you down. Then ten or twelve months ago—"

"Okay, okay," I interrupted hastily. "But those were all things I would have done myself if I'd been able to. Name something illegal I *wouldn't* do myself."

"I don't have that much imagination. And anyway, you wouldn't give away confidential client records to anyone. Probably not even to me. Still want to ask me something?"

"Just for some information out of Lexis." Peppy, giving up on the idea of more hamburger, started exploring the room to see who had been there since her last visit.

"You still don't have a computer? Christ, Vic, when are you going to join the eighties?"

"Soon," I promised. "Very soon. As soon as I get four thousand dollars that isn't marked rent or mortgage or insurance or something. Also I need a new car. The Chevy has ninety-five thousand miles on it and is starting to make horrible grinding noises at high speeds."

"Don't drive it so fast," he advised unkindly. "What do you need off Lexis? Just the officers of a corporation? Spell it for me, okay—one word, right, 'works' not capitalized. One of the paralegals will call you back this afternoon or tomorrow morning. Drink some chicken soup and get a good sleep."

The sleep idea sounded inviting, but first I checked in with my answering service to see how many people I'd kept hanging since Saturday. Lotty had phoned once, as had Furey. Robin Bessinger had called a couple of times.

Maybe Michael had some word on my aunt. I tried both the station and his house and left a message on his machine.

After hanging up I went to the window to stare down at the Chevy. The real reason I'd been skipping my calls was my aunt. Her condition had been pretty marginal when she left the hospital; every time the phone rang I was afraid it was someone with bad news about her.

If she did turn up alive, she'd probably need some nursing care. Maybe I could get Peter to shell out for it, but history didn't make me want to bet on it. Where would I put that kind of money together, though? You'd better not be blowing your transmission or anything really irreplaceable like that, I warned the car. 'Cause it's you and me, babe, for the foreseeable future.

At least I could call Robin. It might be that we'd killed the personal side of our life together, but I ought to be friendly—if I could only play the corporate politics right, I could turn Ajax into a major account.

Robin was in a meeting. With her usual bouncy good cheer the receptionist promised to give him my message. I fiddled with the cord to the blinds. What I really ought to do was call Murray and talk to him about the lack of any Hispanic or black workers at the Alma work site, even though they'd won part of the Ryan contract because they were a minority contractor. But MacDonald had promised me more details about Alma and Roz and I thought I should give him another day before going public. Waiting wasn't my style, though. Why was I being so patient now?

"You're getting old, Vic," I told my wavery reflection in the window. "People didn't used to scare you so easily." Was it his phone call last night or my being trapped in the Prairie Shores last week? It had to be the phone call—I didn't have any reason to connect him with my near death. Except, of course, for the note he'd sent with his greenhouse.

Behind me Peppy was whimpering in frustration. I pulled on the cord to the blinds impatiently, then flicked them shut and looked to see whether she needed to go out. She came over to me, pawed my leg, then went back to the sofa, got down on her forepaws, and whimpered again, her tail waving gently.

"Whatcha got there, girl?" I asked. "Tennis ball?"

I lay down on my stomach and peered underneath but couldn't see anything. She refused to give up. Despite all my assurances that nothing was there, she continued her impatient mewing. Once she got going on something like that she could easily keep it up for an hour. I bowed to her superior concentration and hunted for my flashlight.

When I finally remembered dropping it with my other tools on the floor of the hall closet Sunday night, Peppy was still trying to burrow her way under the couch. I hoped she hadn't found a dead rat, or worse yet a live one. With some foreboding I got back down on my belly to peer underneath. Peppy was crowding me so closely I couldn't see anything at first, but at least no red eyes stared back at me. Finally I saw light glinting off metal. Whatever it was lay out of the reach of my arm.

"Naturally you've seen something that involves moving the couch," I grumbled to the dog.

When I pulled it away from the wall she danced hurriedly

around to the back, tail wagging vigorously. She raced in front of me when the object came into view, sniffed at it, picked it up, and laid it at my feet.

"Thank you," I praised her, rubbing her head. "I hope you think it was worth all that effort."

It was a gold link bracelet, a heavy piece, big enough to be a man's. I pushed the couch back against the wall and sat down to examine the trophy. Two amethysts were set among the links. I turned them over but the backs of the stones hadn't been inscribed.

I tossed it from one hand to the other. It looked vaguely familiar, but I couldn't think of any recent male guests who might have lost it. What men had visited me lately? Robin had come over on Saturday but he hadn't gone near the couch. Terry Finchley and Roland Montgomery had sat there when they came to accuse me of torching the Prairie Shores Hotel on Saturday, but it was hard to imagine how they could have dropped it so it fell underneath. It would be so much more likely for something someone dropped to land in the cushions if one of them had lost it. Still, it wouldn't hurt to ask Finchley.

The only way I could really see it getting down underneath like that was if someone had been sleeping on the sofa bed—when it was pulled out there was a gap between the end of the springs and the floor. Guests of mine had occasionally forgotten a watch or a ring that they'd absently laid on the floor after going to sleep.

Cerise and Elena had been my only recent overnight guests. I thought I'd know if Elena had been carting around such a valuable knickknack, but maybe not. She could have stolen it, after all, hoping to trade it for liquor. Maybe it had belonged to Cerise's boyfriend and she wore it the way girls did when they went steady in my high school. Maybe I should drive down to Lawndale and show it to Zerlina since it was much likelier that Cerise had owned it than Terry Finchley. But would Zerlina know? And if Maisie was standing militantly in front of her, would she even say?

I was feeling better but not nearly well enough to deal with Maisie. Anyway, the bracelet was scarcely the most urgent item on the agenda. I stuffed it in my jeans pocket and looked down at Peppy's expectant face.

"You've been treated badly the last few days by the people who ought to be worshiping you. You'd like to go to the lake, wouldn't you?"

She thumped her tail happily.

# 37

# Hunting
# for Rabbits

I walked along the beach, Peppy dancing around me, dropping sticks for me to throw. It was almost October. The water had grown too cool for me, but she could swim happily for another month if we didn't get any heavy storms.

I ambled along to the rocky promontory jutting east into the water. When I sat to stare at the water Peppy jumped down the rocks to explore for rabbits. It was a pretty steep drop, but she occasionally found them burrowing in the boulders along the shore.

The water had a flat silvery sheen, a flinty shade that you don't see in summer. You can tell the seasons by the color of the lake, even if nothing else in the landscape changes. When it's calm the water seems infinitely enticing, offering to hold you, to caress you until you sleep, as though there were no cold depths, no sudden furies that could dash you helpless against the rocks.

It was helplessness I feared. A life like Elena's, bobbing along without any channel markers to guide it. Or my own the last few days, nibbling circumspectly at the edge of the dam but not daring to dive clean in. Letting myself wait on Ralph MacDonald, for instance. I didn't even know if it was out of fear of him, fear of his veiled threats I'd been doing so. Maybe I was just too worn by my aunt's recent escapades to have energy left for taking charge of my own affairs. It was an ego-salvaging theory, at any rate.

I should overcome my repugnance and pay some attention to Elena's problems, though. It wasn't fair to her or to Furey to just hand her affairs over to him. At least I could hunt out Zerlina to ask again if she knew anyone who would shelter Elena. My shoulders drooped at the prospect.

I could stop by the Central District to see if Finchley recognized the bracelet—and to check on whether Furey had turned up anything on Elena. If he hadn't, I'd organize my own search in the morning, maybe call in the Streeter Brothers to help out. And I could go see Roz—it was time I went on the offensive with Ralph MacDonald. Whether he was connected personally with the fire or not, he had something on his mind; I'd stood passively by far too long.

I stood up abruptly and called to the dog. Peppy gained the top in three easy jumps and danced around eagerly. When she saw we were getting in the car instead of returning to the beach, her tail sagged between her legs and she slowed to a painful crawl.

The Chevy was crawling pretty painfully too. I'd put in more transmission fluid, checked the oil, looked with a semblance of intelligence at the plugs and the alternator. Tomorrow I'd have to make the time to bring it to a garage. And make the money for paying a mechanic and hiring a rental car in the interim.

"Keep moving," I ordered the engine.

The top speed it allowed me this afternoon was thirty-five. I had to stick to side streets, irritating the traffic behind me by keeping below twenty. It took over half an hour to get to the Central District.

"I'm stopping here first because Finchley will be gone later," I explained to Peppy, in case she was accusing me of cowardice. "I'm still planning on finding Roz."

I went in through the entrance to police headquarters on State Street. If I used the station door around the corner, I'd have to explain my business to the watch commander. Of course there's a guard at State Street, but he didn't take as much persuading as a desk sergeant would—especially since he recognized my last name. He'd known my dad years ago and chatted with me about him for a bit.

"I was just a rookie then, but Tony took an interest in the young men on the force. I've always remembered that and try to do the same for the new guys coming up. And gals, of course. Oh, well. You want to go up to the lieutenant, not stand around reminiscing. You know where his office is, don't you?"

"Yes, I've been there hundreds of times. You don't need to call up."

Bobby's unit shared quarters on the third floor at the south end of the building. The detectives had desks jammed behind waist-high room dividers lining the fringe of the room while the uniformed officers shared desks in an open space up front. Bobby held the reins of command in a minuscule office in the southeast corner.

Terry Finchley was finishing a report, banging on a typewriter almost as ancient as my own. Mary Louise Neely, a uniformed officer who worked with the unit, was sitting on the edge of his desk talking while he typed. The typewriter was so noisy, they didn't hear me come in.

Most of the desks were empty. The shift changes at four, so roll call and assignments had long been disposed of. Five is a slow time in the crime world. The cops take it easy then, too, getting dinner or waiting for witnesses to come home from work or whatever else you do when you have a little breather on the job.

The door to Bobby's office was shut. I hoped that meant he'd gone home. I went over to Finchley's cubicle, interrupting Officer Neely as she was describing the interior of an XJS she'd chased down last night. I didn't know if it was the black leather seats or the three kilos of coke she'd found underneath them that impressed her more. Usually ramrod stiff, she was gesturing and laughing, a tinge of color in her pale face.

"Hi, guys," I said. "Sorry to butt in."

Finchley stopped his one-handed banging on the machine. "Hi, Vic. You looking for Mickey? He's not in right now."

Officer Neely retreated behind her colorless facade. Murmuring something about "putting it in writing," she marched stiffly off to the desks in front.

"Only partly—to see if he'd turned up anything on my aunt. She's been missing four days now, you know. I found something at my place this afternoon and stopped by to see if you might have dropped it."

"I didn't know your aunt was missing. The lieutenant must have given Mickey the assignment on the side." Finchley gestured hospitably to the metal chair by his desk. "Take a pew. Want some coffee?"

I shuddered. "My stomach isn't strong enough for the stuff you guys drink." I sat down. "I never saw Officer Neely look so human. I kind of wish I hadn't interrupted."

The policewoman was sitting at a typewriter clattering away with flawless precision, her back straight enough to satisfy a West Point inspection.

"She's the first female in the unit," Finchley explained. "You know how that goes, Ms. W. Maybe she's afraid you see her acting natural, you'll squeal to the lieutenant."

"Me?" I was outraged.

Finchley grinned. "Okay, maybe she's afraid if she acts friendly around you, the lieutenant will think you've corrupted her. You like that better?"

"Much," I said emphatically. I pulled the bracelet from my pocket and showed it to Finchley.

"I found it under my couch," I explained. "You and Montgomery are the only men who've been sitting there lately. I wondered if you'd dropped it."

Finchley looked at it briefly. "Ain't mine. That's pimp jewelry— I hate that kind of stuff. And give Monty his due, it's not exactly his style, either." He scanned my face. "I'll ask him for you if you like."

I hesitated. I hated to admit I couldn't stomach facing the arson lieutenant. On the other hand, how many difficult confrontations did I need to prove I wasn't a chicken? I accepted ruefully.

Finchley was sliding the chain through his fingers. "You know, this really looks more like—" He bit himself off. "I'll ask around."

"Can you just do it with a description? The other person it might have belonged to is the dead girl—the young woman whose family you helped me locate last week. I want to take it down to show her mother in the morning."

"Conscientious little thing, aren't you? You ever think of hiring someone to do some of your legwork for you?"

"Every day." I gestured toward Officer Neely's stiff back. "Maybe I should talk to her. The pay isn't great but it'd make a change from typing reports on cokeheads."

"Hey, if you don't have to type reports, start with me," Finchley protested. He made a careful note of the number of amethysts in the chain and handed it back to me. "I'll ask Monty and—and give you a call tomorrow if I can."

His phone started ringing. "Take it easy, Vic."

"Thanks, Terry. Can I use a phone before I leave?"

He picked up his own receiver and gestured to the desk behind him. I went around the divider and called my answering service.

Lucy Mott had phoned from my lawyer's office with information on Farmworks, Inc.; she hadn't left details with the answering service. Lotty had called. So had Robin.

I tried my lawyer first. Lucy Mott was gone for the day but Freeman Carter was still there, in conference with a client. The man answering the phone offered to take a message, but when I explained I was at police headquarters and couldn't ask for a callback, he went to get Carter.

Freeman thought I'd been arrested, of course, and wasn't too thrilled to learn I was just borrowing a phone. "It's that kind of tactic that burns your name around town, V.I.," he grumbled. "But since you've taken me out of my meeting I'll show you how much better my manners are than yours and dig the stuff out now instead of making you wait."

"I know you've got better manners than me, Freeman—that's why I always stand quiet and serious at your side when I have to go before the judge."

He left me dangling for five minutes or so. A few more detectives wandered in, people I didn't know who stopped to talk to Finchley and eye me curiously. Just as Freeman got back on the line Sergeant McGonnigal walked in. When he saw me his eyebrows shot up in surprise. He didn't wave or detour to see me but kept on his way to Mallory's door, where he knocked and stuck his head inside. I turned my attention to Freeman.

Farmworks, Inc. was an amazing company—it existed without officers. The only name associated with it on the Lexis system was the registered agent, August Cray, at a Loop address. Freeman hung up on my thanks. I sat with the receiver in my hand until the police operator came on asking if I needed assistance. I hung up abstractedly.

I knew that name. I'd heard it fairly recently. I just couldn't place it. It was too late to go traipsing over to the LaSalle Street address Freeman had given me. Anyway, I was too tired tonight to undertake many more errands and I kind of wanted to go see Roz. I'd get over to the north Loop in the morning. When I saw Cray I'd probably remember why I knew his name.

"Can I help you find something, Vic? That's my desk you're burrowing in."

McGonnigal's voice at my elbow made me jump. He was trying for a light note but his voice held a brittle undercurrent.

I held up a hand. "Pax, Sergeant. I wasn't delving into your deepest secrets. I came by on an errand and Detective Finchley told me I could use this phone. . . . Can't we go back to being friends, or at least nonenemies, whatever it was we used to be?"

He ignored the bulk of my comment and asked what kind of errand I had. I rolled my eyes in disgust but pulled the bracelet out of my pocket and went through my saga.

McGonnigal picked it up, then flung it to the desk. "We can go back to being friends or at least nonenemies when you stop playing little games, Warshawski. Now get lost. I've got work to do."

I stood up slowly and looked at him stonily. "I'm not playing games, McGonnigal, but you sure are. You little boys give me a call if you ever decide to let me in on the rules."

Officer Neely had stopped typing to watch us. "You get tired of the Boy Scouts, come see me," I said as I passed her. "Maybe we can work something out."

She flushed to the roots of her fine sandy hair and resumed typing at a furious rate.

# 38

# Running into
# a Campaign

When I got into the Chevy, Peppy looked at me expectantly. I'd forgotten I had her. It wasn't fair to make her sit while I tried to track down Roz, but I was afraid if I took her home I wouldn't be able to goad myself back into action.

"Sorry, girl," I said, turning on the ignition. "Terry and John both know who owns that bracelet, wouldn't you say? So why won't they tell me?"

Peppy looked at me anxiously—she didn't know, either. A small procession of cars was moving north up State Street. I waited for them to pass so I could make a U. The tail of the procession was Michael's silver Corvette. I tried honking and waving, but he either didn't see me in the fading light or chose to act as though he hadn't. I could try to catch up with him to ask him about Elena but I didn't feel like running into McGonnigal again tonight.

I drove north to Congress. The potholes and derelict buildings gradually melted into the convention hotels fringing the south rim of the Loop. After I turned west on the Congress and speeded up, the Chevy gave an ominous whine. My stomach jolted again.

"Not at thirty," I lectured the car. "You gotta get me around town a few more years. A few more days, anyway."

The car paid no heed to me but increased its nerve-wrenching noise as I took it up to forty. When I brought it back down to twenty-five, the engine quieted some, but I really couldn't drive it on

the Ryan. I left the Congress at Halsted and plodded my way north
and west to Logan Square.

Roz Fuentes's campaign headquarters were in her old community organization offices on California Avenue. The front window
held flags of Mexico, the U.S., and Puerto Rico, with the Mexicans
on the left and the U.S. in the middle. Underneath the Mexican flag
hung a huge portrait of Roz, beaming her two-hundred-watt smile,
with the slogan in Spanish and English: "Roz Fuentes, for Chicago."
Not original, but serviceable.

The office was still brightly lighted. We were five weeks from
election and people would be working into the dawn at different
headquarters all over the county. On top of that Roz was still func-
tioning as a conduit for community problems with the city on housing and crime. According to the papers, that was a thorn for the
alderman—a gent of the old macho school—but Roz was too popular in the neighborhood for him to try going head-to-head with her.

Beyond the plate-glass window people were working with the
noisy camaraderie a successful campaign brings in its wake. A dozen
or so men and women sat at desks in the big front room talking,
answering the wildly ringing phones, shouting questions at each
other in Spanish or English. No one paid any attention to me, so I
wandered past the campaign workers to the back, where Roz used to
have a small private office.

Another small knot of people was sitting in there now, a nice
landscape of Roz's multiracial appeal: a white man of about thirty
and two Hispanic women—one plump and fiftyish, the other not
long out of high school—were deep in conversation with a wiry
black woman in horn-rims. I didn't recognize the white man but I
knew the woman in horn-rims—it was Velma Riter.

The four of them fell silent when I came in. Velma, who was
seated behind the beaten-up desk in Roz's swivel chair, looked up at
me fiercely. To call her expression hostile was about as descriptive as
calling Niagara Falls wet—it didn't begin to convey the intensity she
was putting out.

After a puzzled glance from Velma to me, the fiftyish woman
asked, "Can we help you, miss?" She wasn't unfriendly, just brisk—
they were conducting business and needed to get back to it.

"I'm V. I. Warshawski," I said. "I was hoping to find Roz."

The plump woman held out a palm toward the high school grad without speaking; the young woman handed her a typed sheet of paper. She scanned it and said, "Right now she's finishing a community meeting on gangs in Pilsen. After that she's going to Schaumburg for a fund-raising dinner. If you tell me what you need I can help you—I'm her chief assistant."

"You're not content with trying to stab Roz in the back—you're coming in here to put poison in her coffee, is that it, Vic?" Velma spoke up venomously.

The young woman looked flustered at Velma's open anger. She stood up hurriedly and picked up a stack of papers. Murmuring something about getting them typed before she went home, she effaced herself.

"Are these people so close to you that you want me to talk in front of them?" I asked Velma.

"They know you've been trying to smear Roz."

I leaned against the door, my shoulders too tired to keep me upright without a prop. "Have you seen some kind of smear story in the papers or on TV that you can trace to me?"

"People are talking." Velma held herself rigidly. "Everyone on the street knows you want to stab her in the back."

"That wouldn't be because *you* told them that, would it, Velma?" I couldn't bear to look at her angry face; I turned my gaze to a peeling poster on the wall showcasing a quote from Simón Bolívar that proclaimed liberty for all peoples.

"Why don't you tell us why you've come, Ms. Warshawski? We're all close to Roz, we don't have any secrets from each other," Roz's chief assistant said.

I moved uninvited onto the metal folding chair the young woman had vacated. "Maybe first you can tell me your names."

"I'm Camellia Maldonado and this is Loren Richter. He's managing the finances for Roz's campaign."

Richter flashed a perfect Ipana smile. "And I can assure you there's nothing amiss with them."

"Splendid." I put my arms on the desk and propped my chin on my hands. "I'm really exhausted. If Velma's told you all about me, you know I almost died in a fire in an abandoned hotel last week.

I'm still not quite over it, so I'm not going to make any effort to be subtle.

"Two weeks ago at a fund-raiser out at Boots's place Roz made a special point of taking me to one side and asking me not to sandbag her campaign. Since that was the farthest thing from my mind, I was irked to say the least. And it made me think she must be hiding some secret."

"If it was secret, then it was none of your business, Warshawski," Velma interjected.

I sat up at that. "She made it my business. She—or anyway, Marissa Duncan—got me to put my name to a public roster announcing my support. And I backed it up with more money than I gave to all other political candidates this year. If Roz was pulling off something illegal or unethical behind my name, I damned well did have a right to know about it."

I was panting by the time I finished. I took a minute to calm myself and focus my thoughts. Camellia and Loren were sitting stiffly, willing to hear me out but ready to slam the door on me as soon as I'd finished.

"When I started asking questions a long list of people began telling me I was a pain in the ass and to mind my own business. The first, of course, was Velma here, followed by Roz. And then, interestingly enough, Ralph MacDonald, the big guy himself—Boots's pal, you know—warned me off. A little more subtly than Velma and Roz, but a warning nonetheless. And after the fire he warned me again, this time not nearly as subtly."

Ralph's name took them all by surprise. If Boots had told Roz he was siccing MacDonald on me, she'd kept it to herself.

"Well, when I was at Roz's fund-raiser she had her cousin with her—Luis Schmidt—and Carl Martinez, his partner in Alma Mejicana. And it seemed to me that it was they who pointed me out to her, suggesting I was up to no good."

I stopped. Something in that picture, the scene of Wunsch and Grasso huddled with Furey and the two men from Alma Mejicana, was tugging at my brain. If I wasn't so tired, if Velma wasn't so hostile, I'd get it. It was because he'd been talking to Wunsch and Grasso that Schmidt warned Roz. They were all connected, Wunsch and Grasso, Alma, Farmworks. And Farmworks was connected to

Seligman, through Rita Donnelly's daughter Star. Did that mean that Wunsch and Grasso were connected to the arson? My brain spun around.

"We're waiting, Vic." Velma's cold voice interrupted my flurried thoughts. "Or are you trying to embellish your story to make it more credible?"

I gave a bitter smile. "I'll wrap it up fast. And believe it or not as you please, but worse is going to follow soon. Alma Mejicana was on the fringes of the construction business up until two years ago. They had a couple of suits against the county, claiming discrimination in the matter of bids, but they were strictly small potatoes—parking lots, a few sidewalks, that kind of thing. They really weren't big enough for the projects they were bidding on.

"Run the cameras forward. Suddenly they've dropped their suits and by a remarkable coincidence they pick up a piece of the Dan Ryan action. You've got to be a heavy roller to play at that table. Where did they come up with the equipment and the expertise?

"Now Roz is a partner in Alma Mejicana. I'm just guessing this part—" I ignored an explosive interruption from Velma. "I don't know whether she went to Boots or he came to her. But his support has eroded badly in the Hispanic wards. They've been backing Solomon Hayes to oust Meagher as board chairman. As long as they're going with Hayes and the blacks have a different candidate, Meagher can scrape by. But lately it's been sounding like the old Washington coalition is perking up again. And if the Hispanics got together with the black coalitions and united on a black candidate, Boots could kiss his forty years of power and patronage good-bye."

Velma was muttering to my right, but Camellia Maldonado sat with a look of glassy composure, much as an Edwardian lady might have watched a drunk in her living room.

Loren Richter was tapping his pencil rapidly against the chair leg. "That's not news. It's not even a crime."

"Of course not," I agreed. "Coalitions, changing loyalties, that's the name of the game. But Boots isn't ready to turn in his chips yet. So say he went to Roz. If he put her on the ticket, she'd bring in Humboldt Park and Pilsen for him—she's gold here. In return he'd see that Alma got a big piece of county action. They drop their discrimination suits, tie in with a dummy corporation, the work will really go to Wunsch and Grasso, who will share out the profits and everybody's happy. Alma doesn't do a lick of work on the Ryan— I've been there and seen it. They got the bid, they pay everything out to a dummy corporation, and let Wunsch and Grasso supply the equipment and the personnel."

"You don't have any proof of this, none at all. It's a total fabrication," Camellia Maldonado said hotly. "Whatever Velma said of you you're ten times worse."

I got up. "I'm not going to stay to fight it. I'm beat. I just wanted to give Roz a chance to answer before I go to the papers. There's one thing I don't understand, though."

"One?" Velma spat out. "Just one? I thought you understood the whole universe, Warshawski."

I ignored her. "I don't know why Roz thought a story like this would hurt her chances on the ticket. It's just business as usual in this old town. When the story finally breaks the good old boys will breathe a collective sigh that she's not a flaming radical, that she's one of them after all."

I turned on my heel, not listening to the three of them shouting at me. Camellia ran to the door on pencil-heels and grabbed my arm.

"You must tell us what proof you have of this terrible allegation. You can't come in here and drop such a bomb and then just walk off."

I rubbed my eyes tiredly. "It's all there. You just have to go to the Ryan and look at their part of the zone. Although maybe now they know I've been there they'll bring in a few minority or women workers for the photographers. But the real kicker is to visit their offices. They're a sham. There're only three desks occupied in the whole place. You don't run a big business out of a cubbyhole, at least not a contracting business."

Camellia looked at me with such anger that it made my knees feel wobbly. "I've worked for Roz's success for a long time," she hissed. "You're not going to be able to ruin her with your lies."

"Great," I said. "Then you don't have anything to worry about."

I glanced back at Velma, sitting in the swivel chair. She didn't say anything, but dropped her gaze to the desktop. Camellia followed me to the big front room. She was too savvy a campaigner to let the hired hands see a crisis was in the works. She shook hands formally with me at the door, gave me a big smile, and said she'd be sure to let Roz know we'd spoken.

# 39

# Death Rattle

**W**hen I got back to the Chevy I was exhausted past the point of feeling or thinking. In some recess of my mind I knew I needed to see August Cray, to try to understand the connection that apparently lay between Farmworks and Seligman. Even if it hadn't been too late to visit his Loop address I couldn't have gone—I just didn't have the stamina left to talk to anyone else today. All I wanted was to get home to a bath and my bed.

Peppy, curled in the front seat, gave me a look of disgust when I got in. She didn't deign to lift her head—after three hours in the car she didn't think I was good for much.

"Sorry, girl," I apologized. "We'll go home now, General Motors willing."

The Chevy was grinding horribly even at twenty-five. I forced it forward like a knight with a battle-shy horse. It went about as happily. With the car whining and screaming I couldn't follow the frantic line of thought I'd started at Roz's any further. Aside from the noise, I was too nervous that the car might stop altogether to be able to think about anything else.

When I turned onto Racine it went on me, going from a brain-shattering whine to a lurching rattle to a final dead silence. I turned the ignition key. The engine ground horribly but wouldn't catch. Behind me cars were honking furiously—it's well known that the best cure for a stalled engine is for a hundred thousand drivers to blow their horns in unison.

I was less than three blocks from home. If I could push the Chevy to the curb, I could leave it there for a tow truck and walk home with Peppy. Peppy had other ideas. When I opened the door she bounded across the seat divider and outside so fast I was just able to grab a hind leg before she hurled herself in front of a delivery van. I wrestled her to the ground and dragged her back into the front seat.

"You gotta wait five more minutes," I told her. She wasn't buying it. Usually the most docile of dogs, she snarled at me now and I had to wrap her leash around the seat divider to keep her in the car. She stood on the passenger seat barking at me furiously.

My legs had cramped up from tensing them so hard while I drove. When I stood up I almost fell over. I steadied myself against the car door.

"Neither of us is in very good shape, are we?" I murmured to the Chevy. "I promise I won't sell you for scrap if you'll do the same for me."

Cars were moving around me now that they saw I was stalled, but the ones farther back kept up their honking. I was too tired to react to the insistent blare. With one hand on the steering wheel and the other on the doorframe, I tried pushing the car to the curb. Too much strain in the last few days had left my shoulders so weak that I couldn't urge the extra force into them to muscle the car forward.

I leaned my forehead against the roof. Someone across the street was adding to the cacophony on Racine. I ignored him along with the rest until finally over the din of the traffic I heard my name.

"Vic! Vic! You need some help?"

It was Rick York, Vinnie's friend, at the wheel of a VW. I darted across the traffic to explain my plight to him. Vinnie was sitting in the passenger seat with his head pointedly turned away—he clearly didn't think Rick should have tried so hard to get my attention.

"Do you think you could push me up the street? If I can get it back to our place, I can leave it for a tow in the morning."

"Sure, just let me turn around," Rick said, in the same breath that Vinnie announced they were going to be late if they waited around any longer.

"Aw, don't be a turdhead, Vinnie. This'll take us five minutes."

I sprinted back to the Chevy, feeling refreshed just by an offer of help, and waited for Rick to come up behind me. Peppy didn't like this new development at all. She left off barking to leap into the backseat and whimper, then plunged back into the front seat. I undid her collar to keep her from choking, but she jumped around so much that I had a hard time keeping an eye on traffic at the intersections.

I coasted into an empty patch across from my building. Rick honked twice and took off without waiting for my thanks. In the morning I'd find out where he lived and order a bottle of champagne for him. His kindness took the edge off my fatigue, enough so that I was able to give Peppy her due and walk her over to the inner harbor and back.

When I finally returned her to Mr. Contreras it was past eight. He was beside himself: "Let alone I don't know if you're alive or dead, I don't even know where you've gone to come bail you out. And don't tell me you don't need my help. Where would you of been last year if I hadn't a known where to come hunting for you? Even if you don't want me, you might spare a little thought for the princess here. And then people come calling on you what am I supposed to tell them?"

I ignored the bulk of his diatribe. "Just say I'm a secretive bitch who doesn't give you a printout of my agenda every day. Who came calling?"

"Couple of guys. They didn't leave their names—just said they'd be back later."

His disclaimers to the contrary, my neighbor could identify any man who'd come to visit me in the past three years. If he didn't know these guys, they were strangers.

"Probably Jehovah's Witnesses. How'd you come to let them in? They ring your bell?"

"Yeah, they said they got the floor wrong."

"And the side of the building?" I asked affably. "Did they leave or are they still upstairs?"

His tirade changed rapidly to remorse. "My God, doll, no wonder you don't want to trust me with any of your secrets. Here I am falling for the oldest game in the world. They left, but what if someone else let them back in, that Vinnie guy across the hall or Miss Gabrielsen upstairs?"

Berit Gabrielsen, who lived across the hall from me, was still at the cottage in northern Michigan where she spent her summers. Mr. Contreras refused to listen to this idea but insisted on bustling me into his living room while he went up with the dog to check out my apartment. He wanted my keys but I resisted.

"You'll be able to tell if the locks have been tampered with. They're more likely waiting outside the door if they're there at all. And if they are, I don't want you waltzing into their arms—I don't have the energy to carry you to the hospital. Besides, my car is broken."

He was too agitated to pay any attention to me. If I'd thought there was really any danger I would have gone with him, but if my visitors had been sent by Ralph MacDonald they wouldn't come back when they knew they'd been ID'd. I let Mr. Contreras usher me into his badly sprung mustard armchair.

I leaned back in the soft musty cushions, my mind drifting on the verge of sleep. My neighbor's living room wasn't that different from Saul Seligman's—the same soft, overstuffed furniture, the same relics of their dead wives filling every available inch. And except for Seligman's fire irons, the relics were also remarkably similar, down to the studio photos of their weddings.

I felt a tender kind of pity for the two of them, each struggling in his own way to maintain the intimacy their wives' deaths had stripped them of. Seligman had accused me of being like everyone else, wanting him to sell his heart for a dollar, but I—

I sat up in the mustard chair. But I hadn't been paying proper attention to him. That was my problem. Someone had been trying to get him to sell the building. I hadn't heard that; I'd just been letting his plaints flow over me. Mrs. Donnelly knew, though, because it was Farmworks that wanted to buy it.

Her daughter worked there. To help boost her career she'd let them know the building might be for sale? Or she'd given them access to Mr. Seligman? At any rate, something about the sale, or at least about the fire, had brought that little smirk to her face because it reminded her of some special benefit to her daughter Star. But when she went to the man (woman?) she knew at Farmworks, worried because I had a picture of Star, he (she?) had killed Mrs. Donnelly and torn up the place to find any documents relating to their sale offer.

I got up and started pacing around the room, knocking my shins into a shrouded birdcage. Swearing briefly, I ran into the curio case Mr. Contreras kept in the middle of the room under an old bedspread.

Saul Seligman didn't have anything to do with the property management company anymore. He told people he went in most afternoons, but he didn't really leave his home to do much of anything. I'd never seen him with shoes on, only his worn bedroom slippers. Still, he hadn't given Mrs. Donnelly a power of attorney or anything. She would have needed his agreement to sell.

Whoever killed her had left him alone because everyone knew he wouldn't be able to make the necessary connections. He didn't have any documents—those had all gone to Rita Donnelly. She might even have portrayed him as mentally incompetent to her principals.

But why had they wanted the Indiana Arms? What was it about that building that someone cared so much about? It was just a derelict property in the decayed triangle between McCormick Place and the Ryan. Of course that was where MacDonald and Meagher wanted to put their stadium; if they got the bid, the value of any property there would skyrocket.

I came to a stop in front of the birdcage before I could bang into it again. I couldn't believe it. I couldn't believe I could have been so dense for so long.

Old MacDonald had a farm. Of course. He had damned near every other piece of land in Chicago, why not a farm too? He'd have a little holding company that could do deals on the side without drawing the public scrutiny that MacDonald Development inevitably attracted. And why not call it Farmworks? Just the name for someone with a macabre sense of humor. And if the Indiana Arms was the last, or one of the last, bits of property standing in the way of his development, then just burn that sucker down.

Wunsch and Grasso, they did a lot of business for the county. Ernie's daddy had grown up in Norwood Park alongside Boots and the two of them had just naturally kept in touch. Ernie and Ron had started out doing favors for the Dems—in Chicago that could mean anything from hustling votes to breaking the legs of tavern owners who didn't pay off the right people. So when they took over Ernie's daddy's business it expanded along with Boots's career. So if Boots and his pal Ralph wanted them to supply Alma Mejicana with trucks and compressors and manpower for the Ryan project, they'd be happy to help out.

"What's wrong with you, doll?" Mr. Contreras's severe voice behind me made me jump. "You know I ain't had a bird in there in ten years. I only keep it because Clara loved canaries. You thinking of getting a bird, don't. You may not think they need a lot of looking after, like the princess here, but you can't be gone all the time and have any kind of animal."

"I wasn't planning on a canary," I said meekly. "Anybody upstairs?"

"We went up outside your kitchen besides going up inside here, in case you wondered what kept us. Nobody there. Seemed to me someone might have been trying to get past those locks of yours, but they held okay. Maybe you should spend the night down here, though. I'm not going to be real happy wondering what's happening to you."

"I'll be fine upstairs," I assured him. "They know you saw them. They won't come back. Even if they could field a different crew, they'd be too worried that the cops would trace them through you. I'll lock all the bolts and tie a rope across the upstairs landing, okay?"

He didn't like it and went on at some length to explain why. I couldn't tell if he was genuinely worried or if he just wanted a bigger role in my affairs. Whichever it was, I preferred the possibility of a break-in to spending a night on his sagging couch under the empty birdcage.

"I'm sleeping in here, then, cookie. The princess'll bark if anyone comes in and we'll be upstairs in a wink."

I wondered briefly if they'd have a jolly confrontation with Rick and Vinnie in the middle of the night. It might be worth getting out of bed for. I thanked him gravely for his concern and made good my escape.

# 40

# Scared Out of House and Home

I turned on the bath when I got into my own place but my mind was racing too hard for me to relax. I got out of the tub and tried Murray. He wasn't in, either at the news office or his home. I thought about calling Bobby but I could just imagine his reaction. Accusations against the chairman of the county board and his wealthy sidekick? Much worse than stirring up the officers of his regiment. Just not done, Vic old thing—if you had a touch of class you'd understand.

I went to look out the window. Despite my brave words to Mr. Contreras, I felt lonely and vulnerable by myself. I wondered if the two men who'd come calling had indeed meant to waylay me or if they were, in fact, a harmless duo of salesmen. Were they the answer Ralph MacDonald had promised to give me within twenty-four hours? Was that man idling across the street really waiting on his dog or waiting for me to come out?

I dropped the blind and went back to the phone to call Lotty.

"Vic! I've started to become quite worried, not hearing from you for so many days. How are you?"

"I'm not sure. I've got a tiger by the tail and I don't think I'm quite strong enough to wrassle with it."

"What kind of tiger?" Lotty asked.

I told her where my thinking had been leading me. "I'm just a little scared, Lotty. And I keep worrying about my aunt. I think she must have seen whoever they hired to set the fire. She probably tried a little genteel blackmail, she and Cerise between them, and now she's hiding out someplace not very safe. I don't know how to find her. The cops are helping. At least a cop is helping," I amended, remembering that Finchley hadn't even known Elena'd skipped again. "And now my car is dead so I can't . . ."

My thought died and my voice with it. A cop knew Elena had done a bunk because he'd gone to Michael Reese specifically to see her. Just as he'd gotten me to reveal her address two weeks ago so he could go see her then.

The police didn't give two hoots if an aging drunk on her uppers tried to pick up young men in Uptown. Michael did.

McGonnigal's reaction to that gold bracelet came tumbling through my head and I saw it laid out for me in such complete detail that I thought my whole inside would come up through my mouth. I remembered now where I'd seen it before, the time he'd worn it last February when I'd gone to a birthday party the pals had put on for him. McGonnigal thought I'd brought the bracelet around to flaunt my long-cooled affair with Michael. That's why he hadn't told me it was Furey's.

Only Furey hadn't left it at my apartment. Elena and Cerise had. The night they slept there they'd laid it on the floor under the mattress, the way people do. And in the morning, when Cerise was so sick, they'd forgotten it.

"Vic—what's gone wrong? You haven't fainted, have you?" Lotty spoke sharply; I realized I was standing like an idiot with the mouthpiece in my hand.

"No. No. I just suddenly am seeing something that ought to have hit me long ago."

"What you need most right now is a hot meal and a night's sleep. Why don't I come for you—you can have some soup and sleep in my guest room. Then tomorrow you'll have the strength to think of an advanced design in tiger traps."

It was so enticing an offer I couldn't turn it down, even as my mind was churning over Michael. I pulled my jeans on again and flung a few things into my backpack—including an extra clip for the Smith & Wesson.

The night Elena brought Cerise to my apartment was the night of Boots's barbecue. Michael had driven back to my place and was waiting for me there when I pulled up. He'd had a police emergency and couldn't stay, that was what he'd said. A triple homicide. I could check that sometime, if I lived past tonight, but I doubted it had ever occurred.

No—he'd gone into the lobby and found Elena and Cerise sitting there on Elena's duffel bag. They'd come with their tale of Cerise's baby, hoping they could use me to screw a little money from the insurance company. Then they'd seen Michael, put some heat on him. They'd seen him hanging around the Indiana Arms before the fire, had to be. He had the connection to Roland Montgomery. He'd be the one the pals would turn to when they wanted a building torched. Why the pals were involved I couldn't say, except that they did favors for Boots in exchange for contracts. And Michael did favors for the pals because they were all good old boys from the neighborhood.

So Elena recognized him when he came into the lobby after Boots's party. She told him she loved boys with gorgeous eyes and she wouldn't tell anyone she'd recognized him if he'd just help her out, give her a little something so she could buy a drink.

He gave them the bracelet, that was the payoff, but the next day he hunted out Cerise and took her to the Rapelec site, got her shot full of heroin, left her to die. No, that wasn't quite it. He'd gotten the heroin to someone—maybe to the pals or to their night manager. August Cray! The registered agent for Farmworks was also the night manager at the Rapelec site.

Anyway, Michael thought he could get the bracelet back but Cerise didn't have it. That was why Bobby's unit was there so fast once the night watchman had spotted her—he had to be the first person to see her. Another police officer might be able to identify the bracelet if she had it on her.

But then? It didn't explain everything, but it made a certain amount of horrible sense. He needed to find Elena to get her quiet, too, but she'd skipped. When I told her about Cerise she'd hunted him out someplace and he'd said enough to make her know he'd killed Cerise. She'd run for cover. So his whole story about her trying to turn tricks in Uptown, that was made up. Bobby never asked him to find her. That was why Furey had made such a big deal out of my not calling to ask him.

My legs were cotton. They kept bending when I tried walking on them. I had to get to the Streeter Brothers fast—I couldn't leave Elena out on the loose for Furey to find and pick off at will.

I forced myself to wobble over to the phone. When I dialed their number I reached their answering machine. I left a message, trying to sound urgent without being hysterical, and gave them Lotty's number to use in the morning.

When I'd hung up I tried Murray again; he was still out prowling someplace. I checked the street from my window. The man with the dog had disappeared. A few other people were strolling along the block, coming back from their workouts or heading for dinner. I didn't believe any of them were emissaries of Ralph MacDonald with orders to garrote me on sight, but I still waited behind the blinds until I saw Lotty's new Camry screech to a halt in front of my building.

Before going downstairs I called Mr. Contreras to let him know his vigilance wouldn't be required.

He was a tad miffed that I would sleep at Lotty's but not with him. "Anyway, just because you're not home don't mean someone won't try to sneak in to hit you on the head when you get back. I think me and the princess'll keep up our patrol anyway."

Calling to tell him my plans was the farthest I could stretch my humanitarian impulses—I couldn't summon the courtesy to thank him for immolating himself so unnecessarily. It's true he'd saved my life last winter, but it didn't make me any more eager to include him in my work. I trotted downstairs, waved cursorily at the dog and Mr. Contreras when they popped their heads into the hall, and got quickly into the car. I hate feeling scared—it makes me run when I'd much rather be walking.

"So you've ruined that Chevy of yours with your reckless driving?" was Lotty's greeting.

I opened my mouth to retort, then shut it as Lotty made a rakish U in front of a *Sun-Times* delivery van. The driver braked so hard that a bundle of papers flew onto the sidewalk. Lotty ignored his mad honking and cursing with an imperiousness worthy of her ancestors—she once told me they'd been advisers to the Hapsburgs.

Lotty drives as if she were responsible for an ambulance during the Blitz—she sees the roads filled with enemy aircraft that she's either dodging or beating to a likely target. She insists on buying standard transmissions because that's what she grew up with, but she strips the gears so mercilessly that this was her third new car in eight years. Like all rotten drivers, she thinks she's the only person who has a legitimate right to the road. By the time we'd gone the two miles to her apartment, I was thinking I should have stayed at home and taken my chances with Ralph MacDonald.

When we stopped the Camry hiccoughed softly—it knew better than to complain too loudly to her. I followed her meekly into her building, up to the second floor, where a brilliant display of color always knocks me back on my heels when I haven't been there for a time. Lotty dresses in severely tailored clothes—dark skirts, crisp white shirts or sober black knits. It's in her home that her intense personality emerges in rich reds and oranges.

Even though I've stayed there a number of times, Lotty always treats me as a real guest, taking my bag, offering me a drink from her limited repertoire. She almost never uses alcohol herself and keeps brandy on hand only for medical emergencies. I turned it down tonight—my stomach still had a strong memory of the bottle of Georges Goulet I'd put away last evening.

Lotty had a stew simmering on the back of the stove, some kind of Viennese dish reconstructed from her childhood memories. Hearty and simple, it brought back the comforts of my own childhood.

"You must have known I'd be coming when you made this," I said gratefully, cleaning the last carrot from my plate. "Just what the doctor ordered."

"Thank you, my dear." Lotty leaned over to kiss me. "Now a bath for you, and bed. You have black circles the size of craters around your eyes."

Before I went to bed she checked my hands. The blisters were a bit tender from my gripping the Chevy's steering wheel too hard, but they continued to heal. She put more salve on them and tucked me into her cool scented sheets. My last thought was that the smell of lavender was the smell of home.

When I woke up again it was past ten. The sun stuck little fingers of light around the edges of the heavy crimson curtains, striating the walls and floor. In the empty apartment all I could hear was the hum of the bedside clock, an oddly comforting noise.

I pulled on my sweatshirt and padded into the kitchen. Lotty had left a glass of orange juice for me and a note to help myself to food. My long sleep had left me with an enormous appetite. I boiled a couple of eggs and ate them with a great stack of toast.

While I was eating I tried to come up with a design for a perfect tiger trap, but as soon as I started thinking about Ralph MacDonald and Furey and the rest of the gang, I got too nervous for logic or design.

I wished I had the beginning of an idea of where to look for Elena. Maybe she did have some cronies who she could turn to when she hit the bottom of her considerable depths. If she had been in any of the other abandoned buildings on the Near South Side, Furey would have found her by now.

I got up abruptly. Maybe he had. He could have put a bullet through her or strangled her—her body wouldn't be found until the wrecking crews came through a year or more from now.

I went into the living room to use the phone and tried the Streeter Brothers again. The Streeter Brothers—Tim and Jim—operate a security firm called All Night—All Right. I've used them in the past when I had surveillance work too big for me to handle alone. Tim and Jim operate the firm as a collective with a handful of other guys, all big, all with beards. They move furniture as a sideline and most if not all of them spend their spare time reading Kierkegaard and Heidegger. They do a respectable job, but they also make me nostalgic for the dear dead days of yesteryear.

I got Bob Kovacki, whom I knew pretty well, and explained my situation to him. "I need to find her before this mad police sergeant does, but right now I've got a sickening idea he may have flushed her in one of the old buildings on the Near South Side and left her body there. I'd like you guys to look down there first, then we can go over some of her old hangouts."

"God, Vic, we're pretty booked now." I could hear him drumming his fingers on the desktop. "I'll talk to Jim, see if we can shift the schedule any. You going to be around this afternoon?"

"I may be doing errands, but I'll call my answering service every hour. Look—I—well, I don't have to spell it out for you. This is urgent. I know you'll do the best you can, though."

Once I'd arranged a tow for the Chevy I'd rent a car and go to the Near South Side myself. I called my garage and described what had happened. Luke Edwards, my mechanic, tisked lugubriously.

"Doesn't sound good, Vic. You shoulda called me when it first started making that grinding noise. You probably drove the transmission dry. I'll send Jerry over with the truck in an hour or so, but don't hope for too much."

I made a face at the phone. "Don't be so cheerful, Luke—you'll build up your endorphins too high and your brain'll blow."

"You saw what I see every day and you'd be sober too."

Luke always makes his garage sound like the county morgue. I gave it up and told him I'd be waiting for Jerry with the car keys. I quickly washed the dishes and made up the bed. Leaving an effusive note for Lotty, I hiked to my own home.

# 41

# Unlit Fireworks

I felt honor-bound to stop at Mr. Contreras's and inquire into any dark doings in the night. He was intensely disappointed—nothing had happened. Peppy had wakened him around three barking her head off, but it turned out to be just a couple of guys climbing into a car across the street.

I finished the conversation as quickly as I tactfully could and went up to the third floor. No one was lurking there. I called a small local rental company to arrange for a car. They had an '84 Tempo, no power steering, fifty thousand miles. It sounded like a clunker but it was only twenty dollars a day, including taxes, usage fees, franchise charges, and all the other items the big chains stiff you for. I told them I'd be by around one.

My long deep sleep had worked wonders on my sore shoulders. They were stiff but the needles of pain had gone. While waiting for Jerry I got out my small hand weights and did a light set of exercises to loosen them further.

The bright yellow tow truck finally honked in front of my building a little before one—I should have remembered the laws of relativity that apply to garage time and multiplied Luke's estimate of an hour by three.

I couldn't find my car keys. Finally I remembered stuffing them into the backpack, where they'd clattered against the Smith & Wesson. I picked up the whole pack and fished the keys out on my way down the stairs. Mr. Contreras stuck his head out the door.

"Just turning my car over to the tow service," I said brightly, waving good-bye. Sometimes it was easier to tell him everything than to fight him.

Jerry was a small, wiry guy in his late twenties. He owned a towing service but had a contract with Luke and did most of the garage's work. In his spare time he raced slot cars. We chatted a few minutes about an amazing race he'd won in Milwaukee the previous weekend.

"Let me see if she'll turn over this morning, Vic. Save you the price of a tow."

"The car's dead, Jerry. I had to push it the final three blocks home last night." Why can't a car jock admit that a woman might at least know whether her own automobile starts or not.

"Well, maybe we can jump it then. Just open the hood a minute, okay, Vic?"

"Oh, all right." I stomped ungraciously across the street and undid the hood release. It was already loose, which seemed odd. I wondered if I might have pulled it by mistake while I was fumbling around trying to push the car last night.

Jerry turned his truck around and backed up parallel with the Chevy. Whistling between his teeth, he pulled a set of cables from the back of the truck and came over to join me.

It was the looseness of the catch that made me look inside the engine before he hooked up the cables. Still whistling, Jerry was moving to attach one of them to the battery when I yanked his arm down.

"Get that thing away from the engine."

"Vic—what—" He broke off when he saw the twin explosive sticks laid near the coil.

"Vic, let's get the fuck out of here." He spoke with a casualness belied by his white face. He grabbed my arm and shoved me into the truck. Before I'd shut the door he was at the corner of Belmont.

I was trembling so violently, I'm not sure I could have moved without his pulling me. I tried to stop my teeth chattering long enough to tell him to get the police on his truck radio.

"We can't leave that bomb there for any passerby to touch," I said through clenched jaws. "We've got to get the cops."

His face was still so white that his brown eyes looked black, but he coasted to a stop in an empty loading zone near a hardware store. "I don't want to go near that thing again. Dynamite scares the shit out of me. Who you get so pissed off at you, Warshawski?"

While he dialed 911 I opened the truck door and threw up my eggs and toast in a neat little heap on the curb.

It was three-thirty by the time I finished with the cops. After a squad car duo had taken a quick, fearful look at the bomb, Roland Montgomery showed up with young Firehorse Whiskey, whom I'd seen briefly in his office two weeks ago. As the day wore on I never did get the young man's real name.

Montgomery sent for a bomb-removal team. They arrived after half an hour or so in something that looked like a moon mobile. In the meantime a half dozen more squad cars roared in to seal off the area. For a few hours the street had more excitement than it usually gets in a year, what with police cordons and lots of guys in space suits moving in on my car. The networks all sent their vans, and children who should have been in school appeared miraculously to wave at their playmates on the four o'clock news.

When he saw the TV crews pull up, Montgomery got out of the car where he'd been questioning Jerry and me and went over to talk to them. I ambled over to join in. He liked that so little that he tried grabbing the mike away from me when I started to explain how Jerry and I found the bomb.

"We don't have anything to report to the media yet on this device," the lieutenant said roughly.

"You may not"—I smiled limpidly for the camera crews—"but I'm the owner of the car and I have a lot to say about it. I think my downstairs neighbor heard them putting the bomb in around three this morning."

Of course they lapped that up and wanted more. There wasn't anything Montgomery could do about it. "It was the dog who really heard them," I said. "She probably saw them at my car—that's why she started barking. You can ask him all about it."

I gestured broadly at Mr. Contreras, who was standing on the periphery of the crowd with Peppy. Peppy bounded over to me while Mr. Contreras made his way to the eager reporters. Montgomery backed away from the dog and demanded I get rid of her.

"Don't shoot her, Lieutenant," I said. "It'll be on three networks all over the country."

Dogs make a welcome addition to any picture, especially a golden retriever as beautiful and heroic as Peppy. While Montgomery frowned horribly I told the reporters her name and got her to shake paws with a couple of them. They were naturally enchanted.

I fondled the dog's ears and listened to Mr. Contreras explain at excruciating length exactly what it was he'd heard and seen. He also told them how the dog had saved my life last winter when she found me bound and gagged in the middle of a swamp. I was glad I wasn't the one who'd have to listen to it all in order to find one usable comment.

Once the experts had removed the dynamite from the car and whisked it away in a special sealed container, the TV crews departed too. Montgomery's demeanor changed immediately. He sent Jerry off and informed me we were going downtown for a real talk. A trace of sadism in his expression as he took my arm roughly made my stomach churn. Mr. Contreras pawed anxiously at him, demanding to know what they were doing with me. Montgomery brushed the old man back so roughly, I was afraid he might knock him over.

"Take it easy, Lieutenant, he's seventy-eight. You don't need to prove you're bigger and more powerful."

"Bobby Mallory puts up with a lot of shit from you I don't have to take, Warshawski. You button up now and speak when you're spoken to or I'll have you in on an assault charge fast enough to make your smug little head spin."

"Whew, Lieutenant, you been watching too many Dirty Harry movies."

He yanked my arm hard enough to jar the shoulder socket and hustled me to the car. As he was pushing me inside I turned to scream at Mr. Contreras to call Lotty and get my lawyer's name from her.

Down at Eleventh Street, Montgomery took me to a small interrogation room and began demanding to know how I'd gotten hold of a supply of dynamite. When it dawned on me that he was trying to accuse me of rigging my own car, I was so furious that the room swam in front of my eyes.

"Get a witness in here, Lieutenant," I managed to get out in a voice below a scream. "Get a witness in here to what you're saying."

He swallowed a triumphant smile so fast I almost missed it. "We've got a pretty good case, Warshawski. You've been involved in two suspicious fires in the last month. We figure you for a sensationalist. When you couldn't get the kind of attention you wanted out of those fires, you rigged a bomb up in your car. All I want to know is where you got the dynamite."

I wanted to jump up from behind the table and seize his long stork neck and pound his head against the wall, but I had just enough reason left to know he was hoping to goad me over the brink. I shut my eyes, panting, trying to force my temper down—the first time I let it go he'd have me in the lockup for assaulting an officer.

"You've been hiding behind Bobby Mallory for years, Warshawski. It's time you learned to fight on your own."

I felt him moving toward me just in time to back my chair away. The blow he'd aimed for my head got me on the diaphragm.

"I presume this room is wired. Please let the record show that Lieutenant Montgomery just hit a witness in a bombing case," I shouted.

He aimed another fist at me. I slid from my chair under the legs of the table. Montgomery got down on his hands and knees to pull me out, shouting abuse at me, calling me names out of porn flicks. I scooted away from him. He went flat on his abdomen and grabbed my left ankle. I twisted away and got to my feet on the other side of the table.

Just as I staggered upright Officer Neely walked in. Her professional mask cracked at the sight of a lieutenant on his belly scrabbling around under an interrogation table.

"He lost a contact," I said helpfully. "We've both been down there looking, but he started confusing my ankle with his eyeballs so I thought I'd get out of the way."

Neely didn't say anything. By the time Montgomery had climbed awkwardly back to his feet, she had her face composed in its usual rigid lines. She spoke in a monotone. "Lieutenant Mallory heard you were questioning this witness and wanted to talk to her for a few minutes."

Montgomery glared at her, furious at being caught looking like a fool. I felt sorry for her, her career buffeted by being the wrong person to show up at a bad moment.

"I don't think the lieutenant here has anything else useful to say to me. He's got his facts without asking a single question. Let's go, Officer." Unfortunately I didn't feel sorry enough to keep my mouth shut.

I opened the door to the interrogation room and headed down the hall, not waiting to see what Officer Neely would do. She caught up with me on the stairs. I wanted to say something helpful and sisterly to her in support of her law-enforcement career, but I was too badly rattled to think of anything very chipper. She was looking rigidly ahead, making it impossible to know if she was embarrassed, disgusted, or just not very responsive. On the third floor we silently crossed the Violent Crimes area to Bobby's tiny office along the far wall. Officer Neely knocked and opened the door.

"Miss Warshawski, sir. Did you want me to take notes?"

Bobby was on the phone. He shook his head and motioned me to a chair. Officer Neely shut the door behind her with a sharp snap.

Bobby's desk and walls were crammed with photographs—pictures of yellow birds in flight, gap-toothed children grinning as they sported his dress uniform cap, Eileen hand in hand with her eldest daughter as a bride. He liked to shift them around every so often so he could see them with a fresh eye. Ordinarily I hunt for the shots of Tony or Gabriella—or even the one of me at five sitting on Tony's lap. Today I didn't really care. I sat gripping my hands on the side of the metal chair, waiting for him to finish his conversation. Next to Montgomery, Bobby was the last person I wanted to see today.

"Okay, Vicki, tell me what's going on and make it fast. I had a call from your lawyer, which is how I knew you were down here, but it doesn't make me happy to run interference for you with another man on the force."

I took a deep breath and came out with a tolerably coherent version of the day's events. Bobby grunted and asked a few questions, like how come I knew it was a bomb and how long it had taken Monty to get there after Jerry called in the report on his car radio.

When I got to the end Bobby made a face. "You're in an awkward spot, Vicki. I keep telling you not to play around in police business and this just proves my point. You came to me to get you out of hot water you boiled up yourself—"

"What do you mean?" I was so furious, my head seemed to rise a foot from my body. "I did *not*, repeat *not*, put that bomb in my car engine. Someone did, but instead of trying to get a description of the men who did it—who may have done it—from a pretty good witness, the police are trying to charge me with attempted suicide."

"I'm not saying you planted that device, Vicki. I know you well enough to realize you're not that unbalanced. But if you hadn't been playing around with arson and a whole lot of things I told you to stay out of, you wouldn't be in this mess at all."

He looked at me sternly, daddy to naughty child. "Now I'm going to use a few chips on your behalf, Vicki, with a guy who's not too easy to work with. In return I want you to promise me that you are not going to touch this business any further. Let alone the trouble you've got yourself into, since you started in on that fire three weeks ago you've got my whole unit stirred up. You were in last night with some damned piece of jewelry that has the boys in an uproar now. I just can't have it. Do you understand?"

I pressed my lips together. "I brought in a man's bracelet I found under my couch because I though Finchley might have dropped it when he and Montgomery were in last week. McGonnigal flipped out when he saw it because he knew it was Furey's and thought I was flaunting it at him. It was only late last night that I realized it belonged to Furey and came to see what it was doing in my apartment.

"He'd given it to Elena, Bobby, to Elena and the dead junkie you went to see at the Rapelec site two weeks ago. It was just a little extortion, something to keep them from reporting that they'd seen him—"

Bobby slammed his palm hard on the desk. One of the pictures teetered and fell over the side. "I've had enough out of you!" he roared. "That's a loathsome suggestion. You've been treated too easy for too long, that's your problem, so when things don't go your way you manufacture conspiracy theories. You ought to know better than that, than to come in here and try to lay that kind of sh— something like that on me. Now get out and go home. I told you two weeks ago to stop stirring up my department and I meant it. This had better be the last time I see you around here."

I got up and looked steadily at him. "You don't want to know what I've learned? If I'm right, Montgomery and Furey could be involved in one of the ugliest little scandals to hit this department in a long time."

Bobby scowled ferociously. "Spare me. I hear enough trash in here every day without listening to you fling garbage around about one of my own men. I've told you dozens of times that you're in a line of work that's bad for you, and this is perfect proof of it. You don't know how to reason, how to follow a chain of evidence to a conclusion, so you start making up paranoid fantasies. If I tell you I think you need a good man and a family, you get on your high horse, but women your age who don't marry start getting strange ideas. I don't want to see you ending up like that crazy aunt of yours, propositioning young men for the price of a bottle."

I stared down at him not knowing whether to scream or laugh. "Bobby, that psychology was old before you were born, the old repressed-spinster routine, and even if it were true, it sure wouldn't apply to me. I just hope you aren't laying that line on Officer Neely, or about the time I hit West Madison you're going to be facing a harassment suit so big it'll make your head spin. Anyway, if you have to think of me as a crackpot virgin to keep your faith in the department intact, remember when the pieces come breaking around you that I tried to warn you."

Bobby was on his feet now, too, panting, his face red. "Get out of my office and don't come back here. Your parents were two of my best friends, but I'd have broken every bone in your body if you talked to me the way you spoke to them, and look where it's led— how dare you talk to me like this. Get out!"

The last few words were on a crescendo so loud that they must have heard them on the street, let alone in the adjacent room. I managed to keep my head up and my steps steady and even to shut the door gently behind me. Everyone in the room turned to stare as I made the long walk from his office to the unit-room exit.

"It's okay, boys and girls. The lieutenant got a little excited, but I don't think there'll be any more fireworks this afternoon."

# 42

# Mourning Becomes Electra

**I** walked slowly up State Street. Anger dragged at my steps, anger and depression both. Someone laid a bomb in my engine and no one in the police department had tried to get a word from Mr. Contreras about the men he'd seen. Instead, Roland Montgomery assaulted me physically while Bobby did it mentally. Break every bone in my body. Oh, yeah. That's how you get people to stop asking questions and do as you say, you break every bone in their bodies.

I was angry with myself too—I hadn't meant to talk to Bobby about Furey until I had some proof. Of course Bobby wouldn't listen to me spreading stories about his fair-haired boy. It would be hard enough to get him to listen when I could really back them up. And even though I was furious right now with Bobby, I didn't look forward to bringing him that much pain.

Maybe I'd feel better for food. It had been six hours since I'd eaten and I'd thrown that up. I wandered into the first coffee shop I came to. They had a variety of salads on the menu but I ordered a b.l.t. with fries. Grease is so much more comforting than greens. Anyway, my weight was still down—I needed to pack a few carbs to build myself back up.

Because I'd come during off-hours they made up the fries fresh just for me. I ate them first, while they were still hot and crisp. Halfway through the fries I remembered I was supposed to check in with my answering service every hour to see if the Streeter Brothers could fit me into their schedule soon. I carried the last handful of potatoes to the pay phone at the front of the coffee shop.

I got Tim Streeter this time. "We can start for you first thing in the morning, Vic, but we'll need you to brief the boys, give them a description, and maybe show them the kind of place your aunt would likely pick."

My stomach fell. Morning seemed an awfully long time away just now. I couldn't protest, though—they were doing me a mighty big favor. I told Tim I'd meet him at the corner of Indiana and Cermak at eight and hung up.

Maybe it would still be light enough for me to do some hunting on my own tonight. I could stop at August Cray's office and then head home to pick up the Tempo. I called my neighborhood car rental. They closed at six but said they'd leave the Tempo out front for me with the keys taped underneath the front bumper. If someone stole it before I got there they weren't going to be out much.

I paid my bill—under ten dollars, even though I was perilously close to the upscale part of the South Loop—and took the sandwich to eat on my way to Cray's office.

The address Freeman Carter had given me for Farmworks was on north LaSalle. I took a bus up to Van Buren and then got on the Dan Ryan L—it would take me around the Loop faster than any taxi this time of day. It was just on four-thirty when I got off at Clark and walked the three blocks to Cray's building. I hoped someone was still in the office, even if Cray himself wasn't.

I was going against the tide of homebound workers. Inside the lobby I had to move to the wall and scoot crablike around the outgoing throng to the elevators. I rode in splendid isolation to the twenty-eighth floor and made my way on soft gray carpeting to Suite 2839. Its solid wood door was labeled simply "Property Management." They probably ran so many different little firms out of there that they couldn't list all their names on the door.

The knob didn't turn under my hand so I tried a buzzer discreetly imbedded to the right of the panel. After a long pause a tinny voice asked who was there.

"I'm interested in investing in Farmworks," I said. "I'd like to talk to August Cray."

The door clicked. I walked into a narrow reception area, a holding pen really, with a couple of stiff chairs but no table or magazines —or even a window for waiting customers to gaze through.

A sliding glass window in the left wall allowed the inmates to look at visitors without exposing their whole bodies. This was shut when I came in. I looked around and saw a little television camera in a corner of the ceiling. I smiled at it and waved and a few seconds later Star Wentzel opened a door next to the glass panel. Her blond hair was combed back and gathered into a jeweled white clip. She wore a long narrow skirt that highlighted her gaunt pelvic bones. She looked like a high school student from the fifties, not a participant in a development scam.

"What are you doing here?" she demanded.

I smiled. "I might ask you the same question. I came here to find August Cray—Farmworks's agent of record. And here you are, mourning your mother, but putting a brave front on it by coming into the office."

"I can't bring Mother back to life by staying home," she said pettishly. "I don't need you to tell me how to behave."

"Of course you don't, Star. Can we go inside? I'd still like to talk to August Cray."

"He's not here. Why don't you tell me what you want?"

This was clearly a rote line—she rattled it off without the hostility of her earlier remarks. I smiled.

"I came to invest in Farmworks. It's such an up-and-coming company. I hear they're going to get a huge piece of the new stadium project—I want to be a millionaire just like Boots and Ralph."

She smoothed a hand over a jutting hipbone. "I don't know what you're talking about."

"Then I'll explain it to you. Let's go sit down—this will take awhile—your feet are going to start hurting in those spiky heels if we talk out here."

I opened the door and shepherded Star into the inner office. It was a small room with a blond wood desk about the color of her hair. A couple of portables covered the top—one seemed identical to the Apollo I'd noticed in the Alma Mejicana offices on Sunday. Wood filing cabinets filled the windowless walls and spilled over into the narrow hallway. It was a working person's office all right.

I dumped a stack of prospectuses from a chair in the hall and moved it into the office while Star sat in her padded swivel chair behind the desk. Her mouth was set in a mulish line. I expect I looked about the same.

She lifted a thin wrist to examine a weighty gold timepiece. "I don't have much time, so make your spiel and let me get home. My sister and I have to entertain some of Mother's church friends tonight."

"It's partly about your mother that I came to see you," I said.

"You claimed to be a friend of hers but no one at the church had ever heard of you," she said sharply.

"That's because I only knew her in the narrow context of her work at Seligman. Since the fire at the Indiana Arms—I'm sure you know about that, don't you?—I'd been talking to her, hoping to get some idea about who might have set it. She obviously was sitting on some kind of secret. And that secret had to do with you or your sister. After I talked to you at the funeral home on Monday, I was pretty sure that you working here was what she was so pleased about —and so eager to withhold. And that's what I want you to tell me— why she couldn't tell people where you worked."

A ghost of her mother's smug look flitted across her face. "That's none of your business, is it?"

She said it in a saucy little singsong, the way young children do. It got under my skin, goading me to act like a child myself. I put both hands on the desk and leaned forward between the two computers. "Star, sugar, I want you to be real brave about this, but you should know your boss killed your mother."

Little red spots burned in her cheeks. "That's a lie! Mother was killed by some awful mugger who thought the office was empty and—"

"And broke in and stole only the documents relating to Farmworks's offer to buy the Indiana Arms," I cut in. "Come off it, Star. Ralph and Boots are spinning you a line. Your mother learned I'd gotten hold of a picture of you and she was afraid you'd get linked to the fire when I started showing it around. She went to Ralph and told him she was going to have to tell me all about his offer to purchase—she didn't want you taking the fall in case someone *could* connect you with that arson. And he killed her. Or he got someone to kill her. How bad do you want to protect those cretins? Bad enough to let them get away with your mama's death?"

"You're making this up! Ralph and Gus told me you might be around to harass me. He told me what you might insinuate. You think you're so smart, but he's smarter than you."

"Gus?" I started to ask, then realized she must mean August. "One thing's for damn sure—he's smarter than you! Don't you realize that I didn't *know* MacDonald was involved in Farmworks until you told me just now? It was a guess, but it sure was right on target. Shall I guess everything else that happened and you let me know if I'm right or wrong? Or do you want to tell me yourself?"

She pulled herself up in her swivel chair. "You'd better get out of here before I call the police. You're harassing me in a private office and that's against the law."

"Let me make another guess." I pulled her Rolodex toward me and started flipping through it. "You'll call Roland Montgomery's private number and he'll send some uniforms hopping to drag me away. And Star! What a coincidence! Here it is."

"I . . . uh . . ." She started a sentence several times but didn't finish it. "You don't have any proof."

"No," I had to admit. "It's just another guess. But he—or at least Farmworks—is at the center of a whole lot of different action that he'd just as soon the FBI didn't see. They're going to, though, Star, because the *Herald*'s going to print the whole story. And then the feds will come subpoena your files and they'll charge you with conspiring to commit fraud and arson and murder. And then you won't just be a poor little orphan, you'll be a poor little orphan in jail. Only if a jury hears how you let your own mother take the fall for you, they're not going to treat you like a helpless waif."

"Just because my employer tried to buy a building belonging to Mother's employer does not mean he killed her." Her voice was scornful.

"Ralph and Boots really wanted the Indiana Arms, didn't they? Really badly. I know about their stadium bid—that's not a secret. And it won't take too much work to do a proper title search for the stuff back there, so you might as well tell me."

She thought it over carefully, then finally conceded that Farmworks had been buying up property in the triangle behind Mc-

Cormick Place and the Dan Ryan for several years now, positioning themselves for a bid on the stadium. The Indiana Arms was one of the few occupied buildings they hadn't been able to acquire. Star had been keeping Seligman's books for him at the time—she was a CPA. She thought he was foolish not to sell and tried to pressure him.

"He acted like that place meant more to him than his own children," Star said resentfully. "You'd think he'd of been glad to get what they were offering—it would have been so much better for Barbara and Connie than inheriting that run-down junk heap. Even after—after things started going really wrong, like when the elevators broke down and no one would come fix them, he couldn't see it was a losing proposition."

"It had some sentimental meaning for him. So what happened next? You went to August Cray and Ralph and said if they'd hire you, you'd keep up the pressure on Seligman through your mom?"

She tossed her golden hair scornfully. "They made me an offer. They could see I was good, that I was wasted in that nickel-and-dime place."

"What were you supposed to do? Forge a title transfer? Were you good enough to do that? Or just get your mother to keep the heat on the old man to sell?"

She smiled at me coldly. "You'll never know, will you?"

"But then Rita learned that Mr. Seligman had given me a photo that had you and Shannon in it along with his own daughters. And she came to you, panicked. She was afraid if I started showing it to someone who had lived or worked at the Indiana Arms that they would recognize you. What had you been doing down there? Sabotaging the elevators yourself? Or just guaranteeing that no repair company would come fix them? So you told Ralph your mom was getting cold feet and he did the only decent thing—he got someone to kill her."

She sucked on her lower lip, but she didn't shake that easily. "You're in here with guesses and stories. If that's your idea of fun, I'm not going to stop you."

"Yeah, they're guesses and stories, but they're pretty volatile. A more innocent woman might be hollering for cops or lawyers or witnesses or something. But you're taking it all in to see how much I know, aren't you? Well, Boots may have the local cops in his hip pocket, but I don't think he owns the FBI yet."

I got up to go. Star had a strange little smile on her face. "Of course you have to talk to them first, don't you? And even if Boots doesn't have much influence with the FBI, he can make sure they don't listen to you."

My stomach jolted a bit but I said calmly, "Oh, did Ralph and Boots tell you about their joke on my ignition? I found it and I'll be extra careful looking for others. I remember LeAnn Wunsch telling me what a kidder Boots was. I'm only just beginning to really appreciate it."

She barely waited for me to leave before she picked up her phone. I didn't shut the door all the way and stood with my ear against it. She asked for Ralph and said it was urgent and that she'd wait at her desk until he called back. I guess her mother's church friends weren't that important.

# 43

# The Eye of
#    the Hurricane

I stood in the middle of LaSalle Street trying to quell a rising tide of panic. I needed some allies and I needed them fast. It was luck, pure and simple, that had kept me from disintegrating into my component parts today. If I had, Roland Montgomery would have closed the investigation for lack of leads—or painted me as a bizarre suicidal maniac. I'd miraculously sidestepped my fate, but it wouldn't be Ralph MacDonald's last effort to present me with his side of the story, as he'd put it on Monday.

Maybe I was jumping to conclusions in putting Ralph behind the dynamite in my car. Perhaps it was Roland Montgomery—he had ready access to all kinds of incendiary stuff. Or Michael, getting it from Wunsch or Grasso. Michael. My stomach twisted some more. He couldn't have tried to blow me up. We'd never been in love, but we'd been lovers for a brief sweet time. Can you want to think of a body you've caressed torn into jagged chunks of bleeding bones? Or did my rebuff make him want to see me so?

I shook my head, impatient with myself. This was hardly the time or place to sink into a melancholy reverie. I needed to get myself organized. The Smith & Wesson was in my backpack, that was one good thing. Of course I couldn't very well pull it out in the middle of LaSalle Street, but I didn't think anyone was likely to try to shoot me during the evening rush hour. I was just lucky that Montgomery had been so hot to get me in the interrogation room and break my jaw that he hadn't bothered with the usual formalities at the police station. No one had searched me; I hadn't had to surrender the gun and go through the tedious process of producing my permit and getting permission to pick it up again.

I needed to get to a phone but I was too scared of what direction MacDonald—or Montgomery—or Michael—might next attack from to go to my office. That was an easy place to lay a trap. For the same reason I didn't want to go home—or to Lotty's. If MacDonald's mind was running to dynamite, I didn't want him to kill Peppy or Lotty in the effort to destroy me.

I finally flagged a cab to ride the nine blocks to the Golden Glow. Sal would let me use her phone and I wouldn't mind a little Black Label to settle down some of the more extreme lurches my stomach was giving.

As the taxi wove recklessly through the end of the rush-hour congestion, it occurred to me that Ralph probably hadn't ordered the dynamite in my car. Most likely it had happened just like Becket —him running his fingers through his well-cut silver hair and asking tragically if no one would rid him of this meddlesome priestess. It's always that way, I thought bitterly, from Henry II to Reagan—your barons or Oliver North or whoever does the dirty work and you wrap yourself in a mantle of bewilderment and lawyers. I never knew about it, they misinterpreted my instructions.

"You say something, miss?" the cabbie asked.

I hadn't realized I'd been angry enough to mutter aloud. "No. Keep the change."

Murray Ryerson was sitting at the mahogany horseshoe bar drinking Holstein and talking to Sal about the upcoming college basketball season. Neither of them broke off a spirited debate about the NCAA sanctions on the KU Jayhawks when I climbed onto a stool next to Murray, but Sal reached behind her for the Black Label and poured me a glass.

Sal's cousin was taking care of customers at the tables. I sipped my whiskey without offering any opinion on Larry Brown's perfidies or Milt Newman's abilities now that Danny Manning wasn't leading the squad anymore. When Sal and Murray had run out of ideas on the subject, Murray casually asked me what was new.

I swallowed the rest of my drink and accepted another from Sal.

"You almost got your wish to write my obituary today, big guy—someone laid a bomb across my ignition coil."

At first Murray thought I was joking. "That so? How come you're here to tell about it?"

"Really happened." When I got to the part where the head of the Bomb and Arson Squad refused to conduct a proper investigation, he shut me up and went to his car for a tape recorder. He was somewhat aggrieved at missing the story. He'd been at a conference out at the airport all day so he hadn't seen any of the wires or the sensational reports the networks were trumpeting.

I told him everything I knew, from Saul Seligman and the Indiana Arms to the little scam among Farmworks, Alma Mejicana, and Wunsch and Grasso, to Roland Montgomery's strange theory of me setting fire to the Indiana Arms and then blowing myself up in remorse.

When I finished Murray put an arm around me and gave me a sloppy kiss. "You're wonderful, Vic. I forgive you for holding out on me last winter. This is a great story. All it needs is a little proof."

"You don't call a hunk of dynamite proof?" Sal snapped a bottle of Holstein's down in front of Murray. "Her dead body would impress you more?"

"It shows someone wanted to kill her, but not who." Murray drank directly from the bottle. "You didn't copy any of the stuff you found at Alma's offices or at Farmworks did you?"

"I took notes at Alma's offices, but I didn't see any of the books at Farmworks. But can't you track some of this stuff down through Lexis and the Office of Contracts and so on? And get someone in the county to tell you what Roland Montgomery owes Boots? That scares me more than almost anything—you get a big cop dogging you and he can kill you or frame you or any damned thing he wants. I'm shaving my head and growing a beard until this sucker blows up big enough that I'm not the only figure tap-dancing in the spotlight."

Sal offered me the bottle again but I turned it down. I couldn't spend the night at the Golden Glow and I wouldn't survive if I left here too drunk to notice who was walking up behind me.

Murray went into Sal's private office to make some phone calls. It was too late in the day to look up any records in the county building, but he was going to initiate a more thorough search through the Lexis network than Freeman Carter had done for me—now that we were looking for a tie-in between MacDonald or Meagher and Alma Mejicana, Murray could ask the system to pull together combinations of names that hadn't occurred to me earlier.

"So what do you do now?" Sal asked. "Lay low until the storm passes?"

"I think I go home." I interrupted her voluble protest. "I know, I came in scared, crying for help. I'm still scared but—" I broke off, trying to think my inchoate feelings into a semblance of logic.

"It's like this. Now Murray has the story—he can get enough going by tomorrow even maybe to print something Friday or Saturday—if the *Star* isn't too scared of Boots and Ralph. So as soon as Boots and MacDonald see things are coming into the open, they'll be shredding documents like mad, be covering their tracks on the Ryan. They're probably rounding up a truckload of Hispanic and black workers right now with documents proving they've been working there since the first of March.

"If they think it's still just me on my own, maybe they'll try to come get me. And then at least we can nail a few of them in the act."

"You and Murray?" Sal pursed up her face in high disdain.

"I'll do the story—Murray'll make the pictures," I said with a lightness I was far from feeling. "No. I think I'll be okay at home. I was panicking earlier, wondering if Ralph might dynamite the whole building just to get me. But really, he's much more likely to wait until I'm on my own and try something different. My old guy downstairs has been on all the stations talking about the men he saw yesterday—the pair who came calling on me in person and the pair who probably put the bomb in the car. So I can't believe they'll risk anything there again, at least not so soon." I hoped.

A couple of guys in business suits came in and sat up at the mahogany bar on the opposite side from me. Sal went over to fill their orders.

I played moodily with my whiskey tumbler. The one name I hadn't given Murray was Michael Furey's. It wasn't that I wanted to protect Furey, but I didn't have proof—just a string of guesses supported only by logic. His name hadn't even been in Star's Rolodex.

Before I started my own offensive I wanted to know how deep

Furey's involvement went with his neighborhood pals—whether he'd just put some of his daddy's life insurance money into Farmworks when they gave him the opportunity—or done more. Like maybe borrowed heroin from police evidence stores so Cerise could kill herself.

If he'd done something like that—I couldn't imagine trying to break the news to Bobby. I'd tried today without evidence. If proof came in—I shuddered. It just better not be me that lets Bobby know about it, that was all.

When Murray came out of Sal's office I went in to call Lotty to let her know what I was doing. She'd heard the story of my bomb from her clinic nurse, who'd called after watching the six o'clock news and was well and truly alarmed. She wanted me to come stay with her, wait in seclusion until the police caught my assailant, but when she heard what response they were giving me she reluctantly agreed I was making the right decision.

"Only, Vic—be careful, all right? I couldn't bear it if you got killed. Will you think of me before you stick your head in front of a gun?"

"Christ, Lotty, I'll think of me before I do that. Don't. Don't think I'm that careless of my life. I'm more frightened now than I can remember being in a good long while. If Bobby Mallory were paying the least attention to me, I wouldn't touch this business with a barge pole."

We talked a little longer. By the time we hung up I was close to crying. I got up slowly from Sal's desk and went back through the mahogany door to the bar. My palms were tingling with nervousness, but a warm afterglow from the whiskey kept my stomach in place.

The bar had cleared out. Sal was washing the empties as her cousin brought them in from the tables. She finished sticking a row of glasses in their slots above the bar and came over to me.

"You sure you want to take off now, girl?"

"Yup." I stuck my hands deep in my pockets. My right fingers ran into metal. I pulled out the Cavalier keys—I'd forgotten putting them there. The sight of the Chevy logo stamped into their heads increased my nervousness.

Sal isn't given to demonstrativeness but she came around to the front of the bar to hug me tightly. "You be careful, Vic. I don't like this at all."

"It's a far better thing that I do now than I have ever done," I recited in attempted bravado.

"If you die you're not going to land in a better place than you've ever been, so just watch yourself, you hear?"

"Do my best, Sal."

Murray offered me a lift north. "Then maybe I'll just cruise around the block every now and then to see whether you're still alive."

"Shut up, Ryerson," Sal said roughly. "Gallows humor isn't going down well tonight."

We stood awkwardly silent for a few minutes. A late customer came in, breaking the spell. Murray and I left while Sal stirred a martini for him.

Murray and I have a style of banter together that somehow precludes true intimacy. Tonight I was too nervous to respond in kind to his jokes. Too nervous to respond at all. I kept rubbing my palms dry against my jean legs and trying not to imagine what Mac-Donald might do next.

# 44

# An Old Friend Catches Up

**M**urray dropped me at the neighborhood car rental. He waited while I checked the engine—whether out of courtesy or because he was hoping for another dynamite story, since he'd missed the first, I didn't ask. No one could have known I'd called Bad Wheels for a car; it was just my jangling nerves that made me look.

The Tempo's engine ignited with a lurching rumble, but no flames shot out from under the hood. When Murray saw I wasn't going up in smoke, he tore off in his battered Fiero, leaving me drumming my fingers on the wheel in indecision.

The sun had set. It would be light for another half hour or so, not really long enough for me to go hunting Elena with any confidence. If Michael had found and killed her, would it matter that her body lay waiting for me until morning? Of course she wouldn't be alone, exactly—there were all those rats I'd seen last week.

It made my palms and feet tremble when I remembered the little ball of fur I'd encountered groping for my flashlight in the dark. I drove home, parking on Nelson west of Racine and going down the alley to the back of my building.

Peppy set up a terrific barking when I came in the back gate. Mr. Contreras appeared at the kitchen door, holding her on a short leash with his left hand and carrying a pipe wrench in his right.

"Oh, it's you, doll. Gave me a start. I thought maybe someone was sneaking up on you."

"Thank you," I said meekly. "I was just creeping up on myself. I didn't want to be ambushed in the stairwell."

"No need to worry about that. Her highness and I are keeping a sharp eye out."

He let go of the leash—the dog was whimpering in her eagerness to greet me. Her tail was whipping up a great circle—not the portrait of a fierce guard dog. I kissed her and fondled her ears. She danced with me back to the stairs and clattered up with me, convinced this was the prelude to a major run. Mr. Contreras trudged up behind us as fast as his stiff knees would allow.

"What are you doing now, doll?" he asked sharply when he'd invited himself into my apartment.

"I'm trying to remember where I left my flashlight," I called from the bedroom. It had rolled under the bed, I finally saw. Peppy helped me lie flat to pull it out. She ate a Kleenex she found underneath and started to work on an old running sock half buried under the bedclothes.

"Yummy, is it?" I pulled it away from her and went back to the kitchen.

"I mean, where are you going?" the old man demanded severely when he saw me checking the clip to my gun.

"Just to see if I can locate my aunt. I'm worried that she might be dead and lying in one of those vacant buildings behind McCormick Place." Come to that, she'd left the hospital in bad shape—she could be dead without anyone lifting a finger to make it happen. Or lying there unconscious.

"I'm coming with you—me and the princess here." His jaw set in a stubborn line.

I opened my mouth to argue with him, then shut it again. Here was a perfect errand to restore his good humor with me—he could see the action without causing any major havoc. Not only that, Peppy could kill the rats. I accepted his escort graciously and was rewarded with a big smile and a resounding slap on my still-weak shoulders.

"Just don't swing that pipe wrench around," I warned him, locking the grate across the kitchen door. "You're under a peace bond because of that thing, remember?"

He slung it decorously through one of his trouser loops and

headed happily up the alley to the car with me. All the way to Lake Shore Drive and the McCormick Place exit he kept up a happy flow of talk.

"You know, your Chevy's still out front with the hood up. Didn't no one want to touch it. I tried getting that young fellow, the one with the tow truck, to take it off, but he was too chicken. I said, 'Let me do it. I'll hook it up and drive it to the garage for you, you're too yellow to do it,' but he just took off like a bat outta hell, if you know what I mean."

"I know just what you mean." Besides having steering as stiff as an old-fashioned shirt collar, the Tempo roared rather loudly. Bad Wheels didn't pay much attention to exhaust systems—"Drive 'em Till They Drop" was their motto. The noise spared me most of Mr. Contreras's conversation until I parked on Prairie.

Peppy was thrilled to be part of the expedition. She strained at her leash, sniffing every pile of rubble, investigating trash heaps with the solemnity of Heinrich Schliemann. Mr. Contreras was only a hair less enthusiastic in commenting on the general decay around us.

"Been a lot of fires down here."

"Yep," I said shortly. Elena being a creature of rather tiresome habit, she would most likely select a place close to the Indiana Arms, as she had when she'd chosen the Prairie Shores. I was going to look at only one or two of these in the fast-fading light. The rest could wait until morning.

We went first into the warehouse two doors down from the shell of the old hotel. Mr. Contreras's pipe wrench came in handy in knocking out the boarding around the entrance—annoying, since it would make it impossible to get him to leave it at home in the future.

Once inside we let Peppy take the lead. She had a field day chasing rats. I kept my gun out in case one of them turned on her, but there were enough escape routes to keep them from becoming bellicose. After five or ten minutes of sport I called her off and kept her close to me while I explored what was left of the premises.

The interior walls had crumbled, making it easy to go from room to room without hunting for doors. Chunks of plaster lay everywhere. Wires dangled from the exposed ceiling studs. When I ran into one I let out a muffled shriek, it felt so much like a hand trailing through my hair. Mr. Contreras came stumbling through the rotted flooring to see what was wrong.

A giant tractor tire propped against one wall was the only sign that humans had ever been around. I guess it didn't even prove that —only that tractors had been around.

When we got outside it was dark, too dark to make hunting in rotting buildings very smart. And it was too evocative of my near baking at the Prairie Shores for my taste—my clothes were wet with sweat, my hands grimy from touching the decayed walls. I was glad I'd had the dog's support in the warehouse.

Even Mr. Contreras had been subdued by the expedition. He put up a token protest that we shouldn't leave now, just when we were getting our bearings. When I said it was too dark to look farther, he agreed readily, volunteering to return in the morning with the Streeter Brothers.

"Sure," I said heartily. "They'll love the help."

I returned the gun to the back waistband of my jeans and bundled him into the car with Peppy. On the way home he kept shaking his head and muttering comments that drifted to me only sporadically over the roar of the engine—he hoped Elena—roar, roar—not a place for a—roar—you really should do something, doll. I gave the car more gas to drown out what it was I should do.

I found a parking place on Wellington and left the Tempo there. I didn't want to make it too easy for anyone watching me to connect me with the car. I turned down the old man's invitation to dinner and headed up the stairs, shining my flashlight on the treads above me.

Furey was waiting at the top of the third flight. I dropped the flashlight and fumbled for my gun. When he launched himself down the stairs at me, I turned to race back down. Fatigue and injuries slowed me. He got my feet and grabbed my head in a brutal armlock.

"You're coming with me, Vic. You're going to kiss your aunt good-bye and then have a farewell party yourself."

He was sitting on my back. I tried twisting underneath him, biting into his leg. He yelped in pain, but grabbed my hands and cuffed them together. Seizing the handcuffs, he started pulling me down the stairs. I let out a great cry that brought Mr. Contreras and the dog to the door of their apartment.

"I'm going to shoot both of them, Vic," Furey hissed at me. "Interfering with the police in the performance of their duties. You want to watch? Or stop fighting and come along with me."

I gulped in air, trying to quiet my heart enough to talk. "Go in," I quavered at Mr. Contreras. "He'll shoot Peppy."

When the old man came into the hall anyway, brandishing his pipe wrench, Furey fired at him. The wrench flew to the floor as the old man crumpled. As we left I saw Peppy race over to lick Mr. Contreras's face. I was choking on my tears, but I thought I saw him put up an arm to pet her.

# 45

# A Walk on the Wild Side

Furey's car was parked halfway up the block. He jerked the driver's door open and shoved me across the gear box into the passenger seat. I flung up my cuffed hands to protect my face as I fell against the door. My left leg was tangled in the gear stick. I was twisted at an awkward angle, unable to kick at Michael when he thrust my leg onto the passenger side.

At least he hadn't bothered to pat me down. Maybe he didn't know I sometimes carry a gun. If I kept my wits, I might still be able to use it.

A handful of people were out on the street, but they turned studiously the other way when they saw me struggling against him —no one wants to be involved in domestic quarrels. I kept biting off the cry to call the cops. After all, Michael was the cops. What would the patrol units do when they showed up and Michael told them I was a violent prisoner?

"I'm not taking any chances with you, Vic—Ernie and Ron were right about you all along. You're not interested in the things a normal girl is—you just play the odds and wait your chance to jump on a guy's balls."

I leaned back in the leather seat. "You're so brave, Furey, shooting a man old enough to be your grandfather. They have special sessions on that at the Police Academy?"

"Shut up, Vic." He took a hand from the wheel and slapped my face.

"Gosh, Michael, now I *am* scared. You and your friends really know how to keep your women in shape. How about fastening my seat belt so I don't go headfirst through the windshield—you'd have a hard time explaining it to Bobby."

He ignored my request and took off with such a burst that I was flung against the leather. I squirmed awkwardly to fish the seat belt from where it was wedged against the door.

"They kept laughing at me, all the kowtowing I did to you— Ernie said LeAnn talked back to him that way just once and he taught her who was boss. That's what I should have done with you from the start. Out at Boots's barbecue they warned me you were acting sweet just so you could nose your way into our business. Carl and Luis took them seriously—but me! I just couldn't listen!" He pounded the steering wheel, his voice rising and cracking.

I finally managed to snap the metal tongue into its holder. "Three weeks ago, when you told me Elena had been seen soliciting in Uptown, that was a lie, wasn't it? That's why you were so insistent I not call Bobby to talk to him about it."

He turned onto Diversey and moved into the oncoming traffic lane to swoop around the traffic backed up from the light at Southport. "You're so sharp, Vic. That's what always attracted me to you. Why couldn't you be smart and sweet at the same time?"

"Just luck of the draw, I guess." I tried to brace myself against his sudden braking as he cut back into the right lane. "You said you had my aunt. Where did you find her? Down in one of those abandoned buildings on Cermak?"

He laughed. "She was right under my nose. Can you beat that? Right around the corner in my own neighborhood. Eileen had seen her and told my mother and Mother mentioned it to me at supper last night. She'd gone to hide out with one of her old cronies, but her thirst got to her—she just had to go get herself a bottle. I knew sooner or later, if she wasn't dead, she wouldn't be able to put up with that thirst anymore. I just didn't expect it to be around the corner from me. So I hung out all afternoon and sure enough, round about eight o'clock, there she came. I just helped her into the car. She tried sweet-talking me. It was loathsome."

He did sixty through the park to Lake Shore Drive. I suppose the beat cops knew his license plate, or at least called it in and saw it belonged to a detective. The local traffic didn't have that inside track and honked ferociously as they had to swerve out of his way.

"Was she loathsome because of her age or her drinking or both?" I asked.

"Women who think they've got sexual powers that they don't are disgusting."

"She appeals to some guys. Just because she's not your type doesn't mean everyone finds her repulsive."

He turned onto Lake Shore Drive so fast I was flung against him. When I was upright again I said conversationally, "Touching you seems loathsome to me, but I'm sure some women would disagree."

He didn't say anything, just took the Corvette up to ninety, diving in and out of lanes around the other cars, making them seem to stand still in a blur of light. I was afraid I was going to throw up when he braked into the curve at the Michigan Avenue exit. He slowed down then—the traffic was too thick for him to keep up so mad a pace.

"You're cracking, Michael. You're leaving a trail a mile wide. Even if Roland Montgomery's your clout in the department, he can't protect you from the mayhem you're manufacturing tonight."

In the streetlamps along the Drive I could see sweat beaded on his forehead. He made a violent gesture with his right hand but the car swerved; he fishtailed and got us back in our lane by a miracle.

"What is it that Roland owes Boots?" I kept my tone level. "And why did he get you to set the fire—why couldn't he do it himself?"

Furey bared his teeth at me. "You're not that fucking smart, Vic. *I* went to Montgomery. I found him for Boots. All he had to do was get me the accelerant and make sure no one investigated too closely."

"What a good boy," I said, marveling. "Is that when they gave you the Corvette?"

"You don't understand anything, do you? I was prepared—I was willing—you could have lived like LeAnn and Clara—had whatever you wanted—but you—"

"I have what I want, Michael. My independence and my privacy. You've just never understood it, have you, that all those things, those diamonds and stuff, just don't turn me on."

He got off at the Grand Avenue exit and whipped around the curves to the Rapelec complex. He parked the Corvette well away from the street, behind one of the wooden walls blocking the site.

He jumped out and came around to the passenger door. I had thought I might be able to kick him as I got out of the car but he'd handled a lot of rough arrests in his time—he stood well away from the frame and waited for me to wrestle with the seat belt and get my legs out myself. He put an arm around me in a savage mockery of chivalry and hustled me into the building.

I shivered involuntarily when we moved into the inky corridors. We were on the plank-covered ramp I'd walked three weeks earlier up to the management offices. Beyond the naked bulbs lay the gaping hole of the complex. I wondered where my aunt was, if she was still alive, what tragic end was destined for us.

Furey hadn't said a word since we'd gotten to the site. I began to feel boxed in by the silence as much as by my cuffs.

To regain my composure I said conversationally, "Was it because McGonnigal told you I had the bracelet? Is that why you came to get me tonight?"

He bared his teeth again in a violent parody of a smile. "You left your scarf at the Alma offices, Vic. I saw you unwrap it when Eileen gave it to you the day we met. You don't remember it but I do because I thought you were the hottest little number I'd ever laid eyes on. I do want my bracelet back, but I'm not in any hurry."

"That's good," I said calmly, even though my cheeks burned at the idea of being a hot number. "I left it in my apartment. You're going to need a wrecking crew to get in there. You don't get it, do you? Not even being a cop can cover your tracks for you when you've created this much carnage. Not even Bobby will do it. It'll break his heart, but he'll let you go."

Michael hit me across my mouth with the back of his hand. "You need to learn a few lessons, Vic, and one of them is to shut up when I tell you to."

It stung a little but didn't hurt. "I don't have a long enough lifeline right now to learn new tricks, Mickey, and even if I did, yours just purely make me throw up."

Michael stopped in the middle of the gangway and shoved me against the wall. "I told you to shut up, Vic. Do you want me to break your jaw to make you do it?"

I looked at him steadily, marveling that I'd ever found those dark angry eyes engaging. "Of course I don't, Michael. But I have to wonder if beating me while I'm defenseless would make you feel powerful or ashamed?"

He held my shoulder with his left hand and tried to slam his right into my face. As he came forward I kicked him as hard as I could in the kneecap, hard enough to break it. He gave a sharp cry and dropped my shoulder.

I ran down the ramp, terribly hampered by my bound hands. Above me I heard Furey crying out, and then Ernie Wunsch calling down asking what the fuck was going on. I darted into the shadowy interior, stumbling over boards in the dark. I was making too big a racket—no one would have any trouble finding me.

I stopped running and moved cautiously forward until I came to a big pillar, steel with concrete poured around it. I sidled around behind it and stood there trying not to breathe out loud, scrabbling behind me trying to reach my gun. My arms were crossed in their cuffs, though, and I couldn't reach far enough around.

A powerful flashlight stuck fingers out on the floor around me. I didn't move.

"Let's not play hide-and-seek here all night," Ernie said. "Go get the aunt. She'll flush her out."

I still didn't move. A couple of minutes later I could hear Elena's breathless voice, squeaky with fear.

"What are you doing? You're hurting me. There's no need to hold me so hard. I don't know how you were brought up, but in my day a true gentleman did not squeeze a lady's arm hard enough to bruise it."

Good old Elena. Maybe I'd find a happy death, laughing at her incongruous scolding.

"We have your aunt here, Warshawski." It was Ron Grasso speaking now. "Call out to your niece, Auntie."

He did something to make her scream. I flinched at the noise.

"Louder, Auntie."

She screamed again, a cry of genuine pain. "Vicki! They're hurting me!"

"We just broke a finger, Warshawski. We'll break her bones one by one until you decide you've had enough."

I swallowed bile and stepped out from behind my pillar. "Okay, he-men. I've had enough."

"That's a good girl, Vic," Ernie said, moving toward me. "I always told Mickey there was a way to manage you if he just looked for it. . . . Keep the light on her, Ronnie. Little bitch maybe broke Mickey's knee. I don't want her clawing at me."

He came up to me and took my arm. "Now don't you try anything, Vic, because Ron there will just start breaking your auntie's fingers again if you do."

"Vicki?" Elena quavered. "You're not mad at poor old Elena, are you?"

I held out my cuffed hands to her. "Of course I'm not mad at you, sweetie. You did the best you could. You were very smart and brave to hide so long."

What good would it have done to chew her out for not sharing the whole story with me from the beginning—or at least from her bed at Michael Reese.

"They hurt me, Vicki, they broke my little finger. I didn't mean to scream and make them find you, but I couldn't help it." Her face was in shadow but I sensed the tears beginning to fall.

"No, no, sweetie, I know you couldn't." I patted the thin bones in her hands. They were fragile, exposed, as easy to break as sticks of china.

Behind Ron and Elena stood August Cray, the night project manager. "What happened to your security guard? He not in on the kill?" I asked. "And I don't see dear little Star, either. She and I had such a nice chat this afternoon."

Nobody answered me. "We're just going to go for a ride, Vic," Ron said. "You take it easy. There are three of us here and we can make it mighty unpleasant for both of you if you try any of your cute tricks on us."

"Just three of you? What happened to Furey? Did I really get his kneecap? A shot like that takes a lot of practice." I was amazed to hear myself sounding as chipper as a cheerleader. "You know, if he's gone to the hospital, you've got a little problem—if my body's discovered with his handcuffs on, I mean—it's going to be awkward for the poor boy to explain that one away."

"You're not the only one around here with a brain, Warshawski, so don't get your underwear in a bundle over that one." Ernie's sharper voice came from behind me. "Mickey won't leave us holding the bag."

"That's right," I said approvingly. "You're all pals and pals gotta stick together, even unto death, at least the death of a whole lot of innocent bystanders."

"You're no little innocent, Vic, so don't get me shedding tears for you."

We got to the hoist and they bundled us in. Cray operated the controls while Ron and Ernie hovered close to Elena and me. I wished futilely that I'd learned enough Polish to do more than greet my grandmother Warshawski at Christmas. I could have told Elena about the gun and gotten her to slip it out of my back before Ron or Ernie found it, but if I muttered the news to her, they'd hear me and disarm me.

As we rode slowly up my terror and helplessness increased. I could imagine our end, tipped over the side of the building, the accidental death of an unstable wino and her eager but unhelpful niece. I stopped trying to goad the boys with my bright chatter and slumped down on my heels against the elevator wall, my head in my hands.

"What's she up to?" Ron demanded.

"I'm sick," I groaned. "I'm going to throw up."

"Be my guest," Ernie said sardonically.

I made retching noises and collapsed on the floor of the hoist, clutching my stomach with my cuffed hands. Elena fluttered down next to me. "Oh, my poor baby, what would Gabriella say if she could see you? She'd never forgive me. I hope I don't go to heaven when I die, I couldn't bear to see the look on her face for knowing I got you into trouble like this. Come to Elena, baby, come here, Vicki, just lean your head against old drunk Elena and maybe you'll feel a little better."

I sat up and leaned my head against her shoulder. With my voice muffled against her scrawny neck, I told her about the gun. "Wait until we're out of here and in the dark, then pull it out and hand it to me."

Fear had sharpened her wits. She didn't give a sign of having understood me. "Oh, Vicki, yes, whatever you say, baby, just don't cry. That's a good girl."

Maybe she hadn't understood me. I wondered if I should try to repeat the message, but the hoist had slid to a stop and Ernie was urging me to my feet. Still clutching my stomach and moaning, I lurched on the way out and stumbled against the concrete.

We were on the open deck at the top of the building. Around us steel beams sent blacker fingers against the dark sky. We were up twenty-five or thirty stories. A stiff wind made the girders sway and froze my marrow. The sight of open air in all directions brought on a genuine attack of nausea. I fell down, almost swooning.

Elena was on me like a shot, weeping over her poor little Vicki. While Ron tried to wrestle her away her bony hands felt behind me for my gun. He pulled her up, but she had the Smith & Wesson loose and dropped it in front of me. The sharp sound of metal on concrete echoed a thousandfold in my ears.

Ernie and Ron didn't immediately realize what had happened. The only light came from the hoist. I could just make out the glint of the metal and scrabbled madly for the gun. I reached it just as Ernie yanked me to my feet. Fumbling it into my right hand, I slid the safety off with my thumb. I wrenched myself from Ernie and turned and shot him.

Cray was still standing in the hoist. When he heard the shot and saw Ernie fall, he closed the doors and started back down. Ron started dragging Elena toward the edge of the platform. I couldn't make him out except as a bundle of darkness moving along the paler sheen of the concrete. I forced myself to follow him, to fight down the spinning in my head, to place the muzzle in his back and pull the trigger.

A yard from the edge Ron collapsed, falling on top of Elena. I had never killed a man before, but I knew from the way his body lay, crumpled as a dark blob on the concrete deck, that he was dead. I couldn't bring myself to walk close enough to check—but what would I have done even if he had been alive? My hands were still cuffed and the hoist was somewhere below us.

My aunt began thrashing about, trying to move away from him. That finally brought me over to the body. Even a yard from the edge of the deck my head swam. I shut my eyes and managed to roll Ron from my aunt's torso. I brought her with me to the center of the platform.

Behind us the crane loomed up. The pale light of the midnight sky glinted from its long swaying arm. I thought of the hole underneath, going down thirty stories to the bottom of the elevator shaft, and shuddered.

Ernie was still alive. I'd shattered his shoulder. He was losing enough blood to want to get help, but he told me there wasn't any way to bring the hoist up myself. Ernie wasn't inclined to talk much. I tried asking him about his relations with Boots and MacDonald and why he and Ron did so much for them, but he told me I was a nosy interfering bitch and to mind my own business before it was too late. At the same time he was peeved with me for not climbing down to the ground—he told me they nailed ladders into the openings where fire stairs would eventually be poured.

"You could at least try to get some help," he complained. "You shot me—you owe me something."

"Ernie, sweetie, I shot you because you were going to throw me over the side of the building. I'm not climbing down thirty stories of ladders in the dark, especially not with my hands not working."

At that Wunsch cursed some more, this time at his partners. It seems Furey had given Cray the key to my handcuffs—he'd been supposed to undo me right before I went over—they didn't want to run the risk of not getting to me before some passerby did. "Now look at that jerk. Takes off and leaves us alone up here to die."

"I thought you were a real macho kind of guy," I said disapprovingly. "John Wayne would never have lain around pissing at how rotten his pals were just because he'd taken a bullet."

Ernie swore at me, then asked me to take off my sweatshirt to wrap him up, he was getting so cold with blood loss.

"Ernie, I can't get it over my hands. Remember? They're locked together. Anyway, I don't want to hang around up here all night with nothing but a bra between me and the cold cruel wind."

Ernie flung a few more unimaginative epithets at me, then lapsed into silence. I wished Elena would too. Playing a heroine's role for once in her life, my aunt grew loquacious. She went on as though shot full of pentobarbital, talking about her childhood, her quarrels with her mother, what Tony—my father—said when he cut all the hair off her dolls when she was eight.

After a while I thought I might scream at the emotional, inconsequential torrent. Ernie found it so intolerable, he demanded I shut her up.

"She's driving me round the bend with that drivel," he announced. In his own living room this probably got instant results. I could picture LeAnn giggling and saying, "You're so cute, Ernie," but taking her offending friends or children or mother off to the kitchen. I wondered what LeAnn and Clara would do now.

"She's not doing anything to you, Ernie. Listen to her—it'll take your mind off your troubles." I asked Elena to repeat a particularly tangled narrative involving my uncle Peter, a dog, and the neighbor's flower garden.

I don't know how much time passed that way when I heard the hoist returning. It can't have been long, but in the dark, surrounded by the wounded and the babbling, it felt like hours.

I persuaded Elena to stop talking and move with me behind one of the girders. "Just be quiet, Auntie. They may have come back to shoot us and we don't want to give them any help finding us."

"Sure, Vicki. You know what you're doing. Whatever you say. I was never so scared in my life as I was when that boy with the gorgeous eyes picked me up at the liquor store—"

I put a hand over her mouth. "Shut up, darling, for now. You can tell me about it later."

The hoist groaned to a stop. My hands were thick with cold. I was having trouble remembering which was the right and which the left. I counted painfully in my head, trying to figure out how many shots were in the clip. I tried to subdue the tremor in my right hand so I could make all of them count.

I waited for the noise of doors opening or feet on concrete. When a minute had gone by with no sound, I peered around the edge of the pillar. I couldn't see the box-like car inside the frame. Over the wind in the girders and Elena's nervous whispers, I strained to hear. Finally I moved away from her in the dark, ignoring her piteous cry.

To my left I suddenly saw a bobbing point of light. I moved toward it cautiously, keeping my weight on my back foot with each step until I was certain I hadn't come to some unexpected hole.

The light flickered again and went out. Ernie had mentioned a ladder in the stairwell opening. This must be Cray or some other confederate hoping to climb up and surprise us from behind.

My eyes were so accustomed to the dark that I saw the stairwell opening loom in front of me as a darker patch in the black night. I lay on my stomach and watched until the black changed again, a blob crawling up the side to the top. When a hand emerged on the deck I smashed the butt of the Smith & Wesson into it with all my strength.

Cray cried out but leaned against the ladder and brought his other hand up and fired. The bullet went wide in the night but I slid back, away from the opening, as he hoisted himself one-handed to the deck.

I aimed at the dark shape in front of me and fired. Lying awkwardly as I was, the recoil wrenched my right shoulder. I fell over but managed to hang on to the gun. Light shone on me, blinding me, and I rolled instinctively as he shot.

Somehow I managed to get to my feet and around behind one of the girders. Cray kept the light on for a moment but realized when I fired again that it made him as much a target as it did me. When the light went out I dropped to my knees and elbows and scooted to the next girder. I stopped there and listened. Elena had started talking again, in an undertone, the sound just audible above the wind.

"You can get the old woman, Cray," Ernie called in the thread of a voice. "She's jabbering away over here. You can find her by the babble."

Elena whimpered but couldn't make herself shut up.

"You still there, Wunsch?" Cray shouted back. "Keep the faith —I'll have you down in no time."

Cray started circling around behind me in the dark. I couldn't keep track of where he was. I was tired and disoriented and I clung to my girder without trying to figure out his next move. Suddenly he gave a cry, a scream of such panic that my heart thudded violently.

"What happened? Where are you?" Ernie called out.

From the middle of the deck I could hear Cray screaming, his voice muffled, coming from a distance. He had fallen down the opening for the crane, but the safety nets around it had saved him.

# 46

# On the Scales of Justice

I have a hard time remembering what remained of the night. I managed somehow to climb down the slats connecting the deck to the floor below. My arms trembled so violently that I don't know how I made it—more by will than by muscle. And I got the hoist up, after a painful round of trial and error. It wasn't easy to run at the best of times; with one hand it was pure bloody hell. And I got Elena and Ernie into the cage and lowered us down to the ground.

Furey was waiting there but he'd been joined by some uniformed cops. A passing blue-and-white had heard the gunshots and swung over to the site. They were keeping Furey company until the hoist came down. I spent a good chunk of what was left of the night in a lockup at Eleventh Street—I was in cuffs and Furey persuaded the uniformed boys that I'd resisted arrest.

Furey went off to the hospital to get his knee attended to. He had bravely stayed at the construction site in excruciating pain waiting for his pals to come down—it was just his bad luck that the patrol car had shown up first.

I couldn't get the cops who were holding me to understand that another man was on top of the building, in the nets around the crane, and that he had the key to my handcuffs. After a while I gave up trying. I didn't say anything at all except to tell them my name. When they shut the lockup on me I lay on the floor and went to sleep, oblivious to the clamor of the drunks around me.

They got me up about a couple of hours later. I was so sleepy and disoriented, I didn't even try to ask where we were going—I assumed it was for early morning court calls. Instead they hustled me to the third floor, to the Violent Crimes area, to the corner office where Bobby Mallory was sitting behind his desk. His eyes were red from lack of sleep, but he'd shaved and his tie was neatly knotted.

"Is there some reason she's still in cuffs?" Bobby asked.

The men who'd escorted me didn't know anything about it. They said they'd been told I was dangerous and to leave me locked up.

"Well, get them off before I make a report to your commander."

He didn't speak again until they'd found a key that would work on those cuffs. When I was free, rubbing my sore arms, he laced into me with scorching bitterness. He went on and on about me playing at police, ruining his best men, screwing up his department until nobody knew what he was supposed to be doing. I let it wash over me, too tired, in too much pain, too overwhelmed by his fury, to try to form a response. When he'd finally exhausted himself he sat still, tears coursing down his ruddy face.

"May I go now?" I asked in a thread of a voice. "Or am I still facing charges?"

"Go. Go." The word was a hoarse squawk. He covered his face with his right hand and shoved the left in the air as if to drive me from the room.

"The boys here wouldn't listen to me, but there's a man named Cray trapped at the top of the Rapelec building. He fell into the nets around the crane." I stood up. "Can you tell me where my aunt is?"

"Leave, Vicki. I can't stand the sound of your voice tonight."

When I left his office and got to the Eleventh Street entrance, Lotty was waiting for me. I fell into her arms, beyond surprise or question.

# 47

# In Lotty's Nest

**L**otty took the day off on Thursday to look after me. She wouldn't let anyone near me, not Murray nor the networks, not even the federal district attorney. Good Republican appointee that he was, he was slobbering at the possibility of bringing down the Democratic county chairman. With her characteristic flair for detail, Lotty called my answering service and told them to switch calls for me through to her—but she wouldn't let me take any.

When I woke up finally around five I remembered Mr. Contreras. Lotty bundled me into some blankets on the daybed in her living room and insisted I eat some soup before she told me her end of the adventure.

The shot and our scuffle had brought Vinnie and Rick York to the hall. They'd been busy in the back bedroom or they might have arrived soon enough to help out—or maybe to get shot themselves. Anyway, Mr. Contreras had taken the bullet in his shoulder and was able to give Rick Lotty's number.

"He's all right," Lotty assured me. "It would take more than a broken shoulder to stop him—as soon as we got someone to patch him together he had to be sedated to keep from racing off to hunt for you."

"How did you find me?" I asked from my nest on the daybed.

"I called Lieutenant Mallory. Your tiresome neighbor knew who had shot him—I gather he monitors all your male visitors?" She flashed a wicked grin. "A full-time job for him, my dear. Anyway, the lieutenant was not at all disposed to intervene, but he could scarcely ignore the evidence of a man who'd been shot. He finally agreed to call me when they'd located you. I was afraid he wasn't going to push hard enough—you had me very frightened, my dear."

She compressed her lips and turned her head away to regain her composure.

"I was damned scared myself," I said frankly. "I just didn't understand how desperate those boys were getting."

"At any rate, I had done a difficult delivery for the chief assistant federal prosecutor, or whatever her title was, so I rang her up and told her what I knew. I think she organized some resources to look for you, but by then you'd surfaced at police headquarters. What a loathsome place. I tried hard to get in to fetch you, my dear, but they were quite—quite physical in keeping me out."

I got out of my nest to hug her. Lotty has an antigen against police stations—they played too terrifying a role in her early childhood—so it made her effort doubly precious to me.

I asked her about Elena. My aunt had been treated for exhaustion and had her broken finger set, but the hospital released her around noon. After telling me about Elena, Lotty tried to get me to think of other things, like the possibility of a vacation. She pulled out a giant folder of travel brochures—trips to Caribbean islands, to the Costa Brava—various warm and friendly climates that would make me forget the Chicago winter closing in on us.

On Friday, Lotty finally let the rest of the world loose on me. She laid down the law with all her imperial force: Anyone who wanted to see me had to do so on Sheffield Avenue. Unfortunately there were any number of people eager enough to talk to me to meet that condition.

First in line was Alison Winstein, the deputy prosecutor whose life Lotty had saved last year. She took me through what I knew and what I surmised. Like all prosecutors, she didn't feel like giving much back but she did let me know that they had obtained warrants for Alma and Farmworks. They had wanted to subpoena the county contract files but Boots was a pretty wily fighter—neither he nor Ralph would turn over records without a pretty good battle.

After Ms. Winstein left I went through the account of my escapade in the papers. Murray had put together a pretty strong story without talking to me—he'd gotten an exclusive with Mr. Contreras and managed to track Elena down before the hospital released her. I grinned to myself over the interview with my neighbor. Of all the men I know, Murray is the one Mr. Contreras likes least—thinks of him as a snothead and a hot dog. Murray earned his byline on that one.

When I'd finished with the papers I called Robin Bessinger at Ajax. He'd seen the stories and was in a chastened frame of mind. "I'm sorry we questioned your judgment, Vic. You were the pro on this one. I—could we have dinner again?"

"I don't know," I said slowly. "I'll have to think about that. But you could do one thing for me—cut a check for Saul Seligman. I'll take it over to him in the morning."

"We'd kind of like to subrogate against MacDonald and Meagher," Robin said.

"Be my guest. But don't keep the old guy hanging. He's had a rough three weeks, with his favorite old building going and his chief lieutenant getting murdered. I know you can grease those bureaucratic wheels. Drop it off for me on your way home and I'll take it to him tomorrow."

Robin agreed, somewhat unwillingly. It was perhaps the hope of dinner—et cetera—with me that made him agree at all. I was going to have to build up my strength and get over a lot of wounds before I was in the humor for much et cetera.

Lotty had gone to Beth Israel to see her more pressing patients, but she came back at lunch to heat some homemade chicken soup for me. "You're too thin, *Liebchen*. I want to see those purple circles disappear from your eyes."

I obediently ate two large helpings and a few slices of toast. While I was finishing the toast Murray showed up. I didn't much feel like talking to him, but the sooner I did it the faster it would be behind me. And when I'd done I was glad because he knew what had happened to Furey—suspended without pay, out on $100,000 bond for felonious assault on me, Elena, and Mr. Contreras.

"They're never going to prove a case against him with that young girl—what was her name? Cerise? Sergeant McGonnigal did tell me off the record that they're missing some heroin they'd copped in a drug raid a month or so ago. He also figures the department's going to sit on that one."

"What about Boots?" I asked. "How do things look for the election next month?"

Murray made a face. "This is Chicago, sweetheart, not Minneapolis—he got a standing ovation at last night's meeting of the County Board. And the campaign funds are still coming in—too many of those contractors owe the old guy too much. They're not going to jump ship unless he falls below the waterline."

"Has he backed away from Roz?"

"Same story—she's just too popular in the Hispanic wards. Boots lets her go he can kiss the Humboldt Park–Logan Square vote good-bye. And don't forget there's a sizable Mexican population out in the Mount Prospect area—her support isn't all in the city."

"So why did she bother?" I burst out. "Why did she care what I did or who I talked to? That's what burns me. The way people were carrying on I thought she was sitting on bigamy or illegitimate children tucked in an orphanage. Turns out it was just business as usual in this town. I'm sick to death of it, but it's so goddamn usual, why did she think it would matter?"

Murray shrugged his massive shoulders. "Maybe she felt vulnerable. First woman Boots has backed in a big way. First Hispanic. Maybe she was afraid the rules would be different for her. You of all people ought to be able to figure that one out."

"Yeah, maybe." Suddenly I was very tired, so tired that I started drifting off to sleep while Murray asked me something about Elena. I tried to answer coherently but he saw I was struggling.

"You go back to bed, kid. Once more Wonder Woman saves the city. Go to sleep." He patted me on the shoulder and took off, magnanimous because I'd let him garner so much glory.

It was late in the afternoon, after I'd slept a while, that Velma Riter dropped in. When Lotty told me who had come I wanted to dive back under the covers. Instead I staggered to the living room on woolly legs and braced myself for her onslaught.

She stood in the middle of the room twisting a copy of the *Star* around and around in her hands.

"Quite a story you were digging up," she finally said in a voice like dry soil.

I looked at her warily. "It doesn't seem to be hurting Roz much. Of course there's still a month till the election."

"I don't know who I'm madder with—Roz for doing all this or you for turning on a sister and making it all public."

I rubbed my face with the heels of my hands. "I don't have a pat answer for that, Velma. Does being a feminist mean you have to support *everything* your sisters do? Even if you think they're abusing you?"

"But talk to her in private, couldn't you do that?"

"She wouldn't let me. I tried. She just wants those golden apples too bad, Velma. I'm sure she'll do a good job. She'll be better than most, I expect. But she isn't enough of a risk-taker to try for the apples without getting some worms to help her."

Velma flung up her arms. "It's too much. Too much for me, anyway. I should have stayed with photography—it's safer."

I looked at her directly. "Velma—your pictures are honest—and they involve a lot of risk—emotional risk. I'd think you'd want that in any woman you came out in public for. Well, I do. And I won't take it, to be spun around—by *anyone.* And especially not by someone like Roz, trading on old loyalties and asking us to countenance —well, worms."

"She didn't do it for the money, you know," Velma said.

I made an impatient gesture. "I know—she did it for her cousin, family loyalty, wanting Hispanics to have a bigger piece of county action. Just because her motives were so damned wonderful doesn't make me like it any better."

Velma stared at me unblinkingly for a minute. "Well, anyone looking at your body knows you take risks, Warshawski. I'll give you that. I did resign from her staff today. She—she—" The wide, generous mouth crumpled. "She talked to me so sweet, you'd think that voice was every mother in the world singing a lullaby. That hurt. I had to quit."

I looked at her and nodded without speaking. She winked back her tears and left abruptly.

# 48

# The Birthday Party

On Saturday, before I took old Mr. Seligman his check, I stopped at a Pontiac dealership on Western and bought myself a bright red Trans Am. I've never owned a new car before, especially not one with twin exhausts and 180 horsepower. I didn't know what I was going to do for money to pay for it, but when it moved up to fifty with just a whisper of gas it seemed like the car I'd been waiting for all my life.

After that I took my time going north and west to Norwood Park. Eileen had decided to go ahead with the party for Bobby. So much planning had gone into it, involving so much of the neighborhood, that she didn't feel she could turn it off now. The people on either side were lending their yards so there'd be a place for a refreshment tent and for some pipers.

I'd called Eileen to tell her I wasn't up to seeing Bobby, but she'd begged me to come.

"Vicki, try to understand. Michael is his godson. He was like a seventh child to Bobby and his great hope in the department. He was only yelling at you out of his hurt for Michael."

"It doesn't work for me, Eileen. Michael wanted to kill me and he damned near did it. By the time Bobby finished with me I felt he wished it had happened."

"No, no, don't ever think such a thing." Her warm rich voice cracked in distress. "Tony's child? Gabriella's? It was himself he wanted to attack, for letting himself be so betrayed. He—Bobby's a good man, Vicki. A good cop too. You know that. Tony would never have taken him up if he wasn't. But—he's not good at thinking through these things, figuring out why he lashed out at you the way he did. He has other strengths, but not that one. I'm asking you— begging you—to understand and be better than him. It would mean so much. Not just to him, but to me. So if you can't do it for him, will you do it for me?"

And so I found myself ducking under the billboard of Boots Meagher at the corner of Nagle—a smiling year-round fixture proclaiming that "Boots Is Chicago"—and crossing into Bobby's neighborhood. Bobby's neighborhood. Michael's neighborhood. Where my father and uncles and Aunt Elena grew up. Where Boots and Ernie and Ron came from. Where they all grew up together and helped each other out because the one thing you must never forget in Chicago is to look out for your own.

Usually when I cross the invisible line into Norwood Park I feel as though I've gone into Munchkin land, a place of tidy tiny bungalows on minuscule well-tended lots. It's a mirage of a neighborhood —it seems to have nothing to do with the sprawling, graffiti-laden, garbage-ridden city to the southeast.

Today, though, it seemed dead. The October air was gray and the houses looked drab and colorless. Even the bursts of fall flowers in the tidy yards seemed drained of vividness, the bronze mums looking brown, the gold ones merely sickly. I wished I was anywhere in the world but here.

I pulled my new toy into a line with other cars blocking the street. No one would be out ticketing today. I dragged myself slowly up the short drive. Laughter and the sound of bagpipes were coming from the back. A few knots of people had spilled over into the front yard. They smiled and waved at me in the happy camaraderie of a big party and I dutifully waved back.

When I got to the back the crowd was packed into every inch of turf, not just in Eileen's yard but in the two adjacent. A canopy with Bobby's name done up in lights stood in the middle. I couldn't see the pipes or anyone I knew. I stood awkwardly on the fringe until Eileen suddenly came from nowhere and pulled me to her large soft breasts.

"Oh, Vicki, oh, it's so good to see you. Thank you so much for coming. I was afraid . . . Anyway, Bobby's over here. He'll be so pleased—he hasn't said—but you know . . ." Tears sparkled on her long black lashes. She took my hand and made her way through the throng to the densest part, where Bobby stood. Beyond him a piper was playing and the crowd was urging Bobby to dance.

Eileen waited until the howl of the reel had ended before thrusting me forward. "Bobby. Look who's come."

When Bobby saw me the smile died from his face. He looked at me with some combination of embarrassment and rigidness.

"You guys gotta excuse me," he said abruptly to the group around him. "I need to see this young lady for a few minutes."

He took me into the house, a slow procession through the jam of happy neighbors, fellow cops—I even saw Officer Neely looking flushed and relaxed in a bright fuchsia dress—and screaming grandchildren.

Inside the house two of Bobby's daughters were constructing a giant cake. They squealed when they saw him. "Daddy! You know you're not supposed to come in here."

"It's okay, girls—I ain't seen nothin'. I'm just going down to the family room with Vicki for a few minutes. You keep everyone out, okay?"

"Sure, Daddy, but go on before you see something!" They shooed us down the steps.

Bobby had finished the basement himself, installing a bathroom, real floors and walls, building in bunk beds for his two sons when there'd been six children in seven rooms upstairs. Only two of their daughters were still at home, but he'd left the beds for his grandchildren to sleep in—he loved having them stay over.

He turned on a lamp and sat on the red plaid couch next to the bunk beds. I sat in the shabby armchair facing him, next to the fake fireplace. He moved his big hands uncomfortably, trying to think of something to say. I didn't help him.

"I didn't expect to see you here," he said at last.

"I didn't want to come. Eileen talked me into it."

He looked at the floor and muttered, "I said a lot of things I shouldn't have last week. I'm sorry."

"You hurt my feelings, Bobby." I couldn't keep my voice from cracking. "Your golden boy damned near killed me and you talked to me like I was some kind of street scum."

He rubbed his face. "I—Vicki, I talked to Eileen about it, she tried to make sense out of it for me. I don't know why I did it, that's God's truth. Dr. Herschel called me. That's how I knew you were in trouble. You know about that part, don't you?"

I nodded without speaking.

"I knew by then it was Mickey. Well, you'd tried to tell me, but it wasn't until she told me he'd shot the old man that I—don't look at me like that, Vicki, you're making it hard to say this and it's hard enough to start with."

I turned my head toward the cowboy coverlets on the bunk beds.

"I called John and the Finch. They weren't as upset as I was— they knew Mickey'd been acting queer since the day before when you brought that damned bracelet of his in. And they'd wondered about some other things. Of course they'd never told me—I was the lieutenant and he was my fair-haired boy." He gave a harsh laugh. "What was the story on that bracelet? Why did it send him into orbit?"

I explained. "I tried to tell you Wednesday. I didn't know what it was—I don't think he'd worn it around me more than once or twice. He thought—you know, as long as Elena was alive she could link it to him. Well, not just that. She could tie him to the fire at the Indiana Arms. He was the person, too, who knocked us both out and tried to burn us at the other place." I started shivering as the memories hit me. I tried to push them aside but I couldn't.

Bobby grunted and stood up to reach for one of the cowboy coverlets. He tossed it to me and I wrapped myself in it. After a bit my shivering stopped, but both of us sat lost in our own reveries.

At least my last visitor yesterday was benign—Zerlina, again taking three buses, wanted to know how her daughter came to die. She shared a Coke and more of Lotty's chicken soup and wept with me. She shook her head in amazement when she learned Elena had saved my life: "Thought she'd pickled her brain too good years ago to come up with something like that, but the Lord provides when you least expect it."

As if following my thoughts, Bobby asked abruptly about my aunt.

"It's like it all never happened. I stopped by the Windsor Arms —the hotel where she's living now—last night. She was out front with a bottle and a crowd of greasy old men, showing her little finger in a splint and bragging over her heroics. Some people even a whirl-wind won't change, I guess." I laughed mirthlessly.

Bobby nodded a couple of times to himself. "I want you to understand something, Vicki. Try to, anyway. Tony, your daddy, took me under his wing when I joined the force. He must have been a good thirteen, fourteen years older than me. A lot of guys were coming back from the war then, they didn't make it easy on us rookies. Tony looked out for me from day one.

"I thought I could do the same for Mickey and it hurts me, hurts my pride Eileen tells me it is, that I could be so wrong. I keep thinking to myself, what would Tony think, he saw me making such a colossal mistake?"

He didn't seem to want an answer but I gave him one anyway. "You know what he'd say, Bobby, that anyone can make a mess but only a fool wallows in it."

Bobby smiled painfully. "Yeah, well, maybe. Yeah, probably. But here's what you gotta understand, Vicki. I thought the best thing I could do to pay Tony back for all he did for me was look out for you. I never could understand the way Tony and Gabriella brought you up, not making you mind the way my own girls did. And you just didn't seem like a real girl to me, the things you wanted and wanted to do. I'm not even sure I liked you all that well. I just thought I owed it to Tony to look after you."

I thought he'd finished, but he only stopped to crack his knuck-les, get himself over the hump. "So you're not like other girls. Eileen —Eileen never minded a minute, she always loved you like you were her own daughter. But I just couldn't deal with it. And then when you exposed Mickey—he was like my son and you were like an alien monster. But if he'd had your guts and your honesty, he'd never of gone along with those buddies of his to begin with. Never dug him-self that kind of hole.

"So I've had to think about it. Think about you, I mean. Start from the beginning. I love my girls. I don't want them any different from how they are. But you're the daughter of the two people I loved best, next to Eileen, and you can't do things different than you do, shouldn't do them different, not with Gabriella and Tony bringing you up. Do you understand?"

The door at the top of the stairs opened and Bobby's daughter Marianna called down. "Daddy! People are waiting for you!"

"Be up in a jiffy, sugar!" he yelled back. "Don't let them start without me."

He got up. "Okay? Is that enough?"

I stood up too. "Yeah, I think that's enough." I fished in my pocket and handed him a small parcel. "I brought that along for you. Just in case, you know—just in case I felt like giving you a present."

He undid the paper and opened the little box. When he looked inside and saw Tony's shield lying in the cotton, he didn't say anything, but for the second time that week I saw him cry.